Raised in Rockford, Illinois, *New York Times* bestselling author **Erica Spindler** lives in New Orleans with her husband and two sons. She has won several awards for her fiction and her books have been turned into graphic novels and a daytime drama.

Available from Erica Spindler

Shocking Pink

Erica Spindler

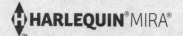

Harlequin MIRA is a registered trademark of Harlequin Enterprises Limited, used under licence.

This edition published in Great Britain 2016
By Harlequin Mira, an imprint of HarperCollins*Publishers*
1 London Bridge Street, London, SE1 9GF

Shocking Pink © 1998 Erica Spindler

ISBN: 978-1-848-45495-8

58-0616

Printed and bound by
CPI Group (UK) Ltd, Croydon, CR0 4YY

I'd like to express my heartfelt thanks and appreciation
to the following people for their help and support
during the writing of this book:

Jessica Schneider and Erin Engelhardt for honestly sharing
their thoughts, feelings, hopes and wishes; for reminding
me what it's like to be fifteen and best friends.

Linda Kay West (as always) for answering m many
questions about the law and legal proceedings.

Dianne Moggy and the amazing MIRA crew
for helping me make this book all it could be.

Evan Marshall for his support, enthusiasm
and incomparable instincts.

And special acknowledgment to Deanna Breheny,
winner of my 'Fantasy Proposal' contest.
Deanna, you and Jim are the greatest!

Prologue

Thistledown, Missouri
1998

The call had come in at 3:01 a.m. An anonymous tip. Something weird was going on over at the Gatehouse development site, the caller had said. They had seen lights.

Something weird, all right. A homicide.

Detective Nick Raphael climbed out of his Jeep Cherokee, stopping a moment to take in the scene. Two black and whites, his partner Bobby's truck and the coroner's wagon. No press yet, thank God. An officer stood guard at the door of the model home, cordoned off with yellow tape.

Nick moved his gaze slowly over the face of the house, then the land around it, careful not to rush, not to take anything for granted. He had learned long ago that rushing equaled missed opportunities. He had learned that good police work required a quick mind, a slow eye and the patience of Job.

He rubbed his hand across his jaw, rough with his morning beard. Funny place for a murder. Or a brilliant one. Located twenty minutes east of Thistledown, in the middle of nowhere, the development was hardly even up and running. It had, no doubt, been created with the St. Louis executive in mind. Only a forty-minute commute to a better life, Nick thought, mouth twisting into a grim smile. In relatively crime-free Thistledown.

Right. And tonight's little event wouldn't do much for the neighborhood.

He brought his attention back to his immediate surroundings. So far, the development consisted of three model homes, this one complete and two others nearly finished. Pool and tennis court just under construction; lots parceled off. No residents yet. Completely deserted.

Not completely deserted, Nick thought. Not tonight. The anonymous tip proved that. So did the stiff.

Nick started for the front door, squinting against the light spilling from the house into the darkness. He greeted the officer at the door, the man's rookie status apparent by his pallor.

"Davis, right?" Nick asked.

The kid nodded.

"What've we got?"

Davis cleared his throat, his color turning downright pasty. "Female. Caucasian. Twenty-eight to thirty-two. The M.E.'s checking her out now."

Nick swept his gaze over the face of the house again. Nice house. He'd bet it'd go for a half a million or more. He motioned with his head. "Everybody inside?"

The kid nodded again. "Straight ahead, then left. The living room."

Nick thanked him and went inside, noting the alarm-system panel as he did. Fancy, all the bells and whistles. It was on but not armed.

He heard voices and followed the sound, stopping dead when he saw her. She hung by her neck, naked, her hands bound in front of her by a black silk scarf. An identical scarf had been used to blindfold her. A tall stool lay on its side under her dangling feet, a short one sat beside it, undisturbed.

"Holy shit," he muttered, the past coming up behind him and biting him in the ass. "Holy fucking shit."

"Raphael. Glad you could make it."

Nick shifted his gaze to his partner. "I had Mara. It

took her baby-sitter a few minutes to get to the house.'' He moved his gaze back to the victim, his sense of déjà vu so strong it disoriented him. Nick forced himself to focus on this crime, this victim. He narrowed his eyes, studying her. She was—had been—a looker. Blond. Stacked. Even in death her breasts stood up high and firm. The blindfold covered too much of her face to be certain, but he'd bet the face had gone with the body. It just seemed to go that way with stiffs, though he couldn't say why.

The coroner stood on a chair, carefully examining the corpse. He stopped working and met Nick's eyes. "Hello, Detective.''

"Doc.'' Like Nick, the M.E. had been around a long time. Long enough to remember. "Talk to me,'' Nick said.

"Not a suicide,'' the doctor said quietly. "Not an accident. Her hands are bound. Kind of hard to string yourself up that way. She definitely had a playmate.''

Nick moved closer. "Do we recognize somebody's work here?''

"We might,'' the coroner said, returning to his examination. "Or it could be a copycat. No outward signs of a struggle. I think we're talking consensual, up to the very end anyway.''

"Right,'' Nick muttered. "Up to the moment the bastard kicked the stool out from under her.''

"Whoa.'' One of the uniforms came up beside them. "What's this 'recognize' bullshit? Have you guys seen something like this before?''

"You could say that.'' Nick moved closer to the body. "Something just like this. Fifteen years ago. Right here in Thistledown. Unsolved.''

As Nick said the words he thought of Andie and her friends, their involvement in that crime. He remembered how they had been all those years ago, young and naive and frightened. But so full of life. And he thought of himself, of how he had been the same way.

Much had changed in fifteen years. He'd changed, in ways he never could have imagined.

"Can you ID her, Nick?"

Using tweezers, the coroner ever so carefully removed the blindfold, dropped it into an evidence bag, then tapped the body. It swung slightly in Nick's direction.

Once again the past stared him square in the face, this time through lifeless blue eyes. Nick sucked in a sharp breath.

Not her. Dear Jesus, it couldn't be.

But it was.

He thought of Andie again. And of the events of fifteen years before. A knot, an emotion, settled in the pit of his gut, one he hadn't experienced in a long time.

Fear. Icy-cold and putrid. Like death.

Aware of the other two men looking at him, waiting for an answer, Nick struggled to find his voice. "Yeah," he managed to say finally, "I know who she is."

Book One

Best Friends - Summer of 1983

1
_____

Thistledown, Missouri
1983

The inside of the car was hot, steamy with the heat radiating from the two teenagers making out in the back seat. The Camaro rocked slightly with their enthusiastic movements. The sound of mouths and tongues meeting and sucking, of sighs and groans and murmured pleasure, filled the interior and spilled out into the June night.

Julie Cooper believed she had died and gone to heaven. She had run into Ryan Tolber, a senior she'd had a crush on the entire year before, on her way to the bowling alley's ladies' room. One thing had led to another, and when he'd suggested she come out to his car with him, she hadn't been able to say no.

Saying no was a big problem for Julie. Or at least that's what her best friends, Andie Bennett and Raven Johnson, told her.

As far as Julie was concerned, saying yes was tons more fun than saying no. And, of course, that was the problem.

"Come on, Julie baby. I'm gonna die if we don't."

"Oh, Ryan...I want to, but—"

He cut off her words with his mouth. He kissed her deeply, spearing his tongue into her mouth, pressing her back against the seat. She thought fleetingly of Andie and Raven, inside the bowling alley and no doubt looking for her by now. Andie would be worried sick; Raven would be mad as hell. Julie knew she should go back into the bowling alley and tell them where she was.

All thoughts of her friends evaporated as Ryan brought his hands to her breasts and began kneading them. "No buts, baby. I want you so bad. I need you."

Growing dizzy with his words and the sensations rocketing through her, she arched toward him. "I need you, too, Ryan."

He slipped his hands under her shirt and cupped and stroked her through her bra. "All last year I liked you. I thought you were the cutest freshman girl of all."

"Me? The cutest?" She gazed into his warm brown eyes, pleased at the compliment, feeling about to burst with happiness. "I liked you, too. Why didn't you ask me out?"

"You were a freshman. That made you off-limits, babe."

She nuzzled against his neck. "But I'm a sophomore now."

"Exactly. And now that you're older, you know what a boy needs." He worked her shirt over her head, then unfastened her bra. Her breasts spilled out into his hands. "Oh, baby," he muttered, his voice suddenly thick. "You have great tits. The best." He pulled a nipple into his mouth while he squeezed and rubbed them. "Say yes, baby."

Julie's head fell back. She wanted to, she really did. It felt so good. Much better than...than anything. She shuddered and curled her fingers into his hair. Besides, it wouldn't be fair to him if she said no now. After all, it was a proven fact boys needed sex more than girls. Starting this way and not finishing, well...it hurt them. She'd even heard that if it happened too often, their penises would go numb and eventually fall off.

And all because she wouldn't go through with what she had started.

That would be awful. She would hate for that to happen to Ryan. Or any guy.

"You're so beautiful, babe. So sexy. I love you. I really do."

She drew away from him so she could gaze into his dark eyes. "You do?" she whispered. "You love me?"

"Sure, baby. I do. I love you so much. I can't bear not to touch you. Let me in, Julie Cooper." He moved a hand to the waistband of her shorts, unfastened the snap and slipped his hand inside. "Let me in."

As his fingers brushed against her sex, she grabbed his shoulders, a low moan escaping her. She lifted her hips slightly so he could get his hand deeper between her legs, even as a part of her recoiled at her own behavior.

You're the devil's own, Julie Cooper. A Jezebel and a sinner.

Her father's voice, his words, ones she had heard hundreds of times before, popped into her head. Cold washed over her, and she squeezed her eyes tight shut, trying to force her father out of her head.

Ryan loved her. That made it okay. It did.

She locked her thighs around his hand, her eyelids fluttering shut, tingling sensations rocketing through her. It felt so good. So incredibly good. Anything that felt so good couldn't be wrong, no matter what her father said.

"Julie!" Someone rapped against the fogged window. "Is that you in there?"

"Get your ass out here!" another voice called. "If you miss your curfew—"

"Your dad's going to kill you!"

Julie's eyes snapped open. *Andie. And Raven. They'd found her.*

Dear God…her curfew.

She struggled to free herself, but Ryan locked his free arm around her waist, pinning her on his lap, his hand still between her legs. "Get lost," he called. "We're busy."

"Julie!" Andie shouted, pounding on the window again. "Are you nuts? Do you want to be grounded for the entire summer?"

Julie froze. Even one minute past her nine o'clock curfew would be met with severe punishment. An image of what her summer would be like passed before her eyes. No friends. No movies or parties or swimming. Hours spent on her knees studying the Scriptures and praying for forgiveness.

Her father at the pulpit, delivering his sermon, pointing at her, singling her out, calling her what she was.

Sinner.

She made a sound of terror. Her dad would do it, too. All of it. Without hesitation.

And if he had even one hint of what she had been up to, he would do worse, the way he always threatened. Send her away. Separate her from Andie and Raven. Send her to a place where she would have no one. She couldn't bear to be alone like that again, the way she had been before Andie and Raven had become her friends.

Julie wiggled free of Ryan's grasp. "I'm coming," she called, scrambling around for her bra and shirt, yanking them on, then refastening her shorts. She found her hair band and pulled her long, wavy blond hair back into a high ponytail, combing it with her fingers. She dipped her fingers into her shorts' pocket for her glasses, dark-rimmed, ugly things she hated and wore as little as possible. She had begged her father for contacts. He had refused, admonishing her sternly about vanity being the work of the devil, then had removed every mirror in the house save for the one in his and her mother's bathroom, which he kept locked at all times.

Glasses clutched in her hand, she looked apologetically at Ryan. "Sorry. I had a great time."

He cupped her face in his palms, his expression boyish and pleading. "Then don't go. Stay with me, babe."

Her heart turned over. *He loved her. He really did. How could she leave when he—*

The door flew open; light from the parking lot flooded

the car's interior. Andie stuck her head into the car. "Julie, come on! It's twenty to nine."

"Twenty to nine," Julie repeated, a shudder of fear racing up her spine.

Ryan caught her hand. "Fuck your old man, babe. Stay with me."

Raven appeared at the doorway then, all but growling at him. "Her old man is *not* who you want her to fuck. Get lost, creep."

Andie grabbed her one arm, Raven the other. They pulled Julie out of the car, slammed the door behind her and tugged her toward the shortcut back to Happy Hollow, the subdivision where all three girls lived.

As soon as they had gotten out of earshot of the car, Julie shoved on her glasses and whirled to face Raven, her cheeks hot with fury. "How could you say that to him? You called him a creep. You…you used *that* word. The F-word. He'll never want to see me again."

"Please." Raven made a sound of derision. "He is a creep, Julie. And the F-word is just a word. Fuck. Fuck, fuck, fuck. There, I said it four times and nobody's dead or anything."

"Do you always have to be so crude? It makes me sick."

"Do you always have to be so easy? It makes me embarrassed for you."

Julie took a step back, feeling as if the other girl had slapped her. "Thanks a lot. I *thought* you were my friend."

"And I thought—"

Andie stepped between them. "Stop it, both of you! If we don't get out of here *now*, Julie's sunk. What's the matter with you guys? We're supposed to be friends."

"I'm not going anywhere with *her*." Julie folded her arms across her chest. "Not until she apologizes."

"Why should I? It's true."

"It's not! Ryan said he loves me. That changes everything."

The words fell between them like a dead cat. Andie and Raven exchanged glances.

"What?" Julie asked, indignant. "Why are you two looking at each other like that?"

"Julie," Andie said gently, "you hardly know him."

"That doesn't matter. With love, that doesn't matter." She looked from one to the other, knowing she sounded almost desperate. Sudden tears stung her eyes. "He said he loves me, and I know he meant it."

"How?" Raven muttered. "By his hard dick?"

Julie sucked in a sharp breath, hurt. "You guys are supposed to be my friends. You're supposed to stick up for me. You're supposed to…to understand."

"We are your friends." Andie squeezed her arm. "And we do understand, Julie. But friends are also supposed to try to protect each other. Guys will…they'll say anything to get what they want. You know that."

"But, Ryan—"

"Look, Julie," Raven cut in, her tone that of an impatient mother with her toddler, "get real. You ran into the guy at the bowling alley. He's never even asked you out."

"He said he liked me all last year. He didn't ask me out because he was a senior and I was a freshman and—"

"And time for a reality check," Raven cut in, rolling her eyes. "Did you, like, take classes in being stupid?"

"Thanks a lot," Julie said, nudging her glasses up to the bridge of her nose with her index finger, her voice quivering with hurt. "I guess it's hard for either of you to believe that a boy as cute and smart and…and as important as Ryan Tolber would like me, ridiculous little Julie Cooper."

"That's not it at all." Andie shot a warning look at Raven. "And you should know that. We think you're the best. We think you're too good for him. Isn't that right, Rave?"

"Way too good," Raven answered. "He's not even in the same league with you."

"Really?" Julie blinked back tears even as she glared at Raven. "Then why are you always so ugly to me? You act like you're so much smarter than I am. Like you know so much more about everything. It makes me feel bad."

"I'm sorry, Julie. It's just that sometimes you act like all you care about is boys and making out. You know, if you keep this up, people are going to call you a slut. Some already do. And it really makes me mad."

"A slut," Julie whispered, her world rocking. "People are…they're calling me a—" She looked at Andie in question, hardly able to see through her tears. Andie would never deliberately hurt her, but she wouldn't lie, either. Andie never lied. "Are people…are they really…calling me that?"

Andie hesitated, then put an arm around her. "We're just trying to protect you, Julie. Because we love you."

Raven joined the other two. "I shouldn't have said those things. I just get so pissed off when I see you setting yourself up to be hurt that way. You're too good for guys like Ryan Tolber. He's a user."

"I'm sorry," Julie whispered, turning and hugging Raven. "I know you're only trying to help me. But you're wrong about Ryan. You both are. You'll see."

"I hope you're right," Raven said, hugging her back. "I really do."

"Guys," Andie murmured, glancing at her watch, "it's almost nine now. Any ideas how we're going to get Julie home by her curfew?"

Julie looked at her friends, the full impact of her situation sinking in. "My dad's going to kill me," she whispered. She brought a hand to her mouth. "He's going to…he'll—"

She started to run. Her friends ran after her, but she didn't pause or glance back, just continued to put one foot before the other. She pictured her father, standing at the kitchen door, watch in hand. She could almost hear his lecture, his litany of criticisms and accusations. His disappointment.

The clock on Thistledown's town square began to chime, ringing out her defeat. *She wasn't going to make it. It was too late.*

Julie stopped, panting, swamped by tears. "Why am I even bothering?" She dropped to her knees, despair overwhelming her. "I've done it again. Screwed up again. What's the matter with me?"

"Nothing's the matter with you." Andie sank to the ground beside her and patted her arm. "Come on, don't give up. We still have a chance."

"No, we don't. Listen to the clock." It chimed the ninth and final ring, the last of it vibrating a moment on the night air before leaving silence behind. "I'm dead." She covered her face with her hands. "He's right about me. I'm no good at all. An embarrassment. A stupid, vain—"

"Don't you say that!" Raven shouted and started to run. "He's not right. He's not!"

Confused, Julie leaped to her feet. "Raven, what are you... We can't make it!"

Andie followed her up. They exchanged glances, then ran after their friend. "Raven," they called in unison, "wait for us, we—"

Even as the words were leaving their lips, Raven fell, landing on her knees, catching herself with her hands, skidding on the road's gravel shoulder.

With a cry, the other two raced to her side.

"Are you okay?"

"You're bleeding!"

Raven ignored them and eased into a sitting position. She gazed at her badly skinned knees and hands. "Not good enough," she muttered, turning her gaze to the rocky ground. She selected a jagged-edged rock about the size of a lime.

Even as Julie opened her mouth to ask her friend what

she was doing, Raven drew her hand back and brought the rock crashing down on her leg. She barely flinched as the rock gouged a bloody path from her knee to her midcalf.

"There," Raven said, her voice quivering. "That should do it."

"Oh my gosh." Julie brought a shaking hand to her mouth, gazing at the growing puddle of blood on the ground by her friend's foot. "Raven, what... Why did you do that?"

Raven lifted her gaze. "I'm not about to stand back and let you take another round of your old man's shit. I've been watching you take it since you were eight years old, and enough's enough. This should take the heat off you." She smiled, her lips trembling. "Your dad can hardly blame you for my accident. Why, despite fear of his reprisal, you did the Christian thing and stayed to help me. Give me a hand, will you?"

Julie grasped one hand, Andie the other. They helped Raven to her feet. She winced as she put her weight on her leg for the first time. "Man, that hurts."

"Come on," Andie murmured. "We need to get that cut cleaned. It looks pretty deep." She bent and peered at Raven's leg. She wrinkled her nose. "It might even need stitches."

Stitches. Julie felt light-headed. *Raven had done this for her. Hurt herself to help her.*

"Do you think?" Raven studied the gash, her face pale. She swayed a bit and grabbed Julie's arm. "Now my leg will match my face," she murmured, referring to the long scar that curved down her right cheek, the result of a car accident when she was six. "Once a freak always a freak."

"You're not a freak!" Julie glanced at Andie, then back at Raven. "You have the hair and eyes of an angel, and you—"

"Have the face of a monster." Raven laughed grimly. "You think I haven't heard the guys call me Bride of Frankenstein behind my back?"

"They're just immature jerks," Andie said quickly. "Don't pay any attention to them."

"Spoken like someone who nobody's ever stared at or whispered about. You don't know what it's like to be different."

"You'd rather look like me?" Andie asked, holding her arms out. "There's nothing special about me. Dishwater-blond hair, brown eyes. I don't even have boobs yet and I'm fifteen."

"Julie got 'em," Raven said, a smile tugging at her mouth. "Julie got everyone's."

Julie felt herself blush. "You do so have boobs, both of you. Mine aren't *that* big."

"Compared to what? Watermelons?" Raven's smile faded. "Don't you guys get it?" She shifted her weight slightly, grimacing. "It doesn't matter what other people think. It doesn't matter if the whole frigging world thinks I'm a freak. All I care about is us, our friendship. I could be the most beautiful girl in the world, but I would be dead without you two. You're my family. And like tonight, family always sticks up for each other. *Always.*"

2

An hour later, Andie stood at her front door, her head still spinning with the events of the night. She couldn't stop picturing Raven bringing the rock crashing down on her leg. Raven had hardly even flinched, though Andie knew it must have really hurt. The gash had bled so much her white sneaker had turned pink.

But it had done the trick for Julie, that was for sure. Reverend Cooper had glowered at them, questioning them about their whereabouts before the accident had happened, obviously trying to trap them into confessing some mortal sin.

Through it all, Julie had looked almost comically guilty, but Raven had hammed it up for the Good Reverend, going on and on about the way Julie had stayed to help her even though Raven had begged her to go ahead and get home.

Raven was the best liar Andie had ever known.

And the best friend anyone could have. Andie didn't think she would have the guts to do something like that, even if it meant saving her best friend's butt.

In the end the worst he had delivered was a stern admonishment for them all to be more careful. Mrs. Cooper had cleaned and bandaged Raven's leg, then driven them both home.

Andie turned and waved to Mrs. Cooper, then let herself in her front door. She shook her head. Raven was always doing stuff like that, charging fearlessly in to help her or Julie, never worrying about reprisals or being hurt.

That's how she and Raven had met. It had been the

summer she was eight, and Raven had just moved into the house next door. She had come upon Andie, surrounded by a group of neighborhood bullies on bikes. Raven had jumped in the middle of them, like some sort of supergirl out to save the day. Andie laughed to herself, remembering how awed she had been even though they had both gotten their butts kicked.

They had been instant best friends and inseparable ever since.

Andie headed for the kitchen, hungry. She plucked an apple from the fruit bowl on the counter. "Mom?" she called, noticing how quiet it was. "Dad? I'm home!"

"In here, pumpkin," her dad answered from the den, his voice sounding funny, kind of thick and tight. Like he had a cold. "Could you come in here, please?"

"Sure, Dad." She ambled for the den, polishing the apple on her T-shirt sleeve. She took a big bite, thinking about the way her dad had sounded. If it wasn't a cold, he was probably pissed off about some dumb stunt her brothers had pulled. Twins, four years younger than she was, they were always getting into something they weren't supposed to.

Brothers, Andie thought. They were such a pain.

Andie found her entire family in the den—her mother, father and brothers. She stopped in the doorway, moving her gaze from one to the next, the bite of apple sticking in her throat. Her mother's eyes and face were red and puffy from crying, her dad's face was stiff, his mouth set into a hard, grim line. For once, her brothers were quiet, their heads bowed and shoulders slumped.

Something was wrong. Something terrible had happened.

"Mom? What is it?"

Her mother refused to look at her, and Andie shifted her gaze to her father. "Dad? What's wrong? Is it Grandma? Is it—"

Her mother looked up then, and the raw fury in her

expression stunned Andie. She had never seen her mother look that way before. Andie took an involuntary step backward. "Mom? Have I done something wrong? I mean, I'm sorry if I'm late, but Raven fell and—"

"Your *father* has something to tell you."

Andie turned to her dad. "Daddy?" she whispered, using the name she hadn't called him in years. "What's wrong?"

"Sit down, pumpkin."

"No." She shook her head. "Not until you tell me everything's okay."

"Tell her, Dan," her mother piped in, voice cracking. "Tell her how everything's going to be okay. Tell her how you decided you don't love us anymore."

"Marge!"

Her mother's voice rose to a hysterical pitch. "Tell her how you're leaving us."

Andie stared at her parents. *This couldn't be happening. Not to her happy family.*

"No," she said, hearing her own panic. "No, it isn't true."

"Honey—" Her dad stood and held out a hand to her. "This happens sometimes. Adults fall out of love with each other. This has nothing to do with you or your brothers."

She heard his words, but hollowly, as if they had come from a great distance. They echoed in her head, mingling with the thunder of her own heart.

Fall out of love? Nothing to do with her?

He was leaving them. Leaving her.

She sucked in a quick, shallow breath, pain a living thing inside her. How could he say that? How could it have nothing to do with her if she felt like she was dying inside?

"This has nothing to do with any of you kids," he continued. "I love you all as much as I always have."

Andie darted a glance at her brothers. They were huddled together, clinging to one another. Pete was crying quietly; Daniel was not. Daniel stared stonily at their father, eyes bright with fury. With her brothers, the lines had already been drawn.

How typical of them, she thought. Though twins, they were as different as night and day. Pete was sensitive, emotional, exuberant; everybody's favorite. Daniel on the other hand, was intense, serious, introverted. Unlike Pete, Daniel would hold his anger in—for days, weeks, months—seething. Daniel was not going to forgive their father easily; Pete already had.

What about her? What was she going to do?

"I'm not moving far away," her father was saying. "I'll be right here in Thistledown. We'll see each other all the time. I've already discussed visitation with my attorn—"

"Your attorney?" her mother cut in, her expression stunned. "You've already seen an attorney?"

"Yes, Marge," he said, swinging his gaze to his wife, "I have."

Andie took another step backward. What had happened? she wondered. How could he look at her mother so coldly? Just this morning they had kissed, they had laughed together.

"I thought it would be best," he continued, "to discuss my rights before I—"

"Best? Rights?" Her mother's voice rose. "Your right to see your children only on weekends and half the holidays? You thought that would be best? Better than coming home to them every night?"

"That's enough, Marge! I don't think it's appropriate to be having this conversation in front of the children."

"Don't you talk to me about appropriate behavior! Don't you dare!" Her mother jumped to her feet. "We're supposed to be a family."

"The marriage just isn't working for me." He made a sound of frustration. "I'm not happy. I haven't been in a long time. Surely you knew."

Andie wrapped her arms around her middle, apple still clutched in one hand. *Not happy?* Her mom and dad almost never fought, had almost never disagreed. He'd kissed her mother when he left for work this morning. He did every morning. And every morning her mom kissed him back, then smiled.

A squeak of pain slipped past her lips. *Now he wasn't happy. Now he wanted to leave them.*

Why? Had she done something to cause this? Had her brothers?

Tears choked her. She didn't want her family to break up. She didn't want her daddy to leave. She loved him more than anything.

"Don't go, Dad," Andie begged. "I want us to stay a family."

He looked at Andie, then the twins. "We'll still be a family, kids. We'll always be a family. Where I live won't change that."

But it would. It would change everything. "I'll help out more," she said quickly, scrambling for a way to make everything all right. "I promise. Us kids, we won't fight." She looked pleadingly at her brothers. "Will we?"

"We won't," they said in unison, shaking their heads. "We promise to be good."

"Honey, it's not—"

"And I'll baby-sit," she went on, not wanting to give him the opportunity to speak, afraid of what he might say. "Whenever you ask, so you guys can go out. And I won't complain about it, I promise. Just give me another chance. I'll show you how good I can be."

"You see, Dan?" her mother whispered, sinking back to the chair, the fight seeming to go out of her. "You see what you're doing to your children?"

He ignored her and crossed to Andie. "Oh, pumpkin." He wrapped his arms around her, bringing her to his chest. "It's not you. It's not your brothers. You guys are perfect.'' He drew back and looked into her eyes. "It's me and your mom.''

Andie fought tears. She glanced at her brothers again, at the way they huddled together. They always did that, they had each other, they were a team. She had Raven and Julie. She shifted her gaze to her mother, sitting alone, her expression devastated. Her parents used to be a team. They used to have each other.

How could her daddy do this? How could he leave them this way? He was supposed to love them, no matter what.

Andie struggled free of her father's arms and went to her mother. She knelt by the chair and wrapped her arms around her. For a moment her mother held herself stiffly, then she sagged against Andie, clinging to her.

"Andie, honey," her father said softly, patiently, "I know you're upset, but in time you'll understand."

"No, I won't." She shook her head, her tears spilling over. "You said family was everything. The most important thing. You lied."

"I didn't lie. I didn't know. Things happen. They—" He looked at his wife. "Marge, help me out here."

She stiffened. "You did this, Dan. *You.* Don't ask me to help you *make it better* now."

"Fine." He moved his gaze from Andie to her brothers, then back. "This is the way it's going to be. I'm sorry, kids, but it just…is. When you're older, you'll—"

"Understand?" Andie lifted her gaze to his, heart breaking. She shook her head. "I won't understand, Dad. And I won't forgive you. Not ever."

For a long moment he simply stared at her, then without another word, he turned and walked away.

3
___

Andie lay on her bed, dry-eyed, completely spent. Moments after her father left, she'd heard his car and had run to the window and watched him go, watching until long after his taillights had been swallowed by the night.

Gone. Just like that.

She rolled onto her side. The house was unnaturally quiet. Still. Her brothers had gone to bed some time ago; her mother was now locked in her bedroom. Usually at this time of night, Andie could hear the muted sound of a late-night talk show coming from the TV in her parents' room or her mom and dad's hushed conversation. Once in a while the phone would ring, or the cat would meow outside her bedroom window.

Not tonight. Tonight it was as if the world had come to an end. Nothing was left for her but her own, agonizing thoughts.

Her dad was leaving them.

He didn't love them anymore, not enough to stay a family, anyway.

Her thoughts, the truth of them, cut like a knife. She sat up, hugging her middle. She glanced at her closed door again, thinking of her brothers, picturing their devastated faces. With a sigh, she climbed off her bed and headed out of her room and down the hall to theirs. She opened their door and peeked inside.

"Are you guys okay?"

"Fine," Daniel answered angrily, glaring at her. "We're not babies, you know."

"I know. But, I...I thought you might want to talk."

"Andie?" Pete rolled onto his side, facing her. "I don't get it. Mom and Dad, they were always so...I mean, I thought they were..."

His voice trailed off miserably, and Andie's heart went out to him. "I thought the same thing." She sighed. "I guess we were wrong."

His face pinched up with an effort not to cry. "Are we going to see Dad at all anymore?"

"I don't know." She looked away, then back. "He said so."

"But he's a liar," Daniel said, sitting up. "He's a stinkin' liar. I don't care if I ever see him again. And neither does Pete."

But Pete did care, Andie could tell. His eyes filled with tears, and he turned quickly away. She scowled at her other brother. "Shut up, okay. You don't know everything."

"I know more than you."

"You wish. You're just a kid."

He jerked up his chin. "Well, I know something about Dad that you don't. It's a secret."

"Sure you do," she said sarcastically. "And of course it's a *secret.* That way you can't tell me."

"I'll tell you. Close the door. I don't want Mom to hear."

Andie made a sound of annoyance but did as he asked. That done, she folded her arms across her chest. "Okay, it's closed. What's the big secret?"

"Dad's got a girlfriend."

For a moment Andie simply stared at her brother, too stunned to speak. Then she curved her hands into fists and took a step farther into the room. "You're lying. Take it back, Daniel. Take it back now."

"I heard him talking to her on the phone. Tonight. He told her that...he told her he loved her. Before he hung up."

"It's not true." Andie struggled to breathe past the lump in her throat. "You're making it up."

"I heard him, too," Pete whispered brokenly. "He said...he said that after tonight—"

"They could be together," Daniel finished, his anger and defiance fading. "He had to take care of us first."

"No. It's not true." Andie backed out of her brothers' bedroom, shaking her head, refusing to believe them. There was an explanation for what her brothers had overheard. Her dad wouldn't do that. He wasn't one of *those* kind of men.

She snapped their door shut, wishing she had left bad enough alone. Wishing she hadn't goaded Daniel into telling what he *supposedly* knew about their father. Her dad wouldn't do that, she told herself again. He wouldn't.

As if her thoughts had conjured him, she heard her father's voice. She swung toward her parents' closed bedroom door, hope surging through her. *He'd changed his mind. He'd come back. He wasn't going to leave them after all.*

She raced down the hall. Pete and Daniel were wrong about what they'd heard; it was a lie. She grabbed the doorknob, ready to burst in without knocking. She stopped short at the sound of her mother's voice.

"—take everything you want now, because I swear to God you're not setting foot back inside this house without a court order."

"Fine, I'll do that."

Andie heard the click of latches being opened. She brought a hand to her mouth. He wasn't staying, she realized. He was packing.

"I'm really sorry, Marge. I never meant for this to happen."

"Spare me the big apology," her mother answered, her voice thick with tears. "I've given you the last twenty years of my life, and you give me 'I'm really sorry'? No thanks."

"What's with the wounded surprise? This has been coming for months. Years, really. It's been over for a long time."

"You have children," she said. "How can it be over? You made a vow to me, Dan." Andie pressed her ear to the door and heard rustling noises, like clothes being dug out of drawers. "A *vow*," she repeated. "Don't you remember?"

"I know," he said heavily, sounding tired, more tired than Andie had ever heard him. "I'm sorry."

"Sorry?" she repeated angrily. "Sorry? If you were sorry you wouldn't do this! There's someone else, isn't there?"

"Marge, don't—"

"Someone you love more than me. More than *us*."

"Stop it, Marge. For God's sake, the children will—"

"That's right, *the children*. Your children. What do you care about them? If you cared, you wouldn't do this."

"I care plenty, and you know it."

"Right. You care. Who's always here for them, chauffeuring them to this class and that field trip? Who gave up a career to raise our kids? *Our kids*, Dan. Not just mine."

Andie squeezed her eyes shut, feeling as though she might vomit, not wanting to hear her mother's words but unable to tear herself away.

"Always playing the martyr, aren't you? You've been throwing your ridiculous little career up in my face for twenty years. You worked at the newspaper as a cut-and-paste girl."

"I was a commercial artist!" her mom cried. "I loved it, and I was good, too!"

"Well, here's your chance to get back to it," he said, slamming what sounded like a bureau drawer.

"I know there's someone else. I've known for months."

"For God's sake—"

"Tell me it's not true, then. Tell me you haven't been

having an affair. Tell me you haven't been screwing around behind my back.''

Andie pressed a fist to her mouth, holding back a cry, praying for him to deny it was true.

He didn't deny it. His silence spoke volumes.

''I bet,'' her mother continued, ''whoever she is, she doesn't have any children. She's unencumbered. No runny noses to wipe, no childish disagreements to break up. Plenty of time to make herself look pretty and feel sexy—''

''I don't love you anymore. I don't love *us* anymore! That's what this is about, it's not about Leeza.''

''Your secretary?'' Her mother's voice rose. ''My God, she's twenty years younger than you are!''

Leeza Martin. Her father's secretary. Andie squeezed her eyes shut, picturing her, young and pretty, wearing short skirts and a bright smile. Andie used to look at her and think she was so cute, she used to look at her and long to be as cute herself.

Pretty Leeza had stolen her daddy.

Andie's stomach turned, the taste of hatred bitter on her tongue. All the time Leeza had been smiling and being so nice to her, she'd been…been…sleeping with her father. Breaking her mother's heart.

Her mother was sobbing, begging him to stay, pleading with him to think of the kids. He made a sound of disgust. ''How could you want me to stay if I don't want to be here? How could you want me to stay only for the children? That's not a marriage. It's a prison.''

Andie sprang away from the door as if it were on fire. The tears, the pain welled inside her until she thought she would burst. She longed to throw herself at him and beg him not to go. To cry and plead. Just as her mom was doing.

It wouldn't do any good. There was someone he loved more than his family, someplace he would rather be than here with them.

He had promised he would always be here for her. Always. He'd told her that nothing in the world was more important than his family, their happiness.

He'd lied. He was a liar. A cheater.

Raven. Her friend would help her; her friend would make everything okay.

Andie turned and ran back to her bedroom. She closed and locked the door behind her, crossed to the window and opened it. With one last glance backward, she climbed over the sill and dropped to the ground.

It was late, the sounds and smells of the night assailed her senses: the perfume of some night-blooming flower; the call of the crickets and a bullfrog; the scream of a horn somewhere in the distance.

Andie picked her way across her yard and through the hedge that separated the Johnsons' property from their's. A car swung out of the driveway across the street, momentarily pinning her in its headlights. Andie froze, afraid that Mrs. Blum, a third-shift nurse at Thistledown General, would see her and call her mom.

Mrs. Blum moved on. So did Andie.

Within moments, Andie found herself below Raven's bedroom window, tossing pebbles up at the glass and praying her friend would come. How many times had Raven come to Andie's window, seeking comfort? Too many to count, Andie acknowledged.

Now it was her. Andie's chest ached at the realization. For the first time ever, her home didn't feel safe and happy, it didn't feel…perfect anymore. For the first time, she wanted to be somewhere else.

The moment Andie saw her friend's face, she started to cry. Raven slid the window up, her expression alarmed. "Andie?" she whispered. "What's wrong?"

"My parents are…they're splitting up."

"No way." Raven shook her head, her expression disbelieving. "Not your parents."

"Yes, they're—" Andie struggled to find her voice. "My dad's...he's leaving us."

Raven leaned farther out the window. "Hold on," she whispered, the breeze catching her white-blond hair and blowing it across her face. She swept it back. "I'll be right down."

A couple minutes later she emerged from the house, fully dressed. She came to Andie and put her arms around her. "Oh, Andie. I can't believe it."

Andie pressed her face to her best friend's shoulder for a moment, clinging to her. "Believe it. He called us all together for this bogus meeting about how much he still loves us and everything."

She wiped her runny nose with the back of her hand. "Then I heard the whole truth later. He's been screwing around on my mom."

Raven gasped. "Not *your* dad!"

"With his secretary."

"That perky little bimbo? She's...she's like a Barbie doll. Your mom's way better than her."

Andie sank to the ground and dropped her face into her hands. "I feel so awful. I don't know what to do."

Raven sat beside her, wrapping an arm protectively around Andie's shoulder. "It's going to be okay."

"How did you make it?" Andie asked brokenly. "After your mom took off, I mean. I feel like I'm going to die."

For a long moment, Raven was silent, as if lost in her own memories. Then she cleared her throat. "You know what I think? That parents suck. Especially fathers."

"I always thought I had the best family in the whole world. I never thought my dad could do—"

"Anything wrong," Raven supplied, and Andie nodded miserably. "You thought he was perfect. A *hero,* or something."

As she spoke, something crept into her friend's voice, something mean. Something Andie didn't recognize. Andie looked at her. "Rave?"

Her friend met her eyes. "But he's no hero, is he, Andie? He's just another prick."

Andie looked away. It hurt to think of her dad that way. It hurt almost more than she could bear.

"Let's get Julie."

"Julie?"

"Why not?" Raven smiled. "Screw 'em all. Let's get out of here."

"But your leg. Can you, I mean, doesn't it hurt?"

Raven glanced down at the bandage and shrugged. "Yeah, it hurts. So what? Worst case, I blow out a few stitches."

Andie swallowed hard. "How many did you get?"

"Twenty. Would have been less but the cut was so jagged. You should have seen my dad, he turned green and had to leave the room." She shook her head. "I don't get human nature. My dad turning green at that? *My dad?* Unbelievable." She got to her feet and held out a hand. "Come on."

Andie shook her head. "You're going to hurt yourself. I don't want that."

"It's for you, Andie. Don't you get it? It doesn't matter if I get hurt, not when it's for you."

Andie agreed without saying a word. She didn't have to ask where they would go after they collected their friend; she knew. To their place, the abandoned toolshed on the edge of one of farmer Trent's fields. They had discovered it two summers ago and immediately claimed it as their special place. Small, dilapidated and smelling faintly of oil, they loved it. Because it was theirs. A place where they could be together and be themselves, away from prying parents and annoying siblings.

Julie lived on Mockingbird Lane, three blocks behind Andie and Raven, in Phase II of Happy Hollow. The two girls wound their way across and around the streets and connecting yards without discovery. Not that there was too much chance of that, the streets were deserted, every house dark and locked up tight.

Andie found the quiet unsettling. She moved her gaze over Julie's street, taking in the row of houses with their unnaturally blank windows. Since R. H. Rawlings, a machine manufacturer and one of the town's major employers, had closed six months before, about forty percent of the Phase II houses were for sale or rent and empty. Of the ten houses on Mockingbird Lane only three were occupied. Many of the empty homes were still owned by Sadler Construction, the builder. Andie had heard her father remark that it was a good thing the Sadlers had such deep pockets.

"It's kind of creepy," Andie whispered. "I keep getting this feeling, like all the houses are watching us."

"They're empty, Andie. Nobody lives in them, so how could they be watching?"

She inched closer to Raven. "They're *supposed* to be empty, but what if they're not? I mean, it would be so easy for someone to hide in one of them."

"And do what? Jump out and grab some poor, unsuspecting teenager? I don't think so."

Andie made a face at her friend's sarcasm. "It could happen. Look at those houses at the end of the circle. There's nothing behind them but old man Trent's fields. And the one on the left's bordered by a wooded lot." Andie shuddered, imagining. "That doesn't spook you at all?"

"Nope." Raven shook her head. "I like that they're empty. There's no nosy old busybody peering out her window at us, scolding us for crossing her yard and threatening to call our parents. I wish they were all empty."

They reached Julie's house, a beige-colored two-story with dark blue shutters, and went around to the rear. Their friend's bedroom was on the second floor, in back. Luckily, her parents' bedroom was on the other side of the house.

They had done this before, though they didn't push their luck. Of all their parents, Julie's father was the toughest. He believed in punishment as a daily cleansing ritual. It didn't matter what Julie did, she always did wrong. He made it clear she always let him down.

When she really *did* let him down, he made his daughter pay in ways that scared Andie. Forcing his daughter to stay on her knees for hours reading the Scriptures, humiliating her publicly, controlling her in ways that went way beyond what any other parents did.

Andie was of the opinion that the Good Reverend Cooper, as she and Raven called him, was obsessed with sin and sinfulness, and that he kind of got off on it. It didn't help that Julie looked more like a *Playboy* magazine centerfold than a regular fifteen-year-old. Andie also thought he was a complete A-hole and that Julie deserved lots better than him for a father. She only wished Julie thought so, too.

Raven scooped up some gravel and threw a few pieces at a time at Julie's window. Within moments, Julie appeared. She saw it was them and raised the window and unlatched the screen.

"What are you guys doing here?" she whispered, then glanced nervously over her shoulder.

Raven grinned. "Come down and find out."

"I don't know." Julie looked over her shoulder again, then back at them. "Dad was pretty suspicious tonight. After you guys left, he asked me lots of questions about how you got hurt. Then we had to pray for purity and forgiveness." She lifted the screen higher and leaned her face out, squinting without her glasses. "How's your leg?"

"Hurts. It's no big deal."

"She got twenty stitches," Andie said.

"*Twenty?*" Julie's eyes widened. "Oh, Rave."

"Forget my leg, okay? Come on down." Raven stuck her hands in her back pockets. "Your dad's going to beat your ass even if you don't come. He'll find some reason, you know he will.''

Julie pushed her honey-blond hair away from her face and grinned. "If I'm going to go down anyway, I suppose I might as well have a little fun on the way. Give me a sec.''

A minute or so later, Julie appeared at the window once more, gave them a thumbs-up, then within moments emerged from her house, locking the door behind her. She hurried over to them.

"Andie's folks are splitting up," Raven said without preamble.

"Oh my God!" Julie swung to face Andie. "It's not true, not your parents!"

Andie's eyes welled with tears. "He told us tonight. He's been...cheating on my mom. With his secretary.''

"No! That little blonde?" Andie nodded and Julie hugged her. "That really sucks, Andie. You know, I always thought your parents were so happy. So perfect. Like one of those TV families. And your dad, I thought he was the best and that you were so lucky.''

Andie started to cry. "So did I.''

"Great, Julie. You made her cry.''

"I didn't mean to!''

"Well, you did anyway. Geez!''

Andie made a sound that was half laugh, half sob, then wiped her nose with the back of her hand. "It's not Julie's fault. I'm just upset, that's all.''

"Let's get out of here," Raven said, "before Julie's dad or one of her tattletale brothers gets up to take a pee and sees us out here.''

They started off, keeping to the shadows until they were well clear of Julie's house. As they neared the bottom of the cul-de-sac, Andie stopped. "Wait." She held up a hand to quiet them. "Do you hear that?''

"What?''

"Music. Shh...there.''

The other two girls listened. They heard it, too.

"Where's it coming from?" Julie asked, frowning. They were standing dead center between the four empty houses at the end of the cul-de-sac.

Andie strained to locate the source of the faint music. It floated on the night air, disembodied, there and then gone. It was odd music, disturbing somehow, with a slow, deep beat that made her pulse pound.

"We shouldn't be hearing music here." Andie looked at her friends. "Where would it be coming from?"

Julie glanced over her shoulder at the rest of the houses on her street. All were completely dark. "This is weird. Everybody on this block is asleep."

"We're not." At her friend's blank glances, Raven giggled. "Guys, get a grip. It's probably coming from a couple blocks away. Sound carries on the night air. Which I should know." She grimaced. "My parents' fights were legendary, all over every neighborhood we ever lived in."

"You're right." Andie laughed, sounding a bit breathless even to her own ears. "My imagination is working overtime."

"But it is kind of creepy," Julie said, rubbing her arms. "It's so quiet otherwise."

Raven laughed. "Come on you chickenshits. Follow me!" She took off in a sort of run-limp-hop because of her stitches; with a sound of surprise, the other two followed her. They cut across the backyard of the last house, then ducked into the twenty-foot stand of trees that separated Trent's farm from Happy Hollow. Once in the open fields, it was easier to see; their shed stood out incongruously against the otherwise flat, barren field.

They reached it, but instead of going inside, climbed onto the metal roof, lay back and gazed up at the black velvet sky. Minutes passed; none of them spoke. Somewhere in the distance a dog barked.

"It's so beautiful," Julie murmured.

Raven murmured her agreement. "And so quiet."

Andie folded her arms behind her head and breathed deeply. "It's like we're the only people in the whole universe. Just us and the stars."

"What if it was just us?" Raven mused. "No asshole parents? Nobody making us be what they want us to be?"

"If it was just us," Andie murmured, "I wouldn't be so sad right now."

"What about boys?"

Andie and Raven looked at each other, then burst out laughing. "Leave it to you, Julie."

"Well, really." She sniffed, sounding annoyed. "We'd have to have boys. You guys might be able to do without…well, you know, but not me."

"Well, I could," Raven said, her tone fierce. "Boys become men. Then they become like your dad or mine." She made a sound of disgust. "No thank you."

Andie looked at her. "They don't have to be that way."

"No?" Raven frowned. "Go ask your mom if I'm right."

The girls fell silent for long moments, then Raven reached across and touched Andie's arm. "I'm sorry I said that."

"It's okay."

Raven propped herself up on her elbow. "Do either of you ever think about the future? Where we're going to be? What we're going to be?"

"College," Andie offered.

"Together," Julie added.

"But beyond that? Like, *who* do you want to be? And what do you want your life to be like?"

"That's easy," Julie said. "I want to be popular. I mean *really* popular. And I won't feel bad about it. I won't feel guilty about being pretty and having fun or about going out every single night if I want to."

Raven sat up and drew her knees to her chest. "I want to be the one who says how it's going to be. I want to be the one other people follow."

Julie giggled. "You'll probably be the first woman president. They'll put your face on a postage stamp or something."

"This face? Please, I'd scare little children."

"Stop that," Andie said, frowning, feeling bad for her friend. "You're gorgeous. The only reason the boys say those things about you is because they can't get anything over on you. They call you freak 'cause they want into your pants and you won't let them."

For a long moment, Raven was silent. Then she cleared her throat. "Do you really mean that?"

"I wouldn't have said it if I didn't."

Raven grinned. "I like that." She inclined her head regally. "I accept your presidential nomination, Julie."

Julie tipped her face toward Andie's. "What about you? What do you want?"

Andie met her friend's gaze. Tears choked her; she struggled to speak past them. "I just want my family back. I just want..." She made a strangled sound. "I used to think of the future and imagine myself married. To someone like my dad. I used to think that's what—"

She bit back the words and sat up, wrapping her arms around her drawn-up knees. "I'd hear about bad stuff happening to other people, other kids' families, but I never thought that could happen to me or my family. I thought we were...protected. Special."

She turned to her friends. "How can he do this to Mom? How can he do this to me? And to Pete and Danny?" Her voice broke. "How?"

Raven scooted over and put an arm around Andie. "It's going to get better."

Julie did the same. "It really will. You'll see."

"No." Andie shook her head. "I feel like nothing's ever going to be okay again."

"You've got us, Andie. That hasn't changed."

"That's right." Julie leaned her head against Andie's. "We love you."

Tears stung Andie's eyes. She held out her hand. "Best friends."

Julie covered it. "More than family."

"Together forever," Raven added, joining her hands to theirs. "Just us three."

"Best friends forever," they said again, this time in unison.

4

Andie passed the next two weeks in alternating fits and states of grief, anger, panic and betrayal.

Her father had completely moved out—his clothes and books, the plaques in his office, his golf clubs and tennis racket. Her mother had taken down every family picture in which he was included, she had emptied the pantry and refrigerator of the foods he and nobody else ate—the whole-grain cereal and Fig Newtons, his beer, the sprouted wheat bread and spicy brown mustard—not just throwing them out, but opening and emptying each one, then smashing the box or breaking the bottle.

Within days it had been as if he had never lived there at all.

Except in Andie's memory. And in her heart. Andie had never realized the effect one person could have on a place, but her father had had a profound one on their home. The house was changed, it seemed empty now. Quieter. Sad. Even the smell had changed.

Her house didn't feel like home anymore.

Even though she saw him on weekends, even though she knew he was trying to make up to her and her brothers, it wasn't the same. She missed him being around. She missed the family—and the father—she'd thought she had. And, as angry as she was at him, as hurt, she still longed for him. She still longed to hear his deep voice call out that he was home at the end of the day, longed to hear the rumble of his laughter while he wrestled with her brothers, longed for the reassurance just knowing he was there had given her. A reassurance she hadn't even realized she'd felt until now, until it was gone. She felt as if his leaving had ripped a huge hole in her life, leaving an empty place that ached so bad she sometimes couldn't breathe.

Danny and Pete felt it, too. Either they were even louder and naughtier than usual or unnaturally subdued. Her mother hardly got out of bed. She was listless, uninterested in her children, friends, food or any of the other activities she used to throw herself into with such energy.

Andie had lost her father *and* her mother.

Andie did everything she could to help, to make her mother's life easier. She never mentioned her dad, never expressed her own feelings of fear or despair. She helped with the house and the cooking and her brothers.

Raven and Julie had pitched in. They'd baked cookies, made beds and run the vacuum for her, they'd run to the grocery whenever Andie needed bread, milk or peanut butter. They were her constants, her anchors. With them she still laughed, with them she shared all her feelings, good and bad.

For the first time Andie understood the devastation Raven must have experienced when her mother left, for the first time she truly understood Raven's fierce loyalty to their friendship.

Raven and Julie truly were her family now.

"Andie? Andie, are you okay?"

Andie blinked, realizing Raven was speaking to her. She moved her gaze between her two friends. They were sitting on Raven's bed, listening to music and eating chips; both were staring at her, their expressions concerned. Andie averted her eyes, shocked at the tears that sprang to them, shocked that after two weeks just thinking of her father could still make her cry.

She forced herself to meet her friends' gazes. "Mom and I…yesterday we went downtown to look for new… sheets for her bed. She doesn't want to…sleep on the old ones."

"I can dig that," Julie said, shuddering. "I wouldn't want to, either. It'd be too sad."

"The thing is," Andie continued, "we were in the car, at the stoplight by the McDonald's, and I...we—" Her throat closed over the words, and she cleared it. She clasped her hands together. "He was in the car next to us. With her."

The other girls squealed with disbelief. "No way!"

"They were...she was...right on top of him. You know, kissing him and—"

Andie bit the words back, unable to go on. She brought her hands to her eyes, wishing she could block out the image of her father and the other woman. "He's not supposed to be kissing anybody but my mom. It's not right."

"It's disgusting!" Julie sat up, indignant. "I still can't believe your dad's doing this. I just can't."

Andie dropped her hands and looked at her friends. "Mom saw them, too. She got hysterical. That was yesterday, and she hasn't come out of her room yet. I called Grandma. She came to help us."

"It's that Barbie doll's fault," Raven said suddenly, narrowing her eyes. "She *stole* your dad."

"I hate her," Andie said. "I wish she was dead."

Raven moved her gaze between the other two. "She's a lying, husband-stealing little bitch and she should be punished. We have to come up with a plan."

Julie leaned forward. "Punished? Like how?"

Andie made a sound of frustration. "Get real, Rave. As much as I like to fantasize about frying the little slut in hot oil, the fact is, my dad left my mom. He left me and my brothers. She couldn't have done it without his cooperation."

Raven shook her head. "She *stole* him. These things don't just happen, Andie. She set out to get your dad...and she did."

Andie thought of the times she, either alone or with her mother and brothers, had stopped by her dad's office. She pictured Leeza's short dresses and tight tops, pictured the way she had hovered around her father, as if trying to keep *them* from seeing him. As if she were his wife and Andie's mom the interloper. Andie remembered being uncomfortable with the way the other woman had looked up at her dad from under her dark lashes, the way she had every so often touched his arm, so lightly it was like a caress.

Andie's blood boiled. Raven was right. Leeza had set out to steal her father. "How do we get her?"

"We could roll her house?" Julie offered, reaching for a handful of chips from the bag between them on the bed. "Or egg it?"

"Worse," Raven said.

"Like what?"

Raven smiled. "We could hit her over the head and bury her in the backyard."

Julie nearly choked on her chips, and Andie slapped her on the back while rolling her eyes at Raven. "Very funny."

"It was just a thought." She propped her chin on her fist. "I'm going to have to think about this."

"Wait a minute." Julie reached for another bunch of chips, turning her gaze to Andie. "Doesn't she have some fancy little sports car?"

Andie thought of the way she had once admired the car and of the way she had wished her dad would get one just like it. Now, no doubt, he could drive it anytime he wanted. Hatred burned in the pit of her gut. "Yeah. A bright red Fiat. She leaves the top down all the time, except when it's raining. She thinks she's so cool."

"Do you know where she parks it?"

"Oh, yeah. At my father's office building. Around back, in the shade from that row of trees."

Julie giggled and clapped her hands together. "I say we key it. Or let the air out of her tires."

"Let's not be hasty," Raven murmured. "We want to do something that'll really hurt her. At the very least, scare the crap out of her. I mean, she stole Andie's dad. That's a lot to be punished for, and a paint job can be repaired.''

"Let's just drop it," Andie said, her stomach beginning to hurt. "We're not really going to do anything, and just talking about her—" She sucked in a quick breath. "Let's talk about something else. Okay?''

So they did. They talked about an upcoming pool party and what they would wear, boys—in particular Ryan Tolber and why Julie shouldn't call him—and the new Michael Jackson music video.

Julie sat up suddenly. "I almost forgot to tell you guys! That music, I heard it again.''

"What music?" Andie asked, rolling onto her side to check the time on Raven's bedside clock.

"You know, from the other night. That was coming from the empty house.''

Andie saw that it was time to go home and make sure the twins were in bed. She sat up and began collecting her things. "It wasn't coming from the empty house. Remember? We decided.''

"But I heard it again," Julie offered. "The other night, when I was walking Toto. Don't you think that's weird?''

"You're weird," Raven said, tossing a pillow at her. "Music coming from empty houses? Wouldn't surprise me if you suddenly claimed you were abducted by little green men. And that they're great kissers.''

"They are." Laughing, Julie tossed the pillow back. "Great kissers!''

Next thing Andie knew, a feather pillow hit her square in the face, knocking her back onto her butt on the bed. With a squeal of surprise, she grabbed a pillow, scrambled to her knees and swung.

It was war. Each girl swung until her shoulders ached, they laughed until their sides hurt so bad they could hardly breathe. Raven was, as always, the last to call "Give!'' and as she took her final shot, her pillow split and feathers flew.

A half hour later, smiling to herself, Andie made her way across Raven's yard and into her own. As she shimmied through a bare place in the row of oleander bushes that separated the two properties, a car passed, music pouring out of its open windows.

Andie stopped, listening as the sound faded quickly away, remembering what Julie had said. She had heard that strange music again. On her quiet little street.

Andie didn't know why that suddenly seemed wrong to her. She didn't know why it felt so...ominous. But it did. Prickles crawled up her arms and she rubbed them. Silly, she told herself, starting off again. She was being silly.

Just because other sounds weren't carrying for blocks, just because the same music had been heard twice, seeming to come from someplace it shouldn't, that didn't mean anything weird was going on.

But what if it did? The prickling of goose bumps returned, this time racing up her spine, all the way to her hairline. What if their imaginations weren't running away with them and someone really was in one of those empty houses?

5

"I've been thinking about what Julie said the other night, about hearing that music again," Raven murmured, two nights later as the three girls sat on Andie's bed, an open *Cosmo* and a half-dozen bottles of nail polish between them, all shades of pink, from pale to shocking. "It just doesn't seem right to me."

Andie reached for one called Blush. She painted her thumbnail, then blew on it. "I was thinking the same thing. Hearing it twice like that, that's got to be more than a coincidence." She held out her hand to inspect her nail, then frowned. "Why do you suppose girls always wear pink?"

"That's just the way it is," Julie said, inching her glasses up to the bridge of her nose. "Girls are pink, boys are blue."

"I suppose." Andie decided she didn't like the shade and reached for the polish remover.

"Guys—" Raven made a sound of impatience "—what if somebody is in one of those empty houses?"

Andie looked at her. "Why would they be?"

"Why indeed? That's the question."

Julie glared at them. "You guys are creeping me out. Stop it. I've got to live there."

"Exactly." Raven sat up. "I think we should check it out."

"Now?" Julie held out her hands. "My nails are wet."

"Your dad's going to make you take it off anyway."

Raven looked at her friends. "What else do we have to do?"

"Nothing, I guess." Andie looked at Julie. "What do you think?"

She shrugged. "Okay by me. I've got to be home in an hour anyway."

After telling Andie's mom they were going over to Julie's house, the girls headed outside. They took the short-cut, angling through several backyards, dodging a particularly vicious Doberman pinscher, dragging Julie away from a couple of guys they knew who were shooting hoops in a driveway, reaching Julie's street within minutes.

They went to the end of the cul-de-sac and gazed at the four dark houses.

"This is so exciting," Andie whispered. "What if we actually discover something?"

Julie giggled nervously. "I'll pee my pants, that's what."

Andie glanced at Raven. "Which one do you think the music was coming from?"

Raven considered the houses a moment, squinting in thought. They were all dark; their windows eerily empty. All four had For Sale signs in the yard, two of them still sported the builder's signs. The one-story ranch houses were modest in size, though equipped with all the latest appliances, conveniences and colors. Though the lots weren't large—not as large as those in Phase I—the developer had taken care to leave as many trees as possible. The big shade trees gave the appearance of a richer, more established neighborhood.

"That one," Raven said finally, pointing to the one farthest left. "It's the most secluded. There, next to the empty lot. And look—" she pointed "—that streetlight's out. If I was up to no good, that's the one I'd want to be in."

The other two girls murmured their agreement and fell into step behind Raven. Darting glances in every direction, they crept around to the back of the house. Julie poked

Andie in the back, making her jump. "Boo," she whispered, giggling.

Andie brought a hand to her heart and scowled at her friend. "Stop that. You about gave me a—"

"Shh." Raven held up a hand. "Listen."

Andie did, heart thundering. A moment later she leaned toward Raven. "I don't hear anything."

Julie put her head close to theirs. "Me neither."

Raven grinned. "Gotcha."

"Very funny."

"Thanks a lot."

Raven laughed softly. "Come on."

They crept to the first window and peered in. The room beyond—it looked as if it was supposed to be a bedroom—was empty. They made their way to the next window, then the next, finding the same thing. An empty laundry room, breakfast room, kitchen.

Then they hit pay dirt. A chair. A single, high-backed, wooden chair, the kind you'd find at a desk or dining table. Only there was no table or desk, no television, lamps or anything else in the room.

It looked strange, parked there, a sort of centerpiece. Andie tipped her head. No, not a centerpiece. A kind of audience to an empty stage.

Andie shivered. "This is the one. I'll just bet."

"Me, too." Raven turned to Julie. "Are you sure no one bought this house?"

"Positive." She rubbed her arms. "My mom was talking about it with Mrs. Green just a couple weeks ago. All four of these houses are still available. Mrs. Green was really weirded-out about it, 'cause there's a chance Mr. Green's going to be transferred and she's afraid they won't be able to sell." Julie sucked in a deep breath. "Besides, the For Sale sign is still in front."

"What now?" Andie whispered. "A few pieces of furniture doesn't mean some ax murderer has taken up residence in an empty house."

"Let's try the door."

Andie held her breath as Raven did, letting it out when she saw that it was locked. Next, her friend tried the windows. They, too, were locked.

"Come on, Raven." Andie glanced around nervously. "I don't think this is such a good idea."

"Just a sec." Raven stood on tiptoe and ran her hand along the top of the door frame. "Bingo," she said, holding up a key.

"Where did you learn to do that?" Andie shook her head. "And isn't this against the law?"

"Is it?" Raven arched her eyebrows. "We have a key. That's not like breaking and entering or anything."

"People go through model homes all the time," Julie piped in. "That's all we're doing."

Raven inserted the key into the lock. Andie took a step back. "You guys, what if somebody really lives here? What if they're home?"

Raven made a face at her. "Wiener. Chicken out if you want, Julie and I are going in." She looked at Julie. "You're with me, right?" The girl nodded, and Raven eased open the door.

Andie watched her two friends slip through the door, then disappear inside the house. She waited, heart pounding. The moments ticked past with agonizing slowness. *What were they doing? What did they see?*

"Guys," she whispered, "what's going on?"

They didn't answer. Andie inched closer to the door, straining to hear her friends inside. When she couldn't, she peeked around the doorway. Still nothing. Feeling like the wiener Raven had called her, she followed them inside.

The door opened onto the kitchen. Adjacent to it was the family room with its one chair, and beyond it, the entrance foyer and dining room. A hallway led to what Andie supposed were the bedrooms.

Creepy, she thought, hugging herself, chilled. Obviously empty, yet something about it felt occupied. She turned slowly, taking in the fast-food bag on the counter, the cups in the sink; hearing the hum of the air conditioner.

"Rave?" she called softly. "Julie?"

"Here," Raven answered. "Come see what we found."

Andie went down the hallway and found her friends in the master bedroom. It was a large room with a vaulted ceiling and exposed wooden beams. There wasn't a bed, just a couple of big floor pillows and a stool, the kind her mom had at the breakfast bar in their kitchen.

And a tape deck. A nice one. Andie crossed to it, squatted and popped open the cassette holder. Nothing.

"The boom box proves it." Julie looked from one of her friends to the other. "This is where the music was coming from. Somebody's using this house."

"But for what?" Andie shook her head. "There's something really weird about this. I don't like it."

"No joke. Let's get out of here."

They started back toward the kitchen. Andie peeked in the bathroom as they passed it. It, too, showed signs of limited occupation. A shower curtain, a cup by the sink. But no towels or toiletries.

Back in the kitchen, Julie shivered. "It's like someone's living here, but not. Like a ghost, or something."

"A ghost?" Raven repeated, pointing to the McDonald's bag on the counter. "Get real, girl. Whoever's using this house is a flesh-and-blood human being."

Which made it all the more scary, as far as Andie was concerned. She crossed to the gently humming refrigerator, opened it and peered inside, squinting at the sudden light. A bottle of wine and a six-pack of beer, some cheese and a bunch of grapes.

Raven peered over her shoulder and grinned. "Beer?"

"Oh no you don't. If you take one, they'll know we were in here."

"So what?" Raven reached around her. "It's not like they'll know it was *us* who—" She stopped, frowning. "What's that rumbling sound? It's kind of like—"

They all froze, as if realizing simultaneously what it was. *The automatic garage door. Opening.*

"Oh shit." Andie looked at her friends. A door opened then slammed. *A car door.* "What do we do?"

"Hide," Raven managed to say, her voice a frightened croak. "Now!"

Andie looked wildly around, her heart in her throat. She grabbed Julie's hand and darted for the walk-in pantry door. She pushed Julie inside, then ducked in behind her, not having time to get the door completely shut before a man entered the kitchen.

Andie held the knob to keep the door steady, her heart hammering nearly out of control. Cracked open about an inch, she was able to watch the man's progress.

He didn't turn on a light, so she couldn't make out his face or features, only that he was tall, dark-haired and dressed casually. He went to the refrigerator and opened it. Light flooded the dark kitchen, though his back was to her. A moment later she heard the pop and hiss of a can being opened. *He was drinking beer. Thank God they hadn't taken one. He would have known they were here.*

He shut the fridge and turned, staring straight at the pantry. He stood unmoving a moment, his eyes seeming to meet hers. Her heart stopped; he started toward her.

Fear exploded inside her. Andie held her breath, dizzy with emotion, certain that her next moment was going to be her last. She squeezed her eyes shut, a bead of sweat rolling down her spine, slipping under the elastic band of her panties.

Behind her on the floor, Julie stirred. *Don't move, Julie. Don't breathe.*

The man stopped in front of the pantry door. He reached out. And pushed the door the rest of the way shut. The latch clicked into place.

He hadn't discovered them.

Now they were truly trapped.

Andie brought a hand to her mouth to hold back her cry

of relief and panic. What did they do now? she wondered, shifting slightly so she could see Julie's face now that her eyes had adjusted to the darkness. And where was Raven?

Julie's eyes were wide and terrified. Andie felt her friend's rising hysteria; it mirrored her own. She fought the urge to scream. To just open her mouth and let out a wail of terror, and then run for it. Past the man. The man who had no business being in this house, in this neighborhood. The man who could be anyone. Or anything. A rapist or murderer.

Instead, Andie held tightly to her control and brought a finger to her lips to signal Julie to be quiet. Her friend nodded and pressed her face to her drawn-up knees.

The minutes seemed like hours. An eternity. As they ticked past, the pantry became hotter, closer. It was like a tomb, an airless box. Andie began to sweat; the urge to scream, to run, grew. She didn't know how much longer she would be able to last.

She counted to ten, then twenty, forcing herself to breathe evenly. She told herself everything would be all right. The pantry was empty. If he didn't hear them, there should be no reason for him to open the door. As long as they were quiet, they would be okay. So would Raven.

She closed her eyes, imagining him there in the dark, drinking his beer. Imagined him turning suddenly toward the pantry door, sensing their presence, their panic. The way a predator in the wild does.

The metallic taste of fear nearly gagged her. She strained to hear him. Every so often she thought she heard him stir, his footfall, his rhythmic breathing. She couldn't be sure.

She held her breath and prayed. *Please, God. Please make him go away.*

The prayer played in her head, over and over again until she suddenly realized she was digging her nails into her palms, that she was light-headed from holding her breath.

At the same moment she realized it had been quiet for some time.

The pantry door flew open.

Her cry shattered the quiet.

It was Raven. With a sob of relief, Andie tumbled out, Julie behind her. They fell into each other's arms, clinging to one another.

"Where were you?" Andie cried. "I was so worried he'd see you!"

"In the dining room. Are you guys okay?"

"Fine. Fi—"

"I want to go home," Julie said, her teeth beginning to chatter. "I want to go home."

Raven caught Julie's hands and rubbed them. "What do you think he was up to?"

"I don't know. It was so weird. He—" Andie bit the words back, new fear taking her breath. "Are you sure he's gone? Are you sure—"

"He's gone." Raven indicated the family room. "He went the way he came in."

Andie looked in the direction Raven pointed. "What if he comes back? He could be hiding, waiting for us."

"Why would he do that?" Raven shook her head. "No, I heard the garage door. He's gone."

"I want to go," Julie said again, starting to cry. "I don't like it here. He could have hurt us."

Andie hugged her. "It's okay, sweetie. He didn't touch us. He's gone. You're fine."

"But he could have! If he'd found us, he could have done…anything. No one knew we were here!"

"Who was he?" Raven asked softly, as if speaking to no one but herself.

Andie turned to Raven. "I didn't get a look at him. Did you?"

The other girl gazed at her for a moment, then shook her head. "You didn't see his face? I thought for sure you had. He was right there."

"It was dark, and when he came close I drew back from the door." Andie pressed a hand to her fluttering stomach. "I think I closed my eyes, too. I was so scared he was going to find us."

"Me, too." Raven let out a long breath. "I was too afraid to peek around the doorway." She laughed, the sound high and excited. "What a rush." She laughed again and crossed to the breakfast counter. "Come see. He left these."

Andie followed her friend. She stared down at what looked like two folded pieces of black fabric.

"What are they?" Andie asked.

"Scarves."

Raven moved to pick one up; Andie caught her hand. "Don't touch it."

"Why not? I'll put them back the way I found them." She shook off Andie's hand and picked one up. It was long and narrow and semisheer. "It's so soft. Feel it."

After a moment's hesitation, Andie did. The fabric slithered through her fingers, as soft as butterfly wings. "My mom has a scarf that feels like this. It's silk."

"Silk," Raven repeated. "Why did he bring these here? What are they for?" She met Andie's eyes. "Who is he, Andie? What's he doing here?"

Andie searched her friend's gaze. "I don't know. But I don't think we need to find out."

Julie came up behind them, white as a sheet. "I don't feel so good. I want to go."

Andie nodded, then nudged Raven who had turned her attention back to the scarf. She seemed almost mesmerized by it and her own questions. "Come on, let's get out of here."

"They're for a woman, that's for sure. But who? Why did he bring them here? And why two of them?"

Julie moaned and bent slightly at the waist. Andie put an arm around her. "Come on, Raven," she said again. "Julie's sick."

As if only just realizing Andie had spoken, Raven looked blankly at her. "What?"

"Julie's sick. We've got to get out of here."

Raven nodded, refolded the scarf, then the three of them left the way they had come in. As they did, Andie glanced back at the dark house. She was never coming back here, she promised herself. Never.

6

For the next few days, all Andie and her friends could talk about was the mystery man and their brush with danger. They were certain Mr. X, as they had begun to call him, was up to no good, but they could only speculate as to what kind. Which, for Andie and Julie, was enough. Neither girl had any desire to get that close to Mr. X or that house again.

Raven, on the other hand, wanted to find out exactly *what* Mr. X was doing. "Aren't you guys even curious?" she asked her two friends. They sat in Andie's front yard, drinking Cokes. Even in the shade, the midday air was stifling.

"Nope. Not that curious, anyway." Andie brought her cold, damp can to her forehead. "I just want to forget it."

"Me, too," Julie added. "I've never been so scared in my whole life."

"Listen to yourselves, guys. You say you want to forget it, but it's all you can talk about. Besides," Raven persisted, "how can we forget it? We were in that house. We know something's wrong with that guy."

"I don't know that." Andie flopped back onto the grass, cursing the heat. "Neither do you. *We* were the ones who were wrong. We didn't belong in there."

"He didn't either." Raven leaned toward Andie. "That house is *supposed* to be empty." She turned to Julie. "Be honest, you thought something about him was wrong. Didn't you?"

"Well...he was pretty creepy." Julie rubbed her arms.

"And Rave's right, Andie. He wasn't supposed to be in there."

"You guys are nuts." Andie sat back up, looking at the two in disbelief. "*We* weren't supposed to be in there. We broke in, for Pete's sake. Get real."

"You get real." Raven drew her knees to her chest. "This is *our* neighborhood. It's Julie's street. What if he's some sort of freak? A murderer or a...a *child molester?*"

"A murderer? A child molester?" Andie rolled her eyes. "The guy drank a beer in a house we *think* is supposed to be empty. Come on, Rave, you're taking this too far."

"I don't think so. Read the newspaper any day of the week. Those freaks are everywhere." Raven lowered her voice. "You don't want that kind of person in our neighborhood, do you? Around Julie's little brothers? Around yours?"

"No, but—"

"Geez, Andie—" Raven made a sound of disgust "—you used to be the one who looked out for everybody. Remember? You used to care about right and wrong. You used to do something about it."

"I still care. But I'm not sure this guy's doing anything wrong. I mean, of course we were scared. We should have been, look what we were doing. Maybe he's perfectly innocent. He probably has every right to be in that house."

"Be honest, Andie. You don't believe that." Raven faced her. "Look me in the eyes and tell me you didn't think the way he came in and sat in the dark drinking a beer was weird? Tell me you don't think there's something strange about a partially filled house that's *supposed* to be empty?"

"And don't forget those icky black scarves," Julie piped in, making a face. "That was so creepy."

Andie closed her eyes and recalled the quiet way the man had moved around the kitchen, the measured sound of his breathing, how he had made her feel, and she shuddered, gooseflesh racing up her arms. She rubbed them, feeling chilled despite the heat of the day. "Okay, okay. He was creepy. The whole thing was weird. So what?"

Raven turned to Julie. "Tell her what you found out."

Julie leaned conspiratorially toward them, lowering her voice to a dramatic whisper. "I asked my mom about the house again, you know, just to be sure. I asked if it had been sold or rented or anything, and she said she didn't think so. She said she had even mentioned that house to Mrs. Butcher, the real estate agent." Julie dragged in a deep breath. "Mrs. Butcher told her all four houses were still owned by the builder."

Andie shuddered again, her chill going clear to her bones. "So, what do we do?" she asked, looking from one friend to the other. "Go to our folks?"

Raven pursed her lips. "And what do we tell them? That when we broke into the house we discovered someone living there?"

"My dad would kick my butt for even looking in a window." Julie shook her head. "If he ever found out what I did..."

She let the thought trail off, but all three knew that the Good Reverend Cooper was capable of any number of horrible punishments, including splitting the three of them up. For good.

"We could say we heard music," Andie offered, rolling her Coke can between her palms, staring at the grass. "We could say we thought we saw someone go into the—"

"Andie!" Julie grabbed her arm. "Look, it's your dad."

He was turning into the driveway. The way he had countless times before. *He was coming home.* "I knew it," she whispered, turning to her friends. "I knew he couldn't do it. He's coming back, you guys."

Raven and Julie exchanged glances. Raven cleared her throat. "Andie, don't get your hopes up."

"Why else would he be here? In the middle of the

day?'' He opened the car door, and she jumped to her feet and ran toward him. ''Hey, Dad!''

He turned and looked at her, his face white with rage. Andie stopped in her tracks, her pleasure evaporating. ''Dad? What's wrong?''

''Where's your mother?'' He slammed the car door. ''Is she inside?''

''I think so. I—''

''You stay here, Andie. This is between me and your mother.''

Andie watched him head for the house, then scurried after him, despite his order that she not. He reached the front door and opened it without knocking. ''Marge,'' he called, stepping inside. Then louder, ''Marge!''

She appeared at the kitchen doorway, her expression lifting at the sight of him. ''Dan? What a surpri—''

''Save it,'' he snapped. ''What the hell are you trying to pull?''

Her face fell. ''Pull? I don't know what you—''

''Don't hand me that bullshit. You know exactly what I'm talking about.''

Andie made a small sound of surprise, stopping only steps behind him. She could count on one hand the times she had heard her father swear. She looked at her mother, confused. If he had come to ask their forgiveness, why was he swearing? If he wanted to come home, why was he so mad?

He fisted his fingers and took a step toward his wife. ''Leeza could have been killed, Marge. Killed. Doesn't that mean anything to you? What kind of person are you?''

This was about Leeza, Andie realized, crushed. He had come here about *her*. Not because he loved and missed his family. Not because he wanted to come home. She inched backward, wishing she had done as her father had asked and stayed outside.

''A snake in her car?'' he continued. ''Couldn't you

have come up with something a little less obvious? Something that didn't point directly at you?''

''A snake?'' Her mother brought a hand to her throat. Andie saw that it trembled. ''You're not suggesting that I…that I had anything to do with that?''

''Are you saying you didn't?'' His voice dripped sarcasm. ''Are you saying you didn't slip a garter snake into her car, knowing what might happen while she was in traffic? Hoping the worst might happen?''

''Dad!'' Andie burst out, shocked. ''Mom wouldn't do that! How could you even say that?''

He swung toward her, paling slightly. ''I thought I told you to wait outside.''

Andie tipped up her chin, furious at him, a smart reply springing to her lips. Before she could utter it, her mother jumped in. ''This is Andie's home. Unlike you, *she* has a right to be here.''

He looked from one to the other, as if just realizing how his accusation made him look to his daughter. ''She could have been killed,'' he said again, voice shaking. ''She's in the hospital, for God's sake. She's—''

''Seems to me,'' Raven said from behind them, ''those are the chances you take when you decide to screw somebody else's husband.''

Andie gasped and swung around. Raven stood in the doorway, eyes narrowed, mouth set. Julie stood a few paces behind her, her face bright with embarrassed color.

Dan Bennett turned, too, trembling with rage. ''How dare you, young lady. *You* have no business here. *You* are not a member of this family.''

''Family?'' Marge repeated, stepping forward. ''You're the one who's no longer a member of this family. I'd like you to leave.'' She crossed to the door and swung it open. ''And don't you ever enter this house without an invitation again.''

He opened his mouth as if to say something further, then closed it, turned on his heel and stalked past Raven and

Julie. Moments later, he backed out of the driveway, tires squealing as he did.

For a full minute no one said anything, then, as if realizing everything that had occurred, Marge cleared her throat. "I'm sorry you girls had to see that." She shifted her gaze to Raven, then hesitated, as if unsure what to say to her.

Raven beat her to it. "I'm sorry I said that, Mrs. B. It just makes me so mad, what he did to you."

The woman's expression softened. "Thank you for caring, Raven. But I can...and should, fight my own battles. All right?"

Raven nodded, and Julie reached out and touched Marge's hand. "We think you're the greatest, Mrs. B."

"That's right," Raven added. "He's the one who should be apologizing. We love you."

Her friends' words seemed to calm her mother. Once again Julie and Raven had come through for her and her family. And once again she wondered what she would do if she ever lost them.

"Thank you, girls," Marge murmured, smiling, though not, Andie saw, without effort. "You're all very sweet. And I...I—" She turned to Andie. "Go on now. I know there are things you girls are wanting to do, and hanging out with an old lady isn't one of them."

Andie's chest tightened. "You're not old, Mom."

"Older than you three," she said firmly. "You go. I have work to do around here, and you're keeping me from it." She gave Andie's shoulders a quick squeeze. "I'm fine," she whispered. "Really. Go on now. We'll talk later."

Andie nodded, turned and led her friends outside. They took their places under the maple tree, not speaking for long moments.

After a time, Julie leaned over and caught Andie's hand. "I'm sorry, Andie."

"Yeah," Raven murmured. "Me, too."

"Thanks." She blinked against tears. "You guys are the best."

Raven leaned back against the grass and smiled up at the blue sky. "At least the little slut learned a lesson."

Andie turned and looked at Raven. "What?"

"The little slut. Leeza. She had it coming."

She had it coming. Andie caught her breath, remembering. The three of them sitting on her bed and talking about ways they could get even with Leeza. Discussing the things they could do to her to make her pay. Discussing the kind of car Leeza drove and where she parked it.

But that had been just...talk. Just the three of them joking around.

Hadn't it been?

A sick feeling in the pit of her stomach, Andie looked from Raven to Julie. Julie was staring at Raven, her expression horrified.

Maybe not.

"Raven," Andie whispered, "you didn't...I know we talked about making Leeza pay, but that was just...we were just kidding around. Right?"

Raven met Andie's eyes. "Were we? Just kidding around? Don't you hate her guts?"

"I do. But...but she could have died."

To that, Andie was greeted by complete silence. Then Raven shook her head. "You said you wished she was dead, Andie. So, why do you care? What if she had died? If you ask me, the little bitch got what she deserved."

For a moment, Andie couldn't speak. She hated Leeza for taking her father away. She did. But...saying she wanted her dead wasn't the same as *meaning* it.

Surely Raven understood that.

"Gosh, Andie, don't look at me like that." Raven laughed and sat up. "*I* didn't do it, for heaven's sake. I'm only saying that I don't care that it happened and neither should you. Look what she's done to your family. To your mom."

"That's right," Julie piped in, looking relieved. "Rave wouldn't do something like that. But I don't feel bad for that little witch, either."

Andie brought a hand to her chest. "For a moment there, I thought you…" She let the words trail off. Something about Raven's expression, something bright in her eyes, made her uneasy. She cleared her throat. "But…how do you think the snake got in her car?"

Raven shrugged. "You said she leaves the top down all the time. I bet that stupid little snake dropped out of the trees she parks under and curled up under her seat for a nap."

"I bet you're right." Julie giggled. "The same thing happened to Mrs. Beasely, from church. Only it was bird poop. It landed right on her head. She got nearly hysterical."

Raven hadn't done it. Of course she hadn't. Andie laughed weakly. "What would I do without you guys?"

"Go crazy."

"Become a total spaz."

The three laughed. "So what do we do now?" Andie asked.

"I say we get back to our little mystery." Raven lowered her voice to an excited whisper. "We watch the house. We figure out what he's up to. That shouldn't be hard. The house is surrounded by trees. My dad's got binoculars—"

"So does mine," Julie offered.

"Good. Then, when we find out what he's up to, we bust his ass. We go to our folks, they go to the police and we're heroes."

Andie drew her eyebrows together. "And what if he's not up to anything?"

"Then we chalk up the whole thing to overactive imaginations."

"It is kind of exciting," Julie murmured. "I feel like Nancy Drew."

Andie had to admit her curiosity was piqued. What if this guy was up to no good? What if he did mean someone harm? She wouldn't be able to live with herself if that was true and she had sat back and done nothing.

"When do we start?" she asked.

"Tonight."

She let out a long breath. "Okay, I'm in. On one condition." The other two looked at her. "We don't go in again. Not ever, no matter what. I mean it, or no deal. Otherwise, I go to our folks. Deal?"

Julie nodded, then looked at Raven. The girl paused a moment, then acquiesced. "Deal."

7

The three friends had made their plan for watching the house. They would spend the afternoons and after-dinner hours, barring any unexpected monkey wrenches, together. They split the rest of the days and nights into shifts, their times determined by their home situations.

Julie took the early-morning watch not only because her house was on the same street as the one they were watching, but also because her dad operated under the belief that most sin took place later in the day. Combined with the fact that the morning hours were busy ones in the Cooper household, Julie had a good bit of freedom before 10:00 a.m.

Raven's dad, on the other hand, gave her an incredible amount of latitude—as long as she was waiting for him when he arrived home from work, dinner on the table and a smile on her face.

Andie filled in the weekday time gaps. Between her mom's job hunting and her constant depression, she hardly even noticed if Andie was around.

Weekends were up for grabs, though; because of increased activity on the street the girls didn't think they would see their mystery man then anyway.

They had found the perfect lookout in a huge oak tree in the empty lot next to the house. A couple of years back, some kids had begun to build a tree house in its big branches, but had been forced to abandon it when the lot's owner had discovered their handiwork. Though nothing more than a wide platform, it fit the three of them comfortably, shielded them from sight and afforded them a clear view of the house's driveway.

So far, however, there had been no sign of their mystery man.

Frustrated, they had decided to try something new. Both times they'd heard the music, it had been late—past eleven. So tonight they had decided to sneak out of their houses and meet at the platform at ten-thirty sharp. It was now ten to eleven.

"Where do you think Rave is?" Julie asked, glancing at her watch.

Andie shrugged. "Maybe she couldn't get out. You know, sometimes her dad stays up late."

Julie caught her bottom lip between her teeth, obviously worried. "You don't think he found out what we're up to? If he did, he'll go straight to our parents. You know he will."

Andie peered toward the street. "Naw. Raven's dad would be the last to find out something. Raven's too smooth to get caught."

"I suppose you're right." Julie shivered and rubbed her arms. "I guess I'm just nervous, that's all."

Andie brought the binoculars to her eyes. The mystery house was as dark and deserted-looking as always. Weird, she thought. The whole thing was weird.

"There she is!"

Andie swung the binoculars to the street. Sure enough, Raven was making her way toward the empty lot at a jog. Moments later, she crashed through the underbrush, heading in their direction.

"We were getting worried," Julie called in an exaggerated whisper.

"Sorry," Raven answered, skidding to a stop under the tree and looking up at them, struggling to catch her breath. "Wait till you hear this, you're not going to believe it. My dad's dating! That's why I'm late. We had to have dinner together. They're going out dancing now.'' She took another deep breath. ''I had to wait for them to leave.''

''Dating?'' Andie scooted to the right to make room for Raven. ''That's hard to believe.''

''No kidding.'' Raven climbed onto the platform. ''I was blown away.''

''I always thought it was sweet,'' Julie murmured. ''The way he pined for your mom. Sitting on your patio for hours, just kind of staring off into space.''

''Real sweet.'' Raven made a face. ''Anyway, I played super nice for this lady, making like my dad was some sort of superhero or something. I felt like warning her instead.'' She brought her hands to her mouth, megaphone-style. *''Caution, asshole ahead!''*

Julie burst out laughing. ''Raven, you kill me. Your dad's not *that* bad.''

''No,'' she said softly, looking her friend dead in the eye. ''He's worse.''

For a moment, all three girls were silent. Andie cleared her throat, uncomfortable. Julie flushed, obviously embarrassed and at a loss for words. They both looked away. It wasn't what Raven had said about her dad, but the way she had said it. The way she always sounded when she talked about him.

Like he was some sort of monster.

Andie had the feeling there was something Raven hadn't told her about her dad, something important. Something really bad.

Andie shook her head slightly, as if to rid herself of the traitorous thought. What wouldn't Raven have told her? They were closer than sisters; they shared everything with each other, they had from the moment they met.

''Look!'' Julie elbowed her hard. ''It's him!''

Andie turned. Sure enough, a car was coming down the hill and turning into number twelve Mockingbird Lane's driveway. Raven had the binoculars, although Andie doubted she could see much in the dark. As they watched, the automatic garage door went up; the car disappeared inside, then the door lowered.

"Did you see his face?" Andie asked. Raven shook her head and Andie let out a frustrated breath. "Darn it."

"You guys," Julie hissed. "Another car."

Andie and Raven turned. *It was. Another car. Pulling into number twelve's driveway, into the garage.*

Raven lowered the binoculars. The girls looked at each other. "Two cars?" they said in unison.

"It's a woman," Raven said. "I saw her. She checked her reflection in the lighted visor mirror while she waited for the garage door to open."

Andie sat back hard. "Holy shit."

"It's a romance," Julie whispered. "A love affair." She sighed. "That's so cool."

Raven frowned at her. "Then why the scarves? Why the music late at night? Why meet in an empty house?"

The three girls looked at each other. "What now?" Andie asked.

"We go down there," Raven answered. "We get some answers."

"And just how do you propose we do that?"

"We peek in the windows." Raven grinned. "How else?"

"No way." Andie looked at Julie who was already shimmying out of the tree. "You guys are crazy. No way am I going down there to peek in those windows."

Five minutes later, Andie followed Raven and Julie around the back of the mystery couple's house. As they approached the first window, they ducked down to avoid being seen. When they reached it, they cautiously eased up to peer over the ledge.

The room appeared to be empty.

They crouched down and went to the next window, then the next, each time with the same results. Andie was beginning to believe the whole thing was going to be a bust, when Raven motioned frantically from the window just ahead.

Andie went, though she couldn't believe she was doing this. Her heart was pounding so fast and hard she felt faint. She continued anyway.

She peered over the windowsill. The room was dark save for the glow from a single, flickering candle. It took Andie's eyes a moment to adjust to the darkness; when they did, she saw the man. He sat in the lone chair in the room, his back to the window.

It was him, she knew. The man from the other night.

Then she saw the woman. She stood several feet in front of the man, arms at her side, still as a statue. She wore a conservative suit—knee-length skirt and short jacket. Her white blouse was high-necked and buttoned all the way up. Her shoes were low-heeled, her hair styled in a conservative bob.

She fit the image of banker or accountant or president of the PTA. Except for one thing.

She was blindfolded.

With a black silk scarf.

One of the ones they had seen the other night, Andie realized, a lump lodging in her throat. Maybe the one she and Raven had touched, the one they had run through their fingers.

A funny sensation settled in the pit of her gut, queasy and uncertain. She looked at Raven and Julie. They met her eyes. The expression in theirs told her that they'd recognized the scarf, too. That they felt the same about it as she.

Moments passed. Andie didn't breathe; the woman didn't move. Then the music started, the same stuff they had heard twice before. With it, the woman began to sway, as if in time to the music, though her movements seemed halting to Andie. Almost uncertain. Or frightened. She brought her hands to the lapels of her jacket. Slowly, she slipped the garment off her shoulders. It dropped to the floor.

She tugged her blouse from under the skirt's waistband, then moved her hands to the collar of her blouse, to the row of tiny buttons that ran from throat to hem. She struggled with them; Andie imagined that her fingers shook. One by one each button slipped through the hole; the delicate fabric parted.

She was stripping. Being forced to strip.

With the realization, Andie's mouth turned to ash, her heart began to thrum. She wanted to jump up and shout—pound on the window to frighten the woman out of the trance she appeared to be in or to frighten away her captor. She told herself to look away or duck down.

She did none of those. Instead, she continued to stare, paralyzed by shock and disbelief as the woman removed one piece of clothing after another.

Stripped down to bra, panties and half slip, she stopped. In the feeble, flickering light of the one candle, shadows danced crazily on her pale skin.

The man stood and left the room, walking past her without even a glance. Andie held her breath. *Run,* she silently urged. *Grab your clothes and go.*

But the woman didn't move. Not a muscle, it seemed to Andie.

What was wrong with her? Why didn't she—

She wasn't a prisoner. She wanted to be there.

Andie brought a hand to her mouth and dared a glance at Raven and Julie. Their faces reflected each of her own emotions—shock, disbelief, a kind of fascination mixed with revulsion. She gazed at them, afraid to speak, willing them to look at her. Hoping if their eyes met, they would all come to their senses and leave this place.

But they didn't look her way, and Andie turned back to the window and the nearly naked woman, standing like a mannequin before it.

Moments passed, though it could have been minutes—

even hours—for all Andie knew. She had lost all sense of time and reality. It seemed like aeons that the woman stood unmoving, half-naked and alone.

The man returned. Again, he strolled past the woman without looking at or touching her. As if she weren't there, Andie thought. As if she didn't matter enough even to glance at.

Andie struggled to see his face before he turned his back to them and sat down, but came up with only impressions: of dark hair and features, of strength and beauty. And of evil.

Rampant and blackhearted. Like the devil Julie's dad was always warning about.

Andie decided she hated him. Fiercely. The emotion reached up and grabbed her by the throat until she felt both choked and exhilarated by it.

He lit a cigarette. The sudden, tiny flame illuminated his profile for a fraction of a second, then left it more inscrutable than before. Smoke curled, snakelike, through the light of the candle at his feet.

The woman moved. She eased the slip over her hips and down. It puddled on the floor at her feet, and she stepped out of it. Next, she brought her hands to the back-clasp of her bra; she struggled with it a moment, then with almost agonizing slowness, she took the garment off.

The panties, small and plain white, came next. She eased them off, then dropped her hands to her sides and stood completely still before the man, as if awaiting his instruction.

Heat washed over Andie; she began to sweat. She had never seen a naked woman before. Not like this, not just…there. She and her friends had changed clothes in the same fitting room, she had seen her mother when she had burst into the bathroom without knocking, but that had been…natural, kind of innocent.

But this was different. Unnatural. Anything but innocent. All of it. The man and the woman. The music. Her and her friends spying on them this way.

Still, Andie didn't look away. The woman was beautiful, pale and slim but with the kind of curves Andie dreamed of someday having. Cheeks burning, she moved her gaze over the woman, stopping with a sense of shock on the dark triangle of hair at the top of her thighs.

Suddenly, Andie became aware of the labored sound of her friend's breathing, the pounding of her own heart, of Julie's fingers wrapped around her forearm in a death grip.

The woman took a halting step toward the man, then another, seeming to feel her way in her darkness. When she reached him, she stopped, paused for a moment, then knelt at his feet.

She lowered her head to his lap.

For one dazed moment, Andie wondered what the woman was doing.

Then she knew.

This wasn't happening, she told herself, sucking in a strangled breath. Not in Thistledown. Not in her own neighborhood.

But it was.

With a squeak of fear, she ducked down, grabbing her friends' hands and dragging them with her. They stared at each other in shocked silence, then looked away, embarrassed and uncomfortable. Andie opened her mouth to whisper something to break the silence, but nothing came. It wasn't so much that she couldn't speak as that suddenly she didn't want to.

The three ran. Away from the window and back to the abandoned tree house in the empty lot. Breathing hard, they scrambled up the makeshift ladder and onto the platform.

Several moments passed in complete silence except for the sound of their ragged breathing. Andie stubbed the toe of her sneaker against the platform floor, the need to speak nearly strangling her. But for the first time in her life, she didn't know what to say to her friends.

Suddenly, Julie giggled. Self-conscious, she slapped a hand over her mouth. Still, she giggled again. Raven and Andie looked at her, and she shook her head. "I can't help it. It was so…" Julie flushed. "You guys, she was… blowing him."

Andie brought her hands to her face. "I can't believe they…I mean, *that? Here?*"

"No joke." Raven drew her knees to her chest. "I've never seen anything like that before. It was wild."

Andie made a face. "And what was that blindfold all about?"

"They're sex perverts," Julie answered, looking at Andie. "I saw a book in the library about it. In the psychology section. It was called sexual—" she thought for a moment "—sexual deviation. I think that was it."

Sexual deviation. Just as Andie couldn't rid herself of the sensation of gooseflesh crawling up her arms, she couldn't shake the image of the woman standing blindfolded and naked in the dark.

She looked at Raven, then Julie. "That woman, why does she do that for him?"

The other two looked blankly at her, then at each other. "I don't know," Raven answered, shrugging. "Because she likes it?"

"But how could she?" Andie continued, wishing she had seen the man's face, wondering if, somehow, she would understand if she had. "It was so…awful. It seemed, I don't know—" She searched for the right word. "Demeaning," she said, finding it. "Like the woman was nothing and he was everything. Like she was a slave and he was her master."

"Gross," Julie said, screwing up her face. "I sure wouldn't do that for anybody."

"No kidding." Raven looked thoughtful. "What do we

Erica Spindler

do now? We could drop it, but it was just so weird...so wrong.''

"Do you think..." Andie hesitated a moment, knowing what she was about to suggest was far-fetched, but feeling as if she had to say it. "I know that the woman...that she showed up alone and all, but do you think she could have been...that maybe she wasn't there of her own free will?"

Julie widened her eyes. "What do you mean, like she was kidnapped?"

"Or being blackmailed."

The other two said nothing, just gazed at Andie, their expressions troubled.

"I don't know," Julie murmured after a moment, her cheeks pink. "Maybe. But why would she do that? What could be so bad that she would get in a car and drive someplace she didn't want to be and do something like *that?*"

"Something really bad," Raven answered softly. "Life-and-death."

Andie glanced down at her hands, realizing that she had them clasped in front of her so tightly her knuckles stood out white in the darkness. She lifted her gaze to her friends', suddenly thinking of something that hadn't occurred to her before. "Guys? Why two scarves?"

The question landed heavily between the girls. They looked at each other.

"He brought two," Andie prodded. "Remember?"

For a moment nobody said a thing, they didn't even seem to breathe. Julie jumped as a creature scurried in the branches above them, then she rubbed her arms, as if chilled.

Raven swore softly. "This guy's a freak. We can't let it go. We've got to figure out what's going on. Agreed?"

Julie hesitated, then nodded. "I'm with you, Rave. We can't let it go."

They turned to her. Andie squeezed her eyes shut, wishing she could stop thinking about the woman, about what she had seen. Wishing she could go back to an hour before she had peeked through that window. If she could, she wouldn't look through it.

But she couldn't go back, as much as she longed to.

Releasing a breath she hadn't even realized she held, she inclined her head. "Agreed."

8

Raven sat in her dark kitchen, awaiting her father's return. She waited up for him even though it was nearly 1:00 a.m., because he expected it, expected it from a daughter to whom her father, her family, was everything.

Absolute loyalty. Complete devotion. Those were the things that mattered.

She hated his guts.

Raven brought a hand to her right temple and massaged the spot, the tiny fist of pain that had settled there. She had headaches often, some blinding in their intensity, but she had learned to live with them. They were a part of her life, of who she was, just as the scar that curved down her right cheek was.

She closed her eyes and breathed deeply through her nose, the events of the night, the events she and her friends had witnessed, whirling in her head. Something important had happened tonight. Something important to her, though she didn't know why she was so certain of that.

Her exhilaration, her excitement, hadn't been sexual. She had been spellbound, but not by the woman and what she had been doing. By him, the man.

Raven rested her head against the chair's high back. Who was he? she wondered. What gave him such power over that woman?

And why couldn't she put him out of her head?

She hadn't been able to since that first night, when they'd all been in the house together. Contrary to what she'd told Andie, she had screwed up her courage and peeked around the corner from her hiding place—and seen his face. He had the features of a hawk, she thought, picturing him, all sharp angles and intense. He was older, not like her dad, but older than any of the guys she knew, probably in his twenties.

Raven frowned and rubbed her temple again, guilt plucking at her. She didn't know why she had lied to her friends, she hadn't planned to. The words, the lie, had simply slipped past her lips.

Andie and Julie were her best friends. They were her family. It was wrong to have lied to them. She had never kept anything from them.

Until now. Until this.

It was for their own good, she told herself. She was protecting them. The way a parent did a child.

But protecting them from what? she wondered. From who?

Raven thought of the man again. He knew many secrets, she was certain of it. Secrets that gave him power—over other people, over life and death. Tonight had been proof of that.

She wanted to learn his secrets.

From outside she heard the sound of a car door slamming. *Her father.* She straightened and turned toward the kitchen door, pasting on an expectant and welcoming smile.

The door opened. Her father stepped through.

"Hi, Daddy. How was your date?"

"Raven, honey." He beamed at her. "You waited up."

"Of course I did." She smiled and stood. "Why don't you sit down and I'll get you a cup of sleepy-time tea."

"Thanks, honey. That sounds good."

He took a seat and she busied herself putting on the kettle and getting out the mugs and tea. "So," she asked, her back to him, "how was it? Do you like her?"

"It was good. She's a nice woman. Did you like her?"

Raven didn't turn. She feared he would read in her eyes

what she really thought—that he was a son of a bitch and she wished he was dead. "Yes, Daddy," she said. "She did seem very nice."

For a moment he was silent. She sensed his gaze on her back, sensed him assessing her every movement, her every word and its inflection. She had played this game with him so long it had become second nature, yet still she lived in fear that he might someday see through her.

And then she might end up as her mother had, trying to run away in the dead of night.

He cleared his throat. "I know what you're thinking, Raven," he said softly. "You can't hide your thoughts from me."

Her fingers froze on the tea bags, and she forced a stiff laugh. "I don't know what you mean."

"Yes, you do. Look at me, please."

Schooling her features to what she hoped portrayed a look of innocence, she did as he asked, turning slowly to face him.

"I know what you're worried about," he said. "You're worried I'll get involved with Marion and things will change."

"No, I'm not." She shook her head. "Really, Dad."

He frowned. "You know I like you to call me Daddy."

"I'm sorry." She clasped her hands in front of her. "Thank you for reminding me."

He stood and crossed to her. He caught her hands, and gooseflesh raced up her arms. She walked a very fine line with him, she knew. If he ever discovered her disloyalty, if he ever even suspected it, he would take care of her. The way he had taken care of her mother.

She swallowed her fear. That wasn't going to happen. She wouldn't allow it to happen.

She was smarter than he was.

He squeezed her fingers and looked her straight in the eyes, demanding that she do the same. "You're worried it will be the way it was with your mother. That's it, isn't it?''

"I guess," she lied. "Maybe I'm a little worried about that.''

He smiled tenderly, and she wanted to retch. "It won't be that way, sweetheart. I promise you. Marion's not the way your mother was. She's loyal. And honest." His eyes filled with tears. "I loved your mother more than anything, Raven. It broke my heart when she left us. You know that, don't you?''

"Yes, Daddy," she whispered, understanding that he had loved her mother that much. Love, it seemed, took many forms. "I know that.''

He tightened his hands over hers and she had to fight not to flinch from the pressure. "Family is everything," he said fiercely. "Loyalty counts above all." He moved his gaze over her face. "No one will come between us. I won't allow it. Do you understand?''

"Of course." She forced an adoring smile. "Family is everything.''

He smiled and brought his hands to her hair, hanging loosely down the sides of her face. He tucked it behind her ears. "Why do you wear your hair this way? You know I like it pulled back.''

"I'm sorry, Daddy. I guess I forgot. Tomorrow, I'll wear those new barrettes you bought me.''

"That's my girl." He bent and pressed a kiss to her forehead, then dropped his hands. "Run along to bed. It's late.''

Just then the kettle screamed. Raven jumped, nearly leaping out of her skin. "I'll get it," she said, swinging toward the stove. She reached for the kettle. "You just sit—''

He caught her hand. "You're nervous as a cat tonight.''

"Just tired.''

"I'll take care of the tea. You go on to bed. I'll see you in the morning.''

"All right." She stood on tiptoe and pressed a kiss to his cheek. "Good night, Daddy."

As she turned and walked away, Raven smiled to herself. One morning, he wouldn't see her. One morning, when the time was right, he would never be allowed to see her again.

9

Julie awakened with a start, a silent scream on her lips. Terrified, she moved her gaze over her dark bedroom, looking for the beast in every shadow, the monster who had come to take what was left of her soul.

After a moment, the outlines of her furniture began to take shape; the silhouette of the tree in her window, the pile of discarded clothes in the corner. Her breathing slowed, her heart with it.

Only a bad dream. Nothing to be really frightened of.

But she was frightened. Julie pressed her lips together, realizing they were trembling. Realizing, too, how close to tears she was. The nightmare had been so real and vivid. So awful.

Her reaction had been worse.

She had been turned on. Sexually aroused, even in her sleep.

Julie rolled onto her side, curling into a ball of misery and self-disgust. The dream had been a reenactment of the scene she, Andie and Raven had witnessed that night. Only she had been the woman, blindfolded and performing for the man. She had been the one who stood before him naked and completely vulnerable, the one who had knelt before him and taken his penis into her mouth.

She should have been ashamed, terrified or repulsed. She should have been desperate to escape.

She had loved it, instead. She had reveled in it.

What was wrong with her?

Just remembering, her body began to throb again. Julie

squeezed her thighs together, wanting to stop the sensations but knowing she couldn't. Knowing that once again, she had lost control and her body wasn't her own.

Julie turned her face to the pillow and moaned, the tingling sensation building between her legs. She rocked slightly, and the folds of flesh at the apex of her thighs rubbed together, a trick she had learned years ago. She had used it in church, at the dinner table, during Scriptures.

Even as she told herself to stop, she rocked harder, squeezed tighter. The tingling ignited, becoming fire. Her mind emptied of everything but the heat, the need for that moment of complete oblivion and electric nothingness.

The moment where Julie Cooper, her life, her body itself, ceased to exist.

It arrived. She brought her fist to her mouth to hold back the sound that rushed to escape. One of pleasure and pain. The pleasure of the moment. The painful truth that in the experience, it was already over.

Back to life. Her life.

Julie Cooper lived.

Pleasure and pain. As the throbbing eased, she thought of Andie and Raven. Julie's eyes welled with tears. What would they think if they knew the truth about her? If they knew what she did, how she touched herself? Would they still want to be her best friends?

They wouldn't; she knew they wouldn't.

Earlier that night, as she had peered in that window with her friends, she had been afraid, so afraid, that Andie and Raven would see how excited she was, that they would know what she was thinking, what she was feeling.

She had been so ashamed, she had wanted to die.

Her thoughts returned to the dream. In it, she had been that woman; she had crossed to the man and had eagerly taken his penis into her mouth.

Remembering, her stomach rose to her throat. Unlike the real scene she had viewed, it hadn't ended there. Suddenly, her blindfold had been stripped away. She'd lifted her eyes.

And seen the hideous, red face of her lover.

She'd had the devil inside her mouth, his penis, his sperm bubbling up, gagging her.

She had clawed at him then, trying to free herself. He had tipped back his massive horned head and laughed. She couldn't escape him. They were joined forever.

You have the devil inside you, girl. You always have.

Julie drew her knees tighter to her chest, her father's voice ringing in her head, the devil's laughter with it. She squeezed her eyes shut, wishing she could blot them out. Wishing she could crawl out of herself, become someone else, someone new and clean and good.

Clean and good. The way she hadn't felt in a long time, not since the terrible Easter morning so many years ago. She drew in a shuddering breath, the memory unfolding in her head. She had been seven years old, standing in front of her bedroom mirror, gazing admiringly at herself. In her new Easter dress, bonnet and white patent-leather shoes, shoes so shiny and bright she could see herself in them, she had felt like a princess. A beautiful princess.

She had giggled and whirled around, her long blond curls swinging with the movement. From downstairs, Julie had heard her two brothers playing, laughing and tussling with each other, from the bathroom down the hall her mother humming "Amazing Grace." The new baby had been asleep in the nursery; her father had been running through his sermon one last time. This was her father's first big sermon for his new congregation here in Thistledown, and Easter Sunday was the most important day on the religious calendar. His new congregation expected something especially rousing today. Julie had heard him tell her mother that he didn't want anything to go wrong. Not this time.

Julie ran her hands over the dress's tissue-like fabric, liking the way it rustled against her legs. Something had gone wrong at their last church, the one in Mobile. Julie didn't know what, she only knew that some men from the congregation had come to see her dad one night, and after they left she had heard her mom crying.

Not long after, they had moved here, to Thistledown and Temple Baptist Church.

Julie pirouetted again, delighted, wishing she could dress like this every day. When she grew up she would, she decided, tilting her head this way and that and smiling at herself in the mirror. She fluffed her hair and pursed her lips, imitating the way she had seen an actress do it on a shampoo commercial. Would the other girls think she was pretty? she wondered. Would they like her?

Maybe today, she thought hopefully, beaming into the mirror, at the egg hunt and picnic after the last service, she would make a friend.

"What are you doing?"

At the sound of her father's angry voice, Julie froze. She dropped her hands and turned slowly to face him, her heart thundering. "Nothing, Daddy," she whispered.

He took a step toward her, his expression thunderous. "I'll ask you once more, daughter. What were you do-ing?"

She swallowed hard, past the sudden knot of tears and fear that choked her. She hated when her father got this way; it scared her. She never knew what answer he was looking for, never knew what she had done to anger him.

"Just...getting ready for...church, Daddy."

"Linda!" he bellowed, vibrant red starting at the place where his clerical collar met his neck and moving upward.

Julie took an involuntary step backward. "Daddy, re-ally, I wasn't doing anythi—"

"Vanity is the work of the devil," he said. "It tempts us, teasing and cajoling until we love ourselves more than God."

She shook her head. "No, Daddy, I wasn't—"

He was across the room so fast she didn't have time to

react. He grabbed her bonnet and snatched it from her head, taking some of her hair with it. She cried out in pain.

"Don't lie to me! I saw the devil in your eyes. I saw the admiration, the self-love for your reflection."

"No, Daddy! Please—"

He grabbed the hem of her dress and yanked it up over her head. She heard the delicate fabric rip, an awful wrenching sound. A sound she felt as if a physical blow. Sobbing, she tried to cover herself, naked save for her underwear and tights. "No...please...I didn't mean to be bad," she begged. "Give me another chance. Please, I—"

He turned her toward the mirror, forcing her arms to her sides so she would face her nakedness. "See yourself, sinner." He shook her so hard her teeth rattled. "What's to admire now, I ask you? Without the Lord, what are you but dirty flesh and foul spirit?"

As if from a great distance, Julie had heard her mother's cry of distress, her brother's muffled giggles. Her father had released her, and she'd crumpled to the floor. Only then had she seen her mother standing in the doorway staring at her with a look of pure horror, her brothers behind her, both of them making ugly faces at her.

A sound of despair had flown into her throat like vomit, and she'd held it back. Just as she'd held back her tears, her self-pity. Such expression was just another form of vanity, her father said. Another form of self-love over God-love.

Her father had ordered her mother to find her something less provocative to wear, something that wouldn't tempt her to stray from the path of righteousness.

She had gone to church that day in a plain brown jumper and scuffed loafers; she had gone marked by sin, so vain and wretched she wasn't even allowed to wear pretty dresses and bonnets like the other girls.

Instead of welcoming smiles, she had been greeted with curious stares from the other children. Their gazes had slipped over her, and they had wondered, she knew, why, on the highest holy day of the year, the reverend's daughter was dressed the way she was.

They hadn't had long to wonder. Her father had told them.

He had been at the pulpit, delivering a rousing sermon. As he spoke, his fiery gaze kept coming back to her.

"You're sinners!" Her father's voice had boomed through the church. Around Julie, people shifted uncomfortably. "He died for you. For your sins. He died so you may live."

He paused a moment, then brought his fist crashing down on the pulpit. "Sinners!" he shouted, swinging his gaze to Julie's, seeming to pin her to the pew.

He lifted a hand and pointed. At her. Directly at her. "Sinner," he said softly. Then louder, "Sinner!"

Julie had gone hot, then icy, clammy cold. Tears had flooded her eyes and she'd sunk down in the pew. She'd heard the hushed murmur move through the congregation, felt those around her ease away, as if afraid of contamination.

If the others hadn't known about her before, she remembered realizing, they had then. And she had known, too.

Dirty flesh and foul spirit. Marked by sin.

Julie made a strangled sound of despair, the past retreating, the hopeless present reasserting itself. If only Andie or Raven was with her now. They would talk to her, make her smile and laugh, make her forget. Who and what she was. They would tell her she was okay.

And for a little while, she would even believe it.

For a little while. She pressed her face to the pillow, longing so hard for her friends she ached, even though she knew in her heart that no one could help her, not even God. She knew it was true, because she had prayed and prayed, but still the devil stalked her.

And one day, she feared, he would catch her. And she would be lost forever.

10

Andie sat at the breakfast table, going over what she had decided in the darkest hours of the night, rehearsing what she would say to her mother. She had to tell her what she and her friends had seen the night before. She had to, no matter what she had promised them.

Andie folded her hands in her lap, trying to appear calm even though her heart thundered nearly out of control. She had hardly slept. She had tossed and turned, unable to expunge the image of the blindfolded woman from her head. Or of the man, sitting like a king, the lord of the woman before him.

Daniel then Pete slammed through the kitchen door, one chasing the other with a squirt gun, both of them squealing with laughter.

Andie jumped, nearly startled out of her skin. "Hey!" she called after them, irritated. "You're not supposed to shoot that thing in the house. And be quiet. Mom's still sleeping."

"No, she's not." Her mother shuffled into the kitchen, a hand to her head. "Up and at 'em." She crossed to the coffeepot, took a mug from the cabinet above and filled it with some of yesterday's cold brew, then set it in the microwave to warm it.

Andie swallowed against the lump that formed in her throat. When her dad had lived here, there had always been fresh coffee. She remembered walking into the kitchen in the morning and its aroma filling her head, welcoming and somehow reassuring.

The microwave dinged and her mom brought the now-steaming and bitter-smelling cup of coffee to the table. Sighing, she sat down.

Andie glanced at her from the corner of her eyes, nervous. She cleared her throat. "Mom? Can I talk to you? It's kind of important."

Her mother didn't look up. "Sure, honey."

Andie opened her mouth then shut it. Was she doing the right thing? She had made a promise to her friends. She had promised not to go to her mother. She had agreed they would investigate more before any of them blew the whistle on the mystery couple and their activities.

They had agreed.

She chewed on the tip of her thumb, indecisive. But that had been last night. None of them had been thinking clearly. Now she was. And what was going on in that house was wrong.

Andie peeked at her mother again. She seemed to have forgotten her daughter was even there. She stared off into space, her expression so sad it broke Andie's heart.

"Mom?" she said softly. When her mother didn't acknowledge her in any way, she tried again, this time louder.

Her mother started. "I'm sorry, honey. What is it?"

"Are you all right?"

Marge Bennett smiled, though to Andie it looked forced. "Fine. It's just…just that I'm tired. I'm not sleeping much, and…"

Her voice trailed off, and her eyes filled with tears. She drew in a choked breath. "It's just hard, you know? I thought we, your father and I…I thought forever meant forever. I thought we were…that we were happy. I was. Completely."

Her mother fell silent for a moment, her gaze turned to the window and the bright day beyond. "I still love him."

Andie stared at her mother, hurting so bad each breath

tore at her chest. Even so, anger at her father coiled inside her, anger and resentment.

How could he have done this to them? How could he have done it to her mom?

As if sensing her daughter's despair, Marge turned back to her. She covered her hand. "I'm sorry, sweetheart. I shouldn't have said that."

"Don't apologize, Mom. It's *his* fault. He's the one who—"

"No," her mother said, cutting her off, "I shouldn't have said anything to you. Not now or the night he...told us he was leaving. I handled that all wrong. And everything since, too." She sighed. "I was so hurt, I wanted to hurt him back, just a little. I used you kids, his love for you, to do it."

"Mom, don't—"

"No, honey, what I did was wrong and not very mature. Your father loves you and your brothers very much."

"Then why did he leave us?"

For a moment, she said nothing, then lifted her shoulders in a defeated looking shrug. "I guess he's not perfect."

"I'll never forgive him, Mom."

"Yes, you will." She touched her cheek. "You will."

When Andie opened her mouth to protest, her mother shook her head again. "I know how tough this has been for you, too. And your brothers." She bent and rested her forehead against Andie's for a moment. "Thank you, sweetheart. For all the help you've been these past weeks. And for being such a good girl for me."

She squeezed Andie's fingers, then released them. "Now, you needed to talk to me about something. What is it?"

Andie shrank back in her chair. How could she tell her mother that her "good girl" had been breaking into empty houses and peeking in windows and watching kinky sex? She imagined her mother's face, her surprise and disappointment, her sigh of defeat. That's all her mom needed, more to worry about, more disappointment.

No, she couldn't do that to her. She wouldn't.

Andie forced a smile. "I just wanted to tell you about the party Sarah Conners is having and ask your opinion about what I should wear. But it can wait."

"Are you sure? We could go to your closet and—"

"I'm sure." Andie stood, bent and kissed her cheek. "This is something I have to take care of myself."

11

Mr. and Mrs. X, as Andie and her friends had begun to call the mystery couple, didn't show again. After a week, the girls concluded that the couple met only late at night, so they gave up all their day watches and returned to their normal summer routine.

As they went to the mall and the movies or to parties at friends' houses, Andie could almost believe that it was a normal summer. That everything was as it had always been between her and her best friends.

But nothing was, or had been, normal since the night they had peered at Mr. and Mrs. X through the window. And everything certainly was *not* as it had always been between the three friends.

Andie glanced from Raven to Julie, then returned her gaze to the tree house floor. The three of them sat at their post, lost in their own thoughts, not speaking. Raven was distracted about anything but their mission. On that she seemed almost frighteningly intent. Julie, on the other hand, was giddy and silly, even more so than usual. In the past days she'd had periods when she couldn't stop laughing, and there were many times she didn't seem able to look her friends in the eyes.

Between their two moods, Raven and Julie had been at each other's throats even more than usual.

Andie herself was nervous and on edge, and spent a good bit of her time with Julie and Raven thinking about Mrs. X and praying that the couple never came back. She had become almost obsessed with them, thinking about them night and day, worrying.

And she spent each day dreading the night. Dreading sneaking out of the house and going to the tree house to wait and watch. She didn't want to see the couple again. She wanted them to disappear from her life, from all their lives.

If they didn't, something bad was going to happen.

Andie shivered and rubbed her arms, chilled though the night was warm. She glanced at her friends: Julie who was staring dreamily into space, Raven who had the binoculars trained on the house next door, waiting quietly, like a cat for its prey.

Andie shifted, her butt sore from sitting so long on the hard platform. "Are you guys okay?"

Raven lowered the binoculars. "I'm fine. Why?"

"You're quiet tonight, that's all."

Julie giggled, and Raven scowled at her. Julie immediately shut up.

"Maybe we should go?" Andie offered.

"Go?" Raven repeated. "What do you mean? We haven't been here that long."

"Long enough," Andie said. "They're not coming."

"How do you know?"

"Just a hunch."

"Well, I think they are."

"Fine." Andie frowned at her friend, annoyed. "We'll wait a little longer."

"Andie," Julie whispered, leaning toward her. "I met the coolest guy at the pool today, when I took my brothers swimming." She lowered her voice a bit more, then giggled again. "I had that icky grandma suit on, the one my dad makes me wear, so I didn't even take off my cover-up. We sat and talked the whole time my brothers swam."

Andie glanced at Raven, then back at Julie. "What was his name?"

"Bryce. He was so cute."

"You didn't make out with him, did you?" Raven asked, not moving her gaze from the house.

Julie bristled. "Right there, in front of my brothers and everybody else? No, I didn't make out with him."

"Never can tell with you."

Julie's head snapped up, her expression hurt. "What's that supposed to mean?"

Raven lowered the binoculars and looked at her. "Sometimes I wonder. I mean, sometimes it seems like all you care about are boys and making out."

"Leave her alone, Raven," Andie said, furious. "It beats what you care about."

"What's that supposed to mean?"

"This," she answered. "Ever since that first night, this is all you can think about. You're obsessed."

"I am not! I only want to figure out what's going on. Who these people are and what they're doing in this house. You just have a weak stomach."

"I do not have a weak stomach!" Andie couldn't believe she and Raven were arguing like this. "I have a feeling something really bad is going to happen to us."

Julie's eyes widened. "Like what?"

Raven began clucking her tongue at her. At them both. "Chickenshits...chickenshits."

"Stop it!" Andie shouted, scrambling to her feet and glaring down at Raven. "You're really starting to piss me off!"

Julie whimpered. "Guys, don't fight. We're supposed to be friends."

Ignoring Julie, Raven launched to her feet and faced Andie. "And I'm getting pretty sick of your pansy-ass whining."

"Whining!"

"That's right. We decided that Mr. X was a freak. We decided to pursue this a little longer. We made a deal."

"Well, we were wrong. We weren't thinking clearly."

"Speak for yourself. I was thinking plenty clear."

Raven fisted her fingers. "Just 'cause your parents are splitting up, you think everybody should do what you want. Well, you're not the only one whose home life is shit, okay? Welcome to the club."

Andie flinched and took a step backward. "I can't believe you said that to me. How could you? You know how much—"

Andie bit back the words, her eyes flooding with tears. She started past Raven, intent on grabbing her binoculars and heading home. At the same moment, Julie jumped to her feet. Andie knocked into the other girl, unbalancing her.

As if in slow motion, Andie watched as Julie swung her arms trying to rebalance herself. A cry on her lips, Andie grabbed for her friend; she wasn't fast enough. Julie went over the side of the platform.

She landed on her side with a sickening thud. She lay there, eyes open but completely still.

"Julie!" Andie cried, her heart in her throat. It didn't look as if she was breathing. "Are you okay?"

She didn't reply, and Andie and Raven rushed down the ladder to their friend. They knelt beside her. "Are you all right?" Andie asked again, voice shaking. "Please... please...tell me you're okay."

"I...I think I am," Julie said, beginning to shake. "But I'm afraid to move."

"Then don't," Andie said. "Give yourself a minute to catch your breath." She met Raven's eyes. She saw her own concern mirrored in her friend's gaze.

"I can't be hurt," Julie whispered. "If I am, my dad's going to find out what we've been doing. He'll kill me." She started to cry then, softly, heartbreaking mewls of despair.

"He won't find out." Raven squeezed her hand. "I won't let him. I promise."

"Okay," Andie said. "Let's see if anything's broken." Carefully, they tested Julie's arms and legs; they had her move her head, fingers and toes, then helped her sit up. She was fine, they realized. Just shaken.

They all were, Andie decided. Even Raven.

Andie swallowed hard. "I'm really...really sorry, Julie. I didn't mean for that to happen."

"I know. It was an accident." Julie drew in a hiccoughing breath. "No more fighting. You're supposed to be best friends. Best friends don't hurt each other like that."

"Julie's right, Rave." Andie looked at her friend, a lump forming in her throat. "Now do you see what's happening to us? Ever since this started, we've changed. We're at each other's throats all the time. Either that, or not speaking at all. This thing's tearing us apart."

Raven stared at her for long moments, then looked away. "I just wanted to figure this guy out."

"I know," Andie said softly, touching her arm. "But it's hurting us. And I don't want to lose you two."

"Please, Rave," Julie said, her voice quivering. "I want to go back to the way we were before."

Raven moved her gaze from one to the other, then nodded. "Okay, guys. Starting now, none of this ever happened."

12

But Raven wasn't about to forget about Mr. and Mrs. X. No matter what Andie said. Andie was wrong. She and Julie didn't understand. They didn't see how important what had happened to them was. They had been given an opportunity, an open door.

To the secrets. The way.

But she saw. She understood.

And that was okay. She was the strong one; she always had been. Andie was a do-gooder with a weak stomach. She worried about everybody, but didn't have the backbone to take a stand. Julie, on the other hand, was a boy-crazy space cadet and would follow whoever was stronger.

In this case, Julie would follow her.

Raven had decided that she and Julie would continue their late-night stakeout of number twelve Mockingbird Lane. They would watch; Raven would learn. And someday she would need those lessons to protect the three of them, to keep her family together.

Raven didn't know when or against whom they would need to be protected; she only knew, deep in her gut, that they would.

It would mean lying to Andie. She hated to do it, but it was for Andie's own good. That made it okay, she reasoned. A necessary evil.

Raven called Julie. And as Raven had known she would, Julie hesitated briefly, then fell right in line with Raven's plan, promising to keep their activities a secret from Andie.

They agreed to meet that night.

13

After her family had all gone to bed, Julie sneaked out of the house to meet Raven. They had agreed beforehand that they would wait for Mr. and Mrs. X for two hours. Two hours hadn't seemed that long to Julie then, but now the minutes ticked past with agonizing slowness. She could hardly sit still. It was as if someone had plugged her in and turned her on, and she couldn't find her Off switch.

Her mind raced; her thoughts whirled. She thought of Andie, Mrs. X, her nightmare, her father. The devil. She was torn between excitement and guilt, shame and arousal. She worked to hide her feelings from Raven, though a couple of times she had caught the other girl looking at her, her expression strange.

Julie swallowed hard. She couldn't bear it if her friends found out the truth about her. *If she kept this up, they would. They would figure it out.*

"They're not going to show," Julie whispered, then glanced guiltily over her shoulder, as if someone stood nearby, listening. "Let's just go."

Raven released a frustrated breath and lowered the binoculars. "It hasn't been two hours. We agreed, remember?"

"I know, but—"

"Shh. Look, a car."

Sure enough, a car rolled down the street. It pulled into the driveway of number twelve. The automatic garage door slid up; the car eased in. The door shut.

Julie's mouth had turned to dust. She fought to speak around the knot in her throat. "Was it him?"

"Her," Raven corrected, lowering the binoculars, frowning.

"Her? Where's Mr. X?"

"Late, maybe. Let's hang a minute, he'll come."

They waited. Five minutes. Ten. Raven shook her head. "Something's wrong. If he was coming, he'd be here."

"Maybe he was in the car, like hiding in the back seat."

They looked at each other, then scrambled off the platform. They made their way through the wooded lot and around the back of the house.

They found Mrs. X. She was alone, blindfolded and naked. She stood motionless in the center of the great room, waiting.

Julie gazed at her, confused, then nudged Raven. "What's she doing?"

Raven didn't glance over, but lifted her shoulders in response, indicating she didn't know.

Julie frowned. "This is so weird. I wonder—"

Raven glared at her, bringing a finger to her lips. Julie swallowed the rest of her thought. Minutes passed, and though she didn't know exactly how many, it seemed like forever.

The night was sticky; their half-crouching positions uncomfortable. A mosquito buzzed in Julie's ear, and she swatted at it, annoyed. Why was she here, bored and hot and being eaten by bugs, when she could be home, curled up in her comfortable bed? It was stupid. This was stupid. She was taking a big chance just being here. And what for? She opened her mouth to tell Raven exactly that, when her friend caught her arm, stopping her.

"He's here," she hissed.

Heart in her throat, Julie popped up and peered over the ledge. Mr. X wore a ski mask. He had a rope. He came up behind Mrs. X; he brought the rope to her throat. Using it, he tugged her roughly against him.

Julie brought a hand to her mouth, shocked and frightened. Aroused. As she watched, he ran the rope over Mrs. X's body, caressing her with it, making love to her with it. Julie watched as the rope coiled around the woman's neck, then slithered over her shoulders, her breasts. Then lower.

He used it as another man might use hands and fingers. He brought it between her legs. Mrs. X arched; her mouth opened, though Julie heard no sound.

Julie's breath came in fast, shallow gasps. Her cheeks were hot, her nipples hard. She closed her eyes, struggling to get control of herself, her runaway thoughts.

When she opened them, Mr. X was binding the woman's hands with the rope, roughly, yanking her arms behind her back. She didn't fight him, didn't struggle or try to break away. Julie didn't understand. Mrs. X didn't fight him, yet it looked as if he was scaring her, as if he was hurting her.

Did he own her? Julie wondered. Was she his slave, his property to do with as he wanted? Or was she in love with him, so in love she would give him anything he asked for?

Julie could understand that; she could imagine herself loving, needing to be loved in return, that much.

She was like Mrs. X.

Just like in her nightmare.

Mr. X forced her to her knees. Then, his intentions unmistakable, he unzipped his pants and pulled out his erection. Tangling his hands in her hair, he forced her to take him into her mouth.

Julie made a small sound, at once shocked and intrigued. Guilt and shame speared through her. She was wet. On fire.

Burning with shame. Guilt. Desire.

She ducked down, breathing hard, unable to watch another moment. Raven didn't move. Julie covered her face with her hands. They trembled.

She was bad. This was bad. Every time she closed her

eyes, she imagined her face on Mrs. X's body, the man's hands, the rope slithering over her skin.

Andie had been right. They never should have come here. This was wrong. She was going to burn in hell, just as her father said.

"We have to go," she whispered. "Raven, please." She reached up and caught her friend's hand and tugged. "Please, Rave. Please."

Raven met her eyes, the expression in them strange, almost feverish. She gazed at Julie a moment, almost as if she didn't know her, then nodded, not speaking again until they reached Julie's door.

Raven touched Julie's cheek. "It's going to be all right," she whispered. "I'll make sure of that."

Julie held her friend's gaze a moment, then nodded and slipped inside, not at all certain of that fact. In fact, Julie had a horrible feeling that nothing was ever going to be all right again.

14

The next week passed in a disjointed, confusing blur for Julie. Her days were spent pretending to be a good daughter and a normal fifteen-year-old. Her nights were spent peering through the window of number twelve Mockingbird Lane, watching acts that alternately shocked, horrified and aroused her.

Julie lived in fear that her father would discover what she was doing; she struggled to deal with what she saw. One time Mr. X would be tender, even loving with Mrs. X, making love with her in the traditional way. The way Julie had dreamed of being made love to. The next he would be cruel. He would torment her with his indifference, he would make her crawl or beg. Those times, he would take her in whatever way or position he chose, no matter how painful.

He was the devil, Julie decided. She was watching the devil himself.

And he was seducing her.

Julie lay on her bed and stared up at the ceiling, too frightened to close her eyes. She feared if she did, her subconscious would take over and she would be once again transformed into Mrs. X.

She didn't want to be Mrs. X. She didn't want to enjoy...that.

But she did enjoy it. It was sick, yet she watched in fascination. She hated it, yet she couldn't stop thinking about it. She couldn't understand why Mrs. X allowed the man to treat her that way, yet she did understand.

Maybe that was what frightened her most.

Julie rolled onto her side, then her back once more. The sheets twisted around her legs, binding them, trapping her. She began to sweat, her heart to pound. She was afraid.

Something terrible was happening to her. Had happened to her. She bit her bottom lip. She wasn't the same person she had been before the window and Mr. and Mrs. X. Her life wasn't the same.

She knew things now. She was afraid for her future. *She was afraid she was like Mrs. X.*

A cry bubbled up to her throat. She wanted to go back. She didn't want to know what she knew. She didn't want him to be in her brain anymore. She pressed her face to the pillow. She wanted to make it all go away.

And she was afraid, too, for Mrs. X. Tonight, Mr. X had been brutal. He had all but raped Mrs. X, then left her bound, gagged and blindfolded. Alone in the dark.

He had gone to the garage and his car, and he'd driven off.

She and Raven had waited thirty minutes; he hadn't returned. Julie had suggested they go inside and free Mrs. X; Raven had scoffed. It was all part of their game, she had said. Julie worried too much.

Did she worry too much? Julie wondered. Or was Mrs. X still there? Now, hours later? Had he left her to die alone in that house, bound and blinded by the silk scarf? Had he left her that way and gone to get a weapon to kill her?

The dark, her fears, pressed in on her. Julie reached across to the bedside table and switched on her light, squinting against the sudden brightness. Next to the light, in a pretty flowered frame, was a picture of her, Andie and Raven. Julie reached for her glasses and slipped them on, then took the framed photo into her hands and gazed at it. The picture had been snapped last summer, when Andie's folks had taken them all camping. They had their arms around each other, they were smiling.

Now, she could hardly look Andie in the eyes. Now,

she and Raven hardly spoke. It was as if there was a glass wall separating the three of them; they could see one another but not touch, not connect. They didn't laugh together, they didn't whisper together, sharing their deepest, darkest secrets.

Now, they kept those secrets all to themselves.

It was tearing them apart. Tearing her apart. But as much as she longed to, Julie didn't know how to stop it.

15

Andie couldn't put Mr. and Mrs. X out of her mind, no matter how she tried. She threw herself into her friends and summer activities, but still the image of the woman on her knees before the man haunted her.

If only she understood what drove the couple, if only she could fathom why the woman allowed herself to be treated that way. If she understood, she decided, she would be able to let it go and move on.

If she didn't, she feared she would go crazy.

She remembered that Julie had said she'd read something in a psychology book about this; sexual deviation, she had called it. Andie decided a trip to the Thistledown Public Library would do the trick.

Andie found a limited amount of information there. It was frustrating, because she needed to ask the librarian for help but couldn't. Thistledown was a small town; the librarian knew her. But more important, she knew her mom and dad.

No sooner would the question be out of her mouth than the librarian would be on the phone to Andie's mom.

Andie didn't consider that an option, so, knowing that her mother wouldn't miss her, she made the two-hour bus trek to Columbia and the University of Missouri. In the sprawling, book-filled building that housed the library she found more information than she would have time to read before she had to catch the bus back home. The librarian didn't even blink at Andie's request and directed her to the psychology section. She explained how to use the microfiche and how to find the bound periodicals.

Sexual deviation, Andie learned, was a behavior that varied from what a society or people called "normal." She learned that some people enjoyed being dominated during sex, others punishing or being punished. She learned that they found the pain, the humiliation and powerlessness exciting. Some could achieve sexual gratification in no other way.

The experts rarely agreed on why these people found dominance, submission or pain pleasurable—their theories ranged from traumatic childhood experiences to environmental influences to genetics. They did agree, however, that sexual deviance had been a part of every culture, back as far as there were records to study.

No closer to understanding, but slightly reassured by the sheer volume of information, Andie checked her watch. She had time for one more article before she left. Her head already swimming with what she'd learned, she thought about passing on the article and going for a Coke instead, then took a deep breath. She had come all this way, she might as well get as much information as she could.

She would just skim it, she decided, looking longingly at the front doors, then back at the scientific journal. Then she still might have time for that Coke.

She flipped open the journal and began to read quickly. A sentence jumped out at her. She stopped, her world tipping on its axis.

Sometimes, death provides the ultimate sexual thrill.

She struggled to calm herself, to catch hold of the fear racing through her. With forced calm, Andie went back and carefully read the entire article. It went on to explain that such instances were rare, though quite a number had been documented. One man had actually killed four partners over the course of three years, before he was caught. During his pretrial psychiatric evaluation, he had insisted that his partners had been willing victims, that they had helped plan the tableau that had been their last and that they had received as much pleasure in the act as he. A half-dozen or so graphic photographs were included.

Andie gazed at the images, stomach lurching up to her throat. She had been right to be afraid for Mrs. X, she knew now. The woman was in real danger.

A sense of urgency pressing at her, Andie snatched up the journal, and went in search of a copier. She found one, dug in her pocket for change, then began photocopying the article, pictures and all. She had to make Raven and Julie understand; had to get them to see the danger Mrs. X was in. She had to make them as certain as she of what they had to do.

They had to go to their parents. They had to.

16

The minute Andie got home, she called her friends. She told them to meet her at the toolshed, a.s.a.p. It was an emergency, she told them. They had to talk; they couldn't chance being overheard.

Within twenty minutes the three of them were sitting cross-legged on the shed floor. Julie looked guilty and nervous, Raven curious. Seeing them now, Andie realized she had hardly spoken to them in two days.

Without waiting for their questions, Andie launched into the reason she had called them together. She told them how she had gone by bus to Columbia and the university library, describing in detail what she had discovered there, finishing with the last, most devastating piece of information.

"Look." She took the article from her back pocket, unfolded it and handed it to her friends, hands shaking. "Our imaginations weren't running away with us. We were right to be afraid. This guy's bad news."

Julie stared at the photocopy, her eyes huge behind her glasses. "Do you think he…he's…going to kill her?"

Andie swallowed hard. "I think he might."

"Oh, God." Julie wrapped her arms around her drawn-up knees and looked pleadingly at Raven. The other girl sent her a warning glance, and Julie moaned and pressed her face to her knees.

Andie watched them, frowning. "What's going on, you guys?"

"Nothing," Raven said smoothly. She handed the article back. "This doesn't prove anything."

"Of course it does. It proves he *could* hurt her. It proves we can't just sit back and do nothing. We have to go to our—"

"Parents?" Raven supplied. "I don't think so." When Andie opened her mouth to argue her point, Raven cut her off. "She likes what they're doing, and if she's not afraid for herself, why should we risk our butts for her?"

"But the article said—"

"That sometimes the dominator can't stop and kills his partner. I know." Raven tossed aside the pages. "But it doesn't say how often, Andie. It could be one time in a million."

"And what if this is that time?"

Julie lifted her head, her expression stricken. "Raven...we *have* to."

Raven ignored her. "This is *Thistledown*, Andie. Not New York. Not even St. Louis. Stuff like that doesn't happen here. Besides, can you imagine what Julie's dad would do if he found out? Can you imagine what mine would do?"

Julie began to whimper, and Andie cut her a worried glance. "I'll keep you guys out of it. I'll tell my mom it was only me."

"Do you really think she'll believe that? The three of us spend almost every minute together, we have, almost all summer. Do you really think she won't *know* the truth."

Andie pressed her lips together to keep them from trembling. She and her friends had never disagreed this way before. It made her feel funny, almost as if she were on trial and they were judging her. Why couldn't they see this the way she did?

Andie scrambled around for another solution. "How about this? Instead of our parents, we go to the police. We make them promise not to tell our folks. We tell them—"

"It'll never work," Raven inserted, flushing. "We're minors, Andie. Get it? *Minors.* The first thing they'd do is call our folks. It's like a rule. And then we're dead. Grounded. Separated from each other, probably. Shipped off to some private school. And for what? Your imagination? To help a woman we don't know, a woman involved in a kinky love affair? I don't think so."

"You can't tell! Please, Andie." Julie began to cry. She bent and pressed her face to her folded knees and rocked, her sobs high and scary-sounding.

Sending Andie a furious glance, Raven went to Julie and put her arms around her. "You've got to drop this, Andie. You're flipping out, or something. I know it's been a tough summer for you with your parents splitting up and all, but don't screw up our lives...our friendship because of it."

Tears flooded Andie eyes. "But what about...what if something happens to her?"

"Instead of worrying so damn much about this Mrs. X, why don't you try worrying about us? We're the ones you're supposed to care about."

Julie lifted her head then, her face blotchy from crying. "Rave, what if she's right? What if he's killed her?"

"Shut up," Raven hissed. "You promised."

"We have to tell her. We *have* to."

Andie's blood ran cold. "Tell me what?"

"I'm sorry, Rave," Julie whispered. "But she could be dead." Her voice rose. "What are we going to do if she's dead?"

"She's not, but if you *have* to, fine. Tell her. I'm not stopping you, am I?" Raven stood and walked to the doorway, now just a big, rectangular hole in the wall. She folded her arms across her chest and glared at them.

Julie looked at Andie, then slid her gaze guiltily away, her chin trembling. "Raven and I went back to the house and spied on Mr. and Mrs. X."

"What?" Andie moved her gaze between her two

friends, not believing what she was hearing, but knowing it was true. "You went back...after we'd agreed that we wouldn't?"

"Raven explained it to me," Julie said, wiping her nose with the back of her hand. "We had to figure out what they were up to, and we didn't want to upset you."

"I see." *Her best friends had lied to her.* She looked at Raven. The other girl met her gaze almost defiantly. That hurt, maybe most of all. "How many times, Julie?"

"A bunch," she whispered, hanging her head. "I'm sorry, Andie. I didn't mean to."

How did one not "mean" to lie? Tears burned Andie's eyes, she blinked furiously against them. "So, why are you telling me now? Why not keep lying?"

Her sarcasm was lost on Julie. She brought her hands to her throat. "Because I'm afraid he's...killed her."

Julie went back, describing in detail the acts she and Raven had witnessed, she told Andie about the rope, about Mr. X's alternating tenderness and brutality. She finished by telling Andie how he had left Mrs. X alone, bound and blindfolded two nights ago.

When she finished, she curved her arms around her middle. "It was so awful. I've hardly been able to sleep since. I keep thinking that Mrs. X...that she might be...that he might have killed her. And now...that article..."

Her words trailed off. They, their meaning, landed heavily between them anyway. Andie paled. "Have you been back since? To, you know, make sure he...didn't?"

"No." Julie flushed. "I just couldn't. Not alone."

"Rave?" Andie turned to the other girl. "How about you?"

She shook her head. "Get a grip, guys. He hasn't hurt her. She likes what he does to her. It's a big, sick game."

"But what if—" Julie struggled to find her voice. "What if she's...her body would be... I've never seen a...a dead body before."

Raven rolled her eyes. "I swear, you guys are losin' it."

"How do you know?" Andie demanded, facing the other girl, suddenly, incredibly angry. "How come you're always right? How come we always have to do what you want to do?" She lowered her voice, hurt. "I thought we were best friends. I thought we were *family*. And I thought that meant something."

"We are. It does. I—" Raven's throat seemed to close over the words and her eyes flooded with tears.

"Best friends don't lie to each other. They don't hurt each other that way."

"I'm sorry," she murmured, bowing her head. As she did, sun caught on the gold barrette that held the hair away from her face. "I don't know what I was thinking. I don't know...how I could have done that to you. You were right, I've been obsessed with them. Can you ever forgive me?"

"Of course I can. I love you, Rave. Just don't ever do that to me again. It really hurt."

Raven promised she wouldn't, and so did Julie. The three hugged. When they broke apart, they exchanged apprehensive glances, knowing the time for a decision had come. Andie spoke first. "We have to check the house out. We have to make sure Mrs. X is okay. Period."

"When?"

"We need to go early, while it's still light. Besides, we don't want to take the chance of running into him." Andie glanced at her watch. "How about now?"

"No way." Julie checked her watch. "My dad's due home in a few minutes. I have an hour of prayers and Scriptures, then dinner and dishes."

"Rave?"

"You know my old man, dinner's a command performance. Seven-thirty's the best I could do."

"Me, too," Julie said.

Andie nodded. "Seven-thirty, it is. The tree house."

17

Andie watched the clock, her feeling of dread increasing with each tick of the second hand. She fought the feeling off, calling herself chickenshit, worrywart. At seven-thirty it would still be light outside, too early for Mr. and Mrs. X to make an appearance. The three of them would go into the house, make sure there were no dead bodies anywhere, then take off. They would be there ten minutes, tops.

And then it would be over, behind them. She could do this, Andie told herself. It was no big deal.

Then why were her hands shaking? Why did she feel light-headed and winded, as if she had just run around the school gymnasium a half-dozen times?

Because she was scared. That they would be caught. That the couple would be there, and she would see them engaged in…what they did. And worst of all, that Julie would be right and they would find Mrs. X, dead. She didn't know if she could handle that. She didn't know if she would be able to live with that on her conscience.

Andie glanced at the clock above the kitchen sink, and her heart leaped to her throat.

Time had run out. Time to go.

She wiped her hands on the seat of her denim cutoffs and forced a deep breath into her lungs. Leaving the kitchen, she went to the family-room doorway. Her mother sat with Danny and Pete, watching some sports show on TV. One her dad used to watch with them.

"Mom?" Her mother looked over her shoulder. "The

dishes are done. I'm going to go hang out with Julie and Raven for a while.''

Her mother smiled wanly. "Okay, honey. Have fun."

Fun, Andie thought a moment later as she cut through her backyard, heading for Julie's street. Her stomach rolled. Tonight was about anything but fun.

Raven was already there and waiting. Julie arrived only minutes after Andie. The three drew in what seemed a collective breath. Andie took charge. "We check the place, then we're out of there. Right?"

The other two agreed, and they made their way to the house, circling around back. They went to the door; Raven retrieved the key from its hiding pace, unlocked and opened the door.

Before she could take a step inside, Andie caught her arm. "We're in and out," she said. "No messing around."

"No messing around," Raven repeated and stepped inside.

Andie, then Julie, crept in behind her. The first thing Andie noticed was the smell—stale, slightly sour. She wrinkled her nose. "What is that?"

"Oh, God…" Julie brought a hand to her stomach. "I bet it's the…I bet it's her!"

Raven shook her head and moved her gaze over the family room and adjoining kitchen. "No body here. No body parts, no blood." At her friends' horrified expressions, she laughed. "You two are the ones who started this gruesome quest. I'm only along to tell you I told you so after."

Together they moved from room to room, checking corners and closets. Nothing appeared different than the first time they had been through.

Until they got to the master bedroom. It had a vaulted ceiling with exposed beams. Thrown over one was a rope.

The end of the rope was tied into a noose.

On the floor below sat two stools, a tall one directly

under the noose, a short one beside it, the kind one keeps in a kitchen, to help with high cabinets.

For long moments, the girls said nothing, just stared.

"What the hell is that?" Andie asked. "I mean, what's it for?"

The three looked at each other, eyes wide. "I don't like this," Andie said, taking a step backward, gooseflesh racing up her arms. "I want to get out of here."

"Me, too."

"Rave—"

Her friend was staring up at the beam and the rope. Something in her expression gave Andie the creeps. She realized that Raven hadn't said a word since coming into this room. "Rave?" she said again, touching her friend's arm. "Let's go."

Raven jumped, startled. "What?"

"This is creepy. Julie and I want to split."

Raven didn't argue. They started back the way they had come. Almost to the back door, they froze when they heard the unmistakable sound of the garage door rumbling shut.

Andie thought she was going to faint. The house's interior was now almost completely in shadow, and she looked wildly around her. Not again, she thought, hysteria exploding inside her. She was not going to be trapped in here again. She grabbed Julie's hand and bolted for the door. She wrenched it open and stumbled out, Julie behind her, almost crying out with relief.

From the house she heard the sound of another door opening, then a man's voice. Followed by a woman's. Andie pulled the door shut and ran for the cover of the adjoining wooded lot.

She reached it and ducked behind a tree, breathing hard. It was then she saw Raven wasn't with them. Her heart flew to her throat, and she looked frantically around them. "Where's Rave?" she asked, sounding as panicked as she felt.

Julie met her eyes, hers wide with horror. They simultaneously realized the same thing.

Raven hadn't made it out. She was in that house with Mr. and Mrs. X.

18

Inside the house, Raven eased closer to the crack between the door and the jamb, heart pounding. When she had heard the rumble of the garage door opening, when she had realized it was *them,* she had turned and run back here, to the bedroom, to the closet.

She drew in a deep, quiet breath, afraid and excited, trembling with anticipation. From her hiding place she could see only a sliver of the room beyond. But she saw the rope. The stools.

Mr. and Mrs. X.

They held each other, whispering things Raven couldn't make out. Mrs. X seemed agitated. Even frightened. Was she frightened of him? Raven wondered. The rope? Or of something else. Someone else?

"Take off your clothes," he said quietly.

Mrs. X shook her head, clinging to him. "I don't want to." Her voice quivered slightly, then broke. "Don't make me."

"Take off your clothes," he said again, this time sharply, setting her away from him. "I don't want to punish you, but I will."

Whimpering, she did as he asked, removing one garment after another, her movements halting. She peeled away the last and stood before him, naked and trembling, head bowed.

"The ring," he said. "Remove it."

Raven pressed closer to the sliver of space, upper lip wet with perspiration. She saw Mrs. X struggling to get a ring off her finger. Her fourth finger. A wedding ring, Raven realized. Mrs. X was married. To somebody else.

"You belong to me," Mr. X said, taking a step closer. "Don't you?"

The woman lifted her face to his. Raven saw that she was crying. "Yes," she whispered.

He reached out and curved his hand around her breast, but not gently, roughly, as if asserting his possession. "You're mine."

"Yes," she said again.

"And I can do anything I want to you?"

She nodded.

He caught her other breast. "Say it."

"Yes. You can do anything you want to me."

"Even kill you."

The words landed flatly, harshly, between them. They reverberated in Raven's head. Her mouth went dry. She flexed her fingers, her heart pounding heavily.

Suddenly, her father's voice popped into her head, clear, accusing. *Cheating whore. Disloyal bitch. I'll kill you before I'll let you leave.*

Raven shook her head, trying to clear it, trying to force her father, the memory, out. Sweat dripped into her eyes. It stung, and she rubbed at them, rubbed until they burned. When she dropped her hands, she was at another door, her bedroom door. She was twelve again, peering through a different sliver of space.

She heard her father. And her mother.

Their last fight.

They had been going at it, on and off, all night. It had finally escalated to the point of no return, and Raven had known from hundreds of times before exactly where it would lead. She had tiptoed out of bed and to her bedroom door to listen.

"I'm going to ask you again," her father had shouted, "where were you today?" Raven had rolled her eyes and mouthed her father's next words, knowing them by heart. "I called and you didn't answer the phone."

"For God's sake, Ron, I went to the grocery store, the dry cleaner, the scho—"

Her words were cut off by Ron Johnson's furious bellow. "Lying whore! If you went to the grocery, why are we out of bread?" A cupboard door slammed; something crashed to the floor. "If you went to the cleaners, where are the clothes you brought home? How do you explain that?"

"I forgot bread! I took my navy dress! Remember, I spilled coffee on it last Sunday. After church. Don't you remember?"

He said something Raven couldn't understand, and her mother cried out in frustration. "I'm sick of your accusations! Sick of having to account for every move I make!"

"Do you think I like this?" he demanded. "Do you think I like having to come home to this? To your lies?"

"Yes! I think you do like it. But I can't take it anymore. Do you hear me?" Her mother's voice rose to a hysterical pitch. "I can't take it anymore!"

Blah. Blah. Blah. Raven made a sound of disgust. Same old story. Nothing ever changed here at 123 Park Lane. Raven turned to go back to bed, when her mother's next words stopped her.

"I'm leaving you."

The words seemed to echo in the ensuing quiet. Raven held her breath, waiting for her father's reply, startled not by what her mother had said, but by the way she had said it. Gone was the desperation, hysteria and fear. In their place was a kind of calm determination. As if, for the first time her mother really meant it. The first time since the night six years ago when she had tried to leave him and crashed the car, the crash that had given Raven her scar. As if she finally had the courage to do it, to leave her husband.

"Like hell," he shouted. "I won't allow it."

"I am, Ron. I'm leaving you. I won't live like this anymore. I won't take your crazy, jealous accusations another da—"

He cut her off with a chilling laugh. "You brought this on yourself by being a cheating, disloyal whore."

"Stop it! You're sick. You need help. Until tonight I was sick, too, living like this. No more. It's over."

"I'll say when it's over. Got that? Me, not you."

"Take your hands off me. I'm done being bullied by you."

Raven crept to the banister and looked over in time to see her mother struggle and break free of her husband's grasp, then run toward the stairs. Raven dared a quick glance at her father before ducking back into her bedroom and shutting the door. He looked stunned, disbelieving, like a kid who had just been told there was no Santa Claus.

It was almost funny. Raven brought a hand to her mouth to hold back a giggle. Like when Dorothy and her friends pulled away the black curtain and found that the great and powerful Oz was nothing more than a little toad of a man.

Her mother passed her bedroom, then her father passed. Raven counted to ten, then cracked open the door and peeked down the hall. Her parents' bedroom door was open, her mother was throwing clothes into a suitcase.

"I just figured out where this sudden backbone's coming from," her father said. "You're going to your boyfriend, aren't you? Your dirty lover?" He dragged the word out so it sounded vile, worse than the ugliest of curses. "Where do you fuck, Sandy? Here? In our bed? When he sticks it in you, what do you think? About me? Our daughter? Or do you just grunt like the pig-whore you are?"

"Stop it." Her mother's voice quavered, and Raven realized how much standing up to him was costing her. "I've never been unfaithful to you. Why would I want another man, Ron? Life with you has been hell."

"Do you really think I'll let you go?" he asked, his words and tone measured. "Don't you know me any better than that?"

"You can't stop me."

"No?" He circled her, his expression openly contemptuous. "You belong to me. You're mine."

She replied by snapping the suitcase shut, dragging it off the bed and starting for the hall. Raven closed the door save for a crack, heart thundering, wondering if her mother was coming for her. She wouldn't go. She was old enough to choose. She wouldn't leave Andie and Julie. *They* were her family. She chose them.

As if her own fears had transmitted to her father's thoughts, he called out, "What about Raven? Do you plan to walk out on her, too?" He snapped his fingers. "Just like that?"

Sandy Johnson stopped and turned. "No, not 'just like that.' I wish she was coming with me, I wish I could bring her with me. I can't. She wouldn't want to go."

"Convenient, Sandy. A lot easier to abandon your child when you tell yourself she'll like it. But lying comes so easily to you."

"Wake up! Our daughter stopped caring about either one of us a long time ago. Don't you see the way she looks at us? Don't you see her contempt for us? Her hatred. She'll be glad I'm gone. She won't have to listen to…to this all the time."

He grabbed her arm. "Without me you're nothing. How will you survive without me to pay the bills, without me to tell you what to do and where to go and what to wear? You need me."

She snatched her arm from his grasp. "You're so convinced I have a lover, well, maybe he'll take care of me. Maybe he'll—"

Ron struck her sharply across the mouth. She stumbled backward, hitting the banister. She grabbed ahold of it to steady herself, then straightened and brought a hand to her bleeding lips. She met his eyes. "That's the last time you're ever going to hit me. I'm leaving you. I should have done this a long time ago. Maybe then my daughter would still have some respect for me."

"I'll kill you if I have to."

Her mother paled. She stared up at him, frozen, her eyes wide. Then she laughed. "You've bullied and intimidated me for eighteen years. You've made it so I was afraid to go to the grocery or a PTA meeting or to call a friend on the phone. I'm done being afraid. And I'm done living this way."

She had snatched up her suitcase and run down the stairs; the back door had opened, then slammed shut. Raven hadn't been able to see her father, he'd had his back to the door, but she had heard his labored breathing, had felt his fury and frustration, had felt them as an almost physical wave of pure emotion.

Then he had followed his wife, his footsteps thundering on the stairs.

A sharp crack filled her head, like a gun going off or a car backfiring. Raven shuddered, jerking back to the present. Back to Mr. and Mrs. X.

The woman was blindfolded with the black silk scarf. Her hands were bound in front of her with its mate. The tall stool had somehow tipped over, and lay on its side on the wooden floor. Mr. X bent and righted it. As he did, he trailed his hand along the seat, the movement like a caress.

Raven swallowed hard, understanding. Mrs. X was completely vulnerable now, totally helpless. And he was all-powerful. He could do anything to her. Ask anything of her. And she would obey.

What a feeling that must be, Raven thought, feeling her own blood and adrenaline pumping through her, to her head, her heart, the tips of her fingers and toes. To be like a king. Or a god.

Mr. X turned, suddenly. His piercing gaze landed on the closet, the sliver of space. On Raven.

He knew she was there. He knew she was watching.

His eyes seemed to meet hers. His were a brilliant, heavenly blue, and Raven felt a connection between them—sharp and electric. A response to more than his good looks, she recognized that they had something important in common, shared something others didn't—and couldn't—understand.

As if they were two halves of the same whole.

He smiled, then turned, severing the connection. He went to his lamb; he led her to the waiting rope. Though Raven could see that Mrs. X was terrified, she did as he instructed her, climbing onto the stool and letting him fit the noose over her head and around her neck.

All the while he murmured words of encouragement and love. Of appreciation. The act reminded Raven of a religious ritual; Mr. X performed his duty with the solemnity of a priest delivering the Sacraments to his faithful followers.

His faithful follower whimpered with fear as the rope closed around her neck, as it tightened. A lamb led to the sacrifice. One wrong move and she would be dead. One easy act of betrayal, and she would be left dangling, her life's breath forever cut off.

An act of betrayal. Like a wife leaving her husband.
Easy. Like a husband taking care of that wife.

Raven scooted backward in the closet, pressing her fists to her eyes. *No.* She didn't want to remember. Not again.

It was already too late. She was there again, at her bedroom door, her father's footsteps thundering on the stairs. She had heard the back door open then slam shut. Heart racing, she had darted out of her room and run to the hall window that overlooked the backyard and garage.

At first she hadn't seen them. The light from the kitchen illuminated little more than the new patio her father had finished staking out that day, the very edge of the driveway and garage beyond.

Then she did. Her mother was at the car, trying to get

the driver's door open. Her father got hold of her shoulders
and dragged her away from it, his face pinched with rage.
Raven wondered why her mother didn't scream. Why she
didn't shout for help. Years of trying to be quiet, she supposed. Years of trying to hide the truth about her marriage
from the neighbors and everyone else.

Her father backed into the bags of cement mix, stum-
bling, knocking the shovel to the ground. Her mother
broke free. She darted toward the car, wrenched the door
open and crawled inside. Before she could get the door
closed behind her, he had her. He dragged her out, toward
the house. She flailed at him wildly, kicking, twisting, finally breaking free.

He grabbed the shovel and called for her to stop. She
didn't. Raven pressed her face to the window, breathing
hard. Her father lifted the shovel and swung, hitting his
wife in the shoulders and back of the neck.

Raven gasped. For one moment Sandy Johnson hung
frozen in space, her expression one of complete surprise.
Then her husband swung the shovel again, connecting this
time with the side of her head.

Raven heard the crack of the metal blade connecting
with bone. Something flew. Blood, she realized, her stomach leaping to her throat. Brains.

Clutching her middle, Raven sank to the floor. *Oh
God... Oh God...* She felt as if she was going to puke,
and she pressed her lips together, fighting the sickness
back. *He'd said he would kill her... He'd said... What to
do...what to do...*

She drew in a deep, shaking breath. *The police, she had
to call the police. They would send an ambulance. Maybe
it wasn't too late.*

Raven inched up and peered over the window ledge. Her
mother hadn't moved. Neither had her father. He stood
above her crumpled form, shovel still in his hand, staring.
Suddenly, he turned. He crossed to the center of the new
patio and began to dig.

What was he doing? Raven drew her eyebrows together, watching him. Then she realized. *He was digging a hole. To bury her mother.*

Raven dropped to the floor again, unable to breathe. She brought her knees to her chest and rocked back and forth. As she did, thoughts and feelings raced through her head, twisting and turning, colliding with one another. She struggled to focus, struggled to make sense of what her father had done.

She squeezed her eyes shut, fighting for an even breath. How many times had her father told her mother he was going to "fix her" for her lack of loyalty? How many times had he told her he was going to "make her pay" for her betrayal or that he would "stop her" if she ever tried to leave him?

Too many to count, Raven realized. Their every fight had included one of his warnings. And tonight, hadn't he warned her first? Hadn't he said he would kill her if she tried to leave?

Raven brought her hands to her ears, covering them, trying to quiet the voices in her head. Her mother hadn't listened. Despite his warnings, she had tried to run away. From him. From her daughter. Her mother had betrayed them, their family. She hadn't been loyal. She had proved that—had proved true all her husband had ever accused her of—by trying to leave them.

So, her father had taken care of her. Like he'd promised her he would.

A strangled giggle had slipped past Raven's lips. The small sound had seemed to echo in the silent house. She had clapped a hand over her mouth, imagining her father stopping his work and lifting his gaze to the house's second story, to this window.

Suddenly, Raven had been afraid. If the police found out she had known, her dad would be sent to jail. And she would be sent away—someplace far from Andie and

Julie. They were her family. She couldn't live without them.

Andie. Julie.

Mr. and Mrs. X.

Raven jerked back to the present. She was pressed into the far corner of the bedroom closet, her breath coming in small shallow gasps, her cheeks wet with tears. She swiped at them, the dark closed in around her, the smell of paint and builder's dust near choking her.

The room beyond was quiet. Deathly quiet. Raven leaned forward and peered out. Mr. and Mrs. X were gone. She blinked, confused, a kind of cold, damp panic setting over her. When had they gone? How much time had passed?

She shuddered and rubbed her arms, cold yet flushed and sweating. Tonight had been a revelation. She was beginning to see now, to understand power. What it meant to have it. What it meant to hold the fate of another human being in the palms of your hands.

She held her father's fate in her hands. She hadn't told anyone what he had done. Not even the police when they had questioned her about her mother's disappearance. Instead, she had held her secret to her, waiting for the time when she could reveal it—reveal him—to the world.

Her secret gave her power. The kind of power Mr. X had, she realized. Over life. And death.

Raven rubbed her eyes, suddenly tired. Drained of the adrenaline and exuberance that had raced through her only minutes ago. A tiny fist of pain settled in her temple. Andie and Julie should be with her. She missed them; they were three, a family.

Her family was falling apart.

The fist of pain grew larger, more fierce. Family didn't keep secrets, they didn't hide things from one another. They didn't argue. But that's exactly what they had been doing. Ever since Mr. and Mrs. X had come into their lives.

Mr. and Mrs. X had come between them.

Raven brought her fingers to her temple. She had to do something; she couldn't live without her friends, her family. She had to take care of them.

But she couldn't go back to the way it had been before, the way her life had been. She had changed. She understood things now that she'd only had glimpses of before. Things her father understood, though she hated him for them. Perhaps that, too, was part of the circle. Hatred and love, like pleasure and pain, hand in hand.

Andie and Julie could grow with her. She would lead and they would follow. Every family had a leader. Someone in whom they could place their trust, their confidence.

She was the fearless one. The clever one. The one who could observe, could look at people and situations with detachment. Without hurt or sympathy or remorse getting in the way, muddying reason.

If only Julie and Andie could be as she was. If only they understood how good it was, what an easy way to live.

But they couldn't. They weren't strong like her. She was the one who would risk anything for those she loved. The one the other two turned to for advice, for solutions, security.

She was the one who understood love and loyalty.

She would take care of her family. No matter the cost.

She would start now. By convincing Andie and Julie that Andie had been right—and wrong. Wrong about Mrs. X being in danger, but right about their needing to forget this whole thing. Right about how it had been coming between them, tearing them apart.

They would be convinced. And she would continue to watch. And learn. Until the day came to act. To take a stand.

The pain in her temple evaporated. Raven crawled from her cramped, dark place. She stood, stretched and smiled. She would take care of everything. No matter the cost.

Raven ran out to where she knew her family waited.

19

Raven hadn't been able to convince Andie that Mrs. X wasn't in any danger, and though Andie had tried to abide by her friend's wishes, she couldn't. No matter how often she told herself that Raven had been in there, that she would know if Mrs. X was in danger, no matter how often she reminded herself of the horrible repercussions should she and her friends be found out by their parents, she couldn't let it rest.

Right was right and wrong was wrong. She believed that. She believed that not acting on conscience was wrong. And her conscience told her that Mrs. X was in trouble and that she had to do something.

So, here she was, at the Thistledown police department. Andie squared her shoulders, lifted her chin and stepped through the double glass doors. She had her story worked out. She had practiced what she would say, how she would explain, keeping as close to the truth as possible without implicating Raven and Julie. She would claim to have acted alone; any heat to be taken, she would take personally.

It would work. It had to.

She crossed to the front desk. The uniformed officer looked up, his expression anything but welcoming. "Can I help you?"

She swallowed hard, struggling to hide her nerves, her doubts. "May I speak to a detective, please? I...I need to report a crime."

"Our detectives are busy, honey. This isn't about your boyfriend breaking up with you, is it?"

Her cheeks heated and she drew herself to her full height, hoping to look older. "Of course not."

"Nature of the crime?" He barked the words at her and she hesitated, confused. "Nature of the crime," he said again, glancing at his watch, impatient.

"A murder," she blurted out. "I need to report a murder."

The officer narrowed his eyes, then nodded and pointed. It was clear he didn't believe her, but obviously the accusation was serious enough to warrant some discussion with a detective. "Sit over there. Somebody'll be right out."

Andie did and within a couple of minutes a man wearing a rumpled-looking suit came and collected her. He didn't smile, but introduced himself as Detective Peters and asked her to follow him.

He led her into the squad room, to a desk littered with papers and file folders. Another man sat on its edge.

The second man smiled. "I'm Detective Nolan," he said. "The brains of this outfit."

Peters scowled. "My partner, the comedian. Have a seat." He indicated the chair directly across from his. Andie took it, grateful because her legs had begun to shake. He extracted a small spiral notepad from his inside coat pocket, flipped it open and looked at her. "Name?"

"Name?" she repeated, swallowing hard, realizing that there was no going back now. "Do I have to tell you that?"

"Yes, you do."

"Andie Bennett."

"Address?" She told him and he wrote it down. "Age?"

She thought about lying but figured they'd find out the truth anyway. "Fifteen."

"You live here in Thistledown?"

She nodded, her mouth dry. "With my mom and...just my mom. And my little brothers."

The detective looked up. The fleshy folds around his eyes seemed to swallow them. "Where's your dad?"

"He and my mom...they split up."

"I see." He made a note. "But he lives in Thistledown?"

She nodded again, uncomfortable already, wishing she had listened to her friends. Now it was too late. She had told the officer out front that she was here to report a murder; she didn't think they would let her say, "Just kidding," and walk away.

Peters tossed down his notebook and sat back. "Okay, Andie, talk to me. The desk sergeant says you want to report a murder. That's a serious statement. You got a body to go with this crime?"

She flushed. "Not exactly."

The detectives exchanged glances. "No?"

"Well, it's not exactly a murder. Not yet."

Peters narrowed his eyes. She wondered how he still managed to see through them. "Then why'd you tell the sergeant it was?"

She clasped her hands together, mostly to keep them from shaking. "I had to talk to you...to someone," she said. "The thing is...I'm afraid, afraid there *will* be a murder." She twisted her fingers together. "And I want to stop it from happening."

"I see." Again, the men exchanged glances. Peters cleared his throat. "I think you'd better start at the beginning, then we'll talk about what we can do."

As Andie began to do just that, another man entered the squad room. He was younger than the other two detectives, with curly dark hair. He wore blue jeans, a khaki-colored shirt and a tie that looked as if it had been picked by a blind man. As he passed them, he nodded in the detectives' direction.

"Go ahead, Andie. That's just Detective Raphael. Our

resident rookie Boy Scout.'' Peters crumpled a piece of paper and tossed it at him. "Done any goods deeds today, Raphael?''

Andie glanced over her shoulder in time to see the rookie smile, catch the paper with one hand and shoot his colleague the bird.

"Hey, watch that, Raphael. We've got a minor here."

Andie turned back to Peters, more nervous than ever. She looked the man steadily in the eyes anyway. "I've seen the bird flipped before, Detective Peters. On occasion, I've even flipped it myself."

The officer behind her chuckled; the one before her looked annoyed. It occurred to her that perhaps the two detectives were trying to unnerve her. She had seen TV shows about cops, and that was a technique they seemed to use a lot.

She cleared her throat, pleased that she hadn't revealed how nervous they had made her. "Do you want me to start?''

"That's why we're here."

So she did, beginning with the music and her own curiosity, then telling them about the man, the black silk scarves, then about the woman, the rope and the violent sex.

She spoke as clearly and as calmly as she could, forcing herself to keep from looking at the floor and mumbling in embarrassment. Peters was staring at her in stunned disbelief, Nolan's thin, bloodless lips were twisted into a smirk, and behind her, the young detective had become as still and silent as a statue.

When she finished, the squad room was so quiet she could have heard a pin drop. After a moment, Peters cleared his throat. "That's quite a story, young lady."

"Quite a story," Nolan seconded.

"Seems to me," Peters continued, "that you've gone and stuck your nose where it doesn't belong."

"What?" She made a sound of disbelief. "But, don't you see—"

"I see a girl who's going to be in a world of trouble when her parents find out what she's been up to." Peters stood. "Raphael, what've you got going right now?"

"Not much."

"I want you to deliver Ms. Bennett to her mother, please."

"Wait!" She jumped to her feet. "Look what I found in the library." She pulled out the folded article and handed it to Peters. "Look, right there. I underlined it."

Detective Peters read it, then held the paper out for her. "So?"

"So?" Her cheeks burned. "It says this kind of...of thing can lead to murder."

"But it rarely does, kid. Take it from me."

She stared at him, angry, humiliated. "You're not going to do anything?"

"Yeah, I'm going to do something. Against my better judgment, I'm going to let you go home without sending you to juvenile or calling your parents myself. This time. Next time I won't be such a nice guy."

"But—" she struggled not to cry "—Mrs X is in danger. I know she is."

"Look, kid, consensual sex between adults isn't against the law. Even when it's pretty sick stuff. Breaking and entering is. Peeping on other people is. Got that?" He leaned toward her. "What I'm saying is, the only one who's broken a law here is you. Now, you seem like a nice enough kid, I suggest you go home to mommy and keep your nose out of other people's private business."

She shook with fury and embarrassment. She got to her feet. "Fine. But when Mrs. X is found dead, I'll tell everyone you could have helped but didn't, *Detective Peters.*"

"Don't worry, sweetheart, that happens we'll call you first and you can come in and give us a detailed account of what you saw." The odious man grinned. "Blow by blow."

She caught his meaning, the double entendre, and heat washed over her. She glared at them. *Jerks! Pea-brained idiots! They made her sick.*

"Miss Bennett?" The Boy Scout touched her elbow. "Ready?"

She jerked her arm away and stalked out of the squad room. She stiffened her spine as she heard Peters and Nolan laugh. One of them made a joke about ropes and blow jobs. The other about that being the only way to cash it in.

The rookie guided her to a squad car. He opened the front passenger door for her, and she scowled at him. "Seeing how I'm such a terrible person, going and sticking my nose in other people's private business, I would have thought you'd put me in back, in the cage."

He grinned. "Do I need to?"

She jerked her chin up. "What do you think?"

"You look pretty tough, but I'll take my chances. Hop in."

She did as he asked, though what she really wanted to do was wipe the patronizing smile from his face. She didn't need his pity any more than she needed those other jerks' sly amusement. This wasn't a joke. She needed their help. Mrs. X needed their help.

Screw them all, she thought, turning toward the window. No wonder people called them pigs.

He went around to the driver's side and slid behind the wheel. "Where's home?"

"Happy Hollow," she muttered, shooting him a furious glance.

"Look," he said, "I don't blame you for being pissed off, but Peters and Nolan really are good cops." The detective turned out of the parking lot and onto Main. "They've just been around so long they've forgotten how to give a kid the benefit of the doubt."

Kid? As far as she was concerned, they were the ones who'd acted like kids. Immature assholes.

As if reading her thoughts, he said, "I may not always agree with their methods, and I know their personalities can grate, but they were right, Andie. The only one who's broken a law is you."

"Lucky me." She folded her arms across her chest and slouched deeper into her seat, feeling completely sorry for herself.

"I think it was pretty decent of them to let you go. I would have called juvenile and your parents."

"Is that why they call you Boy Scout?" she asked, trying to mask her humiliation with nastiness. "You're always doing the right thing? You're always by the book?"

He smiled. "Try to be."

"So, Detective, what merit badge are you working toward today?"

He glanced at her from the corners of his eyes, amused. "You're pretty cocky for a kid who's not more than a hairbreadth away from getting into serious trouble."

"I'm not the one who's in trouble," she muttered, frustrated, turning her gaze toward the window, seeing the entrance for Happy Hollow just ahead. "But nobody wants to listen. After all, I'm just a stupid kid."

For a moment, he said nothing. She felt his gaze. "You're not even the least bit worried about how your folks are going to react to your being brought home by the police? I guess things must have changed, my dad would have whooped my butt. I wouldn't have been able to sit for a week."

She hadn't thought of that—of her mother's reaction to her daughter being brought home by the police.

Andie imagined her mother's expression. Upset and hurt. So much for the daughter who wasn't causing her any trouble. So much for her "good girl."

"You're quiet suddenly."

Andie looked at him. Her only hope. If only she could take back her nastiness. If only she had thought ahead.

She cleared her throat, trying her best to look contrite. "I'm really sorry I acted like a jerk."

"I'm glad to hear it, but no, I won't cut you some slack and let you off a block from your house."

"Please!" she cried, not too proud to beg. "My mom's going through a really hard time. She's... My dad, he—" Andie sucked in a deep breath. "Anyway, it would upset her if I...if I showed up in a patrol car."

"I'm sorry to hear that. I really am. But I have my—"

"Orders?" she filled in bitterly. "Boy Scouts always follow the rules. Right?"

He glanced at her. "You're a minor. It's my duty to make sure you get home safely. I'd be doing you and your parents a grave disservice if—"

"No, you wouldn't. Please." To her horror, her eyes filled with tears. "I'll go right home. I promise. Please," she said again as he turned onto her street. "My mom, she couldn't handle this right now."

He let out a long breath. "You'll forget all about this Mr. and Mrs. X nonsense? You'll stay away from that house? Curb your overactive imagination?"

She opened her mouth to tell him it wasn't nonsense, that her imagination wasn't running away with her, then closed it and nodded. "I promise. I didn't realize how silly I was being. Please?"

The detective muttered something under his breath, swung the car to the side of the road and stopped. "You know, my butt's going to be in a big-time sling if Peters and Nolan find out I didn't deliver you to your door."

"They won't!" She pressed her hands together, prayer-style, pleading. "You'll never see or hear from me again. I promise."

He hesitated, then let out a long breath. "Okay. But—"

"Thanks!" She grabbed the door handle, anxious to get

out before he changed his mind or one of the neighbors spotted her.

"Wait." He caught her arm. "Just in case, I want you to take this." He dug a card from his shirt pocket and held it out to her. "It's got my number at the station and at home. If anything comes up, if you get in any kind of trouble, call me."

Andie stared at the card a moment before taking it. "Okay," she murmured, lifting her gaze to his. "But I'm not going to need it. You're never going to see me again."

20

Nick watched the teenager walk off. He muttered an oath and pulled away from the curb, uncertain he had made the right decision. He had a feeling about Andie Bennett, a feeling he hadn't seen the last of her, that she was heading for some sort of trouble. Bad trouble.

Too late now. He frowned, recalling the story she had told Peters and Nolan. She was too damn young to have seen what she had. Too fresh and unspoiled.

No wonder she was scared. No wonder she was obsessed with the thought that this Mrs. X was in danger.

The world was filled with a whole lot of sick, ugly shit. Most of it that didn't make a damn bit of sense to any thinking, feeling human being, even the most cynical one. Miss Andie Bennett had just gotten a good look at some of the most confusing.

Fifteen was too young to have the rosy glow swiped off the world.

Nick turned onto Main, heading back to the station. He drew his eyebrows together, mentally taking out and examining each piece of the story she had told them. Some of the pieces just plain didn't fit.

First, it didn't make sense that this girl—a girl from a nice neighborhood, one with a strong sense of right and wrong and responsibility—would do the things she said she had done. Illegally enter a house? At night? Alone? He didn't think so. Second, after almost being caught and being scared witless, she'd gone back again? And again? At night? Alone?

No way. Those were the actions of a different kind of kid. An arrogant loner. A kid with little concern for what was moral or for responsibility. One not easily shaken or scared. That kid would not have felt the need to go to the police in an effort to save someone else.

Those could also be the actions of a group of kids. Pack mentality. Several kids together tended to egg each other on, provide moral support and justification.

Andie Bennett had not been alone. At least one other person had gone into that house with her. At least one other person had peeked into those windows, night after night. To his way of thinking, she had been alone only in her fear and sense of responsibility.

Nick pulled into the station's parking lot, parked the car and climbed out. He headed inside, still mulling over Andie Bennett's story. He went to the coffeepot and poured himself a cup.

"Raphael," Peters called, "you get our little voyeur home?"

"Yeah." He added sugar to the coffee and carried it to his desk. "I've been thinking about her story."

"Me, too," Nolan said from his desk, phone propped between his chin and shoulder. "It got me hot. How about you, Peters?"

"Oh, yeah. Wonder who our little party animals are."

"Maybe they like it when people watch." Nolan wiggled his eyebrows. "We could go find out."

Ignoring their fraternity-boy bantering, Nick took a sip of his coffee, the brew thick and bitter-tasting. The pot had been half-full since about ten that morning and had cooked to a consistency of sludge. He wished he'd added a little more sugar. "Some of the things she said don't add up. I don't think she was alone when she watched all those fun and games."

"Big fucking deal." Peters sailed a paper airplane at Nolan. It hit him square in the middle of the forehead.

"Her little friends had more brains than she did, and kept it to themselves."

"That's just it. It took a hell of a lot of guts to come in here today. Think about it. She's fifteen. She figured there was a pretty good chance she was going to get in trouble. She obviously went against her friends' wishes. And she had to sit across from you two assholes and describe what she saw. A lot of guts."

"So?" Peters made a sound of annoyance and leaned back in his chair. "You've got a point?"

"She must have been damn scared. Maybe there's something there. Maybe we need to check this house out, see if it's rented and to whom. Maybe pay the mystery couple a visit."

"And say what?" Nolan laughed. "That we know they're having kinky sex? *'This is the Thistledown police,'*" he mocked, "*'put down your whips, get that dick out of your mouth and come out with your hands bound.'* Get real, Boy Scout."

The other two detectives nearly fell out of their chairs laughing. Nick flushed but held his ground. "Can you guys get your brains out of your crotches for just a minute? What if this woman ends up dead?"

"She won't." Peters stood and pulled on his jacket. Nolan followed. "Your enthusiasm is commendable, Raphael, but your instincts suck. The kid peeped in a window and got herself an education. It was traumatic. Too bad for her. Life stinks. Give it a rest."

Nick got to his feet and stepped into the aisle between the desks, blocking the detectives' path. "How do you know the woman won't end up dead? How?"

Peters's face mottled. "Twenty fucking years on the job, all right? You put in that kind of time before you start questioning my calls. Got that, rookie? Case closed."

21

Jenny was waiting for him. Nick stopped in the doorway of the trendy little bistro to take a moment simply to gaze at his wife. She sat at one of the window booths, staring out at the remnants of the day, the last of the sun spilling over her perfect face. He never got enough of gazing at her, never lost that incredulous feeling in the pit of his gut, the disbelief that she had said yes to him.

He moved his eyes over her, taking in her shiny dark hair and the way it curved softly at her neck, the way she held herself, so still and straight. Elegant, that's what she was. That's what the suit she was wearing, the earrings, the shoes, hell, even the restaurant, that's what they said about her.

Everything about him shouted a kid from a working-class family, a kid from the worst part of St. Louis, more versed in the ways of the street than in the etiquette of trendy little bistros.

Why the hell had she chosen him?

He pushed the thought away, and started toward her. She didn't look his way, her face still turned to the window. Not that the question nagged at him. Not that he was worried. She had fallen in love with him for some strange and mysterious reason. He smiled to himself. Perhaps then, *that* was the question. Why?

"Hello, sweetheart."

She turned. And smiled. He bent and dropped a light kiss on her mouth, then slid into the booth across from her.

"You're late."

"I'm sorry."

"It's all right. I was enjoying watching the people."

He smiled. "I saw. What are you drinking?"

"Chardonnay." She lifted the glass and held it out to him. "Would you like to try it?"

"I think I'll stick with beer, thanks."

She wrinkled her nose. "Nasty stuff. Your loss." She brought the glass to her mouth and sipped. "How was your day?"

"Interesting." The waiter came, took Nick's drink order, then left. Nick turned back to his wife. "A kid came in today. She told us this bizarre story."

"A kid? What do you mean?"

"Teenager. Fifteen, I think." The waiter brought the beer; Nick took a long swallow before continuing. "Anyway, she thinks there's going to be a murder."

"A murder?" Jenny leaned forward, eyes alight. "Here in Thistledown?"

"Involving kinky sex, no less."

"No wonder you found it interesting. Naughty boy." She laughed and took another sip of wine.

"You sound like Peters and Nolan." He frowned, frustrated. "They didn't do anything about it. They wouldn't check out any part of the kid's story. They were too busy making jokes about what she saw. Like a couple of randy adolescents."

"Well, it is sort of...tacky."

"Maybe so, but I still don't get it, you know? Don't they feel any sense of responsibility? What would it have cost them to check out the kid's story." He took another swallow of beer, disgusted. "Jesus."

She sat back in the booth, a frown pulling at her mouth. "Why is this bothering you so much?"

"I don't know." He shook his head. "Probably because I disagreed with Peters's call. There was something about the kid. It took a lot of guts to come in the way she did and tell that story. I keep thinking there might be something to it. Peters basically told me I was full of crap. He pulled rank.''

"He's done this before, Nick. I think you ought to be careful.''

A smile tugged at his mouth. "Careful?''

She bristled, just a bit, at his amusement. "Well, it seems obvious. You're young, energetic and idealistic—''

"Don't forget gorgeous.''

He grinned, and she laughed. "That, too. He's used-up and burned-out. Every time he looks at you, he sees not only what he once was, but what he's become. That can't be pleasant for him.''

Nick cocked his head, studying her. The way she thought amazed him. "Where do you come up with this stuff?''

She shrugged and took a sip of wine. "Like I said, it seems obvious to me. And I have a lot of time to think.'' She glanced toward the window, a shadow moving across her expression. "Too much time.''

"Jen?''

She looked back at him and the shadow was gone. He caught her hand across the table. "Thanks for worrying about me. Peters has an attitude problem, that's all.'' He ran his thumb across her knuckles and felt her small shiver in response. After a year of marriage, she still responded to even his lightest touch. "The problem is, I didn't become a cop to sit around and do as little as possible. Or, even worse, nothing at all. I sometimes think Peters and Nolan did.''

"I hate that you have to take orders from those two bozos. You're too good for the job, Nick. You're too smart.''

He curled his fingers closer around hers, warmed by her confidence in him, but wanting her to understand. "Yeah, they're burned-out and lazy. Yeah, it frustrates the hell out of me. But they know a lot about being cops, and I can learn a lot from them. I *have* learned a lot from them."

Jenny looked at their joined hands, then back up at him, eyes bright. "You could go back to school, Nick. Either at night or full-time. Study to be a lawyer. I'll work, I'll put you through. It wouldn't take that long, and afterward, you'd be—"

"A lawyer," he finished for her, finding that her suggestion rankled—because of her parents, because they hadn't wanted her to marry a guy with such meager prospects. Because they had nearly broken them up.

"I want to be a cop, Jen." He tightened his fingers over hers. "I always wanted to be a cop. Since I was about four years old."

"But why?" she persisted. "A lawyer keeps the law, too. You could prosecute. You'd be making a difference."

"Not the way I do on the street. On the street it's black-and-white. Good guys versus bad guys. In the courtroom, the law is all shades of gray. I can't play the game that way." He leaned toward her, only half teasing. "What's the matter, embarrassed to be married to a cop?"

"Of course not." She sucked in a quick breath. "It's just that you're never home. And when you are home, you're on call. I never know when you're going to be beeped, in the middle of the night, during dinner, while we're making love."

"It's part of the job, hon. It'll get better. Remember, I'm the rookie, I get the shit detail." He smiled winningly, trying to coax her out of her funk. "Besides, your dad was a doctor, nobody gets more night calls than one of those guys."

"You do," she said with a trace of bitterness he had never heard before. "And when he got called, my mother didn't have to worry about the patient pulling a knife or a gun on him."

"Better that than a malpractice suit."

"That's not funny. This is the way I feel." Her eyes

filled with tears; her lips trembled. "I'm afraid. Every time you go out, I worry you won't come back."

"Oh, hon, I'm sorry." He gathered her other hand in his and leaned forward so he could bring both to his mouth. "This is a little town. Being a cop here isn't like being one in St. Louis or Chicago. Yeah, it's dangerous, more dangerous than being a pediatrician, anyway—" he smiled "—but I'm careful. And the hours will get better. I'm damn lucky to have made detective already. I feel like I have to prove myself, put in the long hours, try harder. Do you understand?"

She hesitated, then nodded. "But understanding doesn't help when I'm alone in bed or sitting in a restaurant waiting an hour for my husband to show up." Her voice thickened with tears. "You said family was the most important thing to you, Nick. A home and wife and kids. That's what you said."

He had said that. And he'd meant it. Nick wanted children. A big, loving family. And a house with a white picket fence and a big, shady backyard. A place where his kids could play, a place where they would always feel safe and loved.

He wanted for them what he hadn't had.

He'd had the streets for his backyard and a mother who had worked herself to exhaustion at two jobs, trying to hold the family together after his father died.

"Nothing is more important to me than you, Jen. You and our marriage, our home. The family we make together."

"That's not the way it feels, Nick." She searched his gaze. "I miss you. I'm lonely."

"It won't be forever," he said again. "I promise, sweetheart."

The waiter came then and took their orders. While they waited for their food, they chatted about other things; one of Nick's brothers who lived in Thistledown and the Italian restaurant he was trying to secure financing to open; her mother and father's cruise; their house hunting.

Just as the waiter arrived with their food, Nick's beeper sounded. Jenny's face fell. "It's headquarters, isn't it?"

He checked, then nodded. "It might be nothing, though. I'll call in."

It proved to be something: a missing kid. The parents were at the station, hysterical with worry. He returned to the table, chest tight with regret, but anxious to get downtown. "I'm sorry, Jen, I've got to go."

She glanced away, her expression so lost and lonely it hurt to look at her. "I know."

"Jen, I am. I wish—"

"Just go," she whispered, smiling tremulously. "It's your job, I understand. I'll have the waiter box your meal, and I'll heat it up for you later."

"Thanks, babe." He bent and kissed her. "I'll be home as soon as I can."

22

Andie decided that if the police wouldn't help Mrs. X, she would have to do it herself. A sense of urgency and impending doom pressing in on her, she made a plan to watch from the tree house every night, just to make sure that when Mrs. X arrived, she also left again, safe and sound.

Sometimes Andie had only a half hour to wait, sometimes several hours. However long, the waiting was agony. Boring. Nerve-racking. Each time the couple arrived, her stomach knotted and a headache would form at the base of her skull, increasing in pressure as each minute passed. When Mrs. X drove away, relief would be instantaneous.

Problem was, one night Mr. X drove away.

But Mrs. X didn't.

23

_____

The phone awakened Nick from a deep sleep. It took him a moment to realize that the high, frightened voice on the other end of the line belonged to Andie Bennett. It took him a moment more to comprehend what she was saying.

When he did, he sat straight up, instantly alert. "Where are you, Andie?"

"Olsen's drugstore," she whispered. "The phone booth."

"Stay put." He swung his legs over the side of the bed. "I'll be right there. Five minutes."

Nick dropped the receiver into the cradle and looked at Jenny. She was awake, though barely. "I've got to go."

"It was that kid, wasn't it? The girl you told me about?"

"Yeah." He pulled on his pants, then went to the closet and rummaged in it for a pullover.

She yawned. "You could call Peters."

He stopped and looked back at her. "And why would I do that?"

"It's the middle of the night and he's lead detective. He's the one, officially, who took the girl's statement."

"And he's the one who officially blew her off." Nick tugged a cotton shirt over his head, then began tucking it into his jeans. "I'm not going to let him do it again."

She sat up and pushed the hair out of her eyes. "He told you to drop it, Nick. Isn't there some type of cop protocol or something?"

"Cop protocol?" He grinned. "You worry too much,

hon. The kid called. She's in trouble.'' Nick slipped into his shoulder holster, then grabbed his jacket and crossed to the bed. He bent and pressed a quick kiss to her mouth. ''Go back to sleep, sweetheart. I'll be home in a couple of hours.''

He found Andie huddled in the doorway outside Olsen's, which had closed since she had called him. He pulled up to the curb, leaned over and opened the door. ''Get in.''

With a glance in either direction, she hurried across the sidewalk and scrambled into the car.

''Which way?''

She told him and he started off, glancing sideways at her. Her face was pale, her eyes wide, the expression in them alarmed. She gnawed at her bottom lip and kept clasping and unclasping her hands in her lap.

''I thought you were going to leave this Mr. and Mrs. X thing alone? I seem to remember you promising me you would.''

''I couldn't. I just… I couldn't.''

''Why don't you tell me what happened tonight.''

She nodded but didn't immediately begin to speak. When she finally did, her voice shook. ''I was watching the house. From the empty lot next door. I just watched to make sure…to make sure whenever she arriv—''

''Mrs. X?''

''Yes. To make sure whenever she arrived, she left again. Tonight she didn't.''

''Did it occur to you that she may have decided to spend the night there. It's pretty late.''

''No,'' she admitted. ''But she never has before.''

''So you called me.''

She shook her head. ''First I waited. About ten minutes. Then I went down there and—''

''To the house?''

She nodded. ''I checked the windows. I mean, I peeked through them.''

"Jesus, Andie." He couldn't believe what she was telling him. "You suspect a man of murder, but you traipse down to the scene and peek in the windows. If you were my daughter, I'd spank you."

She blanched. "You're not old enough to be my father, and you don't know anything. I told you, Mr. X had left."

"Sight can deceive, kid. You don't know who might have been in that house. You don't know what kind of people—"

"I'm here, okay. I'm fine."

Her teeth began to chatter, belying her tough demeanor. He decided to back off. "Go on."

"It was dark. I couldn't see anything."

"Did you hear anything. That music? Someone moving around? Anything?" She shook her head again. He glanced at her. "You're sure?"

"Yes."

"Did you try the door?"

"I was too scared."

"Good girl." She directed him to Mockingbird Lane. "Down there?" he asked as he crested the hill.

She sucked in a quick breath. "Yes. The house next to the empty lot."

He nodded, then rolled down the street, pulled into the driveway and cut off the engine. "You wait here. Under no circumstances do you get out of this car." He looked at her. "Got that?"

"Don't worry." She wrapped her arms tightly around her middle. "I'm not moving."

He swung the door open, then stopped, glancing over at her. "This is probably nothing, Andie. But no matter what I find in there, you're through with this. When we're done here, we're going to your parents. Got that?"

"Yes," she whispered, head down. "I've got it."

Nick climbed out of the car and went to the front door. No one answered either the bell or his knock. After glancing over his shoulder to make sure the kid had stayed put, he went around back.

The house, the layout of the land around it, was just as Andie had described. He scanned the surrounding area. The house backed onto farmland. On one side was an undeveloped lot, large and wooded, on the other, another empty house.

The perfect place for a sick little tryst.

He approached the back door, unsheathing his weapon. He knocked. When he got no reply, he tried the knob.

The door swung open.

The hairs on the back of his neck stood up. He had a bad feeling about this, he didn't know why, but he did. Holding his gun in front of him with both hands, he nudged the door wider with his foot.

''Police,'' he called.

Silence answered him. An unnatural kind of silence. One that almost hummed. Mouth dry, heart pounding, he made his way into the house, moving from room to room, careful of the shadows and of his back.

He should call for backup now, he thought. He should get the hell out, and do things by the book. Instead, he kept going, letting his gun—and his instincts—lead the way.

He found Mrs. X in the master bedroom. Hanging from her neck, blindfolded, hands bound in front of her. Black silk scarves. A tall kitchen stool lay on its side under her dangling feet. Judging by the scuff mark on the white wood, it had been kicked out from under her. A shorter stool sat a foot or so away, undisturbed.

His stomach rushed up to his throat. He gagged, forcing the vomit back, forcing himself to cross to the woman to check her vitals though he didn't have a doubt that she was dead.

She was.

He spun away for a moment, bending at the waist, breathing deeply through his nose. His first homicide. His first real death. This wasn't a cadaver at the morgue. It wasn't old Mrs. Trotter who died in her sleep, a small, pleased smile on her face.

No, this was gruesome. It was ugly and violent and…wrong.

He made himself straighten and turn back to the victim. She had been young. And pretty. Not ready to die. She had been—

He stared at her, at Mrs. X, realization dawning with a sense of impending disaster. Holy shit. Holy fucking shit. Even with the blindfold, he knew who she was. He recognized the sexy mole to the right of her mouth, the striking strawberry-blond hair, recognized her from countless pictures in the newspaper and on TV; recognized her from the dozens of police functions he had attended since joining the force two years ago.

Behind him a floorboard creaked. He spun around, weapon drawn. "Freeze, asshole!"

The kid. She stood in the doorway, her eyes on Mrs. X, her face a mask of horror.

"Dammit, Andie! You were supposed to stay in the car. I could have shot—"

Her gaze went to his. "He did it," she said, her voice almost devoid of expression. "He did it, just like…just… Oh my God—" Her voice rose; she started to shake. "He killed her! He killed her!"

Nick hurried to the doorway and put his arms around her, trying to shield her from the awful sight. She fought him, growing hysterical, repeating those same words over and over.

Nick pressed her face to his chest, too aware of Mrs. X hanging there behind them, the smell of death already in the air. Too aware, also, that Andie Bennett was in more trouble than she even imagined.

Mrs. X was none other than Leah Robertson, the police commissioner's pretty young wife.

24

Mrs. X was dead.

Mr. X had killed her. Just as Andie had known he would.

Andie's stomach rolled, and she clung to Detective Raphael, pressing her face to his chest. Just beyond the safety of his broad shoulders, *she* hung. *Dead. Murdered.*

Andie struggled for a deep breath, thankful for the detective's warmth; for she was cold, so cold her teeth chattered. She squeezed her eyes tightly shut, concentrating with all her might on the steady beat of his heart under her cheek and the reassuring sound of his voice.

Try as she might, she couldn't expel the image of Mrs. X's lifeless body.

"Don't look, Andie."

She nodded, her head beginning to swim. "Is she...are you sure she's—"

"Yes, Andie," he answered quietly. "She is."

Tears flooded her eyes. They filled her throat, nearly choking her. She fought to hold them back, the fight leaving her trembling.

Nick laid a hand on the back of her head. "It's okay to cry, Andie. It's okay."

So she did. Sobbed so hard she could hardly catch her breath. Sobbed until her throat and chest ached, until her eyes burned and she was too weak to stand without his support.

Until she had nothing left but small whimpers of despair for a woman she had not known but had wanted desperately to help.

"Feel better?" he asked

She shook her head no, unable to find her voice but certain she would never be okay again.

"Can I get you a glass of water? Do you need to sit down?"

"I just feel…if only I had—"

"You tried to help her," he said softly. "You came to us, you tried to watch out for her. People like this…" He paused, as if struggling to choose the right words. "People like this live on the edge. Sometimes, that's the way they die. You're not to blame."

She shuddered. "Then why do I feel so bad?"

"Come on. I want to get you out of here." He put his hands on her shoulders and turned her toward the door, careful to shield her view of the body.

She let him steer her out of the bedroom and back to the main part of the house. When they reached the family room, he led her to the lone chair. *His* chair.

She stopped, gazing at it in horror, her mind flooding with memories. "No. I don't want… This is where he…where he always sat."

"Mr. X?"

"Yes."

Nick pointed to the window a couple of feet beyond the chair. "And that's the window you watched through?"

"Yes." She curled her arms around her middle. "I need to sit down. On the floor."

She did, and he squatted in front of her, giving her nowhere to look but right into his eyes. "We have to talk." He searched her gaze. "You have to tell me everything, Andie. You have to tell me the truth."

"I have," she whispered, nervously wetting her lips. "I've told you everything."

"A woman is dead, Andie. Murdered. We need to find the person who did this."

"Mr. X did it!" she said, panicked suddenly—that he

didn't believe her, that Mr. X was going to get away with it. Get off free as a bird.

And she wouldn't be able to do anything about it. Just as she had been unable to do anything to save Mrs. X.

"Do you know his name? Where he lives? Or works? Can you even describe to me what he looks like?" She shook her head, and he looked her dead in the eyes. "We need more information, Andie. Your friends might have noticed something you didn't."

"My...friends?" she croaked. "But I told you, I did all this alone."

"I know what you told me and I know you weren't alone in this."

"But I was!" she cried. "I promise, I was!"

He caught her hands. "You didn't break into this house alone, then having been frightened out of your wits, come back to peek into the windows, not once but several times. You didn't do these things alone, Andie Bennett."

Andie caught her bottom lip between her teeth, confused and uncertain what to do. If she refused to tell, would he find out anyway? Would she get into more trouble?

She couldn't tell. She had promised Raven and Julie that she wouldn't. She had promised them that she wouldn't get them into trouble.

"You want us to catch this killer, don't you, Andie?" She nodded, and he went on. "Homicide investigations are very much like putting together a jigsaw puzzle. You have to sort and lay out all the pieces, studying them carefully, looking at their shape and size, trying to determine where they fit. But it doesn't matter how carefully you sort and study, you'll never see the whole picture until you have all the pieces. *All* the pieces, Andie."

Tears stung her eyes, a lump formed in her throat. *She couldn't let her friends down.*

But if she didn't...

Nick squeezed her fingers. "Do the right thing, Andie. You already have, by coming to us, by trying to watch over Mrs. X yourself. Finish what you started. I know you don't want to get your friends in trouble, but you can't protect them anymore. Do the right thing," he said again. "Help us catch this guy."

A tear slipped past her guard and rolled down her cheek. She hung her head, unable to look him in the eyes another moment.

"You weren't alone in this, were you?"

"No."

"Tell me everything, Andie."

So she did. Everything. About her parents splitting and how she had sneaked out to seek comfort with Raven and Julie. About how they had heard the music and become curious. She told him what had happened next and even how she and her friends had argued about what they should do. She told him about the rift Mr. and Mrs. X had caused between them.

"Thank you, Andie." He flashed her a quick, reassuring smile. "You did good. You're a kind of hero, kid."

Once upon a time, she had wanted to be a hero. She had fancied herself one. Now she felt like a snake who had betrayed her best friends. "I promised them I wouldn't tell. I promised them, Detective Raphael." She searched his expression, pleading without words for understanding, for reassurance. "They're going to get in a lot of trouble. Worse than me. A lot worse."

"A woman is dead. They'll understand." He squeezed her fingers, released them and stood. "I have to call this in. Okay? When I do, I'll have them notify your parents. The next few hours are going to be rough."

She dropped her face into her hands. Her life had just changed. Because of her, Raven's and Julie's lives had changed. She lifted her gaze to the detective's sympathetic one once more, though she didn't know why or what she hoped to see in his warm brown eyes.

What she saw scared her. He knew it, too.

Nothing would ever be the same again.

25

Leah Robertson's murder rocked Thistledown to its core. These kinds of things didn't happen in this sleepy little burg. This was a good place to live; a safe place to raise a family. Happy Hollow was an upper-middle-class neighborhood; Andie Bennett, Raven Johnson and Julie Cooper were *nice* girls from good families—not the type of girls who got involved in something like *this*.

But they *had* gotten involved. The public was outraged; they were frightened. They wanted an arrest. A suspect to pin their fears and fury on.

The citizens of Thistledown, Missouri, didn't want to be afraid anymore. They didn't want to have to look nervously over their shoulders and dog their teenage daughters' every step. And they didn't want to have to worry about a sex freak and murderer walking their streets, looking for another victim.

Problem was, a week had passed since the murder, and Nick and his fellow detectives had nothing. No arrest. No prime suspect—other than the mysterious Mr. X, and he had disappeared, as if by magic.

Captain James Randall, big-town cop recently transplanted to small-town Thistledown in search of a better life for his family, was not pleased about that fact, not pleased at all. Right now his usually pleasant face was twisted into a mask of fury and frustration.

This one was personal—the police commissioner's wife was the victim. And Nick knew, shit rolled downhill. In truth, his only surprise was that it had taken a week to reach him. He had been expecting some version of this since the moment he realized that Mrs. X was none other than Leah Robertson.

"Who the hell do you think you are, Raphael?" the captain demanded. "The Lone Ranger, for God's sake?"

Nick, flanked on either side by Peters and Nolan, faced his captain's ire, unflinching. "No, sir."

"No, sir," the man repeated. "Then what the hell were you thinking the night of the tenth? You respond to a late-night call from a teenager about a possible homicide, without calling in. You enter the scene without backup. You put your life, the kid's life and this investigation at risk."

"Yes, sir. Bad call, sir."

But the captain wasn't finished with his tirade—not nearly, judging by his angry flush. "Bad call? Sweet Jesus, Raphael. The radio. You finally decide to use it, and you mention that the victim is Commissioner Robertson's wife. You mention there are teenage girls involved.

"Didn't it occur to you, Raphael, that the department might have liked to prepare a story for the press? Didn't it occur to you how embarrassing this would be for Dick Robertson and the entire department, that perhaps we would have liked our version to hit the streets first, to cushion the blow? Didn't it occur to you how sensitive this issue would be or that the press would jump on it like flies on dog shit? The *National* Fucking *Enquirer* has already run a piece!"

The captain placed his palms on the desk and rose slightly, easing toward Nick, looking for all the world as if the top of his head was about to pop off. "Just *how* did you manage to make detective, rookie? You want to tell me, because right now I don't have a clue."

Peters jumped in. "He knows procedure, Captain. But he's a cowboy, always trying for the big score, wanting all the glory. He should have called me or had dispatch notify me. I would have—"

Randall swung his angry gaze to Peters. "What *would*

you have done, Peters? If you had checked out the kid's story in the first place, Dick Robertson's wife would, in all probability, still be alive and this town wouldn't be in a complete panic.''

The detective's already florid complexion reddened. ''We don't know that, Captain. We could have checked it out and found nothing.''

''Could have. But you didn't. And you're no rookie, Peters. And right now this department looks like we've got our heads up our asses. Dick Robertson wants a suspect and so do the citizens of this town. What do you have?''

Peters started off. ''Leah Robertson's wedding ring is missing. We've alerted all the pawn and secondhand shops within a hundred-and-fifty-mile radius, just in case.''

''It won't show,'' Nick said. ''I'd bet my ass, this guy took it to remember her by. His personal trophy. This was no accident. No fun and games gone bad by mistake.'' Nick stood and indicated the report on Randall's desk. ''May I?''

The captain nodded and Nick opened the folder and pulled out the crime-scene photos, flipping through to a close-up of Leah Robertson's neck. ''Check out the rope burns. See how different from the primary bruise?'' He pointed to a dark, inverted V on the victim's neck. ''They indicate a kind of struggle, as if she twisted her head violently back and forth. The rope fibers embedded in the skin support our theory.''

''Which is?'' The captain didn't hide his impatience.

''That she knew something bad was about to happen before it did. That this S.O.B. taunted her first. He wanted her to know what was coming next. He wanted her to know that she was helpless to stop him.''

''Then he kicked the stool out from under her,'' Nolan supplied. ''Judging by the mark on the stool, he kicked it with considerable force.''

''Nothing accidental about that,'' Peters added.

The captain scowled. "Is *this* what you want me to tell the press?"

"No, sir." Nick cleared his throat. "I've got records doing a search for any like crimes committed in the last few years. We're also checking known sex offenders in the area. We're checking out anyone new to the area, anyone who's arrived in the last six to eight months. Nobody wants to think this crime was committed by a friend or neighbor."

"But they're all secretly afraid it was." Randall flipped the Robertson folder shut. "What about the kids?"

"Questioned repeatedly. Their stories all corroborate. Our suspect is tall, athletically built and has dark wavy hair. None got a look at his face. Or so they say."

"You don't believe them?"

Nick spread his hands. "It seems odd, that's all. But this whole thing is odd. Plus, I don't know what their motive would be for lying."

"Talked to Jackson Sadler, of Sadler Construction, about the house," Peters said. "Leah Robertson rented it two and a half months ago. A six-month lease. She approached them. Sadler's son works for him. Talked to him, too."

"David Sadler," Nolan offered.

"Right," Peters nodded. "He said the same thing."

"They didn't ask any questions?"

"None. You know the situation in this town. Sadler was grateful for the lease. She put down a security deposit and paid her rent on the first of every month."

"He didn't recognize her from the papers and wonder what she was up to?"

Nick shook his head. "An office grunt handled the transaction. Wrote the lease, the whole business. She said no, she didn't recognize the commissioner's wife. Only reads Dear Abby and the funnies, she said. Hates the news."

"This is some mess." The captain made a sound of

frustration and ran a hand over his closely cropped hair. "The parents didn't have a clue what the kids were up to?"

"None. They're nice kids. Their parents trusted them."

Nolan smirked. "They won't make that mistake again, now, will they?"

Nick looked at Nolan in disgust, thinking of Andie and her friends. They had made a mistake, and they were paying a big price for it. A very big price.

The captain swore and stood. "And just what, out of this conglomeration of nothing that you have, do you clowns suggest I tell the press?"

"How about the truth?" Nick offered.

Randall swung toward him, eyes narrowed. "Watch it, Raphael. I still might bust you back to traffic detail. I ought to."

Nick met the captain's eyes evenly. "Then why don't you?"

"Because I need you on this. All of you. But don't push me." Once again, he moved his gaze between the three detectives. "I'll assure the mayor and citizens of Thistledown that we have the situation under control. In the meantime, I want you to get this sick bastard. I want a suspect. I don't care if you have to work around the clock and turn this town upside down, I want this case solved. Got that?"

The man moved his gaze from one to the other, stopping on Nick. "Got that?" he said again.

Nick nodded and stood. "I'll get him, Captain. If it's the last thing I do, I'll nail the bastard."

26

Raven sat on her bed, planning. She weighed her options carefully, weighed the consequences of each of her choices. The consequences of what she was about to do.

Her father had locked her in her room. In the days since Mrs. X's murder, he had allowed her out only to speak with the police and use the bathroom. She had even had to eat meals in her room.

He thought he was so smart. So powerful. It was a joke. He thought he could make her his prisoner. He had forbidden her to see or speak with Andie and Julie, as if he could keep them apart. He had vowed to watch her every move, the way he had been forced to watch her mother. As if to prove his point, he had called Raven the same names: disloyal whore and cunt, liar. And he had struck her, the way he used to strike her mother, sharply, across the mouth.

But she wasn't like her mother.

She wasn't afraid of him.

Raven narrowed her eyes. It was he who should be frightened of her. She held the power of life and death in her hands. His life.

But he was too stupid and arrogant to see.

Just as the police were stupid. And arrogant. They had grilled her about Mr. X, about what she had seen. As if she would tell them anything. As if she would tell them she had seen his face. As if she would hand her teacher, her mentor, over to them.

Raven drew her knees to her chest and rocked back and

forth, thinking of Mr. X, of his games. She understood power now. She understood control. And she would not be punished by the likes of her father. She would not be made a prisoner or be told who she could and could not see.

She was the only one who would have power over her own life.

The time had come. She had nothing to lose. Her family had been torn apart. Raven climbed off the bed and crossed to her dresser mirror. She gazed at her reflection, studying the purple bruise on her cheek, her swollen, bloodied mouth. More evidence. A dose of concrete reality to go along with her allegations.

She had an aunt in Chicago. Her mother's sister, Aunt Katherine. Aunt Katherine had always hated Raven's father. She had been the one who had insisted the police investigate Sandy Johnson's disappearance, the one who had insisted the police question Ron Johnson. Though the police had never found any evidence of wrongdoing on his part, she had never made it a secret that she still thought him responsible for her sister's disappearance.

She had no children of her own and lived in a big house on Lakeshore Drive. Raven had been careful to cultivate that relationship, knowing that someday, maybe, she would need her Aunt Katherine.

She needed her now.

Raven thought of Andie and Julie, her eyes welling with tears. They hadn't been allowed to see each other or to speak since the night of the murder. She feared for Julie, feared the Good Reverend had delivered the worst he had to offer. She mourned for Andie, though she knew, of the three, her punishment would be the lightest. Within a month her mother would have all but forgotten her darling daughter's wayward acts.

In three years they would graduate from high school. As planned, they would go to college together. They would be a family again.

Three years wasn't that far away, she thought, turning and crossing to the window. She looked out. Her father had cut the branches off the tree outside the window. He had torn the trellis away from the side of the house. It was a two-story drop. If she jumped, she would very likely break her ankle. Or worse.

The young detective, she thought, eyeing the drop, the sympathetic one, she would go to him. She would weep into her hands and tell him how her father had killed her mother and buried her in the backyard. She would tell him how afraid she had been. Afraid to tell; afraid her father would do the same to her as he had done to her mother.

Mrs. X's murder had shocked her out of her silence, she would say. She had realized that even if she kept silent, he could do it to her. Sobbing, she would mourn the loss of her mother. Her voice would tremble, her hands shake. And they would believe her. They would pity her.

And her father would, at long last, pay for his crimes.

Three years, she thought again, sliding the window up, climbing onto the ledge. Not that long at all. Not when they had the rest of their lives to be together.

Sucking in a quick, determined breath, she jumped.

27

Within twenty-four hours of Raven's tearful statement to the police, Ron Johnson, respected businessman and devoted father, was arrested for the murder of his wife, Sandy. A search warrant had been issued, the patio excavated. There, the police found all the evidence they would need to put the man away.

Just returning to some sort of normalcy after the Leah Robertson sex-and-murder scandal, Thistledown rocked with the news. Tongues wagged, heads shook, and even the most restrained Thistledownian couldn't walk down the street without stopping now and then to express shock and outrage to an acquaintance. The summer of '83 had given the once-quiet community something to talk about for years to come.

But of all the citizens of Thistledown, none was more stunned by the news about Ron Johnson than Andie. She couldn't believe that her best friend's father was a murderer. She felt betrayed by the fact that Raven had been able to keep such an important secret from her. Best friends knew each other completely; they were supposed to share everything.

For Andie, it was the final blow, the final piece of the puzzle that changed the picture of her future.

Julie was gone already. Whisked away by the Good Reverend to a place far from Thistledown, a place where she would not be tempted to stray from the path of righteousness again, whisked away without even a word to her friends.

Now she was losing Raven, as well.

Andie's mother took pity on her and allowed her to say goodbye to her friend. Raven's Aunt Katherine brought her by on their way to Chicago. Where Raven was going to live. A million miles away from Thistledown. Or so it seemed to Andie.

The two girls clung to one another, whispering, crying, two weeks' worth of thoughts, fears and confidences spilling from them.

"How come you didn't tell me about your dad?"

"I couldn't. I was so scared."

"Julie's gone."

"I know. He sent her somewhere. Did you get to say—"

"No." Andie drew in a shuddering breath. "I'm worried about her. I'm afraid she—"

"The police haven't found Mr. X." Raven lowered her voice even more. "I heard they don't have a single lead."

"I'm so scared. He can't get away with it. He can't."

"I'm going to miss you so much. I feel like I'm dying."

"I don't want you to go." Andie started to cry. "It's all my fault. I'm so sorry."

Finally, Andie's mother broke them gently apart. Andie was sure it was her heart that was breaking apart. If she could go back, take it back, she would. She had tried to help Mrs. X and all she had ended up doing was hurting the people she loved. Her mother and father, her brothers, Raven and Julie. Most of all Raven and Julie.

She would never stick her neck out like that again. Never.

"It's okay, Andie." They clasped hands. "We'll be together again. I'll make sure of it. We're family, remember?"

"Write me every day. Okay?"

"I will." Raven's aunt eased her away from Andie, her own eyes filled with tears.

And then Raven was gone.

Book Two

Shocking Pink - Present Day

blank

page 170

28

Thistledown, Missouri
1998

Dr. Andie Bennett sat across from her patient, listening intently. The woman, Martha Pierpont, had been a patient of Andie's for nearly a year. She had come to Andie seeking a cure for her sleeplessness and anxiety; it had taken months for the woman to admit the real cause for her unhappiness—her husband's cruelty.

It didn't help that Mr. Pierpont—Honest Edward Pierpont—was Thistledown's very popular mayor. As far as influence and power went in this little burg, Ed Pierpont wheeled what there was to be had. Breaking free of a lifetime—in this case, twenty-two years—of fear and intimidation didn't happen overnight. For some it never happened at all.

Andie smiled encouragingly at the pretty, gentle-natured woman. "And what about your daughter, Martha? Where was she during all this?"

"Patti?" The woman wrung her hands. "You know teenagers. She was in her room. She didn't hear a thing."

"Are you sure?" Andie laid her hands on the notepad in her lap. "After all, you say he was shouting. That he shattered a mirror. How could she not hear that?"

Martha shredded the tissue she had clenched in her hands. "She wears those things, you know, those headphones. All the time."

"Martha," Andie said gently, "we've been through this

before. Patti hears everything. She knows what's going on between you two. She knows how he treats you. She always has.''

"I know we've talked about this, but you're wrong. Those headphones...that loud music. She never takes them off.''

"Why do you think that is, Martha? Is she trying to drown something else out?''

Martha glanced down at her skirt and made a sound of dismay. The navy linen was covered with bits of the damp, white tissue. "Look what I've done!" She began to pick them off, her hands visibly trembling. "Sometimes I just don't think.''

Andie recognized Martha's avoidance technique. She had seen it, or a variation of it, many times. Martha's only child was a subject the woman refused to discuss. Honestly, anyway.

"I don't know why I wear navy, I always make such a mess of myself. The only thing worse, of course, is black. I bought the prettiest black silk dress last week, and now I wonder—''

Black silk.

Andie could never hear those two words together and not remember that awful summer of 1983. Much had happened in the fifteen years that had passed since, but she hadn't forgotten it. Not Mrs. X's unsolved murder—she still thought of Leah Robertson that way—not her guilt over her friends' punishment for her actions, not her shock at learning Raven's terrible secret. She still recalled clearly how it had felt to lose the anchor of her family, how it had felt suddenly to be the focus of the town's nastiest gossip, and most of all, what it had been like to lose the people she cared about most.

It had all been fleeting: the gossip had died away, her family had adjusted, and as they had promised one another, she and Raven had been reunited, this time at the University of Missouri, best friends forever.

What a terrible, confusing time of her life that had been. She wouldn't go back to that year for a million bucks.

She smiled to herself. And yet, that summer had brought her to her work, which she loved. Those shocking events, one after another, like physical blows, had sent her scurrying for answers. For a way to make sense of what had happened to Mrs. X and Raven's mom, to her own family. She had needed to understand why people did some of the things they did.

Her friends gone, Andie had buried herself in the library and read book after book. The more she had studied and learned, the more fascinated she had become with human behavior and the workings of the mind. And the more she had read, the more determined that someday she was going to help people who were confused. Or hurting. Or so lonely they thought they couldn't go on.

She had always wondered if Leah Robertson would be alive today if someone had been there to help her.

"...received another one of those letters."

Andie's thoughts snapped back to the present and Martha. "What?"

"Edward received another one of those threatening letters. This one really rattled him."

Andie frowned. "That makes three so far, doesn't it?"

Martha nodded. "The first couple he shrugged off, but this one..." She lifted a shoulder. "I've never seen him so unnerved."

Andie sat forward. "What did it say?"

"That they were going to 'get' him. That when they did, he would be sorry. Not that much different from the others."

"He took it to the police?"

"Just like the others. But whoever's writing them has been really careful. They haven't left any prints or anything. Other than the Thistledown postmark, the police don't have a clue."

"What about the handwriting? Can they determine anything—"

"This was done the same way as the others. Letters cut out of the newspaper and glued down to make words. Like you see in movies." Martha looked away, shuddering. "The police think it's just some crank, but what if it's not?" She met Andie's eyes again. "What if it's someone really dangerous? What if they break in and hurt Patti?"

That was, indeed, terrifying to contemplate, though Andie thought both Martha and Patti had more to fear from Ed Pierpont than some letter-writing stranger. At first, because of Ed Pierpont's grandstanding and nonchalance, it had even crossed Andie's mind that he had sent the letters to himself, as some sort of perverse, attention-grabbing, election-year stunt.

Andie brought the subject back to the reason Martha was there. "Let's talk some more about the other night."

"Do we have to?"

"Of course not." Andie crossed her legs. "Is there something you'd prefer to discuss?"

Martha shook her head and looked away. "It was bad, worse than it's been in a long time. I knew it was going to be by the way he was watching me." Martha brought a hand to the strand of pearls at her throat. Andie saw that her hand trembled. "I felt his gaze on me through the entire party. As if he was assessing my every move, my every word. At one point I had to go into the bathroom because I couldn't breathe, my heart was pounding so hard."

Andie made a note. "Why was that?"

"I knew what was going to happen when our guests left. I knew I had done something terribly wrong. I'd made him angry."

"But had you, Martha? It sounds to me like you were the perfect hostess."

"I know the things that…incite him. I know, but I…forget." She looked at Andie, her expression begging

for understanding. "I smile at someone without thinking.
I say or do the wrong thing. I don't mean to, it just...
happens."

"Like what, Martha? Do you remember?"

She lifted her gaze to Andie's, full of shame. "I remember smiling at George Wimberly. He told me I looked
lovely, that's all. That wasn't disloyal, was it? To smile in
thanks?"

"Of course not. You received a compliment, you said
thank-you. That's good manners."

"Ed didn't think so." She caught her bottom lip between her teeth. "When everyone left he...he started in
on me."

"He called you stupid? And worthless?"

"Yes. And other things. Worse."

"Whore?"

"Yes." She bowed her head. "And he slapped me."

Andie tightened her fingers on her pen, maintaining an
outward calm. "And then what?"

"He...he..." She struggled, Andie saw, to say the
words. "He forced me down onto the...onto the bed, and
he...dragged my legs...apart."

"He raped you."

"No. He's my husband, so it's not, he couldn't
do...that."

"He penetrated you against your will?" The woman
nodded. "Husband or not, that's still rape."

Martha shook her head, eyes brimming with tears, too
steeped in denial to admit what she suffered at the hands
of her husband.

"What he did to you, how did you feel about that, Martha?"

When the woman only gazed blankly at her, Andie tried
again, not about to let her wriggle out of the question.
"When your husband calls you stupid. When he tells you
you're worthless, how do you feel?"

Martha looked away; Andie waited, letting the silence

awkwardly fill the air around them. Every other time she had asked Martha *How do you feel?* her patient had denied her feelings. She had made excuses for herself, for her husband, his behavior. Even so, Andie asked the question every session, as often as she could.

One day, she hoped, Martha Pierpont would face the truth.

"Martha, did you hear my question? How do you feel when he belittles you? When he calls you ugly names and laughs at you?"

The woman froze, her face flooding with sudden, hot color. She flexed her fingers, as if with extreme agitation.

"Martha," Andie pressed, excited, feeling Martha was close to a breakthrough, "tell me how you feel. When he calls you stupid. When he slaps you and forces you to have sex with him, how do you feel?"

"I want to kill him!" Martha burst out, leaping to her feet, trembling with rage. "I want to kill him, and kill him, and kill him!"

Her expression went from enraged to stunned. She brought her hands to her mouth as if in doing so she could take back the words or deny that she had uttered them.

"It's all right, Martha." Andie held out a hand. "They're your feelings, you have a right to them."

"No, it's not all right. I don't." She sank to the couch. "I'm sorry," she whispered, though Andie knew, to no one in particular. "He's my husband, he…"

Martha broke down then, sobbing into her hands. "How can he treat me that way? How? I'm his wife. The mother of his child…"

Andie went to the woman and held her while she wept. This was a major breakthrough for Martha, it was wonderful, though Andie knew that wasn't the way it felt to Martha. Anything bottled up that long was bound to be bitter, foul even, when it came out. It was going to hurt.

But not as much, not as irrevocably, as what Martha had been doing for all these years, how she had been living.

Denying pain always did more damage than experiencing it.

Andie held her patient until Martha's tears subsided and she slowly regained her control. Before she left, Andie again asked her how she felt. And for the first time in all their months working together, Martha's smile was spontaneous, an easy smile, one unfettered by shadows.

"I feel good," she answered, voice husky from crying. "Really good."

Andie felt as though she could walk on air. The woman exited, and she picked up the phone and dialed Raven's number, needing to share the experience with her best friend.

"Rave Reviews. May I help you?"

"Raven, it's me. This a good time?"

"I'm just walking a client out. Can you hold?"

"What's more important," Andie teased, "your best friend or some client?"

"Thank you," Raven murmured, amusement in her tone, "I'll be right with you."

Andie heard her friend schmoozing her customer right out the door. She smiled to herself. Raven had come back to Thistledown despite bad memories, despite her fear that because of her family's notorious past, her interior design business would fail to take off.

Instead, it had taken off like a rocket. Her renown had brought people in; her talent had brought them back. Now she had the state's most successful interior design firm outside St. Louis.

Raven returned to the phone. "You're never going to believe this, that was Sonia Baker just now. She wants me to redo their house."

"Again? I thought they just did it?"

"Two and a half years ago. And she wants the full deal, not just an updating. What can I say? Rich people." Andie heard the snap and hiss of a pop top opening. Raven was addicted to Diet Coke; she drank them all day long. "So, what's up with you, Dr. Bennett?"

Andie smiled. "A patient had a breakthrough this morning. This person has really struggled, and to see them open up that way, it just... I'm ecstatic."

"You get too involved with your patients."

"Says you." Andie laughed. "That's my job, silly."

"I mean it. I worry what you'd do if something bad happened to one of them. I worry you'd freak, or something."

Andie laughed again. "You've been trying to take care of me since I was what? Nine years old?"

"Eight, I think." Raven made a sound of amusement. "The breakthrough, anybody I'd recognize?"

"I can't tell you that, and you know it."

"Sure I do." Raven chuckled. "But I keep trying anyway. Just like to know which nut job my best friend's spending her day with."

Andie shook her head. "You're the one who's crazy. Always have been."

"Is that your professional or personal opinion, Doctor?"

"Both." She grinned. "We still on for dinner?"

"Wouldn't miss it."

"Great. Look, got to run. A patient's due in two minutes. See you at five-thirty."

29

Raven beat Andie to the restaurant. She went to their table, ordered a glass of wine and sat back, thinking of Julie. She had been trying to reach her friend for several days now with no luck. Today a recorded message had informed her that the number was no longer in service.

Julie was in trouble again.

Raven sighed, knowing it was true from so many times before. It was that bastard she had married. The prick had an aversion to work and the last time they'd talked, Raven had heard the edge of desperation in her friend's voice. The same edge she'd heard the other times, just before Julie had come running home, her job or marriage or whatever in shambles, her life in shreds.

Silly, weak-willed Julie. Didn't she realize that Thistledown was where she belonged?

Apparently not.

But one of these days she would. Maybe this time.

The waitress brought her wine, and Raven sipped. From the corner of her eye, she caught the interested glance of a man she recognized from the health club. She turned, met his eyes and smiled. For a moment he looked stunned, then he returned her smile, stood and sauntered over.

With her blond hair, still naturally platinum, her nearly six-foot height and the subtle scar that curved over her cheek, attracting men wasn't a problem for Raven. She had left behind the label Bride of Frankenstein and freak a long time ago. She looked good, she knew it and didn't mind using it. She figured there was nothing wrong with a little harmless flirtation, as long as she never lost sight of what was really important in life.

"Hi," he said, stopping beside her table. "Don't I know you from somewhere?"

Great line. Original. "The gym, I think."

"That is right. I didn't recognize you in clothes." She arched an eyebrow, and he laughed, sounding almost giddy. "Street clothes, I mean."

He couldn't be more than twenty-two. Pretty but dim, she decided. Not good for much but sex. She caught sight of Andie crossing the restaurant. She smiled and handed the boy her business card. "My friend's just arrived, you have to go now. But you can call me sometime."

He looked almost faint. He took the card, mumbled something and walked away.

A moment later, Andie slid into the booth. "Who was that?"

"A very pretty boy."

"He's too young for you."

"You think?" Raven met Andie's eyes, then laughed. "I know. I couldn't help encouraging him though. Did you see his ass in those jeans? Buns of Steel."

Andie shook her head, a smile twitching at the corners of her mouth. "No, I didn't notice."

"Your loss." Raven lifted her wine. "You get tied up with a patient?"

"Mmm." The waitress came over, took Andie's drink order, then walked away. "Somebody called in a crisis. I had to make the time."

"Of course you did." Raven trailed her index finger along the rim of her wineglass. "Have you talked to Julie lately?"

"Not in a week. Why?"

"I've been trying to get her. Today I learned the phone's been disconnected."

Andie frowned. "Do you think this means—"

"I do. Marriage number three is over."

The waitress delivered the glass of cabernet; Andie murmured her thanks. "I'd really hoped he was the one."

"Andie—" Raven shot her a disgusted glance "—you're a shrink, for God's sake. You thought her *third* husband in five years was going to be the one?"

"I know, I know." Andie made a sound of frustration. "It's just, I can't help thinking that one man is better than an endless string of many."

"She's got a problem," Raven said. "There's no doubt about that."

"I wish there was something we could do to help her. I wish there was something I could do. But she refuses to get into therapy."

"I miss her." Raven turned her gaze to the window. "She should just come home."

"Thistledown's not her home anymore."

"Yes, it is." Raven met Andie's eyes once more. "It's more her home than California. She just doesn't realize it yet. She's out there searching for something, and it's right here. We're right here."

"Hello, Raven."

Raven turned to the man who had come up to their table, silently groaning when she saw who it was. *Trouble. With a capital T.*

She smiled pleasantly, pretending not to notice the angry glint in his eyes or the muscle that twitched in his jaw. "Jason. How nice to see you."

"Bullshit." He glanced at Andie, then back at Raven. He leaned closer. "I just want you to know, you're a cold-hearted, class-A bitch."

Unfazed, she arched an eyebrow. "Really? I'm a bitch? What's the matter, couldn't your ego take a *tiny* dose of the truth?"

Spots of color bloomed in his cheeks. "Fuck you."

"Sorry." Raven picked up her glass, ignoring Andie's quick, shocked breath. "But a girl has to have some standards."

His face mottled, a muscle worked in his jaw. For a moment, she thought he might try for a stinging comeback, then he turned on his heel and stalked off. Raven watched him walk away. "What a jerk."

Andie had watched him go, too. She turned to Raven. "Wasn't that the new hotshot forensics guy from St. Louis?"

Raven nodded. "Creepy, huh?"

"A little." Andie glanced over her shoulder again, then looked back at Raven. "He's only been in town two weeks, and you've already managed to break his heart? What happened?"

"Mr. Teeny-Wienie couldn't take a little constructive criticism, and now I'm a bitch. Some men are so sensitive." She opened her menu and scanned it. "What are you going to have?"

"Raven—" Andie nudged aside the menu and looked her friend in the eyes. "Did you tell the man he had a small penis and didn't know how to use what he did have?"

"Not just like that. But you get the basic picture." At her friend's horrified expression, Raven rolled her eyes. "You're about to tell me that wasn't very nice, aren't you?"

"Well, it wasn't." Andie drew her eyebrows together. "Every man is not your father. You have to stop lashing out at them in an attempt to punish—"

"Don't try to shrink your friends, Andie. It's a bother."

"You don't see a pattern here? You haven't noticed the bodies of the bloodied and bruised men you leave in your wake?"

"Look," Raven said, narrowing her eyes, "I fucked him once. The experience left a lot to be desired. I told him so. You don't think he would have done the same to me?"

"No, I don't. Not if he was a decent man."

"So, I'm not a decent person?"

"I didn't say that."

"I think you did."

"Let's not fight."

"No, let's. And as long as we're talking about men, let's talk about you, Dr. Bennett."

"What about me?" Andie picked up her menu. "I'm fine."

This time it was Raven who nudged aside the menu to look into her friend's eyes. "The problem is, there are no men. None. No relationships. No nooky at all."

"I date sometimes. Besides, we're not talking about me."

"Of course we're not. Headshrinkers never talk about themselves."

Andie tossed aside the menu, exasperated. "I don't need a man. I don't want one. I love my work. I have my friends, I have you and Julie and..." She made a sound of impatience. "Okay, so I'm a little hesitant about getting involved in a relationship. So I'm a little nervous about being hurt. Big deal."

"So I'm a little rough on my men. Big deal."

"Point taken." Andie reached for the breadbasket and broke off a piece of a bread stick. "What kills me is, these guys know your reputation, but they follow you around like puppy dogs anyway. Talk about a study in male psychology."

Raven grinned and reached for the half bread stick Andie had left behind. "It's a macho thing, you should know that, Doc. They all think they'll be the one to break the mighty Raven."

"Break?" Andie arched an eyebrow. "Interesting choice of words."

"You're shrinking me again." Raven took a bite of the crunchy stick. "Any romantic prospects at all?"

"No interest at all."

"I could fix you up."

Andie made a face. "With one of your armed-and-dangerous types. No, thanks."

"You'd rather mild-mannered and malleable? Someone less likely to trample your heart?"

"You know me too well." She shook her head, fighting a smile. "What would I do without you?"

"Sink into a pit of psychobabble bullshit. I'm the only one who tells you like it is."

"Ditto, girlfriend."

They laughed, and Raven lifted her menu again, suddenly starving. And completely satisfied. The truth was, she didn't need anybody but Andie, either. All the guys were just larks, diversions, ways to pass a little time.

The waitress came and took their orders, and while they waited for their food to be delivered, then while they ate, they talked about Raven's business and Andie's family: her brother Pete's new baby, Daniel's promotion to V.P. of marketing at the radio station, and her mother's "significant other."

As they finished up, Raven met Andie's eyes. "My dad contacted me again."

Andie's expression was sympathetic. "Another letter?"

"Mmm." Raven wrinkled her nose with distaste. "Begged me to come see him. Spilled his guts about how he loved and missed me. I'm his 'everything,' he said. He pleaded for a picture, for anything."

"Oh, Rave, I know how tough this is for you. What are you going to do?"

"Same as always, nothing. I haven't seen him yet, why break a record?"

Andie was quiet a moment, a frown tugging at her mouth. When she met her friend's gaze again, Raven knew what was coming. She was right. "At the risk of being accused of shrinking my B.F.—"

"B.F.?"

"Best friend." Andie grinned. "I know how much you hate him, but it might be good for you to see him. Just once. It might give you closure."

Raven held up a hand. "First of all, you can't imagine

how much I hate him. Second of all, I have closure. Believe me. I had closure when I was fifteen years old. Mr. X gave me that."

"Hear me out, Rave. Whether you realize it or not, in your mind your dad's still the authority figure. You were fifteen when he went to jail, twelve when he killed your mom. Just a kid. He was bigger than life. All-powerful. He held your whole life in his hands. Those dynamics are changed now. If you went to see him—"

Raven reached across the table and caught Andie's hands. "I don't need to see him, and I won't. I have closure. I left behind the notion of him having any kind of power a long time ago. Okay?"

Andie hesitated, then nodded. "Okay. It's just that I care about you. And I worry."

"I know. Thanks." She smiled. "Let's get out of here. We have to work in the morning."

They paid the bill and left the restaurant, walking out into the mild night.

"It smells like spring," Andie murmured, crossing the parking lot to their cars, parked side by side. "My azaleas are already blooming."

"It'll be summer and hot as hell before we know it." Raven glanced up at the starless sky. "This time of year always makes me think of Julie."

Andie smiled. "Me, too. If you hear from her—"

"I'll call."

"Good." Andie unlocked her car and climbed in. "Talk to you tomorrow."

Raven waited until Andie's car had disappeared around the corner of Main before she climbed into her own car, a BMW Z-3. She took a deep breath, the delicious scent of new leather filling her head.

Good old Aunt Katherine, Raven thought, smiling to herself. What would Raven have done without her?

She started the car, backed out of the parking space and headed home. Except for missing Andie and Julie and the abominable hours of therapy her aunt had forced her to endure, living with her mother's sister had been a breeze. A delight, even.

A widow, her aunt had been left quite well off and had spoiled Raven rotten. She had given her anything—and everything—she had desired. She had sent her to college, allowing her to attend U of M because that's where Andie was going, even though they could have afforded much better; had allowed Raven to make as many long-distance calls to her friend as she wanted; had dressed her only in the best.

Until then, Raven hadn't had a clue what having a lot of money was like. It hadn't taken her but a couple of weeks to learn that it was very, very nice.

When Aunt Katherine had passed away six years ago, Raven had become a wealthy young woman. She had bought and renovated a house in Thistledown's oldest and most exclusive neighborhood and had opened her design firm without having to worry about turning a profit for years to come.

Luckily, she had begun turning a profit almost immediately.

All this and her father was still rotting in prison, no chance of parole in sight.

Life was good. Almost perfect.

Raven pulled into the driveway, her headlights cutting across the front gallery as she did. Someone sat huddled there on the front steps, waiting for her. She caught her breath, realizing, as if her thoughts had conjured her, who it was.

Julie had come home.

Raven drew the car to a stop and threw open the door. She climbed out and started across the lawn, not taking the time to go the couple extra steps to the walkway.

She reached the porch and stopped in front of her friend. Raven saw that her every worry had been justified. Julie looked exhausted, physically and emotionally. She looked as if she had endured the ravages of hell.

Julie smiled, the curving of her lips bittersweet. "Hello, Rave. Got room for a long lost friend?"

"Silly question." Raven caught her friend's hands. "I always have room for you."

Julie's eyes filled with tears; Raven saw that she fought them spilling over. "My marriage, it—" She lost the battle and began to cry. "Rick kicked me out. I didn't know where else to go."

Raven took Julie into her arms and held her. Julie needed her. "You did the right thing, baby. You came home."

30

Raven and Julie sat up half the night talking. Julie let her friend baby and coddle her. She let her pour her a glass of wine and make her a bowl of soup. She let her hover over her like a mother hen, insisting she eat every bite, then when they went into the living room, she let Raven tuck an afghan around her.

Then Julie told her friend everything—about the endless parties, the booze and drugs. She told her about Rick's bouts of violence and her yawning despair. She told her how she had begun turning to other men to ease her pain and how awful doing that had made her feel. Again.

Marriage number three was over. It had been a joke to begin with; she saw that now. Another of her many failures.

She was a failure at everything. A waste. A nothing.

"I even...I even tried to contact my mom. They're in Mississippi, I knew, so I got the number and called."

Raven narrowed her eyes. "So what's new with the Good Reverend? He get kicked out of another church for being a twisted zealot with a God complex?"

"I don't know." Julie looked at her hands. "Mom answered the phone, but he took it away from her. He told me I was 'dead to them' and hung up."

She looked in Raven's eyes once more, her own brimming with tears. "So, I figured I should be dead. I'm nothing but a failure and an embarrassment, the marriage was over. I figured, why not?

"I almost did it, too," she whispered, shredding her wet

tissue, unable now to meet Raven's eyes, afraid of what she would see in them. "I had the pills in my hand. I took the entire handful, all of them. Just opened my throat and swallowed them all."

Raven made a choked sound. Julie dared a glance at her friend and saw she was as white as a sheet.

She looked quickly away. "Then I panicked. I stuck my finger down my throat and puked them all up."

"Thank God." Raven brought her hands to her face for a moment, then dropped them. "Why didn't you call? Julie, honey, I would have been on the first plane out to L.A. Don't you know I'd do anything for you?"

She would, too. Julie's eyes welled with tears. *What had she done to deserve such loyalty?* "I couldn't face you. I thought...I thought you would hate me. I didn't want to lose you."

"So, you would rather be dead? You didn't think that I—" Raven bit the words back. "Damn, I need a cigarette. Want one?"

When Julie nodded yes, Raven went in search of her pack. Raven had been a sometime smoker for years—she had a cigarette when she felt an urge or when it was convenient. But tobacco had never gotten the best of her.

Nothing ever got the best of Raven.

Hopelessness pressed in on her. Andie and Raven were both so strong and smart. She looked at their lives and saw one good choice after another, one success after another. And when she looked at her own, she saw weakness and failure.

"Found them." Raven returned to the room, waving a pack of Virginia Slims. She took one look at Julie, and her smile faded. "What's wrong?"

"I was just..." Her throat closed over the words, and she swallowed hard, forcing them out. "Why do you even bother with me, Rave? I'm a total failure. I couldn't even kill myself."

"Don't say that. Don't even think it." She crossed to

Julie and knelt before her. She folded her hands around Julie's. "Thank God, you didn't succeed. Thank God. If I had lost you...I think I would have died myself. Don't ever try that again. Do you hear me? If you do, I swear, I'll knock you silly."

Julie giggled, suddenly feeling better. "Kind of hard to do if I'm dead."

Raven laughed, too. "I'll follow you to the other side and do it. Don't doubt it for a moment."

"What about those cigarettes?"

Raven lit one and handed it to Julie, then lit one for herself. For a moment they smoked in silence. "You're here now. Everything's going to be okay."

Julie searched her friend's gaze. "Is it? I'm so tired, Raven. I feel so...empty."

"Yes, it is. You're going to stay with me. As long as you need to, to get back on your feet. You can stay forever, if you want. I love you, kiddo. Andie loves you. We're always here for you. Don't ever forget that again."

Julie closed her eyes a moment, making a sound of exhaustion and relief. "I was hoping, praying, you'd say that." She opened her eyes and smiled weakly at her old friend. "I promised myself that if you and Andie forgave me, if you would have me back, I was going to stay this time. For good."

"For good?" Raven repeated, doubt clear in her tone. "You've said that before and—"

"I mean it, Rave." Julie sat up straighter, mustering all her resolve. "I'm cleaning up my act. I'm giving up the men, the parties. I want to come home. I want to feel good again, the way I used to, when we were all together."

"You've made me so happy," Raven murmured, laying her head on Julie's lap. "We're a family again. Together forever."

31

Detective Nick Raphael and his partner exchanged knowing glances. No doubt that the piece-of-shit scumbag sitting across from them at the interrogation table had done the deed in question. So what that they only had a so-so witness? So what that the junkie proclaimed his innocence with the earnestness of an altar boy?

At eight fifty-seven the night before, the junkie had charged into the Gas 'N Sip, knocked the old lady manning the register senseless and emptied the cash drawer. He'd scored less than two hundred bucks and put the lady in the I.C.U. in a coma.

Nick had been at the job too long not to *know*. Call it a cop's sixth sense, call it instinct, or just years of experience. He knew.

Judging by his partner's expression, he did, too. And Detective Bobby J. O'Shea had been a cop just as long as Nick.

They were going to nail this piece of crap. Unfortunately, the mom-and-pop convenience store had not yet installed a security camera. Next week, the owner had said. He'd already bought the equipment. Too bad. If they had, Nick wouldn't be here trying to work a confession out of this no-good slimeball.

He'd be trying to work one out of some other slimeball.

Nick glanced at the suspect. Still, it wasn't going to be that hard, more of an annoyance, really. As far as IQ went, this guy hadn't had much before the drugs fried his brain.

"You want to try that again, Jacko," Nick said. "I'm

having a hard time buying your alibi. You were home watching TV last night? Alone?''

"That's right. It's the truth. Every word, I swear."

Nick made a sound of disgust. If only he had a nickel for every time a guilty-as-hell perp had said that to him. He'd be too rich to be working this job, that was for sure. "You swear? On your dear departed mother's grave, right?''

"Yeah." The guy reached for a cigarette. "That's right."

"Look, we've got a witness." Nick laid the flat of his hands on the table and leaned toward the junkie. "This witness saw you leaving the scene. Running from the scene, actually.''

"So?" He dragged on the cigarette. "That ain't a crime.''

Nick ignored him. "You needed a fix. You see the Gas 'N Sip. You see there's nobody around but this one old lady. You grab a tire iron from the trunk of your piece-of-shit car, go into the store and knock the hell out of the woman. Then you empty the drawer." He leaned closer, not stopping until they were all but nose-to-nose. "That's what happened, isn't it, Jacko?''

"Nobody saw nothin'." The perp's words slurred slightly. "I wasn't there."

"She's in I.C.U.," Bobby said. "In a coma. She dies, that's first-degree.''

"I don't know shit about that. It has nothin' to do with me.''

Yeah, right. "How long do you think a junkie like you'd last in the pen? No more score, Jacko. Cold turkey.''

"Yeah," Bobby added. "Ever want to be somebody's girlfriend before? Ever squealed like a pig?''

"An admission of guilt would show the courts you felt remorse.''

"Yeah." Bobby inclined his head in agreement. "Could

be the difference between a rehab facility and the state pen.''

''I mean, it wasn't your fault, right? You were hurting, you needed a score. A good lawyer might even get you off.''

Nick pushed away from the table. He nodded at Bobby. His redheaded partner was as big and broad as a bear. His size alone had intimidated the weak into confessing. ''I need some air.'' He smiled at his partner. ''You have my permission to beat the shit out of him while I'm gone.''

Bobby stood and stretched; the junkie's eyes widened and he pressed back into his chair. Bobby grinned. ''I'll take that under consideration, partner. It's been a dull day, I could use a little pick-me-up.''

Nick crossed to the door, then looked back at his friend and smiled. ''Don't leave any marks.''

''I never do, buddy-boy. That's the sign of a real professional.''

Nick left the interrogation room and headed out front. Bobby O'Shea might look like King Kong, but he was one of the least aggressive cops on the force. In all the time Nick had worked with him, he had never seen Bobby use unnecessary force with a suspect. Nick chuckled to himself. Of course, he never had to. Most of their perps took one look at Bobby O'Shea and peed their pants.

Nick and Bobby had been working together for four years now, and they were well suited. For Nick, interrogation was about being clever, about reading your suspect and outsmarting him. It was about understanding human nature and playing to weakness, to ego, to fear. The threat of physical violence was a part of that; he used it often. But he had never resorted to striking a suspect.

''Hey, Raphael,'' one of the other detectives called. ''How's it going in there?''

''Same old bullshit.''

''Nail him, okay? That lady in I.C.U., she's a neighbor of my mother's.''

"You got it." Nick nodded and stepped outside. That was the thing about Thistledown, every victim was somebody's friend or neighbor. Crimes weren't anonymous here, they touched people you knew, people you cared about. It made it all real. It made it frightening.

That was good. When people were aware of crime, they helped do something about it. It was one of the things that made Thistledown a good place to live.

Not that the city hadn't changed in the past ten or so years. It had, growing by leaps and bounds because of its relative proximity to St. Louis, just an hour east. It had become a bedroom community for executives for whom the commute to and from the city was a trade-off for less crime, better schools and a slower pace of life for their families.

Problem was, they had brought some of the big-city filth with them, and Thistledown was no longer the quiet little burg it had been. Nick saw his job as not only cleaning up what was on the streets now, but trying to keep the encroaching muck at bay. He did that by making life in this little town unbelievably uncomfortable for criminals.

It was a balancing act. Sometimes he skated pretty close to fifth- and sixth-amendment violations. He tried not to step over the line; he believed in this country, in the Bill of Rights, in freedom. He also believed that the criminal-justice system favored the criminals and that crime was out of control because of it. A balancing act, he thought again. But if he had to favor one side over the other, the victims and the law-abiding citizens had it, hands down.

Nick tipped his face toward the sky and breathed deeply. The May day was perfect, sunny and warm with a mild breeze that stirred up the scent of flowers from the green space across from the station. He breathed deeply, wishing he was in the park with Mara, his six-year-old daughter.

He smiled to himself, thinking of her. Nearly seven years ago, Jenny had finally consented to have a child. She had already been pregnant at the time—an accident—but

Nick hadn't cared how it had happened, he was just thankful it had.

Weird, how things changed. At first, he and Jenny had both been eager to start a family. But they had decided to wait—until they had a house, until they were financially secure enough that Jenny could quit work to become a full-time mom. Then, when they'd reached that point, Jenny had hesitated. They had begun to fight. She resented his job, the time he spent away from her and home. Every time he'd brought up children, she had said the same thing: if he was hardly home now, why should she believe that would change with children?

Fate had intervened, thank God. He loved his daughter more than he had known it was possible to love.

He did this job for Mara. Whenever he became convinced that dirtbags like the one in the interrogation room with Bobby were winning, he thought of his daughter. Whenever he wondered what the hell he was doing working within a system that consistently failed, he thought of his daughter.

One less bad guy on the street—even if only for a matter of hours—made the streets safer for her.

Mara was the reason, too, that he and Jenny were still together. Their relationship was more a war than a love affair these days.

Love affair? Nick shook his head. He found it difficult even to think of his marriage in that way. Once upon a time he and Jenny hadn't been able to get enough of each other. He remembered rushing home at the end of the day, just needing to see her face. Touching her had been heaven on earth.

Funny, back then just being together had been enough. They hadn't needed to be doing anything, not even talking. Just having her at his side had made him content.

Now, being together was the problem. They argued about everything. Jenny refused to understand him. He said white; she said black. She challenged his every thought, his every belief, his every dream.

She couldn't see that what he did was more than a job. Because of him—of what he did or didn't do—a killer or a rapist or a drug dealer could be free to walk the streets. The more he tried to explain, the wider the fission between them seemed to become.

What had happened to them? he wondered. How had they wandered so far from where they'd started?

He drew his eyebrows together in thought. It had begun with Mrs. X's murder. He could look back and see it as clearly as if he had taken a snapshot. He had become obsessed with the murder, with catching Leah Robertson's killer. He had begun putting his job before his marriage. He'd never stopped, he supposed.

Nick thought of his daughter again, and again a smile touched his mouth. He would fight to hang on, for Mara. Married people stayed together. They worked things out. He had been lazy; he had given in to the urge to ignore his and Jenny's problems instead of confronting them head-on in an attempt to heal their relationship.

No more, Nick decided. Tonight he and Jenny would talk. They would begin working things out. They had been going through a rough patch. A bad cycle. All couples did occasionally.

Buoyed by his own resolve, he checked his watch. Bobby had had the perp all to himself for about twenty minutes. Time to give his partner a little backup, turn up the heat a bit.

Whistling under his breath, he headed into the station.

32

In the week that had passed since Martha Pierpont's last session and her breakthrough, Andie had wondered repeatedly about the woman. She had worried about how she was doing and whether her anger had resurfaced or remained suppressed. Andie had been anxious to see her again to determine how the woman had weathered the emergence of her true feelings.

"How was your week?" Andie asked Martha after they both sat down.

"Fine," the woman answered, shifting in her seat. "Good. Why do you ask?"

Andie smiled. "Well, besides the fact that hearing about your week is what I do, something pretty significant happened during your last session, and I thought it might have affected your mood."

"Significant?" Martha looked at her blankly. "I don't understand."

Full armor, solidly in place. "Your outburst, Martha. You were quite upset."

"I'm sorry, Dr. Bennett. I still don't know what you mean."

Andie frowned. Martha looked completely blank. Was this a form of denial? Of avoidance? Or did she really not remember what had happened?

"You said you wanted to kill your husband. When he abused you."

For a full ten seconds, Martha stared at her. Then she shook her head. "I did not."

"But you did, Martha. Three times. You almost shouted it. You sobbed after."

"You're mistaken. I would never say that. *Never.* Edward is my husband. Killing's wrong."

"Expressing rage," Andie said gently, "expressing hurt, anger or disappointment is not the same as acting on it. It's all right to be angry, Martha."

"Of course it is." The woman looked away. For several moments, she was silent, then she looked back at Andie. "Edward got a gun."

"A gun." Andie made a sound of surprise and dismay. "Oh, Martha, is that a good idea?"

"He was afraid…" She clasped her hands in her lap. "He got another letter. Whoever sent it said that…that he was going to kill Ed. Slit his throat while he slept."

Andie instinctively brought a hand to her own throat. "So, he got a gun."

"Yes. He keeps it in the nightstand by the bed. Loaded, Dr. Bennett."

Gooseflesh ran up Andie's arms. "I don't like this, Martha. Statistics show that more people are killed or wounded by their own guns than the people they're trying to protect themselves from."

"That's what the police said." She looked at her hands, then back up at Andie. "I tried to talk him out of it. I begged him to hire a bodyguard instead, but he…he said it wouldn't look good. He said it would make him look like a coward."

The coward he was, Andie thought.

"I'm afraid for Patti. What if he—" Martha bit back the words, stood and crossed to the window.

"If he what, Martha?"

"Nothing. It's just dangerous to have a loaded gun in the house. She's a teenager, you know. With teenagers, accidents happen."

Martha began to roam the office, touching this and that, obviously lost in her own thoughts. As Andie watched her, she became aware of a certain lightening of her patient's mood to a kind of repressed excitement that seemed to emanate from her.

"Martha?" she queried. "Is there anything else you'd like to talk about?"

The woman stopped and met her eyes. "Are you coming to the benefit Friday night?"

She referred, Andie knew, to the benefit for the Edward Pierpont Women's Shelter. "Of course. I'm bringing my friends Raven Johnson and Julie Cooper."

"It's funny, isn't it? Ironic, I mean."

"What's that?" Andie asked, though she thought she knew.

"That Edward sponsored this project. That he went to the mat for it with the council. A halfway house for abused women?" A smile tugged at her mouth. "What do you think he would do if I was the first woman who checked in? Wouldn't that be just too sweet?"

"You could be," Andie said softly.

"He'd kill me."

The way she said the words, so matter-of-factly, made Andie's blood run cold. She couldn't help thinking of Raven's mother. She shook the sensation, and the memory, off. "That's what he wants you to think, Martha. He wants you afraid, he wants you to feel powerless. He knows if you're afraid and feel helpless, you'll stay."

"You don't know Edward the way I do. He means it, Dr. Bennett. I know he does." She began to shake. "I tried once, a long time ago, and he...he almost did."

"You could get protection."

"He's the mayor."

"He's still bound by the law."

She shook her head again, becoming visibly upset. "I don't want to talk about this."

Andie tried again, anyway, afraid for her patient—living with a violent man, one who now slept with a loaded gun.

"What about Patti? Aren't you afraid that one day he'll turn his anger and abuse on her? Statistics show—"

"No!" Martha cut her off, voice high and tight. She clenched her hands into fists. "She's his daughter. He wouldn't do that. He wouldn't!"

Andie could have pointed out that Martha was his wife and that fact didn't stop him from hurting her, but she didn't. The woman had to come to her own realizations, in her own time.

Andie just hoped she came to them before something terrible happened. Something irreversible.

33

Friday night arrived. Andie had to admit to a fair amount of girlish excitement—it had been ages since she had gone to a black-tie affair, and far longer than that since she had gone to one with Raven and Julie. She figured the last one was their freshman homecoming dance.

Andie laughed to herself. Boy, did that make her feel ancient.

She checked her watch and saw that she had better get moving. Raven had insisted on hiring a limousine for the three of them, and her friends should be arriving any minute. She slipped into her dress, a black-and-white number with stiff, shimmery fabric and a short skirt, fastened it, then slid into her pumps. She was clipping on her earrings when the bell rang.

Raven and Julie were on the doorstep, Julie in a flouncy, deep purple dress, Raven in stunning, unrelieved black. "Hi," Andie said, smiling. "You guys look gorgeous."

"So do you," they responded in unison, then burst out laughing.

"This is such a blast from the past," Julie said. "I feel like a kid again, going to the Spring Fling."

"I forgot about that one," Andie murmured. "All we need now are three pimply-faced boys."

"And those funky corsages."

Julie laughed. "Remember, my dad let me go but only with my cousin?"

"And you weren't allowed to dance."

They all laughed. Andie locked the door, and the three

hurried out to the limo. Raven had a bottle of champagne on ice. She popped it and poured them a glass.

"Together again."

They tapped glasses and sipped. The wine was fine and dry, a California brut; the bubbles tickled Andie's nose and went straight to her head. She murmured her appreciation. "When we were fifteen, we didn't have stuff like this."

"Spiked punch at the dance. That's about it." Raven wrinkled her nose. "Remember how that tasted?"

That memory led to another and another. In what seemed the blink of an eye, they had arrived downtown and the driver was opening the car door for them. The Bakers, one of Thistledown's oldest and wealthiest families, had opened their grand old family home, a turn-of-the-century revival structure, for the benefit. Everybody who was anybody in Thistledown had purchased a ticket. A town this size could support only a small number of these types of affairs, and when one came along, those who could afford to attend, did.

Andie made her way through the crowd, nursing a glass of champagne, pausing to talk to the president of the chamber of commerce, her internist, the high-school principal. She caught sight of Martha. She looked fabulous. Effervescent and smiling, the mayor's wife made the rounds, touching this one on the hand or arm, making small talk, laughing. The consummate politician's wife, Andie thought. An asset worth more than gold.

Andie studied her. She had always thought Martha an attractive woman, but she hadn't realized before that she was beautiful. She usually dressed conservatively, in dark or muted colors, because Edward preferred it. Not tonight. Tonight she wore a vivid red dress, in a bold, off-the-shoulder style. It certainly wasn't the black silk Martha had mentioned.

Andie shook her head slightly. A beautiful woman. A good person. Smart. Charming. Why had she allowed herself to be trapped in an abusive marriage? Andie asked herself the question even though clinically, as a psychologist, she understood how it had happened. But personally, with her heart, she didn't.

Martha deserved so much more.

Every woman did.

From the dais, set up in the front parlor, Janice Petrie, president of the city council, tapped the microphone, cleared her throat and welcomed everyone to the benefit. Andie wandered that way. As she did, she caught sight of Julie, flirting outrageously with the owner of the local department store. Then she saw Raven ease between the two and gently but firmly steer her from him.

Andie shook her head. Some things never changed.

Edward Pierpont began to speak. "This shelter is an idea whose time has come. It first occurred to me while reading the tragic story of Tammy Reed, a Thistledown resident, the mother of three, stalked, then murdered by her estranged husband. She had nowhere to turn. No one to turn to. Things like that must not happen in Thistledown, not ever again."

Applause and murmurs of support rippled through the audience. Edward waited for it to die down, then continued. "The Edward Pierpont Women's Shelter will provide a safe house for women like Tammy Reed, women caught in destructive, abusive relationships, women who are afraid for themselves and their children, women who have nowhere else to go."

Women like your wife, Andie thought, watching him, his hypocrisy turning her stomach. She shifted her gaze to Martha, standing beside him on the dais, face turned toward him, the picture of the devoted and dutiful wife.

Looking at them together—the solicitous way he treated her, his possessive glances, the way he looped his arm around her—no one would ever suspect the true nature of their relationship.

They appeared the perfect, loving couple; he the perfect, loving husband.

Sometimes, things weren't what they seemed. Not at all.

Raven came up beside her. "I take it you didn't vote for him," she murmured, close to her ear.

Andie turned slightly to her friend. "How did you guess?"

"Something about you looking like you want to puke."

"That obvious, huh?"

Raven leaned toward her again. "Julie's on her way to having drunk too much. You know Julie, once that happens there's no stopping her. You want to blow this scene?"

"You got it." Andie lowered her voice more. "If I have to listen to *him* much longer, I will puke."

They collected Julie and went out to where the limo waited. "What now?" Andie asked as they settled in, checking her watch. "It's still pretty early."

"I have an idea," Raven said. A devilish smile tugged at her mouth. "Are you guys game?"

Andie and Julie exchanged glances. "This could be dangerous."

"Illegal."

"Or immoral."

Raven laughed and leaned toward them. "Remember the shed in farmer Trent's field? Remember that night we went out there, climbed onto the roof and looked up at the stars?"

"I haven't thought about the shed in years," Julie murmured.

"Me neither," said Andie. "God, I loved that place."

"Let's go there now."

Andie shook her head. "Big problem, Rave. Farmer Trent's field is Happy Hollow, Phase III."

"No problem at all." Raven leaned forward and gave the driver directions. Within ten minutes they were winding their way through the streets of Phase III.

"Pull over here," she announced suddenly. The driver

did and she opened the sunroof, stood and stuck her head through. "I think this is it."

Andie and Julie followed her up. "I think you're right." Andie pointed. "That's should be Mockingbird Lane, over there."

"Come on, let's climb onto the roof."

"Raven, you've got to be kidding."

She looked at the driver. "When we're all through, close the moon roof, okay? And no fair looking up our skirts while we're climbing out."

The driver laughed and promised he wouldn't, and Raven kicked off her shoes and shimmied through the roof. "Hand up the champagne."

"This is nuts." Andie handed up the bottle, then their glasses.

Julie giggled. "I can't believe we're doing this."

Laughing, they followed Raven onto the roof of the limo. When the opening had eased shut, they all lay back and gazed at the stars.

"Just like the old days," Andie murmured. "All's right with the world."

Julie propped herself on an elbow. "That night we did this, that was the night we heard the music for the first time."

"The night my parents split up."

"The night I got stitches in my leg." Raven made a sound of contentment. "Remember our wishes that night? In a way, they came true."

"We're still friends," Andie said.

"I never doubted we would be," Raven added.

Andie drew a deep breath, letting the mild night air fill her lungs. "I remember how...devastated I was about my folks. I thought the world was ending."

"But it went on."

"Yeah." She looked at Julie. "Did I tell you my mom's dating this really great guy? Not only is he handsome and well off, but he's wild about her. He's been spoiling her rotten.''

"It's about time, I say." Julie smiled. "Your dad's still with Leeza, isn't he? After all these years?''

Raven made a face. "I still think she's a home-wrecking slut-bitch." The other two burst out laughing, and she sniffed. "Well, I do.''

"Okay." Andie turned to her friend, beside her on her right. "Did you put that snake in her car? Tell the truth. It always seemed just a bit too much of a coincidence.''

Raven widened her eyes as with extreme innocence. "Me?''

"Yes *you*. Come on, inquiring minds want to know.''

She hesitated a moment, then nodded. "Yup, I did. I saw this little green snake in our garden, so I scooped it up into a coffee can, went down to your dad's office and set it free in her car." She met Andie's eyes. "I did it for you, Andie. And your mom.''

The girls stopped laughing. A sensation walked up Andie's spine, like ice-cold fingers.

At her friends' uncomfortable silence, Raven stiffened, defensive. "I thought she would be scared, squeal, maybe wet her pants. I didn't know she'd get in a wreck. How could I? Besides, no real harm was done.''

"Her squealing and wetting her pants." Julie giggled. "It's a picture.''

"She has tried to be nice to me and Dan and Pete," Andie said reflectively. "Sometimes, I get the feeling she really wants to be a part of our lives, you know. Like she wants us to share things with her, like she wants us to love her. I just can't. I don't bear her any ill will, but—''

Raven made a sound like a buzzer going off. "Wrong. Time for an honesty alert, Dr. Bennett.''

"Okay—" Andie laughed and held out her index finger and thumb, about a quarter of an inch apart. "Maybe just a little ill will. But sometimes I feel sorry for her, too. Like maybe she knows she made a mistake, and her life hasn't turned out to be quite what she wanted.''

Andie was silent a moment. ''They never had kids together. She confided to me once that Dad told her he'd already done that, that he had his family and didn't want another.''

''Wow, that's cold.'' Julie sat up. ''Poor Leeza.''

Raven snorted and refilled all their champagne glasses. ''Poor Leeza, my ass. She made her choices.''

''I suppose.'' Julie sighed. ''I guess I'm sympathetic because I've made so many bad choices myself.'' She grinned. ''Chester, Frank and Rick, for starters. My ex-husbands, the three stooges.''

Her smile faded. ''Seriously, if we'd been doing this a month ago, when Rick and I…I don't think I could have handled it. I would have looked at you two and felt like such a failure. But now…I feel hopeful.'' She looked from one friend to the other, eyes brimming with tears. ''I'm glad I'm part of your lives, guys. I'm glad to be back. I'm going to make it, I am.''

''Oh, Julie.'' Andie hugged her. ''I love you. And I'm glad you're back, too.''

''A toast.'' Laughing, sounding almost giddy, Raven held out her champagne flute. ''To us.''

''To us,'' Andie and Julie chorused, tapping their glasses against Raven's. ''To the future.''

34

It took Nick a week to act on his resolution to begin patching things up with Jenny. He had gotten involved in a particularly baffling string of robberies and had spent more time on them than he had intended. When he'd come home at night, he had needed to devote his attention to Mara, and by the time she'd been tucked in, he had been too whipped to face a heart-to-heart with Jenny.

Today, however, there'd been a break in the case. Arrests had been made, so he'd decided to knock off early, go home to his family and begin his and Jenny's reconciliation. He'd stopped at the florist on the way and picked up some flowers for her. Nothing fancy, just a colorful spring bouquet, something to break the ice. While there, he'd had the woman put together a small bunch of daisies for Mara. From the florist, he'd gone to the Chinese takeout and gotten everyone's favorites, even that sickly sweet chicken dish Mara loved.

Nick parked in his driveway, surprised to see Jenny's car on the street instead of in the garage. He tooted the horn, a custom he and Mara had gotten into. Most days she barreled out to meet him, though a few he found her playing with a friend or in front of the TV, glued to a favorite cartoon.

Today was one of those exceptions. He collected the flowers and food and headed inside.

"I'm home," he called, setting the bag of takeout and his keys on the entryway table. The mail was there and he shuffled through it, then frowned, suddenly aware of how quiet it was. No music or TV. No high-pitched giggles or pots and pans being moved about in the kitchen.

He glanced around. *Where the hell was the dog?*

Jenny emerged from the hallway that led to the bedrooms. She had her purse and travel bag slung over her shoulder. "I hope those weren't for me," she said.

He realized he had the two bouquets of flowers cradled in his arms. "For you. And Mara." He laid them on the table beside the bag of food, then turned back to his wife, a sinking sensation in the pit of his gut. "What's going on, Jen?"

"I'm leaving you."

He stared at her, not believing his ears. She'd said it so matter-of-factly, so bluntly, as if it meant no more to her than taking out the garbage. "You can't mean that."

"But I do." She made a sound of contempt. "The only surprise here should be that I didn't do this years ago."

"What about Mara?"

"What about her?"

"Think what this will do to her, Jen. Jesus, for once stop thinking about yourself."

"Thinking about myself!" Spots of hot color flew to her cheeks. "You're the one who—" She bit back the words. "I am thinking of her. Living with parents who hate each other is a poor way to live. I want better for her."

"Is that what you think? That we hate each other?"

Her expression softened. "Maybe not. We just hate living with each other."

Nick glanced around, mouth dry, a kind of numbness coming over him. "Where is she, Jen? Where's Mara? I want to see my daughter."

"You will. Mara and the dog are at my mother's." Jenny readjusted the travel bag's strap. "I didn't think it would be right to subject Mara to what was sure to be a scene. I didn't want her to feel like she had to choose."

"Afraid she would choose me?"

Jenny flushed. "She's six, she doesn't get a choice, Nick."

He closed his eyes a moment and sucked in a deep, calming breath. It wouldn't do to get into a knock-down-drag-out fight with Jenny. She had made up her mind. He had to find a way to change it. "All couples have problems," he said softly. "We need to work harder on solving ours, that's all."

She laughed. "You make it sound so simple. We don't have a few little problems, Nick. We have nothing. Nothing in common. Nothing except sex, anyway. And we've even lost that."

"I haven't been here enough, I admit that. I ran from our differences instead of trying to understand them." He lowered his voice. "Instead of trying to understand you. I'm sorry."

She cleared her throat. "I am, too."

He took a step toward her. "It'll work, Jenny. We can make it work. We can patch this up."

"Patch things up," she repeated. "Like an old flat tire."

"No." He took a step toward her. "Like something worth saving."

"How do you propose we do that, Nick? Between your job and Mara, you don't have time for me." When he opened his mouth to protest, she held up a hand to stop him. "I'm not jealous of the time and attention you lavish on our daughter. I'm glad. You're a wonderful father. But before Mara, your job took all your time. You made room for her, but not me."

"I'll try harder," he said quickly. "I'll change."

Her eyes flooded with tears. "Don't you see? You shouldn't have to 'try harder.' You shouldn't have to 'change.'"

"Jen—"

"You don't love me, Nick. Not the way you love being a cop. Or now, the way you love your daughter."

"That's not true, Jenny. It's not."

"No? When's the last time you've thought about me during the middle of the day? When's the last time, in the middle of an important investigation, you've thought about us making love, or decided to drop everything and give me a call?"

"You're not being fair."

She narrowed her eyes, looking suddenly furious. "I'm being more than fair. And I'm being honest. I want more, Nick. I deserve more."

"More," he repeated, angry, too. Angry that she could so cavalierly discard their family. "A bigger house. A finer car? Like your dad gives your mom?"

She hiked up her chin. "That would be nice, sure. I grew up with the best things. Having anything I wanted. But you know what, I would have settled for being number one. I'm tired of waiting."

"Settled? I guess that about says it all."

"I guess it does."

He fisted his fingers. "You're not taking my daughter away from me."

"I already have." She started past him, heading for the door.

"Dammit, Jen..." He caught her arm. "You can't do that. I'll sue for custody."

"Oh, please." She jerked her arm free. "You think any judge would give you custody? With the cop's hours you keep? With the life-style? I don't think so."

"I love my daughter. I won't live without her."

"She'll be close enough for visitation."

Visitation. Stolen hours with Mara, here and there. He nearly choked on the thought; it welled up inside him in a wave of fury and disbelief. "Doesn't family mean anything to you? Doesn't this family?"

She reached the door and opened it, then looked back at him, her expression devoid of anything warm. "You only see one way to live, Nick Raphael. Only one way to love. That's all you've ever seen. It's always been your way or the highway."

"What's to discuss? Married people stay together. Families stay together. It's important. It's—"

"How can you not see the truth? Listen to you. You refuse to acknowledge anyone else's ideas or feelings. When are you going to learn to compromise? To bend? When are you going to see there are shades of gray in the world?"

"Not about this."

"Goodbye, Nick." She hiked her bag higher on her shoulder and stepped through the front door.

He watched her walk away. And then, suddenly, he knew. It hit him like a thunderbolt.

Jenny had someone else.

Nick flew after her, catching her as she swung the car door open. He reached around her and slammed it shut. "Who is he, Jenny? I know you too well. You wouldn't have the guts to do this otherwise."

Her face flooded with color; he saw that he was right. "Son of a bitch. You've been cheating on me?" He took a step toward her, flexing his fingers, furious, betrayed. In all the time they had been together, no matter how bad it had sometimes been between them, he had never cheated on her. And he'd had opportunities, lots of them.

"Is this what 'shades of gray' are all about?" he asked, voice shaking with rage. "Fucking another man? Walking out on your marriage so you can be with somebody new?"

"Don't be so sanctimonious."

He laughed, the sound bitter even to his own ears. "I think I have the right about now. Don't you?"

"I'm leaving."

He caught her arm roughly, hanging on to control by a thread. "Who is he, Jenny? You might as well tell me, because I'm going to find out anyway."

She hesitated a moment, then nodded. "All right. It's my therapist."

Her shrink. He pictured her with the man he had met several times, a real smooth operator; a professional man who drove a sleek foreign car and wore European suits that probably each cost more than Nick's entire wardrobe.

The kind of guy Jenny should have married in the first place. The kind of guy her parents had wanted her to marry.

Nick pushed the thought away, focusing instead on the overtime he had worked to pay for those high-priced shrink sessions. The off-duty gigs, thankless hours spent at restaurants and bars and high-school football games, hours he had wanted to be home with his daughter.

He'd done all that so his wife could be with another man.

So she could fall in love with another man.

"I could beat the shit out of you right now."

She smiled, the curving of her lips brittle, contemptuous. "But you won't, Nick. You're not that kind of man."

She opened the car door again, tossed her bag inside, then climbed in. She started the car and looked back up at him. "You're not sorry to see me go, Nick. If you don't realize it now, you will. I'm filing for divorce tomorrow morning."

35

Nick opened his eyes, realizing the phone was ringing. He looked around, disoriented. Then he remembered. He was in Mara's room. After Jenny left, he'd gotten drunk. Stinking, fall-down, lousy drunk. Not too mature, but he'd figured he was entitled. What else was a guy supposed to do after his wife told him she had been screwing her shrink and then left him, taking his daughter and the dog with her? Yeah, sure, he was entitled.

Shit. Fuck. Son of a bitch.

Nick groaned and sat up. His mouth felt as though he'd mopped the kitchen floor with it. He passed a hand over his face and peered at Mara's Minnie Mouse clock. 1:12 a.m.

How long had he been out?

He swung his legs over the side of the bed and stood, his head screaming a protest. The phone rang again, shrilly insistent, slicing through his brain like a knife. "Okay, okay," he muttered. "Give me a break here."

He went next door to his and Jenny's bedroom, grabbed the receiver and brought it to his ear. "Raphael here," he managed to say, his voice thick.

"Rise and shine, sweetheart," the contralto voice of the dispatcher said. "Got a homicide."

Nick came fully alert. "Where?"

"One Concord Place."

"Ritzy."

"You could say that. The victim's Mayor Pierpont."

Somebody had whacked the mayor? "On the way."

Fifteen minutes later, Nick arrived at the Pierpont house. The first officers had secured the scene; Nick saw Bobby's pickup truck, but not the coroner's wagon. A crowd of what looked like neighbors had gathered.

Funny thing about murder scenes, Nick thought, climbing out of his Jeep, crowds of the curious always gathered, no matter the time, no matter the area of the city. It was like this weird energy floated on the air. For no reason at all, people woke up, they went to their windows and saw that something awful had happened, and they wandered out to find out what. Or to get a closer look. Like rubberneckers on the highway.

It complicated his job immensely. And even without complications, this one was sure to be a circus.

Speaking of which, the press arrived, spilling out of the news vans like clowns out of a burning house. He ducked under the yellow tape, ignoring a reporter's shouted question, and headed up the flower-lined, brick walk. He let himself in the front door. Compared to the chaos outside the house, inside was deathly quiet. A half-dozen officers moved through the place, collecting evidence, taking photographs and talking quietly with one another.

Martha Pierpont—he recognized the mayor's wife from seeing her on television with the mayor—sat on the couch, huddled under a blanket. Her teeth were chattering. A teenage girl, probably the daughter, sat beside her, though they didn't touch in any way. The girl stared blankly ahead, her cheeks chalky white.

Shock, Nick thought, turning and starting for the back of the house, looking for Bobby.

He found him—and the honorable Mayor Pierpont—in the master bedroom. Bobby looked up from his notepad and frowned. "Man, what happened to you? You look like warmed-over shit."

"Thanks." Nick stopped beside his partner and glanced at his notes. "Jenny left me. She took Mara and the dog with her."

"Damn. I'm sorry."

"Thanks." Nick struggled to focus on the scene. "What do we have?"

"One dead mayor. Shot five times. Another bullet embedded in the wall by the window."

Nick crossed to the body and drew in a deep breath through his nose. Ed Pierpont was laying in a pool of blood, brains and assorted other gore. Half of his face had been shot away.

"Grisly, yes?" Bobby placed his hands on his hips and shook his head. "I didn't vote for the guy, did you?"

"Nope. Didn't trust him." Nick met his partner's eyes. "Suspects?"

"Confession. Wife says she did it. He was coming after her, said he was going to kill her. So she got his gun and shot him."

"But she didn't mean to kill him, right? She was terrified for her life. She didn't know what else to do."

Nick's sarcasm wasn't lost on his partner. "You got it, buddy. Self-defense, all the way."

"Who's the girl?"

"Their daughter. An only child. She called it in, pretty hysterical call. When we got here, the wife's still holding the gun. We have to pry it out of her hands. Check this out."

Bobby squatted beside what was left of Honest Ed Pierpont. Nick followed him. He pointed to the area that had been home to the mayor's crown jewels. "Crime of passion, all right. Shot her husband's pecker off."

Nick's stomach rolled. "But she wasn't aiming. Just wanted to stop him."

"Oh, yeah. One of those lucky shots."

"Where the hell's Doc?"

"Right here," the medical examiner said, coming up behind them. "Don't get your panties in a wad, Detective Raphael. I'm not as young as I used to be." He took a good look at Nick and his bushy eyebrows rose. "You look like hell."

"His wife left him," Bobby offered.

"Sorry to hear that." The M.E. cleared his throat. "I lost two that way. I blame the work."

"It wasn't the work," Bobby said, his expression solemn. "He's an asshole. I wouldn't want to live with him."

Nick made a sound of irritation. "Don't worry, I wasn't going to ask. Now, if you two are done dissecting my shitty personal life, we've got a homicide here."

"So we do." The M.E. knelt beside the body. "Why don't one of you cowboys fill me in."

Bobby did the honors while Nick went into the other room to talk with Martha Pierpont. Just as his partner had said, she confessed to having killed her husband. In self-defense. He was trying to kill her. All she could think was that this time he was going to do it, he was going to kill her. Something inside her had snapped.

In terror, she had run to their bedroom, dug his loaded gun out of their bedside table, pointed it at him and fired—continuing to pull the trigger, even after the gun was empty.

The shots had awakened their daughter, Patti, and she had come running. It was the girl who had called 911; she who had let the police in; she who had led the police to her father's body.

As he questioned Martha Pierpont more, he learned that she had been under a therapist's care for more than a year now. She wanted to see her, Martha said. Her name was Dr. Andie Bennett.

Andie Bennett. A name out of his past. A person he hadn't thought of in a long time now.

Nick experienced a momentary pang of curiosity and surprisingly, of pleasure. He hadn't known that she'd settled in Thistledown after college, or that she had become a shrink, though there was no reason he should have.

Nick had kept up with Andie and her friends for a while

after Leah Robertson's murder. Because of the case. And because of his own personal interest in the girls. He'd known what had happened to the three, that they had been torn apart. And he had felt badly for them, especially for Andie. She'd been a nice kid caught in a bad situation.

Once, about six months after the murder, he had stopped by to check on her. She'd been doing fine, her mother had said. In school, trying to put the notoriety—and horror—of the experience behind her.

She had called Andie from her room, though neither mother nor daughter had seemed happy to see him. So, he'd let it go. The kid hadn't needed him coming around, dredging up the past.

Now, it seemed, fate had determined that their paths cross once again. If this Dr. Andie Bennett was even the same girl.

Nice girl, Nick thought again, remembering her honesty and conscience, recalling her open, wholesome face. Too bad she'd chosen such a scumbag profession. He'd had a general dislike for shrinks even before his wife had decided to sleep with hers. He'd been in the middle of too many cases where the defense had brought in some high-priced, mumbo-jumbo-talking headshrinker who'd gotten a criminal off or easy time. It really burned his ass.

No doubt Dr. Andie Bennett would try the same thing with this case. Nick narrowed his eyes. He'd be damned if he'd let go that easily.

First thing in the morning, he would pay a little visit to Dr. Andie Bennett.

36

Andie's morning had all the makings of a blockbuster disaster flick. Because of the previous night's indulgences, she'd overslept. When she had finally made it out to the kitchen, she'd started the coffeemaker but forgotten to put on the carafe; in her rush, she had run two pairs of new hose and her neighbor's cat had left a dead bird on her doorstep, smack-dab on top of the morning paper. To finish it all off, somebody was at her front door.

"I'm coming, I'm coming," she called, trying to walk, put on her earrings and fasten her belt all at the same time. She got the belt taken care of just as she reached the door.

A greeting died on her lips as she swung the door open. Two men stood on her front porch. Both wore dark sunglasses, sport coats and jeans. One was the size of a house, with flaming red hair. The other, nearly as big, had dark hair and a jaw that looked as if it had been carved from granite. Neither smiled.

The morning had just taken a turn for the worse.

"Dr. Andie Bennett?" the dark-haired one asked.

"Yes." Andie cocked her head slightly, recognition plucking at her. She found something familiar about the man. Something about the way he held himself, the shape of his head. The sound of his voice.

The man flashed a badge. "Police. Detectives Raphael and O'Shea. Could we speak with you a moment?"

Detective Raphael. Nick Raphael.

Her mouth dropped, and he smiled, though the curving of his lips lacked warmth. "Hello, kid."

"Detective...this is a surprise." She shook her head. "It's been a long time."

"It has. May we come in?"

"Of course." She stepped aside and swung the door wider. "I'm afraid I don't have much time. I'm running late this morning."

"This won't take long."

She led them to the living room. Interestingly, O'Shea was the curious one, openly looking around, checking her place out. Nick, as if indifferent to where she lived and what she had become, kept his gaze trained straight ahead, not even glancing slightly to the right or left.

She motioned towards the sofa, offering them a seat. Nick refused, so she stayed on her feet as well. O'Shea sat down and began idly thumbing through a magazine.

Then she realized what they were doing—good cop, bad cop. O'Shea might look like a linebacker with an attention disorder, but she would bet he missed nothing.

But why were they here? She looked at Nick Raphael. "Am I in some sort of trouble?"

"Depends on your point of view. Last night one of your patients was involved in a homicide. We need to ask you some questions, that's all."

She stared at him, stunned, then glanced from one detective to the other, waiting for the *Just kidding!* It didn't come.

"One of my patients?" she said. "You're sure?"

"Martha Pierpont."

"Oh my God." She brought a hand to her mouth and took an involuntary step backward, a dizzying sense of déjà vu sweeping over her. "He killed her," she whispered. "He did it, didn't he?"

"Who, Dr. Bennett?"

"Her husband, of course. He killed Martha."

Nick and his partner exchanged glances. Nick cleared his throat. "No, Dr. Bennett. She killed him."

Andie took another step backward, feeling behind her

for a chair. She found it and sat down. *Martha Pierpont? Killed her husband?*

Impossible.

Andie lifted her gaze to the detective's. "Is this some sort of joke?"

"No ma'am, she's in jail."

"There must be some mistake. Martha Pierpont couldn't muster enough rage to chew out a rude salesperson."

Nick took out a pocket-size notebook and a pen. "And you know this from working with her?"

"Yes, I—" Andie swallowed the words, realizing what she was doing. "Martha and I have worked together, yes."

"For just over a year?"

"Just under, actually."

"Is it true that Edward Pierpont was an abusive husband?"

"I'm sorry, Detectives, but that information is confidential."

"Is it true she was seeing you to help her deal with her lousy marriage? With her rage?"

"Again, confidential."

Nick's eyebrows shot up. "Are you referring to doctor-patient privilege?"

Andie bristled at the sarcasm in his tone. "Yes, as a matter of fact, I am."

"Convenient."

"I don't much care for your tone, Detective."

"Yeah, well, I don't much care for your line of work."

She stood and motioned toward the front door. "If that's all?"

"It's not." He smiled again, a tight twisting of his lips that was more grimace than smile. "According to your patient, her husband was an abusive, violent son of a bitch. Last night, she says, he came after her. Threatened to kill her, in fact." Nick Raphael leveled Andie with an icy stare. "Does that sound about right?"

Andie felt sick. "You seem to have already formed an opinion, Detective, so why don't you tell me?"

He ignored her sarcasm. "Anyway, according to Mrs. Pierpont, she was frightened for her life. She needed to protect herself. So she got her husband's handgun and shot him six times—"

"Five," Bobby corrected. "One bullet missed its mark."

"Five times?" Andie whispered, sitting back down. "Are you sure?"

"She shot him in the genitals, Dr. Bennett. Believe me, she's not the first wife to take aim at that particular spot, she won't be the last. That's textbook crime of passion, Dr. Bennett."

"I wouldn't know about that."

"Was Mr. Pierpont sexually abusive to his wife?"

"That's confidential."

"She shot off his face, too. Also classic crime of passion."

"Half his face," Bobby corrected again. "She probably missed. 'Course, it was kind of hard to tell, what with all the blood and brains and stuff."

They were toying with her now, trying to upset her into revealing something she ethically could not. Something she would not. She got to her feet once more. "I'm sorry, Detectives, but I'm out of time."

"Just a couple more questions. When was your last session with her?"

"A day and a half ago."

"At that time, did she say anything to you that would lead you to believe she meant to kill her husband?"

"No."

"And before that?"

Martha's words rang in her head. *I want to kill him! I want to kill him, and kill him, and kill him!*

But to say the words was one thing, to act on them another. Martha Pierpont did not have what it took to kill somebody.

Andie believed that with every fiber of her being.

She shoved her hands into her pockets so the detectives couldn't see that they trembled. "As I explained already, I'm unable to discuss anything having to do with my treatment of Martha Pierpont. Now, if you don't mind, I'm late."

"Are you sure there's nothing else you'd like to tell us?"

"There's nothing else I can tell you, Detective. I'm sorry."

"Sorry, my ass."

"Nick—"

Nick ignored his partner's warning and took a step toward her, his already hard mouth thinning more. "Is it fun hiding behind your so-called ethics? How does it feel to know you help criminals get back out on the street? How does it feel to know you're part of the reason crime pays."

She met his gaze. "*Criminals* like Martha Pierpont? Please."

"She murdered her husband, Dr. Bennett. She shot him at point-blank range, five times. Yes, she's a criminal."

Andie's cheeks heated. "So what are you saying, Detective Raphael? That my patient was not acting in self-defense? That she killed her husband in cold blood?"

"Let's just say it wouldn't surprise me, Dr. Bennett."

A furious retort jumped to her lips; she swallowed it. He wanted her to get angry. He wanted her to hotly defend Martha and perhaps let something slip that he would twist to use against the woman. "You've changed, Detective. No longer the Boy Scout, I see. You've become just like those other detectives. The ones who had no heart." She crossed to the door, opened it and swung it wide. "Good day."

Bobby stood and the two men crossed to the door. Nick took a step through, then stopped and turned back to her. He handed her his card. "If you think of anything that's not...privileged, give us a call. We'd appreciate it."

37

For long moments after the two detectives left, Andie gazed at the card in her hand, reminded of the past, so clearly it took her breath. She ran her thumb across the slightly raised printing, remembering her first meeting with Nick Raphael and how different he had been from the other detectives, the ones who'd had so much fun at her expense.

She could hardly believe that the tough, emotionless man she had just spoken to was the same one who had helped her all those years ago, the same man who had used his body to shield her from the gruesome sight of Mrs. X, the same one who had jumped to her defense with the press, the one who had come to see her months after, just to make sure she was all right.

What had happened to Nick Raphael? Where had all that anger and hard-edged cynicism come from?

Sadness moved over her. All these years she had remembered him and his kindness to her. The memory had been special. Important. Like a spot of light in an otherwise frighteningly dark time.

Andie crossed to the front door and the sidelight to its right. She gazed out at the day, at the street. Even his face had changed, she thought. It, too, had become harder, leaner. Etched by time and hard-earned experience, by the loss of rosy-eyed youth.

Is that what he thought when he looked at her? she wondered. How did she compare to the girl he had known? Did he think her attractive? As attractive as she found him?

Andie shivered suddenly and rubbed her arms. The past didn't matter. How Nick Raphael had or hadn't changed didn't matter. Martha Pierpont was in trouble, big trouble. Martha needed her.

Checking her watch, Andie turned away from the window and hurried to grab her purse and briefcase from the kitchen counter. She would call Missy from the car and have her begin canceling and rescheduling her morning appointments. Then she would give the police a call and see how soon she could get in to see her patient.

Less than an hour later, Andie faced Martha across a battered metal table at central lockup, a lump in her throat. Martha looked ten years older than she had just two days before; she looked as if she had walked down the corridors of hell and had lived to tell the tale.

Andie reached across the table and covered Martha's hands with her own. They were as cold as ice. "Are you all right?"

"He's dead. Edward is. Have you heard?"

"Yes, Martha," Andie said gently, "I heard. Can you tell me what happened?"

The woman's hands began to shake. "I shot him. I don't know how many times, but more than once."

I shot him. Andie swallowed hard. Until now, until Martha uttered those words, Andie hadn't believed it was true. "That's what the police said."

"You talked to the police?"

"They came to my home this morning." Andie gave Martha's hands a reassuring squeeze. "You needn't worry, Martha, anything we've discussed during your sessions is privileged."

"I didn't mean to do it." Her voice quivered. "I just wanted him to stop."

Andie rubbed Martha's hands trying to warm them. "Tell me what happened."

Martha nodded, drew her hands away and dropped them into her lap. "We hadn't even gotten home from the benefit when he started in on me. I'd never seen him that angry before. He was going to punish me, he said. When we got home. He was going to make me pay.''

"Punish you for what, Martha? Did he say?"

She shook her head. "I don't know. I did something... I don't know."

"It's all right," said Andie reassuringly. "Go on."

"As soon as he pulled into the drive, I jumped out of the car and ran for the house. I was going to lock myself in the bedroom. I got the front door open and stumbled inside. But he was right behind me."

She struggled to continue, her eyes wide and blank with remembered terror. Andie found herself drawn into the horror of the scene.

"He...he caught me in the hallway. He knocked me down. I was pleading, begging for him to...to let me go. He got his hands around my neck and starting choking me."

She brought a hand to her throat, and Andie saw the bruises. She shuddered. "I remember looking up at him and thinking that this was it, that he was going to do it. He was going to kill me. His face was red and his eyes...they were bulging out. The whole time he was yelling...screaming at me."

She made a small, helpless motion with her hands. "I kicked and clawed. I broke free and scrambled to my feet. I ran to our bedroom, I got his gun. He was right behind me. I shouted for him to stop. To stop or I'd shoot."

She met Andie's eyes. "He laughed at me, Dr. Bennett. He said I didn't have the guts to do it. He said I was a stupid, worthless cunt and he was going to kill me.

"He kept coming. He kept laughing. Something inside me... I couldn't take it anymore. I...I pulled the trigger. Again. And again. And then he just...he stopped."

Andie swallowed hard, stunned. Only yesterday, she would have sworn Martha incapable of such an act. But the human psyche could be pushed only so far before it snapped. ''What happened next?''

''I don't know, not exactly. Patti was screaming. And then there were people…police.'' She bowed her head. ''They brought me here.''

Martha looked around her as if remembering where she was, as if seeing once more the concrete walls, the guard, the steel door. ''Now, my baby is all alone. And when I go to prison, she'll have nobody.''

''Don't think about that, Martha. You've got a good lawyer, from what I hear the best around, and from what you're telling me you shot Ed in self-defense. The court recognizes spousal abuse as a legitimate reason for self-defense. If you feared for your life, you were only protecting yourself.''

''What if they don't believe me?'' Martha whispered, refusing to be consoled. ''Everybody liked Edward. They won't believe me. I'll go to prison and Patti will be alone.'' She started to cry.

Andie went around the table and put her arms around the woman, aware of the guard's unwavering gaze. ''I'll testify. So will Patti. You've got bruises, Martha, that's proof. You're going to beat this thing. It's going to be okay.''

''Will you go see her, Dr. Bennett? Will you go see Patti?'' Martha drew away to look into Andie's eyes, pleading. ''I'm so worried about her. Will you just make sure she's okay?''

Andie agreed, of course. She learned the child was staying with Martha's mother, a widow who lived in an old neighborhood close to downtown. Andie called the woman, Rose Turpin was her name, introduced herself and asked if it would be convenient for her to come by. Mrs. Turpin not only said yes, she sounded near tears with gratitude. Andie told her she would be there as soon as she could, but that it might take a while.

A while turned out to be an understatement. It wasn't

until much later that afternoon that Andie was able to clear her schedule to visit the girl. By the time she pulled up in front of the grandmother's bungalow, she was exhausted. She had seen back-to-back patients, trying to fit in as many as she could, not leaving herself time for anything but the quickest bathroom break. Raven had called three times, Julie twice, both to find out if she had heard about Mayor Pierpont's murder.

Finally, Andie had squeezed out a minute to call her friends back; they had been shocked at Andie's involvement, then hungry for details about the murder. It had been all she could do not to snap at them, particularly Raven. Her friend thought everything was a big joke and had cavalierly blown off Andie's concerns over Martha's actions and her own accountability.

Andie couldn't blow off her own concerns. She felt responsible. She should have been able to do something to stop it. But she hadn't, and now all that was left for her to do was try to help Martha and her family after the fact.

Andie turned off the engine and looked up at the house. A woman stood in the open doorway. Rose Turpin, no doubt. Martha's mother.

Andie held up a hand in greeting, got out of the car and went up the walk.

"Thank you for coming," the woman said, wringing her hands. "I'm so worried about Patti."

Andie smiled reassuringly. "I hope I can help. I'll try."

"Come in." Mrs. Turpin led her inside and to the front parlor. The drapes were drawn, the lights off. Lines of sunlight peeked around the edges of the heavy drapes.

Patti huddled in a big wing-back chair, completely closed in on herself, her knees drawn up to her chest, arms around her knees, face pressed to them. A sitting version of the fetal position.

Mrs. Turpin switched on a table lamp. "Patti," she said gently, "there's someone here to see you. Dr. Bennett."

The girl didn't acknowledge her in any way. Andie took

another step into the room, carefully closing the distance between them. "Hello, Patti. I'm a friend of your mother's. She asked me to look in on you."

Patti glanced up. "Her shrink, you mean."

"That's right, I'm her therapist. But I think of her as a friend, too." Andie took a seat on the sofa across from the teenager. "How are you, Patti?"

The girl shrugged.

"I saw your mother this morning." Patti lifted her gaze for a moment, but only a moment. "She's worried about you."

Patti tightened her arms around her knees. "I'm okay," she whispered, then drew in a deep, quivering breath. "Is she...is she all right?"

"She's hanging in there."

Patti said nothing. Andie waited, using the moments to study the girl. Andie had seen her out and about before; Martha had shown her photographs. But until this moment, Andie hadn't realized how alike mother and daughter were. Patti had the same soft, pretty features, the same petite frame and gentle voice.

Andie cocked her head slightly. It surprised her that Edward Pierpont hadn't turned any of his rage his daughter's way.

It would have only been a matter of time, she thought, suppressing a sigh. Abusers like Ed Pierpont rarely excluded other family members, particularly ones of the same sex, from their violence and rage.

If it hadn't happened already.

The thought caught her by surprise, though Andie couldn't imagine why, it was so obvious. It troubled her. What if Edward had turned his fury on his daughter? What if Martha had become aware of the abuse and been forced out of her state of denial? It could explain Martha's sudden courage; it could have facilitated her tenuous hold on reality to snap, the way she had described.

Andie clasped her hands in her lap. She was drawing

conclusions without anything but hunches to back them up. But, if what she feared was true, Patti was going to need a friend.

Andie cleared her throat. "I thought maybe we could talk about what happened."

"I told the police everything."

"That's not what I mean. I want to help you."

"No one ca…" Her eyes filled, and she pressed her lips together. "I don't want to talk about it."

"I understand."

"No, you don't. You can't."

"I want to understand, then. I really do. Maybe if you explained it to me—"

"I said, I don't want to talk about it!" Patti leaped to her feet and faced her, visibly shaking, hands clenched at her sides. She opened her mouth, as if to say something more, then turned and ran from the room. Moments later, Andie heard a door slam shut someplace in the house.

Andie shifted her gaze to Patti's grandmother, hovering in the doorway, her expression devastated. "Give her time," Andie said softly. "She's had a terrible shock."

The woman nodded, then met Andie's gaze. "Would you like a glass of iced tea?"

"Thank you." Andie stood. "That would be nice."

Andie followed the older woman into the kitchen. Rose Turpin motioned to one of the high stools at the breakfast bar. "Have a seat." Andie did and the woman got out a pitcher of tea and two tall glasses. She filled them both with ice and looked at Andie. "Lemon? Sweet?"

"Lemon, please."

The woman nodded, got a lemon out of a fruit bowl on the counter and expertly wedged it. She filled the glasses and garnished both with a sprig of mint. She did it all with the mindless movements of someone who has done the same thing hundreds of times before.

"Here you go," she said, setting the glass on the counter in front of Andie. "It's sun tea."

Andie sipped, murmured her appreciation and waited, knowing Martha's mother had not asked her into the kitchen simply to offer a refreshment.

"The bail hearing's set for tomorrow. Marti's lawyer said that considering the circumstances, he believes the judge will set it at a reasonable amount."

"She'll be going home then? Or coming here?"

"Coming here. We thought it would be easier on Patti." The grandmother looked down at her hands, wrapped around the sweating glass. "I don't know what to do about Patti, Dr. Bennett. She won't talk to me. She's barely had anything to eat or drink since she got here."

"It hasn't been that long. Not even twenty-four hours ago her whole world turned upside down."

The woman brought a trembling hand to her mouth, struggling, Andie saw, to compose herself. "What should I do about school? She still has about a month before summer vacation. I hate to have her miss, but to go ba…"

She let the thought trail off because she knew as well as Andie did, that Patti would not be going back to Thistledown High until next year. If then.

"Talk to her teachers. Get them to send home her lessons, hire a tutor if you have to."

"All right."

"Does she have any friends she can talk to?"

Rose shook her head. "Not the kind of friends who would understand. My granddaughter was a bit of a loner."

Andie understood, probably better than most. When she had lost her best friends she, too, had been a loner. And she, too, had been forced to face terrible gossip with no one to talk to.

"How are you doing, Mrs. Turpin?"

"Me?"

"Yes. I know this has been a shock for you, too. It's an awful thing."

"I don't believe she did it. Not my baby. Not my sweet

Marti. She couldn't have done that to Ed.'' Rose looked at Andie as if challenging her to disagree.

Instead, Andie concurred. ''I find it difficult to believe also. But the facts speak for themselves. She did do it.''

At Andie's words, the fire drained out of the woman. ''I know. They say the gun was in her hands...that she...that she shot him five times.''

''Because she feared for her life. Don't forget that, Mrs. Turpin. It wasn't murder, it was self-defense.''

The woman nodded, eyes bright with tears. ''I will. Thank you.''

Andie drew a careful breath. ''Can I ask you a question?''

''I suppose.''

''Did you know Edward was an abusive husband?''

The woman looked away. ''Yes, I knew.''

''Did you urge your daughter to leave him?''

Rose Turpin shook her head. ''No, I...'' She spread her hands. ''He was a good provider. An important man. I just thought, if she tried harder, if she... He would...stop.''

Andie counted to three before responding. She wasn't in the judgment business. She was here to help and support. ''Ed's abuse,'' she said softly, ''was about *him*, Mrs. Turpin. Not about your daughter. Ed Pierpont was ill, and nothing your daughter did invited that kind of treatment.''

An awkward silence fell between them; Andie acknowledged that the time had come to go. She stood. ''The tea was delicious, thank you.''

''You're welcome. Will you...come by again?''

''Of course.'' She smiled. ''I'll stop by tomorrow to look in on Patti. If she needs to talk in the meantime, here's my card.'' Andie dug one out of her purse and handed it to Rose. ''You can reach me anytime, day or night. Don't hesitate to call.''

''Thank you, Dr. Bennett.'' Mrs. Turpin walked her to the door. There, Andie turned and met her eyes once more.

"As far as you know, from what you observed, was Ed a good father?"

"I suppose so. He seemed like most fathers."

"Was he ever abusive to Patti? Did Martha ever say?"

"I don't think so," she said after a moment. "I mean…no, I'm sure he wasn't. Martha wouldn't have stood for it."

"What do you mean?"

"Just that. She wouldn't allow it. She told me more than once that if Edward ever laid a hand on Patti, she would get Patti away from him. No matter the cost."

Andie thanked the woman and walked away, wondering if that cost had been Edward Pierpont's life.

38

"It's awful, Andie. Just awful." Julie bopped into Andie's office, flopped onto the couch and gazed up at the ceiling. "That poor woman. From what I've heard, her husband deserved what he got." She glanced over at Andie. "Raven thinks so, too."

Andie shook her head. Julie had been doing that since they were kids, using Raven's opinion to validate her own. "So she said."

"It's all anybody can talk about. Did you see? You've been mentioned in the paper every day. For the past week."

"Don't remind me, it hasn't been great for business. Besides, the whole thing is too much like... Never mind."

"What?" Julie eased onto her side and met Andie's eyes. "Too much like the past?"

Julie said that so easily. But she hadn't been here; she didn't know what it had been like to be stared at and whispered about everywhere she went. Julie didn't realize just how long the memories in Thistledown, Missouri, were. "Yeah, the past."

"Well, I think it's kind of cool." Julie returned her gaze to the ceiling. "Is this where your patients tell you all their secrets?" She snuggled into the sumptuous leather. "I could live on a couch like this."

"Some of my patients think they do." Andie smiled, amused and charmed by her friend. It had been fun having Julie back in town. It had been like old times, the three of them acting more like teenagers than grown women with responsibilities.

Especially Julie. Of the three of them, Julie had changed the least in the past fifteen years. She had long ago exchanged her glasses for contacts, but other than that she seemed every bit the giddy teenager at thirty she had been at fifteen.

In her tight blue jeans and clingy T-shirt, her mane of long blond hair streaked and tousled, she looked the part, too.

But Andie knew the problems, and the pain, Julie's flighty, devil-may-care exterior masked.

"How are you doing?" Andie asked her.

"Great. Fabulous." Julie folded her arms behind her head. "Raven's been a dream. She's better to me than a mother."

Coddling her. Clucking over her like a mother hen. Fine for a while, Andie thought. But in the long run, it wasn't an answer to Julie's problems.

"I got an apartment, did you know? Raven helped me with that, too. I'm going to pay her back."

"Really?"

"No, I am." Julie sat up and swung her legs over the side of the couch. She fluffed her hair. "I have a job interview today. At the country club. The guy I talked with on the phone said that with my experience, I should have no problem being hired."

"Waitress?"

"No, bartender at the club bar. He said they make great tips." She laughed and fluffed her hair again. "At least the young, cute ones do. I think I still qualify, don't you?"

Andie made a sound of concern. "The bar? Oh, Julie, I don't know about that."

"I know what you're thinking, Andie. But I've given up men. I have. I'm a changed woman."

"Julie, honey, you can't just *give up* an addi..." Andie let the words trail off. What she wanted to tell her was, you couldn't just give up an addiction. Even one you denied you had.

Andie had realized several years back that Julie was a sex addict. She had made her diagnosis during one of Julie's between-marriage visits, when she had been home long enough for Andie to spend some time with her. Julie used men and sex the way other addicts used pills or booze. As a way to forget, to validate, to escape. And like many addicts, Julie wasn't ready to admit she had a problem, not one that had a hold of her anyway.

Andie had been heartsick at the realization and had tried to talk to her friend about it. Julie had become defensive, she'd retreated deeply into denial and accused Andie of being jealous. Because Andie had never been married. Because men didn't like Andie the way they liked her. Because Andie wasn't as sexy, as open, as fun.

Her friend's words had cut Andie to the core, and hard feelings had been between them for months. Andie had decided then and there that friendship and therapy didn't mix. If Julie ever admitted she had a problem, Andie would be the first to try to help. She would recommend a therapist; she would even pay for her friend's sessions. Until that time, however, she would look the other way, supporting Julie as best she could without enabling her addiction. And without having to push the issue.

"Good for you, Julie," she said, forcing a smile. "I just want you to be happy."

"I know you don't think I can do it, but I can. I'm done with cruising." She took a deep breath, excited, almost manic. "I've turned my life around, Andie. I'm here with you and Raven. You guys are all I need."

At Andie's silence, she laughed, undaunted. "Just you wait. I'll show both of you. You're looking at the brand-new Julie Cooper."

39

The bar was empty. It usually was this time of day during the week, Julie had discovered. On weekdays, women populated the club early in the day and over the lunch hour, men in the late afternoon and early evening. The couples and the die-hard drinkers came in at night.

Julie's favorite time of day was when the men started filtering in off the golf course. They were boisterous and raunchy; they made her laugh and left her great tips.

But it was so much more than that. She liked men, and they liked her. It had always been that way. Raven and Andie didn't understand that. They didn't understand what it was like for her. It was almost as if she were a lightbulb, men the switch. They lit her up, they turned her on. Around the opposite sex was the only time Julie felt special.

Of course, those late-afternoon hours offered her more of an opportunity to score. They would, anyway, if she was still doing that.

She wasn't.

Annoyed with her thoughts, Julie grabbed the TV remote and started surfing. Talk show. Talk show. Cartoons. Bad soap. She muttered an oath and switched off the TV.

Nothing to take her mind off sex.

Or rather, her current lack of it.

Julie breathed deeply through her nose, a jittery, nervous sensation in the pit of her stomach. It had been five weeks since she'd had a man. Five weeks without the mindless, exhilarating rush she got from scoring. She was going crazy. She couldn't eat or sleep, she thought about sex constantly. She thought about doing it with every man who came into the bar, even the fat, bald ones.

She was almost out of control.

No, she wasn't. Julie squeezed her eyes shut. She hadn't acted on her thoughts. That meant she was in control. All she had to do was keep saying no, keep focusing on Raven and Andie and the promises she had made to them both.

She could do this. Raven said she could. And Raven knew everything; she always had. All Julie had to do was lean on her friend, and everything would be all right.

"Hi. You open for business?"

Julie opened her eyes. A man, tall, dark-haired and stunningly handsome in his tennis whites, sauntered into the bar. Julie smiled, the jittery sensation moving straight south. "Sure am." She set a coaster in front of him. "What would you like?"

The man—she guessed him to be somewhere in his mid-forties—returned her smile, his gaze sliding from her eyes to her chest. "That's a rather loaded question."

She laughed and flipped her hair over her shoulder, knowing she was coming on to him but helpless to stop herself. "To drink, I mean. What can I get you?"

"A beer's good," he murmured, bringing his gaze back to hers. "Draft."

"You got it." She took a mug from the freezer, filled it and set the foaming beverage in front of him. As she did, she looked him directly in the eyes. "Can I get you anything else?"

"Maybe." His smile promised heaven on earth. Julie found herself mesmerized by it and by his hypnotic blue gaze. "You're new here."

She leaned against the bar, a telltale twitch of awareness between her legs. "Just started a few days ago. Everybody's been real friendly."

"That's us. Given the opportunity, we can be real

friendly.'' He looked at her name tag. ''So, where you from, Julie?''

''Most recently, California. Originally, Thistledown.''

''Came running home to mama?''

''No.'' She shifted slightly and the crotch of her jeans rubbed against her clitoris. The sensation all but took her breath. ''I burned out on the California scene, and I have friends here.''

Just then a group of men entered the bar. They caught sight of the man and howled. ''David,'' one roared, ''you wuss! Should have known you'd be in here, dressed in your pretty whites, instead of out with the real men on the course.''

''What real men?'' he shot back, laughing, unperturbed.

The rowdy group, several of whom she already recognized both as regulars and heavy drinkers, took a table in the corner. They had, obviously, been drinking for some time already.

''Julie—'' one motioned the table ''—beers all around, babe.''

''Coming right up, guys.'' She looked apologetically at David. ''Duty calls.''

He leaned toward her, eyes crinkling at the corners with amusement. ''Uncivilized beasts, aren't they?''

She wetted her lips. ''Uncivilized can be good. Depending on the time and place.''

He slid his gaze to her breasts again, then lower, to the vee of her thighs, outlined clearly in her tight white jeans. She caught her breath, immediately on fire. Aching. Wet.

He leaned toward her. ''Uncivilized can be dangerous, Julie. You like it dangerous?''

''Come on, babe,'' one of the guys from the corner table called. ''We're dying of thirst here. And, David, man, get your ass over here. You're keeping Julie from her work.''

He shot her a quick smile, then started toward the men.

She watched him go, then busied herself getting beers for the table, cursing herself as she did. Why had she said those things? She had all but offered herself to him right there.

What was wrong with her? She wasn't doing that anymore. She wasn't.

She brought the tray of beers to the table, then stood and talked to the guys a while, laughing and flirting, the whole time focused on David's silence, his speculative gaze on her, on the electricity that seemed to crackle between them.

Talk at the table died an awkward death. It was as if the other men had suddenly noticed the current between her and David. Her cheeks flamed, and she took a step backward, mumbling something about needing to get set up for the evening crowd.

She walked back to the bar, aware of the men's gazes on her ass as she did. Aware of David's gaze. She swallowed hard, excited, feeling about to burn up. She had promised Raven she was finished with her previous life. She had promised Andie she would be careful, that she would think before she got involved with another man.

She was the new, improved Julie Cooper. She had made it five weeks. She couldn't give in now; the hardest part was behind her.

She wanted the hardest part inside her.

Julie began to sweat and grabbed a rag and began wiping down the bar. No more men, she told herself sternly. No cruising for sex. No more.

From the corner table came a burst of laughter. She could pick out David's laugh, could feel it. It rippled along her nerve endings, deep, exciting. Full of promise.

She pressed herself against the corner of the bar well; if she moved just so, the top of a bottle brushed against her crotch. She imagined it was David's hand, David's finger. She imagined it was his nose as he buried his tongue deep inside her.

She thought of her friends, her promise to them. Her throat tightened with tears, despair. She could do it. Raven said so. Raven said this was her chance to turn her life around. All she had to do was try. All she had to do was say no.

Even as she told herself not to, she glanced at the men, at David. He was different, she thought. Special. She didn't know why, but he was. Call it instinct or a premonition. But she had a feeling about him. That they were connected somehow, that they were meant to meet.

That he would change her life.

She struggled to breathe evenly. She had told herself that before, Julie reminded herself. Hadn't she? With husband number one, two and three, with countless men in between.

She turned her back to the group, pretending to be straightening the bottles of liqueurs. She reminded herself of her failed marriages. She called herself the names she had been called by countless others, starting with her father. Whore. Slut. Jezebel. Cunt.

The words hurt. She hated them, hated that they were true.

And they were true. She knew it, so why fight what she was? She would never win, never be anything better than what she was.

Julie turned and looked at the table of men again. As if sensing her gaze, David looked up. Even as she told herself to look the other way, she smiled—her ''yes'' smile, the one that left no question about what she wanted.

''I have to visit the stockroom,'' she announced, dragging her gaze from David's and directing it to the entire table, her words sounding forced and false even to her own ears. ''Anybody need anything? I'll be a few minutes.''

They didn't and she exited the bar, counting every step, her legs feeling at once leaden and featherlight. She reached the stockroom, unlocked it and went inside, leaving the door ajar.

As she had hoped he would, David followed her. She

turned and faced him, breathing hard, a feeling of fate, of inevitability, rolling over her like thunder.

He closed and bolted the door behind him. "So, little Julie," he said softly, "tell me now. Do you like it dangerous?"

She took a step toward him, sweat beading on her upper lip, rolling between her breasts. She brought her hands to the waistband of his shorts, first to the button, then the zipper. As she brought herself to her knees, she lifted her gaze to his. "What do you think?"

A moment later, at nothing more than the feel of him in her mouth, she came violently. In that moment, she remembered what it was to be alive, vibrantly, exhilaratingly alive.

And she remembered what it was like to be dead.

Julie Cooper was a dead woman.

40

Andie sat across from the man, listening carefully as he explained why he had sought her out, jotting down an occasional note as she did. His name was David Sadler, and he had found her through, of all places, the newspaper and the numerous mentions of her name in regards to the Pierpont case. Having a patient in jail for killing her husband didn't seem much of a testimonial to Andie, but apparently David Sadler had a different opinion.

He had sought her out in the hopes of getting help with his abnormal sexual appetite.

"I can't leave women alone," he said. "All it takes is meeting a woman's eyes, hearing her laugh, catching a glimpse of her breasts, and I can't think about anything but scoring with her. And it doesn't stop with just thinking about it, I make it happen. It doesn't matter if I'm in love with someone else, if I'm married. Nothing."

He looked down at the floor, then back up at her. "This…it's ruined every relationship I've ever had. Even my relationship with my family."

"What brought you here, David?"

"I told you, the newspaper—"

"That's not what I mean." She smiled gently. "What brought you to this place, to seek help."

He looked away again. "My father died recently. We'd had a falling-out over my behavior with women." He took a deep breath. "More than ten years ago I left Thistledown to run the St. Louis arm of the business. In all that time we'd barely spoken, and then only about the business. And now he's dead.''

"I'm sorry."

"Thank you." A smile of gratitude touched his mouth. "You've probably heard of my family, we're Sadler Construction."

"Of course." Andie inclined her head. Sadler Construction was responsible for just about every development in Thistledown since the 1960s. "Your father was liked and respected. He donated a considerable amount of time and money to Thistledown's many charities."

"He was that kind of man." David laced his fingers together. "Now that he's gone...I guess I see something I didn't before. I regret the years we spent apart. I regret...everything." He looked back up at Andie, his expression tortured. "Do you think you can help me?"

"I can try, David. You've already taken the first, and sometimes hardest, step. You've admitted you have a problem. You've sought help. That's big, David. It's important. Over the next weeks and months, I want you to remember that."

"So, you'll work with me?"

"Yes. Of course."

He smiled and Andie caught her breath. She had thought him attractive before, dark wavy hair, silvering at the temples, tall with an athletic build. But his smile was totally charming. It transformed his face into a boyish, little bit naughty delight.

Obviously he'd never had to worry about attracting women. Which, no doubt, had facilitated his illness.

Andie stood and held out her hand. "Missy will make you an appointment. It's been very nice meeting you."

He followed her to her feet and grasped her hand. "One more question, Dr. Bennett. I have to be assured that anything I say will be strictly confidential. As I'm sure you understand, I'm well known in the community and can't risk news of my...problem getting out."

"Put your mind at rest, David. All our work together is confidential. Even my patient list is privileged." She walked him to her office door and opened it. "Missy," she said to her receptionist, "David needs an appointment for later this week."

The young woman nodded and reached around to hand her several pink message slips. As she did, her low-cut blouse gaped at the neck, revealing the curve of her breasts, spilling over the top of her lacy bra. Andie slid her gaze to David Sadler. She was not the only one who had noticed.

Andie's cheeks warmed. She would have to speak with Missy about what she wore. Considering this particular patient's problem, she would have to be more aware of her own clothing choice from now on, as well.

"Raven called while you were in session," Missy was saying. "She said it was important."

"Thanks, Missy. I'll call her back now." Andie smiled at David. "See you next time."

Andie returned to her office, went right to the phone and dialed Raven. Her friend picked up right away.

"Hi," Andie said. "What's so important?"

"Have you checked your mail yet?"

"No, I've been with a patient."

"Get it. I'll hold."

Something in her friend's voice told her this wasn't a joke. She put Raven on hold, buzzed Missy and asked her to bring in the day's mail, then reconnected with Raven. "What am I looking for?"

"You'll know it when you see it."

Andie arched her eyebrows. "A mystery, huh? Okay." Just then, Missy entered the office, carrying the stack of mail. She handed it to Andie.

"Got it," Andie said, propping the phone to her ear. She leafed through the pieces. "Investment broker, yuck. Postcard from my mother." She turned it over and scanned it. "She's having a very nice time, saw Disney World.

Pete's new baby's gorgeous. Video-club offer. Another investment broker. Don't those guys sleep?''

She stopped at a plain white envelope, addressed to her and marked "Personal." Pay dirt, she would bet. Andie ripped it open. Inside was a newspaper clipping, yellow with age. She swallowed hard, prickles of fear tripping up her spine.

She unfolded the newsprint, knowing what she would find, but needing to see it anyway.

Three Girls Implicated in Kinky Sex, Murder.

"You found it, didn't you?" Raven said. "The clipping from fifteen years ago?"

"Yes." Andie stared at the piece, at the photo of her and her friends, at another of Leah Robertson, before her death.

"Who do you think sent it?"

Andie looked at the envelope. There was no return address but it was postmarked Thistledown. "I don't know."

"It gave me the creeps." Raven let out a long breath. "I don't like this, Andie."

"Did Julie—"

"Yeah. And she's pretty shaken up. You know Julie."

She did know Julie, and this was the last thing her friend needed right now. In truth, it was the last thing any of them needed.

Andie drew her eyebrows together. "It's probably the Pierpont case, Rave. My name associated with another sensational murder. Detective Raphael's, too. This town has a long memory."

"You're probably right."

But it was weird, Andie had to admit. Disturbing. Why would someone target all three of them, simply because of the Pierpont case? Her, she could understand. But not all three of them.

She lowered her eyes to the clipping, suddenly realizing something. "Rave, is yours a photocopy or the real thing?"

''Real thing.''

''Is it the 'Three Girls Implicated in Kinky Sex, Murder' story?''

''Yup. So was Julie's. Yours?''

''Guess?'' Andie muttered.

Someone had collected and saved actual clippings, three alike.

She heard Raven's sudden intake of breath and knew that her friend had just made the connection. For a moment, both women were silent. Then Raven spoke. ''So, Andie, you're the headshrinker. Are we dealing with some sort of a wacko here, or what?''

41

Raven took extra care dressing that morning. Today she had the biggest interview of her career. David Sadler, of Sadler Construction, had called out of the blue, requesting an appointment. His company had broken ground on an exclusive gated community twenty minutes outside of Thistledown, toward St. Louis. The project was aimed at the big-city executives who wanted to move their families to a more rural setting; the location, strategically located minutes from the interstate, cut the commute by at least a third, in some cases by half. They were looking for a design firm to do the model and spec homes, he said. He and the owner of the last firm, a big name from St. Louis, had not seen eye-to-eye, and he had canned them.

Rave Reviews had been recommended to him. He needed somebody fast.

Raven was thrilled. This was a job that would rocket her from a one-woman outfit to a medium-size firm with several designers under her. With Sadler's development on her résumé, she could pitch other like-size projects. No more small-time residential. No more rich housewives whining about cost, no more having to deal with atrociously bad taste or impossibly boring spaces.

Raven took one last glance in her mirror, eyeing her legs, which in the short skirt and sheer hose she'd chosen, seemed even longer than they were. With a satisfied smile, she fluffed her hair and turned to go. David Sadler was a man, and she had heard, a womanizer. She wanted this job, and if a short skirt and an accidental glimpse of something forbidden would help her land it, so be it. She believed in using the gifts she had been given. All of them.

She headed outside, locking the front door behind her. Of course, she would never depend on feminine wiles to land a job, they were like the dessert that came after a spectacular gourmet meal, the butter-cream frosting on a perfectly baked cake.

Raven opened the car door, tossed her briefcase onto the front passenger seat, then climbed in. She had done her homework. After sixty years in business, Sadler Construction was more than solvent, it was rock-solid. They were responsible for nearly every commercial building and residential development in Thistledown, including Happy Hollow, her childhood stomping ground. The company had satellite offices in St. Louis and Memphis, both doing very well. Until Jackson Sadler's death three months before, David, his only son, had run the St. Louis outfit.

Asking around, she had heard a bit of gossip about the family. David Sadler was an infamous pussy hound and had gotten himself in a number of scrapes over women, either with their fathers, husbands or the juvenile authorities—although the last had been a one-time mistake. Raven had also heard the elder and younger Sadler had not gotten along, and that David's stint in St. Louis had been a banishment.

She turned onto Second Street, recalling her conversation with Sadler. He was home now, he'd said. And ready to take the company into the next century. He needed a design firm to make the leap with him. From what he'd heard about her, he had a feeling Rave Reviews was just the firm he'd been looking for.

She smiled, determined. She planned to confirm his feeling this morning. She wanted this job.

Raven pulled into the parking area beside the building that housed her company, a restored Victorian bungalow. She saw that her assistant, Laura, had already arrived. She had instructed the woman to order a small tray of European pastries for the meeting with Sadler, brew some of the Kona coffee she had picked up in Hawaii and freshen all the flower arrangements. Laura was nothing if not dependable.

She swung out of her car and headed inside. "Laura," she called, "I'm here."

Laura came rushing out from the back, her cheeks flushed, eyes wild. Her mouth worked, but no sound came out. In her hot-pink and orange sheath, she looked like a bright-colored bird, startled out of its hiding place.

Raven laughed. "Laura, what in the world's wrong with you?"

"I'm afraid I've caused her to become quite undone. Raven Johnson, I presume?"

Raven realized immediately what was wrong with her assistant. David Sadler had arrived early. Very early. She turned slowly to face him, working to mask her annoyance. Her gaze met his. Her world rocked.

The man standing before her, hand extended and smiling politely, was none other than Mr. X.

42

Much later, Raven sat alone in her dark bedroom. She huddled in a corner, her three-hundred-dollar silk skirt bunched up around her thighs, her back pressed against the wall, remembering.

She was fifteen again, hidden in the cramped closet of the empty house, peering through the inch-wide crack between the door and the jamb. Waiting. Heart thundering. Afraid. Excited.

She moved closer to the sliver of space, anxious to catch a glimpse of him, Mr. X. She trembled. She prayed, the waiting interminable.

Finally, she heard his voice. David's voice. Deep and silky smooth. Powerful. Raven's heart leaped; she pressed closer to the door.

He had come. The woman was with him. He told Mrs. X what he expected her to do, quietly, brooking no disobedience. The rope awaited, its end tied into a noose. Beneath it a step stool, her lifeline.

Mrs. X was naked. Blindfolded, her hands bound in front of her. Raven saw her trembling. She pleaded for mercy.

David told her again what he wanted, this time sharply, as if annoyed. Mrs. X stepped onto the stool, sobbing now. Begging for her life.

For all her tears and pleading, however, she was a willing lamb. She did as he asked without a fight.

Murmuring words of love, of praise, David slipped the noose over her head, then fitted it around her neck. He tightened it to the point it caused discomfort, Raven saw. Tightened it to the point that the slightest move constricted her windpipe, cutting off her breath.

Then he made love to her, with his hands and mouth. Mrs. X cried out in pleasure, and pain, as he brought her to orgasm again and again, until, Raven saw, she hardly had the strength to stand.

Raven pressed the heels of her hands to her eyes, fighting back the memory, knowing how it would end, with Mrs. X's body twitching with her last breath of life.

She didn't want to go there, not again.

She didn't have a choice. The past had sought her out.

Raven dropped her hands. She opened her right. On her palm lay a circle of gold, a symbol of eternity, of everlasting love. A wedding ring. *Mrs. X's wedding ring.*

That last day, Raven had seen it there, lying on the dresser. It had caught the light, seeming to wink at her. In one of those decisions made without conscious thought, she had grabbed it and tucked it into her shorts' pocket. As a prize, she supposed. A memento.

Now it could be so much more.

David Sadler was Mr. X. The man the police had been wanting for fifteen years. The man who had haunted Raven's thoughts and dreams for that same amount of time. She had looked for him every day of each one of those years, expecting to see him on a crowded sidewalk or across a busy restaurant.

Instead, he had found her. Raven dropped her hands and rested her head against the wall. Mr. X. The only man she had ever felt a real connection with. From him she had learned what it meant to hold another's life and fate in your hands, he had shown her that sex was power and never to relinquish control of people or situations.

Without even knowing she was near, he had changed her life, had taken all the pieces of her and rearranged them so she was stronger, smarter, more courageous.

This morning, he had smiled at her, in the way she remembered from all those years ago. And she had known what he was doing. He hadn't sought her out because of her firm or some recommendation, though she had grabbed the job with both hands when he'd offered it to her.

No, he had purposely sought her out because of her connection to his past. Probably as a way to relive his kinky affair with Leah Robertson.

Raven smiled. She knew this man. She knew how he thought, what got him off. Working with her, knowing she was the one who had watched him dominate Leah Robertson, would sexually excite him, the sick bastard.

He liked power, being the one holding all the cards. He had arrived early in an attempt to gain immediate control of the situation. And her.

Too bad for him that it was she, not he, who had control of this situation. She who held the power of life and death over another. Over him.

Wouldn't he be surprised to know that?

She giggled and brought a hand to her mouth, not liking the way the sound invaded the silence. This was too yummy, really. For even though he knew from the publicity of the time that she was one of the girls involved with the Mrs. X murder, he, like the rest of Thistledown, believed she had never seen his face.

But he was not anonymous. She brought both her hands to her mouth, now not able to contain the giggles. They broke free, becoming wild laughter. In a bizarre twist of fate, life had offered her her father, all over again. Her father had thought his actions anonymous. He had believed his nasty little secret had been his alone.

And all along she had known. She had held her secret to her, waiting for the right moment to reveal it to the world.

The waiting had been delicious. It would be just as delicious with David Sadler, her Mr. X. She could use her secret anytime, any way, she chose. All it would take was a word to the right person, a sudden memory, a well-placed call or note. The ring, Mrs. X's ring, showing up in the wrong place, at the most inopportune time.

Yes indeed, she was the master now, he the student. David Sadler had just better watch his step, or he could find himself every bit as dead as Mrs. X.

43

Andie had been working with David Sadler for a couple of weeks, and she found him to be a complex and disturbing man. He had a voracious sexual appetite and described women as a tasty smorgasbord to be consumed and forgotten. At times in his life, she had learned, it hadn't been unusual for him to have sex three or four times a day, with different partners. By his own account, those had been some of the darkest days of his life.

At their last session, he had hinted at something new, another aspect of his relationship with women—a need to control them. Psychologically and physically. He had touched on some sexual experiences involving domination, submission and bondage.

Also disturbing to Andie was her sense that David Sadler was toying with her somehow. That he was enjoying their sessions in a prurient sense, studying her reactions to the tales of his exploits. As if he was being sexually stimulated by their time together.

Sometimes she caught him watching her—while she took a call, as she spoke to her receptionist, or in some other unguarded moment. When she did, something about his expression made her feel naked.

During his sessions, David either paced, energy and tension emanating from him in near palpable waves, or he sat absolutely still, so contained Andie wondered how he could even be the same man from the moment before.

He also had the disconcerting habit of looking Andie directly in the eyes, intently and for uncomfortably long periods. When he stared at her that way, Andie sometimes found herself perched on the edge of her seat, fighting the urge to look away. The directness of his gaze challenged somehow; it was male, territorial and aggressive. He made her feel exposed, totally vulnerable.

She'd never had a patient who made her feel that way before. That in itself was unsettling. She had decided her own reactions to the man would help her understand and help him. He was a sexual predator. She was certain his behavior in therapy, the movement and stillness, the unnecessarily long, intimate gazes were all part of how he acted out his addiction.

Now he was pacing.

She watched him a moment, noticing the way he flexed his fingers with each step, the way he every so often paused to cock his head or roll his shoulders. "Is anything wrong, David?" she asked quietly. "You seem agitated today."

He stopped and turned to her. "Not upset. Excited. Something wonderful's happened."

"Why don't you tell me about it?"

"I met someone. Someone special."

"A woman?"

"Yes." He began pacing again. "One of the special ones."

She made a note of his language, then laid down her pen. "Go on."

"When I see a woman, I get these feelings." He stopped and looked at her. "You know what I'm saying, right?"

"No, David," Andie said. "I don't know. Tell me."

He swept his gaze over her, seeming to linger a moment on her breasts. One corner of his mouth lifted. "Are you sure you can take it? You seem kind of uptight."

"If I can't, then I shouldn't be your therapist. And we'll both know. Go on."

"Okay." Still he didn't look away. "I think about fucking her."

Andie made another note. She met his eyes again. "All women, David? Every woman you see?"

"Pretty much." He smiled and swept his gaze over her again, and she realized that to this man she was another item on that sexual smorgasbord. "But some women are special. That's what I'm saying."

Andie arched an eyebrow. "Explain this to me. Special in what way?"

He crossed to the couch and sat down. For long moments, he said nothing, just stared at her. She wondered if he somehow got off knowing he was making her wait for him to speak. She jotted down her question.

"Some women," he began softly, "I don't know, I sense something about them. They have something special...something that excites me."

"Can you define it? Are they more overtly sexual? Prettier? Smarter?"

"Nothing like that." He crossed his legs. "They're more open to me."

"Open? But not sexually?"

He shook his head. "There's something childlike... needy..." His lips curved up. "They're...vulnerable."

Something about his small smile and the way he said the words made her skin crawl. She cleared her throat. "And that attracts you?"

"Yes."

He stood again and crossed to the bookcase. He ran a finger along the spines. Andie found something almost cloying about the gesture. "Why, David? Why does that attract you?"

He didn't turn. "Because I know I can own them."

Own them. She was grateful his back was turned and he didn't see her grimace. She noted his response, underlining it. "I don't think I know what you mean by 'own,' David."

"Sure you do." He turned. "Some women are selfish.

They won't give you anything. They won't share anything but their pussies.''

"And that's not enough?"

"What do you think?"

"It doesn't matter what I think, David. This is about you."

"No, it's not enough."

"So, when you're making love with these wome—"

"Fucking," he corrected. "I don't make love with those women."

"The ones who aren't special?"

"That's right."

"Do you ever make love? With any of your women?"

"As opposed to just screwing?"

"Yes."

"Sometimes. With the special ones. The most special ones."

"The vulnerable ones," she murmured, her mouth dry, her heart fast. "The ones you can own."

"Yes." He sat back down. "You're starting to understand me, Dr. Bennett. That's good."

Was it? she wondered. It didn't feel good. It felt slimy, like the underside of a rock. "But there's something I don't understand, David. How do you own someone?"

"They give you everything. Their hearts and souls." His extraordinary blue gaze met hers. "Their very lives."

A chill slid up her spine. She fought the shudder that followed.

He smiled. The curving of his lips was almost reptilian. "I'm upsetting you."

"Of course not," she lied, checking her watch. "We're almost out of time."

"What would it take to upset you, Dr. Bennett?" He folded his hands in his lap. "What would it take to make you blow that unflappable cool of yours?"

She arched an eyebrow. "Is that what you want, David? To upset me?"

"Fear's an aphrodisiac, Dr. Bennett. So is helplessness. You should try them."

She ignored that. "And is control, David? An aphrodisiac?"

"Yes."

"Maybe I would prefer to try that, then."

"It doesn't work that way."

"No? How does it work?"

He didn't answer, instead he stood and circled behind her, to the window, forcing her to shift to an awkward angle to see him. Forcing her to squint against the light. "If I told you I like to tie women up, that I like them to be completely helpless when I make love to them, would you think me sick? Or just perverted?"

"I don't call my patients names, David. And I don't label them, except in the clinical sense."

"The clinical sense," he said. "Of course. Terms like dysfunction."

"That's right." She made several notes. "Let's talk about your family, David. What was your mother like?"

He looked at her and laughed, then shifted his attention to the window and the bright day beyond. "That was awfully obvious, Doc. Couldn't you come up with something a little trickier?"

"We're not playing a game here. I'm not trying to trick you." She tilted her head slightly. Watching him carefully. "Why don't you want to talk about your mother?"

"I didn't say that. But no, I don't want to talk about her. Or my father."

"Why not, David?"

"I want to talk about sex. It's a lot more interesting."

"You don't think the two are related?" she asked. "At all?"

"I didn't fuck my mother, if that's what you're asking. Despite what Freud or Jung or any of those other bullshitters say about people like me, I didn't want to, either. Nothing oedipal here."

"You came to me to seek help with your sexual appetite, that indicates to me that you believe your behavior is abnormal. That you believe you have a problem. I'm trying to help you learn where the problem came from. Family and childhood is our most likely place to start."

"Not for me."

He was angry, she noted. Furious enough that a muscle jumped in his jaw. She waited to see where he would go next.

"When I make a woman come, I want them to know that I gave them that. A gift. A gift I could choose not to give them next time. They should thank me." His lips lifted. "They do."

"And you get—" Her voice sounded choked, and she cleared her throat. "—pleasure from this?"

"Of course. It's pleasurable to know that what I give them, I can take away. I can make them come or make them suffer."

"Suffer?"

"Wait. Deny them release." He changed the subject. "You didn't ask me an important question, Dr. Bennett. You didn't ask me who my special new someone is."

"That's none of my business, and I really don't want to know."

"Are you sure?"

"Yes."

"Absolutely?" he teased. "Last chance. You'd think she's special, too."

Suddenly, an image from her past filled Andie's head. The image of Mrs. X, naked and blindfolded, hands bound in front of her and waiting.

Waiting for a man with dark hair, a man she had put her trust in.

Mrs. X had given that man everything.

Everything.

Andie's breath caught. She stood, so suddenly her notepad and pen dropped to the floor. "Our session's over,

David.'' Her hands were shaking. She slipped them into her jacket pockets and forced a stiff smile.

He bent and retrieved the notebook and pen. As he straightened, she thought she felt his breath stir against her legs. She took a step backward, gooseflesh slithering up her spine.

He handed her her things. ''Are you all right, Dr. Bennett?''

''Fine.'' She hugged the pad to her chest, wanting him out of her office and away from her. ''I'll see you Friday.''

''Who knows,'' he murmured, smiling, ''maybe even before?''

44

Martha Pierpont had hired a local defense attorney named Robert Fulton to be her counsel. Although born and bred in Thistledown, he was well-known throughout the Midwest and had handled a number of high-profile murder cases. Andie had gone to school with him, but as he was a few years older, she had only a vague recollection of him.

Insisting she had nothing to hide, Martha had authorized Andie to work with the attorney. Despite her misgivings Andie had agreed to meet with him at her office after hours to talk about Martha's case.

"Would you like a glass of wine?" Andie asked him. He was sitting on her therapy couch and looking a bit uncomfortable. She smiled. "Some of my patients prefer the chair."

He returned her smile. "Funny, all of my clients try to avoid it. The chair, I mean."

She laughed, liking the mild-mannered attorney—everything from his round, wire-rimmed spectacles to his casual business attire. She could almost hear Raven mocking her, teasing her about going for the ones who would be so grateful for a date they would never break her heart.

She pushed the thought away, irritated that her best friend knew her so well. "You're funny."

"Thanks. Shrinks always tell me that."

She laughed again and crossed to the wet bar. "Very funny, actually."

She poured two glasses of cabernet, brought him his, then took her seat. "So, tell me. What's going on?"

He took a sip of wine, murmured his appreciation, and set it aside. "You know we entered a plea of not guilty?" Andie nodded and he went on. "I'm going to argue she acted in self-defense. Edward's habitual abuse, leading up to the events of that night, will be the cornerstone of our defense. We have to prove she feared for her life. Your testimony will be absolutely essential. You, more than anyone, know the abuse she lived with, about his bouts of violence and rage. You and Patti."

"If it's what Martha wants me to do and you as her counsel believe it's best for her, of course, I'll do whatever's necessary."

"But you're not comfortable with it?"

"I'm fine with testifying, no problem. It's this whole thing I'm not comfortable with." Andie made a sound of frustration and set her wineglass on the coffee table. "Let me tell you about Martha Pierpont. She's a gentle woman, timid really. A textbook example of a victim of long-term spousal abuse. She has all the characteristics. Denial of the true nature of her relationship with her husband. Low self-esteem. Guilt, as if, somehow, the abuse was her fault. Her real feelings frightened her, and she kept them carefully controlled. The times they escaped, she would be immediately apologetic."

"Hardly the profile of a woman who shoots her husband five times at point-blank range."

"Exactly."

"She could have snapped?" he offered. "Taken one too many blows or insults?"

"I think she snapped, no doubt about it. It's what caused her to snap that has me guessing." Andie drew her eyebrows together. "What Martha told me of that night, that fight, was awful, but no different than dozens of others she'd told me about."

She met Robert's gaze. "Most abusers aren't killers.

The newspapers bring the ones who are to our attention, they sensationalize them. But the truth is, the great majority of abusers out there, and there are a lot of them, last stat I saw was about six million in the U.S., don't want to kill their spouses or lovers. They want to control and punish them.''

"I'm aware of the statistics," Robert murmured, "and so will the prosecution be. But that doesn't matter, what we have to prove is that in her mind, at that moment, she feared for her life. That she believed he was going to kill her."

"I wonder if there's something she's not telling us."

She had his full attention now. "Like what?"

"I don't know." Andie shook her head. "But something's niggling at the back of my mind. Like a mosquito bite I can't quite reach to scratch." She shook her head again. "It could be that I'm still reeling from this having happened. That I haven't been able to deal with it yet, on an intellectual level. Or it could be something more."

She looked him dead in the eyes. "I wonder if Patti could be involved somehow."

Robert didn't miss a beat. "You think Edward might have turned his abuse on Patti?"

"Maybe. Martha loves her daughter fiercely, and I believe she would go to any length to protect her. It could have been the final trauma, the proverbial last straw. When he started in on Martha that last time, the walls she had built to protect herself began to fall."

"It could help our case." Excitement edged into his tone. "A mother protecting her child, that's powerful stuff to present to a jury. But we'd need proof. We'd need Patti's testimony."

"Don't get excited yet, I could be all wet." Andie told him then about Martha's outburst, her saying she wanted to kill her husband, then her immediate regret and apology after. "The weird thing was, at our next session, she had no recall of it ever happening. In fact, she denied it vehemently. Became highly agitated. It was as if she had totally blocked it out.''

"And you believed her?''

"Yes.'' Andie drew her eyebrows together in thought. "It was as if she was stretched to the breaking point already.''

"Which works with your theory. Had you talked about Patti that day?''

"A great deal.''

He was silent a moment. "We'd have to be very careful. If the prosecution gets a hold of that outburst...'' He shook his head. "They'll sell it as premeditation. And the jury could buy it. That's a whole new ball game, Andie. And the only way to keep that out, is to keep you off the stand. And right now, without you, we don't have a hell of a lot. No 911 calls, no hospital reports. I'm still digging, though.''

Her phone rang. "Excuse me,'' she said, standing and crossing to the phone. "It could be a patient.'' She picked up the receiver and brought it to her ear. "Dr. Andie Bennett.''

Complete silence greeted her. The hair on the back of her neck prickled. "Hello,'' she said. "Is anyone there?''

"Is this the Dr. Andie Bennett from the newspaper?''

She didn't recognize the raspy, slightly slurred voice on the other end of the line. "Yes, it is,'' she said coolly, her guard going up. "Can I help you?''

"You like watching, don't you, you little cunt?'' The man cleared his throat. "You know everything, but you lie.''

Andie froze, stunned. Her eyes went to Robert Fulton.

"What is it, Andie?'' The lawyer stood and took a step toward her. "What's wrong?''

"Nosy little bitch,'' the caller continued, all but spitting the words at her. "I'm going to take care of you. Just wait, you'll get yours, you little whor—''

"Who is this?" she managed to say, her voice a croak. "Why are you—"

"Maybe you'd like a noose around your neck. Just like—"

Andie slammed down the phone, then brought her trembling hands to her mouth. *Leah Robertson.* That's what he had been about to say. Maybe she'd like a noose around her neck, just like Leah Robertson.

The caller had been Mr. X.

Dear God. The other calls she had tried to ignore must have been from him, too.

"Andie?" Robert touched her arm, and she jumped. "Are you all right? Who was that?"

She opened her mouth to answer, but found she couldn't speak. She shook her head, crossed to her chair and sat down.

She brought her head to her hands and, breathing deeply through her nose, struggled to regain a modicum of control. When she had, she looked at the attorney.

"Who was that?" he asked again, taking the seat across from her. "You look like you've seen a ghost."

"I've heard from one," she murmured. "It wasn't his first call, either, though the other times he didn't say anything."

"Then, how can you be—"

"Certain it's the same person? The breathing. He clears his throat often. Like he has sinus problems." She turned her gaze to the phone, shivering. "I don't think he's even aware of it."

"What did he say?"

"That he was going to get me. He said that maybe I'd like a…a noose around my neck."

Robert frowned. "I don't like the sound of this."

"It gets worse." She drew in a deep breath. "I want to show you something." She went around to her desk, opened the top drawer and took out the fifteen-year-old clipping she had received in the mail.

He glanced at it, then back up at her. "I remember this, though I wasn't that much older than you at the time. A few years." He handed it back. "What about it?"

"I received that in the mail three weeks ago. Anonymously. So did my friends Raven Johnson and Julie Cooper. They're the other girls who were involved in that whole Leah Robertson debacle."

"Small towns don't forget."

"That's what I thought, too. Until today. He said I 'liked watching.' He asked if I was the Dr. Bennett from the paper." She hugged herself, feeling chilled to the bone. "Then he said that thing about the noose."

"Who do you think he is?"

"Mr. X."

"Don't jump to conclusions. It could be a prank. It's probably one of Ed Pierpont's fans. The *Herald* reported this morning that you'd be testifying for the defense. That could have ticked somebody off. I've actually gotten threatening calls on several occasions."

"Really?" she asked hopefully, feeling immeasurably better. In her book, an irate kook was better than a sadistic murderer, any day of the week.

"Oh, yeah. One guy promised he was going to tear out my liver." He grinned and patted his midsection. "Still here, all in one piece."

"There you go, being funny again."

"Besides, Andie, why after fifteen years would this Mr. X surface and start harassing you and your friends? That doesn't make any sense." Robert shook his head. "The book's never closed on a murder case, and I'll bet your Mr. X knows that. Stirring up trouble only opens him to discovery."

"Thank you." She let out a long breath and brought a hand to her chest. "You're right. I wasn't thinking clearly."

"Of course you weren't. You were frightened." He recapped his pen and slipped it and his legal pad into his briefcase. "Have you mentioned the calls or clipping to the police?"

"To the police?" she repeated. "No, I..." She shook her head. "I didn't think it was necessary."

"Consider it, Andie. Even though this is probably nothing, you need to talk to the police. This way, you're protected. If you need them, they're up to speed."

"I'll think about it."

"Good." He collected his briefcase and stood. She followed him to his feet and walked him to the door. "I'll keep you informed about what's going on."

"Thanks. I'll make myself available to you."

"Good." He started through the door, then hesitated, meeting her eyes once more. "Would you like to have dinner?"

"Dinner?" she repeated.

"Yes. Tonight."

She opened her mouth to say yes, but found herself making an excuse instead. "I'm really tired tonight, Robert. Rain check?"

"Sure. Another time." He started through the door, then stopped again. "Call me after you speak with Martha, if what you suspect about Patti is true, it could really help us. This case isn't going to be easy to win, Andie. We need all the help we can get."

45

Raven could barely contain her excitement as she walked along beside David Sadler. The Gatehouse development was fabulous; the kind of project she had dreamed of being a part of. A community made up of wooded cul-de-sac lots starting at three-quarters of an acre. The development bordered a natural stream on one side and a state park on the other. Gatehouse would be made up of homes of no less than thirty-five hundred square feet. The average, David predicted, would be forty-two hundred. Three different models were under way, two of them nearly structurally complete.

"The pool and clubhouse will be there." He pointed past her to the left. "And over there—" he shifted a bit right "—the tennis courts. Come, I'll show you through the houses."

By the time they had finished the tour of the last—and most complete—model, Raven's head was swimming with ideas, and she longed to be back at her shop, putting those ideas to paper and digging through catalogs and sample books.

The houses had taken her breath away. Soaring vertical spaces. More windows than walls. Vaulted ceilings with exposed beams and banks of skylights. Open-concept rooms that flowed one into the other, separated by columns and partial walls.

All they needed was the touch of a gifted designer. All they needed was her.

"What do you think so far?" David asked as they finished their tour in the kitchen of the last model.

"I'm more than impressed." She moved her gaze over the room. "I'm blown away. And itching to get started."

A smile touched his mouth. "That's exactly what I'd hoped you'd say." He went to the pantry and opened the door. It was a walk-in, big enough to house enough food for a small army. "In case you didn't notice, throughout the house we included plenty of roomy closets and other storage spaces. You never know what you're going to need to hide in them."

Pathetic, Mr. X. You'll have to try harder. She arched an eyebrow, enjoying the advantage of knowing exactly what he was trying to do. "Maybe even children?" she murmured, her tone bland.

He looked surprised, then laughed. "You don't like children?"

"They're all right. I've never given them much thought." She went to the bank of windows that looked out over the back of the property. This model was going to have a swimming pool; the ground had been cleared. "What decisions about the interior have you already made?"

"None."

"None?" she repeated, incredulous. "Surely you've ordered flooring and light fixtures and—"

"Nothing." He turned to her, smiling. He reached out and trailed a finger along the shoulder of her pewter-colored satin blouse. The garment's flamboyant fabric was countered by its severe design. "I need it all, Raven. Everything."

She didn't flinch at his touch; she found it neither pleasant nor distasteful, more a curiosity. It was hard to believe that at one time she had thought this man almost a god. "All? What exactly are you referring to?"

"Window treatments, furnishings, accents. Everything. Potential buyers must walk into this home and see it as it could be, start to finish. We don't have a lot of time, though." He gestured around them. "As you can see, this model is about ready and I want to start selling sites as soon as possible."

"That's the name of the game, of course."

"It's your baby now, start to finish. With my approval of creative and budget, of course. Don't worry, though, you'll find I'm easy to please."

She thought of what she knew about David Sadler and his particular tastes. "I rather doubt that."

He laughed again, the sound silky smooth. "Any ideas yet? I'd love to hear them."

"With pleasure," Raven murmured, only too happy to give voice to the pictures in her head. "We can't go too formal, not with all the windows in this one. I'd like to bring the outdoors inside even more. Wood floors throughout, with the exception of the kitchen, bathrooms and laundry area, which I see in an earthy-color tile."

"Buyers like carpeting," he murmured. "It's warm. Sensual."

"No problem. We carpet the bedrooms and the formal living room, a thick pile, something sumptuous. A light neutral. For the walls—" She paused a moment, thinking. "—there's that wonderful khaki color that's so popular this year. Combine that with white trim, tinted with the tiniest touch of lavender, and the walls will positively glow.

"We need painted wooden blinds in here, definitely. Maybe throughout." She narrowed her eyes in thought. "I'm going to check into light fixtures made of that weathered iron. Brass would be too formal, too cold for this house. I'm thinking, too, of subtly distressed walls. I know a fabulous painter who'll work cheap."

She turned to David and found him watching her, his expression amused. She frowned. "Is something funny?"

"Not at all. You look excited." He cocked his head to

the side, studying her. "I like it when your eyes heat that way."

"I love what I do. And as I'm sure you know, this is an incredible house. And a wonderful opportunity for me." She skimmed her gaze across the bank of clerestory windows above their heads. "What's the sun exposure for this room, do you know? I'd love to leave those uncovered, but not at the expense of too much heat in the afternoons."

"You're quite beautiful, Raven. In an icy sort of way."

She laughed, unoffended. "Was that supposed to be a compliment?"

"Definitely. I like all types of women."

He wasn't flirting with her, she knew. He was toying with her, trying to unsettle her. She fought back a laugh. The man was so obvious. Really. How had she ever thought him a master player? How could she ever have looked up to him?

"I'll bet you do." She turned and crossed to the unfinished cooking island and the rolls of blueprints there. He followed her, stopping so close behind her she could feel his breath stirring against her hair.

"What would it take to thaw you, Raven Johnson?"

"It's not possible." She turned and met his eyes, again noticing what an extraordinary blue they were. "Ask any man in town. Raven Johnson is one coldhearted bitch."

"I'm not any man."

She laughed, giving him points for balls and persistence, if not for style. "No, you're not."

"It's a control thing with you," he murmured. "You're afraid to let go."

"Not afraid. Uninterested." She shrugged. "Sorry, Mr. Sadler. But I like being on top."

He tipped his head back and laughed. "I could accommodate you. A strong woman doesn't scare me."

As long as that strong woman didn't mind being trussed up like a Christmas goose. "I doubt that. Every battle can have only one commander. And that's always me. And, unless I've missed the mark completely, you fancy yourself the one in charge.''

He rested against the island and folded his arms across his chest. ''Comparing love and war? Interesting.''

''Love is war. I learned that a long time ago.''

He stared at her a moment, then chuckled. ''Going to bed with you would be interesting, I think. How about it?''

''I must say, David, that's one of the most romantic propositions I've had, but I think I'll pass. Just for curiosity's sake, though, if you did get me in bed, what would happen then?''

''That would be entirely up to you.'' He smiled. ''Maybe a dream come true.''

Or maybe a nightmare. She turned back to the blueprints and spread one out. ''What's this?'' she asked, moving her gaze over the schematic. ''Not a house.''

''The pool house. Nice, isn't it?'' She murmured her agreement and he continued. ''I didn't want just another one of those innocuous, almost shedlike pool houses you see in all the developments.'' He reached around her and peeled off the next blueprint, one of the clubhouse's elevation. ''I integrated it and the clubhouse with the architecture of the neighborhood. They'll look like the houses, only smaller.''

''And the inside?''

''Pretty typical. Functional.''

''All an illusion, then.''

''Mmm.'' He traced his finger along her scar. ''How'd you get this?''

''Knife fight.'' At his expression, she laughed. ''Car wreck. When I was six.''

''A plastic surgeon could take care of it.''

''Why would I want to do that? It helps me remember.''

He frowned. ''The accident?''

''No, my mother.''

''Funny thing to remember your mother by.''

"Not for me. She made a lot of mistakes, and she ended up dead. The scar reminds me of her mistakes."

"So you don't make the same ones?" He made a sound of appreciation and shook his head. "I'm going to enjoy working with you, Raven."

"Are you certain about that, David? Because I'm telling you here and now, you're not going to get me in the sack."

"Don't be so sure of that. I always get women in the sack. It's what I do. It's a gift."

"Is it?"

"Mmm." He leaned toward her. She smelled the spicy scent of his aftershave and the cool mint of his mouthwash. He met her gaze evenly but didn't smile. "I'm a lady-killer, Raven Johnson. I suggest you don't forget it."

46

Julie lay on her back on the bed, naked, her bound hands anchored to the iron headboard with a rope.

David sprawled on his side beside her, fully dressed, in complete control. He trailed a feather along her collarbone, then lower, over and around her nipples, then down to her belly. He dipped it between her thighs.

She gasped and arched up off the bed. The rope tightened. He drew the feather away.

Julie whimpered for more, and David laughed softly. "Beg," he murmured, hiding the feather behind his back. "Beg me for what you want."

"David," she whispered, her cheeks hot with shame. "Please."

"Please, what?"

"The feather. More."

"Not good enough." He smiled and brought the feather to her lips. She smelled herself on it. He leaned closer. "Tell me where you want me to touch you, Julie. Tell me how you want me to bring you pleasure."

"My breasts. Touch them."

He complied. She sighed and pressed her head back into the pillow, the sensation like a delicious whisper against her skin.

"My belly and thighs."

Again, he followed her instructions. Only this time he inched lower, across the tangle of tight blond curls at the apex of her thighs. He dipped between them, then darted away.

"More." The breath shuddered past her lips. She spread her legs and undulated her hips, telling him without words what she wanted. "Lower, David."

"Bad girl, Julie." He drew his hand away. "You know you have to be specific. Tell me what you want me to do with this feather."

"Touch me...there. Between my legs."

He laughed and leaned toward her, his eyes alight with amusement. "More specific, honey. Tell me what you want me to touch."

She opened her mouth, but couldn't utter the words. She had never had to ask for what she wanted, not specifically, not with words. She had asked generally—I want to make love, fuck, screw. But not...this.

He shook his head and sat up. "Why can't women name their own body parts? I don't get it. Vagina. Cunt. Pussy. Snatch. They all mean the same thing. They're all beautiful. Say it, Julie. Use whichever you like best. Tell me what you want."

"I want..." She sucked in a deep breath, ashamed but aroused. Aroused in a way she had never been before. The sheet beneath her hips was wet with her own juices. Her entire body quivered, as if she were some sort of live tuning fork. "Please touch my...vagina."

"Nope." He laid the feather on the nightstand. "I don't want to now."

A strangled sound of shame and fury flew to her lips. "You bastard! You promised."

"That was your interpretation." He laughed again, mocking her. "Besides, I can do whatever I want. You're quite incapacitated right now."

She arched her body up off the bed, fighting against the rope, tears of frustration stinging her eyes. "I hate you! Untie me, you son of a bitch!"

He acted as if he didn't even hear her outburst. She redoubled her efforts, though the rope tore at her wrists. She twisted and kicked, the whole while cursing and pleading, begging and threatening. Through it all, David just watched her, a small satisfied smile on his mouth.

His amusement infuriated her. His smug arrogance. When he untied her, she would kill him. She would take the rope and torture him. Picturing that, she fought harder, until her muscles and lungs screamed protest, until she was panting and sweating and spent. She went limp, the fight draining out of her.

"If you're quite done," he murmured after a moment, "I have another surprise for you." He opened the nightstand drawer and took out a square of fabric. He opened it carefully, lovingly. She saw that it was long and gossamer. And black.

A black silk scarf.

Her heart stopped. Fear took her breath. She stared at the fabric, frozen, remembering the past, remembering Mrs. X.

"I'm going to blindfold you now."

"No." She shook her head, panic pounding through her. "No, David, please…not a blindfold. Anything…anything but that. I'm afraid of the dark."

His lips curved up. He leaned over and took one of her nipples into his mouth, sucking at it as a baby would, longing for nourishment. Pleasure speared through her; the sound of it trembled on her lips.

"Sweetheart," he murmured, lifting his head, "you shouldn't tell me what you're afraid of. Now I have to do it."

"No!" She twisted away from him, kicking at the bedclothes with her feet.

"Enough of that," he said, slapping her thigh sharply. She cried out as pain ricocheted through her. "I don't want to punish you, but I will. Do you understand?"

She nodded, tears welling in her eyes, spilling over.

"I want you to do this. I expect you to do it. For me." He let out an impatient-sounding breath. "Now, can you be a good girl?"

"Yes," she answered, voice shaking.

"That's my girl. Close your eyes."

She did, though her every instinct shouted that she not. He laid the fabric over her eyes. "Lift your head, my love." She did, and he expertly and quickly tied it behind her head, making her darkness complete.

He kissed her then, deeply, passionately, as if he wanted to swallow her whole. "You look beautiful," he murmured, drawing away. "Thank you, my darling." He moved his hands and mouth over her, worshiping, praising. "Thank you."

Seconds ticked past. Julie's fear trickled away. The total black became erotic. It enveloped and surrounded her, like a womb or dark sea. Reality slipped away; she was left with nothing but David's hands and mouth and the velvet black.

He brought her to the brink of orgasm again and again. Each time he stopped short, she cried out, begging for release. And each time, he refused to give it to her.

He brought his face to hers; their breath mingled. When he kissed her, she tasted herself.

"I know you, Julie Cooper," he murmured. "I know who you are."

But who was he?

Mr. X?

He moved away from her. The mattress dipped as he got off the bed. She waited a moment, for him to speak, to move, to reveal himself to her. He did not, and a sliver of fear pierced her tranquil dark womb.

"David?" she whispered. "Where are you? Say something."

Silence. She turned her head from the right to the left, panic bubbling up inside her. "David...please."

Then she heard the snap of a lighter, the hiss of the flame touching tobacco. A moment later, she smelled the smoke. "David—"

"But you don't know me, baby. You don't know me at all."

A chill washed over her. "Don't say that, David." Her voice trembled. "I don't like it."

"Does it frighten you?"

"Yes." She pressed herself against the mattress, realizing suddenly how vulnerable she was.

"Do you trust me, Julie?"

"Come back to me," she whispered, voice quivering. "I don't like being alone." *Alone. In the dark. A lock clicking into place.*

"Do you trust me?" he asked again.

"Yes, but—"

"No buts. You either trust me or you don't. You're either with me or you're not." He returned to the bed and sat on the edge. The cigarette smoke stung her nose. He moved slightly and she felt the heat from the lit tip of the cigarette at her breast, her nipple. If she drew in a deep breath, the tip would touch her, she would be burned. She shrank back against the bed, making herself as small as possible.

"You can't have it both ways, Julie. What's it going to be?"

The spot of heat became intense. Her eyes burned with tears. Fear swelled inside her. Fear of the dark and of helplessness. Fear of being alone. Of losing David.

She couldn't live without him.

He moved the cigarette closer. Julie bit down on her bottom lip to keep from whimpering. She trusted him. He wouldn't hurt her. She believed that. She cried it out to him.

"Good girl." He got off the bed and crossed the room. She followed him with her head if not her gaze. She heard him move something on the dresser, then realized what it was. An ashtray.

"Think back, Julie. Think back fifteen years. Tell me what you saw."

"Saw," she whispered. "I don't know what you mean."

"Yes, you do." He circled the bed. "Leah Robertson."

For a fraction of a second, she didn't know what or who he was talking about. Then the realization filled her head. Her blood went cold.

As if reading her thoughts, he laughed. "I told you, I know who you are."

She squeezed her eyes shut, heart thundering. No, he wasn't. She knew he wasn't.

"Tell me, Julie. I read all the newspaper reports, I saw the news clips on TV. Now I want to know everything from you. When you looked through that window, what did you see?" He trailed his fingertips across her mouth, as if coaxing words to spill out. "Were you aroused? Did you wonder what it would be like to be her? Did you fantasize about them? About being her? Did you masturbate afterward? Hiding the truth from your friends and family? Afraid...knowing they wouldn't understand.

"You hated yourself," he continued. "Didn't you, my love? You thought there was something wrong with you, that you were bad. Sinful." He brought his mouth to hers, tenderly, lovingly, all but drinking from her lips. "I understand. I can make you happy, Julie. I will. But you must give me everything I ask for."

Tears welled in her eyes. They spilled over, soaking the silk scarf. He did know her. Everything about her. How could he see into her soul this way? How?

"I could do anything to you right now. Anything I wanted, anything that is pleasurable to me. You're helpless. Like that Leah Robertson was. Does that frighten you?"

Don't hurt me, David. Please don't hurt me.

She didn't speak the words aloud, but he heard them nonetheless. "Trust," he whispered. "Tell me, Julie. Tell me what you saw. You and your little friends, so fresh and pink and unspoiled."

He leaned closer; he lowered his voice more. "Shocking, wasn't it, my love?" He brought his hands to the apex of her thighs, to her pink, her sex. He curled his fingers around her, possessively, lovingly.

She gasped and arched; he laughed, low and deep in his throat. "Tell me, my sweet. Tell me what you saw."

Julie reached into her memory and pulled out fragments of moments, images that had haunted her all these years. With her mind's eye she saw Mrs. X, alone in the dark. Naked and helpless. She saw Mr. X bending her over a chair, taking her from behind. She saw the woman's mouth on his penis, the rope slithering over her skin, coiling around her breasts.

As she remembered, she told David, haltingly, at times overcome with tears. Finally, her memories were spent and she fell silent, trembling, panting as if she had run miles without a break.

"Do you know what I like, Julie? Can you imagine?"

She turned her head in his direction. "Who are you?" she asked. "Tell me who you are, David."

He was silent. Still. Then she heard the distinctive sound of a belt being unbuckled, a zipper being lowered. He climbed onto the bed and straddled her. "Someone who knows you." She opened her legs, and he thrust into her. "Someone who loves you."

She couldn't hold him with her arms, so she wrapped her legs around him, gripping as hard as she could, digging her heels into his lower back.

"Imagine for me, Julie. Imagine what I like."

She did, but the only thing she could imagine was a woman dangling from the end of a rope.

The woman was her.

47

"Good morning, David." Andie smiled at her patient. "How was your weekend?"

He jumped to his feet and began to prowl around her office. "How was yours?"

"Fine." She noted his agitation. "Is there some reason you don't want to talk about your weekend, David? Did something happen that we should discuss?"

"Is there some reason you don't want to talk about yours?"

"We're not here to talk about mine."

"Of course we're not." He flung himself back onto the couch and gazed up at the ceiling. "I've been reading about you in the paper."

"Have you?"

"Yes. That woman who killed her husband, are you going to get her off?"

"I'm not a lawyer, David. You know that."

"Her husband sounds like he was an abusive bastard. Some men don't have a clue how to treat women."

She arched an eyebrow, intrigued with his comment, considering his own history with the fairer sex. "But you do?"

He met her eyes. "Of course. I love women. That's the reason I'm here."

"Is it? I thought you were here because you have a need to sexually conquer and dominate every woman you meet."

He ignored that. "So," he asked, sitting back up, "do you think Pierpont got what he deserved?"

"Do you, David?"

"I want to know what you think."

"This isn't about me."

"But I want to know. Do you think he deserved what he got?"

"I'm not at liberty to discuss this case."

"But you must have an opinion."

Some sessions David was like this, edgy and confrontational. Angry. He wasn't the first patient to have reacted this way; he wouldn't be the last. Therapy was an intense, penetrative process, it ripped away protective masks and broke down walls. Many didn't give up those masks and walls without a fight.

"For me," she said quietly, "guilt or innocence is rarely black or white."

He laughed and shook his head, his expression disgusted. "That's easy, isn't it? It's cheap."

"Why do you say that?"

"Because it is. You never have to put yourself on the line, do you, Dr. Bennett?" He paused. "You're just watching."

Watching. The word, the way he said it, the expression in his eyes, slid over her like ice water. "I don't know what you mean," she managed to say after a moment.

"Yes, you do." He smiled. "Watching. Keeping a safe distance from the action. Observing life rather than taking part in it."

"Is that what you think I do? Is that what you think our sessions are about?"

He laughed, the sound high and almost girlish. "You know what I think? That you get off on our sessions." He laughed again. "My therapist, the voyeur."

She held on to her calm despite the unease pulling at her. "That seems a rather odd word to use to describe your doctor. Is there something we need to talk about?"

"I'm from Thistledown, you know. I was here back then. I know about you and your friends. About that summer."

"That summer?"

"The summer the police commissioner's wife was murdered. As you can imagine, that was of great interest to me."

Andie's heart began to pound. "What do you know about that?"

"I told you. I lived here. I read the paper, listened to the news. You and your little friends got yourselves a real education, didn't you?"

"Is that all you know, David?" she asked, looking him dead in the eyes. "What you read in the paper?"

"Why do you always answer my questions with a question?"

"It's my job."

He rested his elbows on his knees and leaned toward her. "What's your personal life like?"

"We're here to talk about your personal life."

"Watching again. No wonder you became a shrink."

She stiffened, her cheeks growing hot. "That's why you sought me out, David. Presumably, anyway."

He saw that he had gotten under her skin and grinned, obviously delighted. Andie scolded herself for allowing that to happen and forced herself to relax.

She was in control here; what would his knowing a bit about her hurt? Besides, some patients liked to know a little innocuous personal information about her. It was comforting to them; it helped establish an open atmosphere of sharing.

But those patients hadn't made her feel so uncomfortable. Those patients hadn't made her feel like a bug under a glass.

Andie shook that thought off. She laid her notebook aside, leaned back in her chair and smiled at him. "All right, David, what would you like to know about me?"

"Do you have a boyfriend?"

Of course he would go to that first. "No. Not now."

"Why?"

"Not interested."

"At all?"

"Not enough to get involved."

He jumped on the word and pretended to jot it down in a notebook. She had to admit, she found that irritating.

"Do you enjoy sex?" he asked.

"That's a little too personal."

He ignored her. "Or do you just lie there, not getting *involved?*"

She worked not to show her dismay. It had been so long since she'd had sex, she wasn't sure whether she had enjoyed it or not. She could hardly remember if she had gotten involved. She hoped she had, though something in her gut told her she had not.

She fought squirming in her seat. "There's more to a relationship than sex, David."

"There's trust," he said softly. "Sharing. Giving everything. If you were in love, would you give everything, Dr. Bennett? Or would you just...watch?"

That word again. Watch.

Her caller's word.

She changed the subject. "Did you see your special someone this weekend?"

"I don't want to talk about it."

"Why not?"

"Because I don't want to, okay!" He jumped to his feet and began to pace. "Can't you ever leave well enough alone? Pick, pick, pick. I hate that."

Andie watched him a moment, thinking suddenly that she understood. "Were you with more than one woman this weekend, David? Is that what this is all about?"

He froze. One moment became several, then he turned slowly. He met Andie's eyes. The expression in his took her breath—that of a tortured soul. "I don't want to hurt her, Dr. Bennett. I don't want to hurt her the way I've hurt other women.''

Mrs. X. Hands bound, blindfolded. Hanging from her neck, dead.

The blood rushed from Andie's head, leaving her light-headed, dizzy with fear. She began to sweat, to shake. He meant hurt emotionally. He did.

Andie told herself that, over and over, even as the image of Mrs. X played in her head.

David stopped in front of her. He got on his knees and gathered her hands in his. "Help me, Dr. Bennett," he begged. "You have to help me. I don't want to hurt this girl, I don't. I love her.''

48

Andie's thoughts were chaotic as she pulled into her driveway later that evening. Her session with David had lingered with her like a chill that wouldn't go away. She had found herself glancing repeatedly and nervously over her shoulder, the feeling of being stalked so strong that several times she had felt it as a prickling sensation at the back of her neck.

You just watch, don't you?

I think you get off on it.

Her obscene caller had said almost the same thing. Could it be they were one and the same person? The co-incidence of two different people, within a matter of weeks, saying such similar things? She didn't think so; the coincidence was too great.

Andie turned off the engine, took her key from the ignition but didn't make a move to get out of the car. She glanced toward her house, seeing instead David's tortured expression as he looked up at her.

I don't want to hurt her, Dr. Bennett. I don't want to hurt her the way I've hurt other women.

Andie brought her fists to her temple. That couldn't mean what she feared it meant. David Sadler was a sexual predator; he used women, he had an unhealthy need to control and dominate them. But he wasn't a killer.

Was he?

I don't want to hurt her.

Help me, Dr. Bennett. You've got to help me.

Andie shuddered and glanced at her cell phone, mounted

on the car's console. She didn't want to be alone tonight; maybe she and Raven could go out to dinner. Scolding herself for being a wuss, she flipped open the phone and dialed Raven's office. When she got no answer there, she tried her house. Again, no answer.

She hung up without leaving a message, started to dial Julie, then, figuring she would be working at the club on a Friday night, gave it up.

Alone it would be. Ignoring the sinking sensation in the pit of her gut, Andie collected her briefcase and the patient tapes she had brought home to transcribe, opened the car door and climbed out.

Tonight, she decided, she would let herself wallow in neuroses. She would put on her jammies and eat something ridiculously fattening but completely comforting. She smiled to herself, feeling a hundred percent better already. What was it about fatty, sugar-laden food that could turn a girl's mood around, just like that?

She went up the walk, noticing the begonias and marigolds for the first time in days, enjoying the soft twilight shadows and the smell of freshly cut grass. She shook her head, amused at her own behavior. All day she had tried to talk herself out of being unsettled, the moment she had faced her feelings, they had all but gone away. She should practice what she preached more often.

Andie climbed the stairs to her porch and crossed to the front door. She inserted her key, then reached for the mail. She leafed through it, stopping on a catalog from her favorite clothing outlet, then tucked the bundle under her arm and twisted the key.

She heard the music a moment before she swung the door open. The almost hauntingly erotic melody spilled over her, memories with it. Of the potent sounds and smells of the summer night. Of the breathlessness of youth. Of innocent curiosity and of the way it had mushroomed into shocked disbelief, then icy fear.

Mr. and Mrs. X's music.

With trembling fingers, Andie pushed the door the rest of the way open. She stepped inside, heart thundering. Shadows gathered in the corners and at the edges of the room, full of dark possibilities.

Someone had been in her house. Someone who remembered Mr. and Mrs. X.

Someone who wanted her to remember, too.

Her briefcase slipped from her fingers, hitting the floor with a thud, the package of cassette tapes with it. The mail scattered.

Andie crossed to the stereo; she turned it off and popped out the compact disc. The silence was sudden and complete. From somewhere in the house came a stirring; the creak of a floorboard, the quiet whoosh of a breath being expelled. She froze, the hair on the back of her neck standing up.

She looked over her shoulder, toward the hallway that led to the bedrooms. Again, she heard a sound, this time like a carefully placed step.

The oxygen left her body in a rush. *She wasn't alone.*

Her heart stopped and she inched backward, toward the door, her gaze on the dark corridor, fear a living thing inside her.

A shadow moved.

With a cry of distress, she turned and ran.

49

Raven hummed under her breath as she made her way down the apartment building's long corridor to Julie's door. She should have called her friend first, but it was Friday night, she had been passing by Julie's building and, knowing her friend had the night off, had figured she would be eager to go out and do something.

Just like old times, Raven thought, stopping in front of her friend's door. They would pick up Andie and hit the town, the three musketeers on the prowl again.

Raven lifted her hand to knock; Julie's door flew open a moment before she did.

"Rave!" Julie exclaimed, looking surprised. "What are you doing here?"

"It's Friday night. I thought we could get some dinner and drinks and go from there."

Julie peered past Raven, down the hall. "Where's Andie?"

"Don't know. She didn't answer at home or her office, so I left a message. We can swing by her place and get her on the way."

"Oh." Julie shifted from one foot to the other. "Didn't you have a date tonight?"

Raven smiled. "Canceled it. The guy was a geek. Besides, I thought it would be more fun to be with my best friends. Just like old times, Friday night, time to howl."

"I'm not doing that anymore. Remember?" Julie shifted again. "No men."

"Who said anything about—" Raven lowered her gaze.

Julie was dressed for a night out—short denim skirt, tight white T-shirt, fuck-me pumps. Her purse was slung over her shoulder, her full lips lined and painted.

She was dressed for a night out, all right. But not for one out with the girls.

Heat crept up Raven's cheeks. "Where are you going, Julie?"

"Nowhere."

"Nowhere," Raven repeated, the blood thundering in her head. "Dressed like that?"

Julie flushed. "I was going…into…work."

"I thought you had the night off."

"I did…I mean, I do." She wet her lips. "I mean, I told Joe I'd come in, just in case."

"Just in case what?" Raven snapped. "He needs a blow job?"

Julie paled. She looked guilty as sin. Raven felt as if the top of her head was going to pop off, she was so angry. After everything she had done for her friend, Julie repaid her like this? By sneaking around? With lies?

"So, Julie," she asked, "who are you fucking these days? Joe? Someone else? Everyone else?"

"How can you say that to me?" Julie cried. "You're supposed to be my friend."

"How? History, babe. I know you."

Julie wrung her hands. "That's not it. Joe expects a big rush tonight. Because of some golf tournament at the club. He was afraid he'd be shorthanded, so I said I'd come in. If it's busy, I'll work. If not, I'll go."

Raven took a step closer to her friend. "You made a promise to me. You made a promise to Andie. No more men. No more cruising. A promise, Julie."

"I know, Raven." She let out a trembling breath and backed up a step. "I owe you guys everything. I wouldn't… I'm not cruising. I'm not."

Raven narrowed her eyes, studying her friend, unconvinced but wanting to give her the benefit of the doubt.

Wanting to so badly it hurt. Julie was her family; she loved her.

"You're being straight with me, Julie? You're not screwing around?"

"Of course I am—" She flushed. "Being straight with you, I mean." She smiled tremulously. "I love you, Rave. Gosh, without you, I don't know where I'd be."

Raven smiled. She reached out and tucked an errant lock of Julie's silky blond hair behind her ear. "Your hair's pretty tonight. Did you do something to it?"

"Lightened it." Julie's lips lifted at the compliment. "You really like it?"

"I wouldn't have said so, if I didn't. *I* don't lie, Julie." Raven dropped her hand. "You probably need to go?"

Julie checked her watch. "I should."

"I'll walk you out."

Julie locked her apartment door, and they started down the hallway. Raven slipped her arm through her friend's. "So, the job's good?"

"I like it. I'm making good money and everybody's real nice."

"Not too nice, though?"

"No." Julie shook her head. "Not too nice."

They chose the stairs over the elevator, and moments later stepped out into the evening. The soft black sky sported neither stars nor moon, not yet anyway. The friends crossed the parking lot, stopping beside Julie's car.

Raven let out a long breath. "I wish you could come. It'd be like old times."

"I know. I do, too." Julie jiggled her car keys, obviously anxious to take off. "I'll bet Andie's home by now, though. She'll be able to go with you."

"Sunday morning for coffee?"

"Great. Not too early, though. I'm closing Saturday night." Julie climbed into her car, stuck the key in the ignition and turned it. The car sputtered to life. "Have a good time."

"I'll call."

"Great. See ya." She smiled at Raven, waved and started off.

Only problem was, she headed away from the country club.

50

The Thistledown Police Department hadn't changed much in the fifteen years since Andie had last been inside. The same beige-colored walls, the same scarred linoleum flooring and battered furniture.

The smells and sounds were the same, too: of coffee left hours too long on the burner and of sweat, of phones ringing, scuffling feet and the occasional shouted obscenity.

She had never wanted to set foot in this place again.

Now, here she was.

Andie swallowed hard and crossed to the desk sergeant. He, too, seemed unchanged, an updated replica of the one from all those years ago. "Excuse me."

He looked up. "Can I help you?"

"I need to see Detective Raphael," she said, her voice shaking. She sounded more like a girl of fifteen than a woman of thirty. The scary thing was, she felt like one, too. "Is he in?"

"He's in." The man narrowed his eyes. "Name?"

"Andie Bennett. Dr. Andie Bennett."

"Have a seat. I'll tell him you're here."

Andie sat, clutching her purse in her lap. She sucked in a deep breath, trying to relax. Trying to get the music out of her head, working to shake off her fear and the feeling of violation that held her in its grip.

She focused on the tangibles: the calls, the clipping, the music. They were all related; it didn't take a rocket scientist to figure that out. She had been singled out, either because of her past or because of her involvement in the

Pierpont case. People who sent threatening letters and made obscene calls were rarely rapists and killers. Typically, they didn't have the guts to challenge someone face-to-face, they channeled their anger and dissatisfaction anonymously.

Typically. Rarely. There were always exceptions.

Someone had been in her house.

That didn't fit the statistics and norms, now, did it?

"Bang! Bang! You're dead!"

Andie jumped, and a squeal of childish laughter followed. She swung in the direction of the sound. A little girl peeked around the water fountain at her. She had a mop of curly dark hair and big brown eyes. She wore a tin badge and a holster with two shiny six-shooters. She was obviously playing cops and robbers.

Andie smiled and put a hand to her heart as if she had been shot. The child giggled.

"Miss Mara," the desk sergeant boomed, "you're not bothering anybody, are you?"

"Of course not," she said, sounding adult. After casting a squinty-eyed stare at Andie, she turned and sashayed toward him, shoving her pistol back into its holster. "Just taking care of some of the bad guys. Gotta keep 'em off the streets."

Andie brought a hand to her mouth to stifle a laugh. The girl would no doubt be highly offended if she laughed. After all, Andie knew from experience, getting the bad guys was serious business.

She watched as the child circled behind the sergeant's desk and began poking around. He hardly even noticed. She was obviously a regular here at the station, one of the officers' kids.

Even as she wondered whose, she found out. Nick Raphael's.

"Daddy!" the little girl cried as he walked into the waiting area. She launched herself into his arms.

"Mara." He gave her a big hug and kiss. "How's my little deputy doing?"

"Getting the bad guys," she said proudly, then pointed a chubby finger at Andie. "Got her."

Laughing, Nick turned. He met Andie's gaze, and a lump formed in her throat. In that moment, he wasn't a cop. He was a father. A father who was head over heels in love with his daughter.

The emotion in his eyes, his tender fun-loving manner with his child were at odds with the hard-ass cop who had visited her house just a couple of weeks ago. The cop who had flatly told her he thought her profession a sham and her patient a cold-blooded killer.

Andie stood. The connection, the unexpected moment of communication, was broken. His smile died, his expression hardened. Once again he was the unbending cop with a chip on his shoulder.

He kissed his daughter again and set her on her feet. "A few more minutes, sweetie. Now, don't ease up on your post."

After the little girl had assured him she wouldn't, Nick crossed to Andie. "Hello, Dr. Bennett. What can I do for you?"

"Detective, I—" She realized she hadn't a clue what to say or how to begin. She also realized he didn't like her very much, and in all likelihood, would tell her she had an overactive imagination and send her on her way. "I'm not sure where to start."

"Is this about the Pierpont case?"

"Maybe. Or it could be about the—" She took a deep breath, feeling a bit like an idiot for what she was about to say. "I don't know. It could be about the Robertson case. Leah Robertson."

For a full moment, he simply stared at her, as if assessing not only her every word, but each flicker of her eyes, the way she held her head, her stance. As if deciding whether she was telling him the truth. Then he nodded. "Come with me."

After he asked the desk sergeant—Murphy was his name—to keep an eye on Mara, he led Andie into the squad room. He pointed at the rickety-looking chair in front of his desk, then went around and sprawled in the one behind it. He leaned back, looking totally relaxed. Relaxed to the point of boredom.

He infuriated her.

"Why don't you start from the top," he said.

"All right." She clasped her hands together in her lap. "Some...strange things have been happening to me. Tonight—"

"What sort of things?"

"Obscene phone calls for one."

"Considering your line of work, how strange is that?"

She stiffened. "I'm not a 1-900 number, Detective. I'm a psychologist. No, obscene calls are not a usual occurrence."

"It was a straightforward question," he murmured, his expression and tone suggesting that she was an excitable female. It certainly *had not* been a straightforward question but she hadn't come here tonight to argue semantics. "What makes you think this might have something to do with the Robertson case?"

"It started with a fifteen-year-old newspaper clipping about Leah Robertson's murder. Someone sent it to me. Anonymously. They sent one to Raven and Julie, too. Those are my friends, the ones who—"

"I remember who they are."

"Then the calls started. And tonight...when I came home, someone had been in my house, and I—" She swallowed hard, remembering the sounds of a footfall, an expelled breath, a shadow moving in her dark hallway.

She began to tremble, and she gripped the arms of her chair to steady herself. "I thought they were still there. I heard...something, so I came here."

He drew his eyebrows together. "What do you mean, someone was in your house? Someone broke in?"

"Yes. They left music playing. Mr. and Mrs. X's music."

He sat forward. The front legs of his chair hit the floor with a thud. "You're sure, about the music?"

A laugh bubbled to her lips. "Quite sure."

He took out a pocket-size notebook and flipped it open. "Let's go back to the calls. Is the caller a man or woman?"

"A man, I think."

"When he calls, what does he say?"

"The first few calls, nothing. There was just this... creepy breathing on the other end of the line. But the last call, he said I was just watching. He said that I watched but I didn't tell the truth."

"Do you have any idea what he meant by that?"

"None." She let out a short breath. "Anyway, he finished by saying that...that maybe I'd like him to put a noose around my neck. Just like...just like Leah Robertson."

For long moments Nick Raphael said nothing, then he narrowed his eyes. "How long ago was that?"

"A couple of weeks."

"And you're just coming in now?"

The disbelief in his tone had her cheeks burning. She felt like a jerk. "I was afraid I was overreacting. I mean, my name's been in the paper a lot. And there are a lot a people out there with sick ideas of what's funny. I never thought...I didn't think I was in any real danger."

"But you do now?"

"Yes! Someone was in my house. Someone I don't know. They touched my things, God only knows what things. They left music playing on my CD player. Mr. and Mrs. X's music. Don't you think I should be here? Don't you think I'm just a little bit unnerved?"

"You don't have to get so riled up, Dr. Bennett. I'm

only trying to get your take on the situation. I can't assume anything.''

She took a deep breath. "I'm sorry. It's been a big night.''

"Have Raven and Julie received the same calls?''

"No. Whoever it is, they seem to have singled me out.''

He jotted down something in his book. "Tonight, did they take anything?'' he asked. "Was anything disturbed?''

"Besides me?'' she asked. "Not that I know of. I went inside, then thought I heard someone and ran out.''

"They were still there?''

"I was sure I heard—'' She brought a hand to her temple. "I thought so.''

"You did the right thing. I'm sure they're long gone by now, but I'll send a uniform home with you to make certain.'' He glanced down at his notebook, as if scanning the notes he had already taken. "Do you have any idea who your mystery man could be?''

"No. But I...I have this pa—'' She stopped. "Never mind.''

He looked up at her sharply. "You have what, Andie?''

She hesitated, a sinking sensation in the pit of her gut. "I have this new patient. He...he's been talking a lot about sexual subservience and bondage. Things he said... I was reminded of Mr. and Mrs. X. And I get the feeling...I sometimes think he's toying with me. Playing some sort of a game. I think he gets off on it.''

"Good. That's a start. Name?''

"Excuse me?''

"Your patient's name. I'll pay him a call first thing, ask him a few questions.''

She swallowed hard. "I can't tell you his name. That's—''

"Privileged information,'' he said sarcastically, flipping his notebook closed. "Then what am I supposed to do with this?''

"I don't know." She made a sound of frustration. "But I can't divulge a patient's name. It's completely unethical."

"Would you rather be dead?"

Color flooded her cheeks and she jumped to her feet. "Thank you for your time, Detective Raphael. I'll see myself out."

"Dr. Bennett…Andie, wait." He followed her to her feet. "I'll get a uniform to go home with you and check it out. Make sure nobody's in your house. He'll write up a report."

"Thank you," she said stiffly. "I appreciate it."

"And look, I want you to keep me informed of what's going on. That means, I want to know if you get any more calls or clippings, I want to know if you have any more uninvited visitors."

She rubbed her arms. "Don't worry."

"Wait here. I'll get a uniform to follow you home." He started off then stopped and looked back at her. "And in the future, Doctor, if someone says they're going to put a noose around your neck, don't wait to report it until they're actually trying to do it."

51

Nick felt funny about turning Andie Bennett over to another officer, though he knew the other cop would do no less than he would have, nor could he do any more.

She was in good hands, he told himself, walking away. Perfectly safe. This was his weekend with Mara; he wasn't going to start it by keeping her waiting half the evening while he checked out something that was going to turn out to be nothing.

If only the woman hadn't alternatingly looked completely lost and bravely defiant. If only he hadn't realized how alarmed she had been, how torn between fear and her professional ethics.

He shook his head and told himself he was imagining things. She wasn't a fifteen-year-old kid anymore, she was a grown woman, a professional. She had a handle on this, no big deal.

Sure, she did. Dammit.

Nick stopped and looked back. She hadn't moved from the spot by his desk where he'd left her. She had her arms curved around her middle and wore an expression that had a lump forming in his throat. *Dammit to hell and back. Why tonight?*

"Daddy!" Mara shouted, catching sight of him and barreling around the corner. "Are you done? I want to go now."

He caught his daughter to him and hugged her hard. "What's wrong, no more bad guys?"

She pouted. "I got 'em all." Mara tugged at his hand. "And I'm hungry, too."

"Okay, baby, just one more thing." He looked back over his shoulder. "I just have to—"

Andie Bennett was gone. She had probably been assigned the uniform—Wilkens, most likely—and had exited with him. He could take off now with a clear conscience.

He smiled at his daughter. "You ready to go have some fun?"

Within minutes, they were on the road, Mara safely buckled into the seat beside him, chattering about everything and nothing.

He glanced at her, realizing how much he had missed times like this. Time they had spent together on a daily basis, doing routine things, ones he had taken for granted.

Just being together, he thought. He missed their just being together.

"Who was that lady, Daddy?"

"What lady?" he asked, turning off Main and onto Park.

"The one you talked to. Inside."

He grinned at her. "I thought you said she was a bad guy?"

Mara looked at him, exasperated. "I was just pretending, Daddy. If she had been a bad guy, she would have been wearing handcuffs."

Nick laughed. His daughter, how her mind worked, never ceased to amaze him. "How'd you get so smart?" he asked.

She shrugged. "Dunno. Who was she?"

"An old friend." Nick found his own description of his and Andie's relationship amusing—in a way, they were old friends, though they had shared nothing more than a handful of horrendous hours together. What, he wondered, would Andie call him? Not friend, he was sure. Probably something like *major pain in the ass.*

"She came to see me about police business."

"What business?"

"None of yours." He stopped at a red light, reached over and tapped the end of her nose with his index finger. "What do you want to eat tonight?"

"Hot dogs."

He made a face. "Try again."

"Pizza?"

The light turned green; he started off. "Uncle Tony's?" he asked, referring to his brother Tony's Italian restaurant, Bella's.

She thought a moment. "Okay. Daddy?"

He cut her a glance from the corners of his eyes. "Hmm?"

"That lady, your friend—" she shifted in her seat "—she's pretty."

Nick suppressed a chuckle. Mara obviously had something on her mind. And when she wanted something, be it answers, attention or a new toy, she could be like a bulldog with a rib bone. She would not be sidetracked or deterred, not for long, anyway. She was like him in that way. Jenny called it mule-headed, but he thought it a good quality, one that had helped him immensely in life.

"Yeah," he said, slowing to take a right onto Whitman. "I suppose she is."

"Not as pretty as Mommy, though."

He made a noncommittal sound. Right now, he wouldn't describe his soon-to-be ex-wife with any words that were proper in the company of his daughter. Truth was, he couldn't even think about Jenny without gritting his teeth.

"Do you like her?"

"She's nice." He glanced at Mara, then back at the road. "Did you like her?"

She shrugged. "I don't like Bernard. He's not fun like you."

Bernard Jameson, Jenny's wife-stealing, family-wrecking prick of a boyfriend. Nick tightened his fingers on the steering wheel, struggling to get hold of his fury.

The man had seen more of Mara lately than he had, her own father.

"He's not your daddy," Nick snapped. "He's not supposed to be as fun." Even as the sharp words passed his lips, he regretted them. He smiled at his daughter, trying to lessen their sting. "Your daddy's especially fun."

Her shoulders drooped, as if in defeat, and she turned toward the window and gazed silently out.

Nick frowned, a thought occurring to him, one that scared him to his core. He took a deep breath, choosing his words carefully. "Bernard's not...he's not mean to you, is he? He doesn't...hurt you in any way?"

Mara glanced at him, then lowered her gaze to her lap. She shook her head.

"You're sure? Because if he is, Daddy will take care of it. I promise you, baby, I'll make everything okay."

She nodded, fiddling with her seat-belt buckle. "That's not it, it's—" She looked at him, eyes swimming with tears, chin quivering. "When do Mommy and I get to come home? I don't like where we live. I want to be with Mommy *and* you."

Nick's heart broke. From what he had gleaned, Jenny and her shrink-boyfriend were all but living together. It infuriated him, but there was nothing he could do. His lawyer said that unless he wanted to get really nasty with Jenny, thus subjecting Mara to a muckraking war, he was not going to get full custody. Even with a war, he might lose, having done nothing but made his situation worse.

At least this way, he was guaranteed partial custody; Jenny had already agreed to it.

He pulled the Jeep to the side of the road, shifted into park and turned toward his daughter. "Come here, sweetheart." She scooted over, and he drew her onto his lap. "I'd like us to be together again, too. More than anything. But your mother, she has other ide..."

He let his words trail off. He wanted to bad-mouth Jenny. He wanted to tell Mara exactly what had happened, laying the blame just where it belonged—squarely at his wife's feet.

He wanted to do that so bad the words pressed at his chest, demanding to be said.

But Mara loved her mother. And as much as he wanted to punish and hurt Jenny, he didn't want to hurt his daughter.

And criticizing Jenny would hurt Mara. In the long run, it would hurt them all.

He sighed and hugged her. "Mommy and Daddy had problems together. And Mommy was really unhappy."

Mara nodded. "She used to be crabby a lot. She never used to smile."

But she did now. Mara's words took his breath away. Bernard could make his wife smile, something he had been unable to do. "That's right," he continued, his voice thick. "And when that happens, sometimes a mommy and daddy have to live apart."

"Forever?"

He heard the hope in her voice. He wished he could reassure her, wished he could tell her it wouldn't be forever. But that would be a lie. He and Jenny would never get back together. Not unless Jenny came to her senses, anyway. And begged. "Most of the time, yes, it's forever. Do you understand?"

She let out a long, trembling breath. "I guess."

She didn't, he knew. How could she? At six, her view of life and people was pretty basic—like it or don't, want it or not, naughty or nice. He put a finger under her chin and tilted her face toward his and smiled. "But you know something? Even though your mom and I are apart, we love you just as much as we always have. To us, you're the most important thing in the whole world. You always will be."

She smiled and hugged him. "I love you, Daddy."

"I love you, too. Come on, let's go get that pizza."

Mara scrambled off his lap and back to her seat. Once

she had rebuckled her safety belt, Nick pulled away from the curb. As he did, he realized where they were—a block and a half from Andie Bennett's house. By now, the uniform would have done a complete inspection of her property; he might have found something.

Could this guy harassing Andie Bennett be Mr. X?

"Kiddo," he said, turning to his daughter, "how about we make one more quick stop before Uncle Tony's?" When she started to frown, he added, "But you'll have to bring your badge and six-shooters. It's police business."

Moments later, Nick and Mara reached Andie Bennett's house. Light blazed from every window. She and Officer Wilkens stood on her front porch talking; his cruiser was parked behind her car in the driveway. Obviously, her place had checked out.

Nick pulled up to the curb; he and Mara climbed out.

"Hi!" Mara called, racing up the walk, toy gun in hand. "Police business!"

"Detective?" Wilkens said as Nick approached, obviously surprised to see him. "Is something wrong?"

"I was in the area and decided to see if you found anything."

"Nothing," the officer said. "If someone was in there—"

"Not 'if,'" Andie corrected, cheeks bright with color. "Someone entered my house illegally and left that music playing."

"Don't go getting riled up, Dr. Bennett," Nick said, meeting her eyes. "If I thought you were making the whole thing up, I wouldn't have sent Wilkens. And I wouldn't be here now. It was a poor choice of words on Officer Wilkens's part. Isn't that right, Wilkens?"

"Right," he said automatically. "Sorry, ma'am."

Nick turned back to the officer. "Did you dust for prints?"

"Yup. Found nothing but this." Wilkens held up a

clear, plastic evidence bag. It contained a compact disc. *The* compact disc.

Nick gazed at it a moment, thinking of the past, of Leah Robertson and her unknown killer, more than likely Andie and her friends' mysterious Mr. X.

Could he have done this?

"Point of entry?" he asked.

"Could have been anywhere," Wilkens answered. "Most of the windows were unlocked, so was the back door."

When both men looked at her, Andie made a sound of irritation. "This is Thistledown, for heaven's sake." She held up a hand when Nick opened his mouth to scold her. "I know, I know. It's locked up tight now and will stay that way. Believe me."

"Good." Nick nodded. "Anything missing that you noticed? Anything disturbed?"

She rubbed her arms, as if chilled. "Not that I saw."

"If there's nothing else, Detective," Wilkens said, "I've got another call."

Nick told him to go, then turned back to Andie. "You okay?"

"As okay as can be expected, I guess." She let out a long breath, glancing uneasily at her house. "I know no one's hiding in there, but I feel...funny about going inside. I don't know if I'm afraid they'll come back or if I just have the creeps because someone was in there in the first place."

"It's natural to feel that way. But, if it helps, my guess is they won't be back. Whoever did this didn't want to meet you face-to-face. You probably scared the life out of them when you arrived home before they'd gotten out. They wanted to frighten, not hurt, you."

"But why?"

"I don't know. I don't have enough information even to speculate with any confidence."

"But if not the Robertson case, then why the music?"

Nick glanced at Mara; she was hiding behind a shrub, pretending to ambush some bad guys, then he looked back at Andie. "Whoever is doing this might be using the past as a way to get under your skin."

"Thanks," she muttered. "I feel so much better now."

"You could give me the name of that new patient of yours, the one who—"

"I can't," she said, cutting him off. "No matter how funny I feel about this whole thing."

Mara zoomed by, making motor noises. She stopped and looked up at Andie. "Maybe you feel funny 'cause you're hungry." She rubbed her stomach. "I've got the rumblies."

Andie looked at her as if surprised—or disconcerted—by the comment, then laughed. "Maybe you're right. My tummy's rumbling, too."

"You can come eat with us! We're going to my uncle Tony's for pizza."

"Uncle Tony's my brother," Nick explained. "He owns Bella's."

"I've driven by it before, but never tried it."

"Best Italian in Thistledown."

Mara clapped her hands together. "Can she, Daddy? Can she come with us?"

"Thanks, Mara," Andie said, shaking her head, "I'd really like to, but I don't think—"

"Come with us," Nick offered. "Really. We'd love to have you join us."

Even as he heard himself saying the words, he couldn't believe they were his. This was his and Mara's evening together, the first all week. The last person he wanted to spend it with was Dr. Andie Bennett.

Judging by her expression, she was as surprised by the invitation as he was. She opened her mouth to refuse; he saw "no" forming on her lips.

She said yes instead.

"You will?" he repeated, not quite believing what had just happened. "Join us, I mean?"

"Sure. Why not?" She looked down at Mara and smiled. "Thank you for the invitation."

Bemused, Nick glanced from his daughter to Andie and back. For better or worse, it seemed, he was having dinner with Andie Bennett. "All right then," he said, motioning toward the car. "Shall we?"

52

Andie insisted on taking her own car, and followed Nick and Mara to the restaurant. The whole way, she berated herself for having accepted the invitation. What had she been thinking, agreeing to have dinner with Nick Raphael and his daughter? Besides the fact that she was quite sure she didn't like him, there was the little matter of his wife to consider. What would the woman think about her husband and daughter dining with another woman, however innocently?

She shook her head, thinking of Raven, imagining what she would say. Her friend would, no doubt, have a good laugh over Andie having dinner with a man she had repeatedly called the enemy over the past couple of weeks. The same man she had also described to her friend as cold, arrogant and a pain in her backside. She would have a good chuckle over the fact that he was married, as Andie was constantly lecturing Raven about steering clear of attached men—a thing Raven had absolutely no conscience about.

Andie smiled suddenly, recalling Nick's expression when she had accepted his invitation. It had been almost comical. She didn't know who had been more surprised and dismayed—him or her.

Andie saw Bella's up ahead, and her smile faded. She knew why she had agreed to this dinner, one that any other night she would have refused. She had been afraid to be alone in her own home. Even though Officer Wilkens had checked every closet, nook and cranny and proclaimed her house free of intruders, the idea of spending the evening alone in her house had scared her silly.

Not alone, she thought. With the specters of Mr. and Mrs. X. With the memory of Mrs. X's unsolved murder.

Reason enough, she decided, to be out with a man she hardly knew and didn't like, a married man with a daughter and no doubt, a bushelful of his own problems. Hopefully, by the time she got home, she wouldn't be thinking of Mr. and Mrs. X anymore. Hopefully, by the time she got home, she would be thinking about what an annoying, overbearing man Nick Raphael had become, and not about the fact that a stranger had been in her house, a stranger connected in some way to a fifteen-year-old murder.

Andie pulled into the restaurant parking lot behind Nick, then into the parking space next to his. Okay, she thought again, firming her resolve. It wouldn't be fun, but it would serve a purpose.

Within twenty minutes, Andie saw how wrong she had been. Mara was a delight. Precocious. Smart and funny. Andie had laughed more in the last few minutes than she had in a week.

And Nick, once he'd relaxed, wasn't nearly the ogre she had made him out to be. In fact, she found him rather charming.

Or maybe, she thought, laughing as she watched the two arm-wrestle, it was the father and daughter together she found charming. Nick loved his daughter so much. The emotion shone from his eyes and echoed in his every word, gesture and expression.

Watching them together reminded her of the way it had been between her and her own father. Before he had left them for Leeza. Before everything had fallen apart.

The waitress, a pretty girl of about sixteen, came over. "Hi ya, Uncle Nick," she said, snapping her gum. "Hi, Mara." She set a box of crayons and a coloring book on the table in front of the girl, then looked at Andie, openly checking her out. "Hello."

Nick introduced her. "Andie, this is my niece, Sam. Sam, Dr. Andie Bennett."

"Nice to meet you," Andie said, smiling.

The girl looked at her a moment more, as if deciding whether she was going to sanction this meal, then nodded. "Nice to meet you." She handed them menus. "You want a beer, Uncle Nick?"

Nick looked at Andie. "You like red wine?"

"Love it."

He looked back at his niece. "Bring a couple glasses of your house red."

The girl arched her eyebrows at that, then bent to Mara. "Shirley Temple?"

Mara didn't look up from her coloring. "With extra cherries."

As Sam started to walk away, Nick called to her. "And tell that no-good brother of mine to come out. He owes me money."

When the girl disappeared into the kitchen, Andie turned to Nick. "I feel kind of funny about this. Your family must think, I mean...this is perfectly innocent, but—"

"My wife and I are separated."

"Oh," she said, surprised. She supposed she shouldn't be. She should have suspected by the fact that he and Mara were out together on a Friday night that he was divorced or separated, but she hadn't. Something about him seemed married to her. For one thing, he still wore his ring.

"I'm sorry," she murmured.

"Don't be. It's old news."

Not that old, Andie thought, noticing the way Nick's mouth thinned and the defensive glint that raced into his eyes.

"Mommy and Bernard are in New York," Mara piped in. "They're bringing me something from the biggest toy store in the world."

Bernard? A boyfriend, most probably. That answered

one question—Nick and his wife had been separated long enough for her to have begun to date. But, had he?

Andie sneaked a glance at Nick. Judging by his thunderous expression, he had not.

Nick's brother came out of the kitchen and greeted them with much fanfare. Older and heavier than Nick but nearly as handsome, he gestured broadly and spoke loudly. His voice rang through the restaurant.

"Who's this, baby brother?" He stared with open curiosity at Andie.

"A friend," Nick answered. "Dr. Andie Bennett, my brother Tony."

"Pleased to meet you," she said.

"Welcome." He grinned, a speculative gleam in his eyes. If Nick noticed, he didn't comment. "Any *friend* of my little brother's is a friend of mine."

Tony beamed at her another moment, then turned and shouted, "Bella, come meet Nick's friend."

Nick leaned toward her. "Bella's his wife. You'll love her, she's the greatest."

She was, indeed, the greatest. Friendly and energetic, with a tart tongue and, Andie would bet, a temper to match, she held her own with the boisterous brothers.

Sam brought the wine, set the glasses on the table and looked at her parents in disgust. "I've got orders in, you know. Can't we save the family reunion for another time?"

"Kids," Tony said, shaking his head as she marched off. "They have no sense of what's really important in life."

His daughter, two tables over, heard that. "Tips," she called back, scowling at him. "That's what's important."

"She's right." Bella playfully slugged her husband. "The kitchen awaits. You and Nick can argue over baseball another time." She smiled at Andie. "It was nice meeting you. Come and see us again."

Andie said she would, then the woman held her hand

out to Mara. "Sweet pea, come help your aunt Bella make your pizza. You can put anything on it you want."

Nick watched them go and made a face. "Prepare yourself, there'll be cherries on the pie. And lots of them."

Andie laughed. "Your family's great."

"Is that what you call it? I always thought insane a better description."

She laughed again and took a sip of wine. It was good, full-bodied with a fruity finish. "Not insane, trust me. And I should know, I'm a shrink."

His lips lifted. "But you've only met a couple of them. I have three brothers and two sisters. We tend to be loud and damn obnoxious when we're together. My mother had her hands full. What about you? I can't remember if you had any siblings?"

"Two brothers. Twins. Four years younger than I am."

"Are you close?"

She thought about it a moment. They were, but not in the way Nick and his brother Tony were. She told him that. "Because they were twins, they did everything together. They were each other's best friend and brother. Plus they were boys, and I'm—"

"Not."

She smiled. "Exactly. Besides, I've always had my friends Raven and Julie. They're like sisters to me."

A high-pitched squeal came from the kitchen, and Andie's lips lifted. "Mara's so cute. And so smart. You must be very proud."

His smile was both spontaneous and wistful. "I am. The day she was born was the best day of my life." He laughed, looking embarrassed at having revealed so much to her. "Uh-oh, there goes my macho-cop image."

"I think it's really sweet."

"Sweet?" He rested his chin on his fist. She decided then and there that he was gorgeous. Flat out to die for. "Just what I always wanted to be. I'll be picturing myself that way the next time I wrestle some scumbag to the ground.''

"Don't worry, I can imagine you doing that. You don't have to pull out your gun to prove what a tough guy you are.''

"Pull out my gun?'' One corner of his mouth lifted into a lopsided grin.

She flushed, realizing what she had said, the double entendre. "You know what I mean, your weapo—'' She bit the word off, then burst out laughing. "I'm sorry.''

"That's okay.'' He grinned. "I don't mind talking about my weapon. Anytime, Andie.''

She shook her head, not believing they were having this conversation. "Anyway, what I'm trying to say is, your tough-guy image is safe with me.''

"I appreciate that.''

Another excited squeal came from the kitchen, and Andie glanced that way, then back at him, thinking aloud. "It must be hard, not seeing her all the time.'' She brought a hand to her mouth, embarrassed. "I'm sorry. That's none of my business.''

"Forget it.'' His expression tightened. "And, yeah, it is hard. It stinks, as a matter of fact. But it's out of my hands.''

"I shouldn't have said anything.'' Andie made a small, fluttering motion with her right hand. "It's none of my business. I'm sorry.''

He took a swallow of his wine, working, she thought, to appear nonchalant and failing miserably. He shot her a tight smile. "I shouldn't have snapped that way. I'm a little pissed off at my wife. She decided our family wasn't worth saving. I felt differently.''

"How long ago did it...happen?''

"A couple months.''

A fresh wound. Too fresh for her to be sitting here, feeling all cozy and comfortable, thinking the things she was about him. A girl could get in a lot of trouble that way.

She could get her heart broken.

"What about you, Andie Bennett? What have you been doing for the last fifteen years?"

"Not much. College. Graduate school. Opened my practice."

"Just hanging out, huh? Wasting time."

She lifted a shoulder, amused. Charmed. "That's about it."

"No husbands along the way? No kids?"

"Nope. I left the husbands to Julie. She's done the till-death-do-us-part thing three times. And counting."

"Ouch."

"Exactly."

He toyed with his wineglass. The deep red liquid dipped and swirled, catching the light, at times appearing red, other times almost purple. "And your other friend—Raven—are you still close?"

"Best friends." Andie laughed and tucked her hair behind her ear. "That sounds so high school, doesn't it? But we've been friends so long we're more family than friends. We share everything, do everything together."

He met her eyes. His crinkled at the corners with amusement. "Interesting."

She caught his meaning and flushed. "Everything within reason."

"She's done well for herself, hasn't she? Seems I heard something about a business. What was it? Something to do with—"

"A design firm. Interior design. She's really good."

"I'll remember that next time I need paint swatches and throw pillows."

Andie laughed. "I've got a big picture of you picking out throw pillows. And, yes, she's done amazingly well. In fact, she landed the new Gatehouse development job."

Nick cocked his head, eyebrows drawn together in

thought. "Isn't that odd, though? Considering the trauma she lived through?"

"Yes. And no. The human mind is an incredible thing. Some people endure terrible trauma yet emerge seemingly unscathed. They go on to lead productive, happy and relatively normal lives. Others experience trauma that appears much milder, but the damage to their psyche is much greater."

He took a swallow of his wine, his expression rapt. "But how do you know who's made out okay and who's—"

"Screwed up?" she filled in. "Simple. By looking at their lives. Are they productive? Happy? Do they live within the confines of 'normal' society? Are their relationships with other people stable and healthy?"

Andie took a sip of her wine. "Raven and I have talked about this. She believes our friendship, and her friendship with Julie, is what kept her together. She believes we were—and are—her emotional anchors."

"And you believe that's true?"

Andie drew her eyebrows together. "Why wouldn't I?"

"That's not what I meant. As a psychologist, you believe that's true, that her evaluation is correct?"

Andie trailed her finger along the edge of the red-and-white-checked tablecloth. "It's not that unusual, actually. As humans, we find something to cling to, to give our lives a center or focus. For some it's God, some family, others a job or a goal. For people who have lived through severe emotional trauma, that need is greater, perhaps. They cling tighter, harder."

He was silent a moment, as if studying what she'd said, then met her eyes once more. "Just out of curiosity, what would happen if those emotional anchors were taken away?"

"I'm not sure I follow."

"Someone like that, if their anchor is suddenly taken away. What happens?"

"Again, it depends on the person. Nothing could happen. The person could find new anchors, maybe learn to depend solely on themselves.''

''Or they could go bonkers?''

''Bonkers?'' she repeated, arching an eyebrow.

''Yeah, you know, like opening fire on a school yard full of kids or turning into an ax murderer.''

''Are you mocking me?''

''Who me?'' He pointed at his chest. ''Not at all.''

He did his best to look innocent, instead he reminded her of a jock caught in the locker room with his hand up a cheerleader's skirt—guilty as sin.

He leaned toward her, eyes alight with interest. ''So, what do you think, Andie? Could that send someone into a tailspin?''

''I suppose the trauma could be great enough. It could be another betrayal or disappointment in a long line of them. But, that kind of thing's quite rare. For the most part, people are what they seem to be.''

''What you see is what you get? Is that it?''

''Basically.''

''And you don't think you can be fooled? You don't think a slick sociopath can put a mask on for the world, one no one sees beyond?''

''No one?'' She shook her head. ''Perhaps not the layperson. Casual friends, acquaintances, co-workers. Usually, people like family, those who are really close to the person, they know something's terribly wrong, but they deny it. They accept that person's behavior as different maybe, but okay. Not dangerous.''

''Like the serial killer who liked to kill and mutilate animals as a child.''

''Exactly. The family thinks it's weird, but they call it a stage and shrug it off. But fool a trained mental health professional?'' She shook her head. ''I don't think so. Not if they have time to really observe them.''

''That's where our opinions differ, big-time, Dr. Bennett. A slick criminal, they can wrap you psych-nerds around their little fingers. You don't have a chance. I see it every day.''

"Psych-nerds?" She tilted her head, more amused than annoyed. "Every day?"

"That's right." He finished his wine. "They get you guys all involved in if their mommies put them on the bottle too soon or potty-trained them before they were ready. You argue that their fathers were cold and their mother's cruel. When you do, you miss the facts, lady. They're criminals. They hurt somebody. They should pay."

"First off, I don't think our opinions differ just there, Detective Raphael." She brought her wine to her lips, a smile tugging at her mouth. "You're wrong, by the way."

He laughed and leaned back in his chair, folding his arms across his chest. "I'll bet you think criminals can be changed, too. I bet you think you can save them."

"I think they can change, yes. Save's too judgmental a term for me."

"Too judgmental?" He laughed again, this time without amusement. He leaned forward and the front legs of his chair hit the floor. He lowered his voice. "If you saw the shit I see, day in and out, you wouldn't say that. Some people are bad, Andie. Period. The have no conscience. They hurt others without remorse. Kill without provocation. They are totally selfish, amoral beings. If that makes me judgmental, so be it."

Silence fell between them. He gazed at her, his expression unreadable. She realized what it must be like to be a suspect, sitting across the interrogation table from him, having to look into those eyes, eyes that seemed to see all the way inside her.

She wondered what he saw when he looked into her eyes. She wondered if he saw how attractive she found him, how intriguing. She shifted in her seat, suddenly uncomfortable, feeling exposed.

"What about Mr. X?" he asked suddenly. "Could you have changed him?"

At the mention of Mr. X, Andie thought of David Sadler. Of his plea for help.

"I don't know." She lifted her shoulders. "How could I? But I've always wondered about both of them. Particularly her. If Mrs. X had sought treatment, would she be alive today?"

"It really bugs me that we never solved that case. That guy's a killer. And he's still out there." Nick looked away, then back at her, pinning her with his intense brown gaze. "I want to get him, Andie. I'm going to get him someday, I know it. He's going to do it again, he can't help himself. And when he does, he's mine."

Just then, Mara burst through the kitchen doors. At the sound, Andie jumped, startled. They both swung in her direction. She carried a small pizza. Sam was beside her with a larger one.

"Mine has cherries!" Mara cried, skipping toward them. "And pineapple, too!"

From that point on, adult conversation ceased and pandemonium reigned. Mara dug into her candied pizza, eating more than Andie would have thought a six-year-old could. She insisted her dad and Andie try a bite, and Andie had to admit it was awful.

At one point the child had tomato sauce from her chin to her nose, and better situated to help out, Andie had wet her napkin in her glass of water and wiped the worst of it from her face. As she drew away, she noticed a couple at the next table looking at the three of them.

They caught Andie's eye. "Your little girl is adorable," the woman said. "How old is she?"

Nick swung to face them. "Six."

The man put an arm around his wife and smiled. "We're expecting our first."

"Congratulations," Andie murmured, a lump forming in her throat.

The couple thought she, Nick and Mara were a family.
They thought that she was Mara's mother, and that Nick
was her husband.

The lump became a boulder, and she struggled to
breathe around it. What would it be like to be a wife and
mother? she wondered, casting a surreptitious glance at
Nick, then Mara. What would it be like to be part of a
family?

Andie felt a sort of pinch, deep in her gut. A twinge of
longing, she realized with a sense of shock. An ache for
motherhood, for love and commitment, things she had
never longed for.

Dear God, what was wrong with her?

Her shock turned to a kind of wonder, a warm, fuzzy
sensation.

"You're not eating," Nick said to her. "Not hungry?"

She looked down at her plate and realized she hadn't
even finished her first piece of pizza. She looked at Nick,
her cheeks warm. "I'm starving," she said, and with an
almost giddy laugh, dug in.

53

Andie and Nick talked until the restaurant was empty save for Tony, Bella and a few of the kitchen staff. They talked about his marriage, her decision to become a psychologist and some of the strange situations she had encountered along the way. They talked about his job and her friendship with Raven, Julie's troubles and a host of Mara's firsts.

Hours before, Mara had crawled onto Nick's lap and fallen asleep. She fit snugly onto her father's lap, and while they talked, he rocked slightly and stroked the child's hair.

When it became apparent that they were keeping Tony and Bella from being able to go home, they said their good-nights and headed outside. The night was cool, the sky a velvety, star-studded black.

Andie walked with Nick to his car. His arms filled with Mara, she unlocked the door for him, then helped him get the child tucked into her seat with the buckle fitted around her. Mara moaned a little when Nick made the transfer, then turned her face to the seat and fell back to sleep.

"She's getting too big for me to keep doing that." He shook his arm and flexed his fingers, working to get circulation back. "My arm's asleep."

"Has she always been that way? Able to just fall asleep anywhere?"

"Yup. Restaurants, movies, shopping carts. Once, she fell asleep at a bowling alley, the sound of pins exploding all around. When she's tired, she sleeps." He glanced up at the sky, then back at her. "I'll walk you to your car."

She smiled. "It's right here."

"Humor me, okay? I'm old-fashioned."

She laughed and shook her head. "All right."

He walked her around to the driver side of her car. "I had a nice time, Andie."

"I did, too, Nick. Thank you." She lifted her gaze to his, realizing that she wanted him to kiss her. Wanted it rather desperately.

She told herself to get a grip. The last thing she needed in her life was a macho cop with a ready-made family. A cop who wasn't even divorced. One who wasn't even *that* separated.

He shoved his hands into the front pockets of his blue jeans. "You'll be okay? Going home, I mean?"

"Fine." She swallowed hard, going home the last thing on her mind.

"If anything happens, anything at all, call me."

"I will."

"You have my card?"

"I do."

He lowered his eyes to her mouth. Her breath quickened. Even as she called herself an idiot, even as a dozen different warnings rang in her head, she lifted her face slightly to his.

He leaned toward her. She tilted her face a fraction more toward his; her eyes fluttered shut. For one agonizing, wonderful, terrifying moment, she waited. And wanted.

And then it was over. He reached around her and opened her car door, then took a step backward, away from her. A sound of frustration, of disappointment jumped to her lips. She swallowed it, cheeks burning with embarrassment.

"Thanks again," she said, quickly, turning her back to him and climbing into her car. "See you around."

She drove away, telling herself not to look back. Promising herself she wouldn't. She had already embarrassed herself enough. Dear Lord, she had all but thrown herself at him. She couldn't have told him what she wanted any more clearly if she had been wearing a sign.

She would not, absolutely would not, look in her rear-view mirror to see if he was watching her drive off.

Instead, she was even more obvious—she looked over her shoulder.

He was already gone.

54

Andie pulled into her driveway, her head filled with confusing thoughts of Nick, his daughter and their evening together. She turned off the engine and leaned her head against the back of the seat and closed her eyes.

It had been a long time since she'd thought about a man in the way she had thought about Nick Raphael tonight, a long time since she'd thought about kisses and dates and one thing leading to another. Why now? she wondered, a sinking sensation in the pit of her stomach. Why him? A man who was neither really free nor right for her.

He hadn't wanted to kiss her.

She acknowledged that a part of her was bitterly disappointed by that fact, another relieved. What if he had kissed her? Would one kiss have led to another evening together? Or nothing? Which would she have wanted more?

She opened her eyes and looked at her house. Light blazed from the windows, reminding her of the events earlier, reminding her how she had come to be with Nick Raphael at all that evening.

Her head filled with memories, of Mr. and Mrs. X, their music, of Mrs. X's lifeless body dangling from the end of a rope.

Andie climbed out of the car and started up the walk, wishing she was anywhere but home, having to do anything but go into her house alone. She had been right about one thing—being with Nick had taken her mind off the past and her own fear.

But only temporarily.

She stepped onto the front porch and crossed to the door. She jiggled her keys nervously. She could call Raven from her cell phone, tell her what was going on and ask if she could sleep over. Or, she could call Julie. She would be home from work by now. That way, she could come back in the morning, when it was light. One of her friends could come with her.

Andie stiffened her spine, feeling like the chickenshit Raven used to accuse her of being. This was her home. She wasn't about to be scared away by some pervert who had an ax to grind with her. Besides, it was perfectly safe. A police officer had checked every square inch for her and found no intruder lurking in a corner or closet; afterward, she had locked every door and window.

Before she could give herself the time to wimp out, she shoved her key into the lock, twisted it and swung the door open. Taking a deep breath, she stepped inside.

She had left at least a dozen lights burning. She said a silent thank-you for that, turned and closed the door.

From behind her came the distinctive pop and hiss of a soda being opened.

Andie spun around, heart in her throat, scream on her lips.

"Where the hell have you been?"

Raven. It was only Raven.

Andie brought a hand to her throat. "My God... Raven...you nearly scared me to...death."

Andie went to the sofa and sat down, her legs shaking so badly she wondered how she had gotten there. She dropped her head into her hands and breathed deeply, light-headed with fear.

"Geez, Andie, maybe you better slow down on the caffeine."

A hysterical laugh bubbled to her lips. Andie lifted her gaze to Raven's. "I didn't see your car.... I didn't expect..." She held her hands out. "Look at me, I'm shaking like a leaf."

She drew her eyebrows together. She and Raven had exchanged keys to each other's place so they could help each other out—to meet an inconveniently timed delivery, to check on things when they were out of town, for emergencies.

Emergencies. She caught her breath, thinking of her mysterious visitor. Maybe he had visited her friends, too. "What's wrong?"

"Besides being worried sick about you?" Raven crossed to the couch and glared accusingly down at her, Diet Coke can clutched in her hand. "I didn't know where you were. I've been calling for hours. Where have you been?"

Andie took a deep breath and told her about the break-in, the music and hearing someone in the house, about going to the police station.

Raven set her soft drink on the coffee table, looking shaken. "My God, why didn't you call me? I would have come right over."

"I tried. I got your machine. I didn't want to alarm you, so I hung up without leaving a message."

"Well, you did alarm me. When I couldn't reach you, I imagined all sorts of things. Jesus, Andie. I guess I wasn't far off." Raven searched her expression. "Are you all right?"

"Except for being pretty shook up, I'm fine." Andie let out a long breath. "What's going on, Raven? First the calls. Now this. Why is this happening?"

"And why only you?" Raven shook her head. "What did the police say?"

"Nick was concerned, but he didn't have any answers. He sent a uniform over here to check out the house, make sure whoever broke in was gone."

"Nick Raphael? That macho jerk?"

Andie jumped to his defense. "He's not so bad. Besides, he's a good cop."

"Since when?" Raven made a face. "Look at his track record. He let Mrs. X's killer get away."

"You know as well as I do, he wasn't in charge of that case."

"Yeah, they took him off it 'cause he screwed up so bad."

"He did not! The whole thing was politically motivated, and you know it. The press jumped on the story like rabid dogs, and the department needed a scapegoat."

Raven narrowed her eyes. "Why are you defending him?"

"I'm not, I—" Andie choked on the denial, realizing suddenly that was exactly what she was doing. And why.

A smile tugged at her mouth, and she leaned toward her friend, anxious to tell her about her evening, about Nick Raphael, about her feelings. "You're not going to believe this, Rave. We had dinner together. Nick and I."

"Excuse me?" Raven arched her eyebrows, openly incredulous. "You had dinner with Mr. 'Shrinks are the scum of the earth?'"

"Yes, can you believe it?" Andie laughed and grabbed her friend's hands. "I had the best time. It was amazing, Rave. He's amazing."

She squeezed her friend's fingers, feeling like a schoolgirl—giddy and silly and a bit out of control. "We talked about everything. His being separated, me being a shrink. Everything. And his little daughter, Mara, is so cute. Raven, I swear, I don't think I've ever seen a cuter little girl. She's smart, too. Really smart."

Andie released Raven's hands and stood, too energized to sit still. She crossed to the bay window, then turned back to her friend. "I met his brother and sister-in-law. And they were really nice. You know what I mean? The kind of people you would love having as family."

She laughed. "Nick and I discussed my work. We discussed our differing opinions about psychology and the law. And it was okay that we felt differently about things. It was cool, it really was.''

Raven sat stone still and silent, so Andie rushed on, telling her friend about how she had caught the couple at the neighboring table looking at them and how she'd felt this longing—to be a mother, to be part of a family. And about how she had wanted Nick to kiss her good-night.

''You are part of a family,'' Raven said suddenly, standing.

Andie blinked, becoming aware that Raven looked upset. That she hadn't uttered a word until now. ''What?''

''You are part of a family. Me, you and Julie.''

''I know.'' Andie made a fluttering motion with her hands. ''That's not what I meant, not that kind of family.''

''Oh, I understand. You meant a happy little domestic thing. Woman as servant and doormat.''

Andie froze, hurt. ''It doesn't have to be that way.''

Raven laughed, mocking her. ''My, you do have it bad.''

''Why are you acting this way?''

Raven crossed to the window, stopping beside Andie but not looking at her. She gazed out at the night a moment, then turned and faced Andie once more, her expression furious. ''So, did you fuck him?''

Andie recoiled at Raven's crude question. ''Sometimes you really tick me off. You know that?''

''Well,'' she pressed, ''did you? Was he good?''

''I'm not talking about sex, Raven.''

''What are you talking about? *Love?*'' she mocked. ''Taking vows? Something like *till death or a fox in a short skirt* do us part?''

''Screw you, Raven,'' Andie said, shaking, hurt beyond words by her friend's nastiness. ''I think it's time for you to go.''

''What about his kid?'' she went on. ''Think his little

darling will welcome you with open arms? Did you welcome Leeza that way?''

"It's not the same thing!" Andie cried, tears choking her. "I'm not the other woman. Nick's already separ—''

"Get a grip. To the kid, you're still the other woman." Raven laughed. "Thought you didn't like your men armed and dangerous. This guy is both, big-time. He's got heartbreaker written all over him."

"You don't even know him!"

"Do you?"

"You're a fine one to talk. You date all the time. You don't care if they're married or separated or have a dozen kids."

"That's just it, Andie. I don't care. I play games. I screw around. You—'' she snapped her fingers in front of Andie's face ''—one dinner and you're ready to marry him."

"I didn't say I wanted to marry him! I enjoyed his company, I liked being with him. Why is that so wrong?''

"It's not. It's just—'' Raven made a sound of regret and caught Andie's hands. "I'm sorry. It's just that I know you. And I love you. I don't want to see you hurt."

"I won't be hurt."

"That's what your mom said, I'm sure. But in the end she was hurt, so badly it took her a long time to recover."

Andie's eyes filled with tears, remembering. Leeza had taken her father away from them all. And even though she was an adult and understood that no one can *take* someone away, that her father had made his own choice, and that if it hadn't been Leeza it would have been someone else, she still blamed the woman.

"The man's married, Andie. All your life you told me you would never get involved with a married man, or one who had children from a previous marriage. Because you knew what it was like to be that kid. I don't want you hurt,'' she said again, bringing Andie's hands to her cheek. "You're too special, Andie. And you're too important to me. I won't let you do it to yourself."

Andie slipped her hands from Raven's, crossed back to the couch and sat down. Being with Nick went against everything she had ever promised herself about men, dating and marriage. What had she been thinking?

She hadn't been. She had enjoyed his company; she'd found him interesting and attractive and for the first time in forever, she had wanted to be with a man.

"You're right," Andie whispered. "I don't know what got into me."

"You were frightened," Raven said. "He was there, he made you feel safe, he took your mind off what had happened."

Andie looked at her hands. "I guess so."

"I need to talk to you about Julie."

"What?" Andie blinked, confused. "What?" she said again.

"I think Julie's up to her old tricks again. When it comes to men, that girl has no loyalty. No self-respect. She's not like us at all."

Except for her little slipup tonight, Andie thought. How could she have been so stupid? Nick Raphael was off-limits. If she gave him the chance, he would break her heart. She leaned her head back against the couch, aching, feeling drained, as if someone had taken a vacuum and sucked the very life out of her.

"Andie? Did you hear me? I think Julie's involved with someone."

"She has an illness," Andie murmured, tired. So tired it hurt to stay here and have this conversation. "An addiction. She can't just quit because we want her to. She needs help."

"Why don't you talk to her? You're a specialist in this area."

"She doesn't want to face the truth. She isn't ready."

"So, you're just going to let her get involved with someone and run off again? Don't you care enough at least to talk to her?"

Andie held back what she wanted to say—that she wanted Raven to leave, that she wanted to be alone. That right now she didn't like Raven very much.

Guilt speared through her at her own thoughts. Raven had been a good friend for a long time, and if she had been less than sympathetic tonight, well, maybe Andie had needed a kick in the pants.

It didn't feel that way, though. It didn't feel that way at all.

She sighed. "I'll talk to her, okay?"

Raven smiled brightly. She crossed to Andie and gave her a big hug, acting as if nothing had happened between them. Acting as if she hadn't cut out Andie's heart and left her to bleed to death.

"See?" Raven said cheerily. "Everything's going to be fine. Just like it's always been."

55

As Andie had promised Raven she would, she went to see Julie the very next day. She caught her friend having morning coffee, not yet completely awake. She looked like hell warmed over. Andie told her so.

"Thanks. Same to you." Julie smiled and swung the door wider. "Come on in. Excuse the mess. I'm rebelling against that whole cleanliness-is-next-to-godliness thing."

Andie stepped inside and followed the other woman to the kitchen. Julie hadn't been kidding about her place being a mess—the tiny apartment was in total disarray. Clothes and magazines and empty Coke cans were strewn about. Dishes were stacked in the sink, take-out cartons littered the counter. Once upon a time, Julie had been a neat-freak. In fact, she had always taken great pride in how she and her things looked.

"Are you sure you're all right, Julie?" Andie asked, eyeing her. "You don't look yourself."

"I had a little too much to drink last night." She dragged a hand through her hair. Andie noticed that it shook. "Want some coffee? I just made it."

"Sounds good."

Julie took a mug out of the cabinet, filled it with coffee and slid it across the counter to Andie.

Andie reached for the mug, then stopped, her heart leaping to her throat. A raw-looking, reddish mark ringed Julie's wrist. Not quite a bruise. More like a...

A rope burn.

Andie struggled to find her voice, struggled to find

enough calm to speak without an edge of alarm or condemnation. "What happened to your wrist?"

Julie lowered her gaze. Her eyes widened a bit, as if seeing the mark for the first time herself. She drew her hand away. "I don't know." She lifted a shoulder. "It's nothing."

"It's not nothing." Andie reached out a hand. "Let me see."

Julie folded her arms across her chest. "It's fine. Really."

Andie searched her friend's expression, a sinking sensation in the pit of her stomach. "What are you doing, Julie? What have you gotten yourself into?"

"Nothing. For heaven's sake." She turned her back to Andie and refilled her own coffee cup. "One little bruise and you're ready to call out the cavalry."

Julie was lying. And, true to form, not very well. "Let me see your other wrist."

"I said it was nothing," she snapped. "Drop it, okay?"

"Raven's right, isn't she? You're involved with someone. Who is he, Julie?"

"So that's why you're here," she said, ignoring Andie's question. "I should have known she didn't believe me. I should have known she would send you running over here, like some trained watchdog."

Andie stood and went around the counter. She caught her friend's hands and held them out. Identical marks circled both of her wrists.

"These are rope burns." She looked Julie dead in the eyes. "Aren't they? Don't lie to me."

Julie wrenched her hands away, wincing. "It's my life, okay? Not yours, not Raven's."

"We're not trying to run your life, we care about you. You've been hurt so much, you're vulnerable and..." Andie sucked in a quick breath. "What you're doing is dangerous, Julie. Really dangerous. You should know that. Mrs. X ended up dead. Or have you forgotten?"

"I haven't forgotten, I...I think about her, Leah Robertson, all the time. I think about them, you know?"

"I know," Andie said softly. "I do, too."

Julie passed a hand over her eyes. "Do you ever wonder if it wasn't chance that we were there, that we were the ones who saw them?"

Andie drew her eyebrows together. "If not chance, Julie, then what?"

"Maybe it was us because...because it was our own futures we were seeing."

"Stop it, Julie. You're scaring me."

"But why was it us, Andie?" She searched her expression, her own desperate. "Why?"

"Because it was, that's all. It doesn't have anything to do with us except when we allow it to."

"You're right, of course." Julie smiled, though to Andie it looked forced. "Sometimes my imagination gets the best of me. It always has."

"Is it your imagination? Tell me the truth, Julie. Who is this guy? What are you into?"

"Just a guy, okay. And I'm not into anything dangerous, Andie. Harmless games, nothing heavy. I promise you, I'm not that stupid."

Andie hesitated, wanting desperately to believe her. "You're sure? Those marks on your wrists don't look harmless to me."

"I'm sure. I'm in control of this." She laughed and gave her a hug. "Promise me you won't tell Raven."

"You know I can't do that."

"Please, Andie. I'm in love with him. I am. And he loves me, too."

Andie bit back a sigh. She had heard those exact words from Julie many times before, too many to count. Julie looked to being loved by others as a way to validate herself, her behavior. She looked to love as a way to feel good about herself. It was all part of her addiction.

This time it was Julie who caught Andie's hands, Julie

who begged. "I can't bear for her to know. She'll be so mad at me. She'll be disappointed that I...that I let her down again."

"Raven loves you, Julie. She's worried, like I am. And she'll be glad that you trusted her enough to—"

"No, she won't." Julie shook her head again. "She's not like you, Andie. She expects me to be better than I am."

Andie's heart broke for her friend. In that moment she hated Reverend Cooper, hated him with every fiber of her being. The man should be in jail for the psychological abuse he had heaped on his daughter. But the law only acknowledged physical attacks, though blows to the spirit were every bit as damaging, maybe more so.

"You are good, Julie. Do you hear me? You're strong and smart and kind. You deserve to be loved." Her friend's expression said it all, but Andie didn't give up. "You deserve to be loved," she repeated. "You deserve kindness."

"So, be kind to me. Keep my secret, just for a little while. You'll understand when you meet him."

Andie searched her friend's gaze. "When Julie? When will I meet him?"

"Soon. I promise. So, will you do it? Keep this from Raven?"

Andie sighed. She didn't like having to lie to one friend to keep the confidence of another. It made her feel uneasy and disloyal. Indeed, Raven would be furious—and hurt—if she found out. And she would, eventually, find out.

But Julie was right. Raven expected more from Julie than she was able to give. When it came to friendship, Raven kept demanding standards.

"All right," she said, heart sinking. "I'll keep your secret. For now."

"You're the best!" Julie hugged her. "Thank you!

Thank you. You and Raven are all I've got. I don't want her to be mad at me.''

"No, we're not all you have. You've got you, Julie. And that's a pretty wonderful thing." She reached out and cupped her friend's cheek, a sense of urgency pressing in on her, a sense that Julie was on a clock. And that her time was running out. "I don't want anything to happen to you. You've got to promise you'll be careful with this guy. That you'll play it smart."

"I will. I promise." Julie smiled and hugged her. "You'll see, Andie, this guy's the one who's going to change my life forever."

56

Nick couldn't stop thinking about Andie Bennett. He had enjoyed their evening together—the easiness of their conversation, the sound of her laugh, the way she had treated Mara, with warmth and respect, something adults didn't always show children.

Most of all, he had enjoyed the way he caught her looking at him, as if she wanted to eat him up. That look had gone straight to his head, from there dead south.

It had been a long time since he'd had dinner—or anything else—with a woman who had looked at him like that. From that moment on, he'd been able to think of little but how she would feel in his arms, his bed.

Why hadn't he kissed her? He'd wanted to. More than he'd wanted anything in a long time. She wouldn't have said no. Hell, she had all but sent him an engraved invitation.

Nick frowned. He'd called himself a number of names in the week since then, jackass among them. But the fact was, it hadn't felt right. Not the time or the moment, not being with her.

It wouldn't work. *They* wouldn't work. Not that he was looking for a relationship, he wasn't. Which was precisely the problem. Andie Bennett wasn't the type of woman who jumped into bed with somebody on a whim. And certainly not a still-married, Italian cop with a ready-made family and a bad attitude.

Nope, Andie Bennett would want a lot more than a few

laughs and a quick trip to paradise. She would expect a lot more.

He smiled to himself and passed a hand across his jaw, realizing he needed a shave. And when had he become such an expert on Dr. Andie Bennett? For all he knew, she slept around as a matter of course. For all he knew, still-married, Italian cops were her specialty.

Yeah, right. And so were little green men from Mars.

"Nick, buddy, heads up." His partner tossed a couple of reports on his desk, then folded himself into the chair opposite Nick.

Nick smiled. "What's up, Bobby?"

"Same old shit. What about you?"

"Business as usual."

"That so? Then why have you been sitting here, staring into space for fifteen minutes? One might even call it mooning." His partner grinned. "What're you mooning over, Nick? Or should I say who?"

"Kiss mine," Nick said good-naturedly. He had made the mistake of telling Bobby about his dinner with Andie. Ever since, the other man had taken every opportunity to razz him about it.

Nick shuffled aside the reports, reaching for the Pierpont file beneath them. Before he'd gotten sidetracked by thoughts of Andie Bennett, he had been mulling over a couple of puzzling facts about Martha and Edward Pierpont.

"You aware of these?" Nick asked, referring to the four threatening letters Edward Pierpont had received in the last months before his death. He slid them across the desk.

Bobby scanned them. "Anonymous, right? No leads."

"Right." Nick frowned. "Got the last one two weeks before his death. It prompted him to buy a gun and keep it loaded by his bed."

"What are you thinking?"

Nick lifted a shoulder. "That it's odd. A little over a

week after buying a gun to protect himself from an anonymous threat, he's killed with that very gun.''

"By his wife.''

"Exactly.''

Bobby tossed the letters back onto the desk. "You thinking premeditated?'' He shook his head. "She has the bruises. The kid corroborates her story. Pierpont was out of his head that night. The kid heard him say he was going to kill his wife. I'm not saying I buy into the self-defense shit, but premeditated? That's a stretch, buddy.''

Nick let out a long breath. "Yeah, I know.'' He glanced down at the file, something nagging at him. "But it still bothers me.''

Bobby whistled low, under his breath. "Don't look now, partner, but you've got company.''

Nick looked up. Andie Bennett stood in the doorway of the crowded squad room, talking to one of the uniforms. The man pointed Nick's way, and she started toward him.

He watched her approach, acknowledging pleasure at seeing her, acknowledging attraction. He caught Bobby grinning at him, and scowled. "Fuck you.''

"Sorry, buddy, I'm already spoke for.'' Bobby reached into his breast pocket and tossed something at him. Nick caught it. *A package of breath mints.*

"Just in case you get lucky.''

Nick dropped the roll of candy on his desk and stood. "Andie, hello.''

"Hello, Nick.'' She smiled and turned to Bobby. "Detective O'Shea.''

Grinning now from ear-to-ear, Bobby stood. "It's good to see you again, Dr. Bennett.''

Nick ignored his partner and motioned toward the chair. "Have a seat, Andie.''

"Thank you.'' She took it and looked at him. "How's Mara?''

"Good. She asked about you. She was upset with me that I didn't wake her up to say goodbye the other night.''

Bobby made a sound, a cross between a cough and a laugh, and Nick glared at him. "Aren't there some criminals you're supposed to be busting?"

"Not that I know of." Bobby leaned back in the chair, folding his arms behind his head, making himself nice and comfy.

Nick cleared his throat. "No, I definitely think there's something you're supposed to be doing."

Bobby widened his eyes in exaggerated innocence. "Oh, I get it. Crime. Bad guys. My job." He stood and smiled at Andie once more. "I hope to see you again real soon, Dr. Bennett. Real soon."

Nick watched him walk away, then turned to Andie. Her cheeks were pink. "You have to excuse my partner, he suffers from the delusion that he's funny."

Her lips lifted. "I could help him with that. Delusions are one of my specialties."

He laughed and rested his elbows on the desk. "How are you, Andie?"

"Good. Fine. And you?"

"Same." *Damn, she was pretty.* Nick fought the urge to drop his gaze to her mouth or any other part of her that might get him into trouble. "I meant to call, to see how you were doing. It's been a crazy week here."

She shrugged, brushing off his apology. "Don't think twice about it." She reached in her purse and took out a plain white, business-size envelope and held it out. "I got this today. I thought you'd be interested."

Speaking of delusions—there went his, the one about her coming here today because she couldn't resist him.

Nick took the envelope. "Is this what I think it is?"

"Yes."

He opened it and pulled out the contents—a fifteen-year-old newspaper clipping, one he recognized. One he, Andie and her two friends were named in.

Murder Still Unsolved, Teens Questioned.

Across the article's text someone had scrawled one word: *Liar.*

Nick arched his eyebrows. "Interesting."

"What do you think it means?"

"Whoever sent this seems to believe somebody didn't tell the truth fifteen years ago. Any idea who that might be, Andie?"

She shook her head, looking frustrated, scared. "He said nearly the same thing that time he called. He said that I 'knew everything, but I didn't tell the truth.''" She frowned. "But I don't know what he's talking about, Nick. Fifteen years ago I told the police everything. So did Raven and Julie."

"You're sure?"

"Yes." Her voice rose slightly. "I'm sure."

"Can I hang on to this?" She nodded and he slid it back into the envelope.

A moment of silence fell between them. She lowered her gaze to the desk; it landed on the Pierpont file and the collaged letters, lying on top.

"Did you know about those?" he asked.

She hesitated, then nodded. "Yes. Martha mentioned them and that Edward was...unnerved."

"Frightened, you mean."

"Yes."

"You know he'd bought a gun to protect himself?"

Again she hesitated, and again, he suspected, to decide whether answering broke her oath of confidentiality. She must have decided it didn't. "Yes," she murmured, "I knew."

"How did you react to the news?"

"I was uncomfortable with it. For obvious reasons." She shifted in her seat. "Why don't we change the subject, Nick?"

He smiled. "For obvious reasons?"

She returned his smile, looking relieved. "Yes."

"One last thing, though." He leaned forward, trying his

best to adopt his demeanor of the other night, to resurrect their friendly camaraderie—and feeling like a heel for it. "You don't find it odd that he died by his own gun, only a week or so after having bought it?"

She stiffened. "I find it tragic, Detective."

"You don't think it's odd that Martha Pierpont encouraged him to buy a gun, despite the fact that he was violent? Despite the fact that there was a teenager in the home?"

Andie drew her eyebrows together. "What?"

"Odd," he repeated, "that Martha Pierpont encouraged her violent, abusive husband to keep a loaded gun by their bed? The store clerk who sold them the gun said she encouraged him to do it when he hesitated."

She struggled, he saw, to compose her features. He wondered why.

"I don't know anything about that," she said after a moment, collecting her purse. She started to stand. "But I do know this conversation is inappropriate for me to be having."

"Anything new with your kinky patient?"

She blinked, surprised by his sudden shift in conversation. "Nothing I can talk about. You know that."

He got up, making a sound of frustration. "Dammit, Andie, I don't like this. What if he's the one who's sending you these clippings? What if he's the one who broke into your house?"

"I can't give you his name." She curled her fingers around the strap of her purse. "I can't."

"What if he's a killer?"

The sentence landed heavily between them. She paled. "He's not," she said, her words lacking conviction. "I know he's not."

"How?" Nick took a step toward her. "How do you know he isn't the one who sent the clippings? How do you know he's not the one who called you, the one who broke into your home and left Mr. and Mrs. X's music playing? How do you know he's not Mr. X?"

Andie started to shake, though he saw that she tried to hide it from him. "I think I would know if he was," she said. "I work with him, Nick. The therapy process, it's…intimate. He couldn't hide the truth from me."

Intimate. He didn't like the word, what it suggested. Not in connection with Andie and this guy.

Nick stood and came around the desk to stand directly before her. "You're wrong about him. He could hide the truth, he could. I see it all the time. If he's a killer, you're keeping him from justice. And you're putting your own life in danger. Do you want to die, Andie?"

"No." She wet her lips. "Of course not. But I've taken an oath, I can't break it."

Nick leaned toward her. He caught a whiff of her perfume, something flowery and bright. It went straight to his head. "What's that oath worth, Andie? Tell me, is it worth dying for?"

57

Andie watched David Sadler as he roamed her office, touching her things, moving them slightly, making them his own. She breathed deeply through her nose, working to calm herself. Nick had scared her. She couldn't stop thinking about what he'd said.

If he's a killer, you're keeping him from justice. And you're putting your own life in danger. Do you want to die, Andie?

Swallowing hard, she returned her attention to David. Had it been him in her house the other night, touching her things the same way he was now, forcing himself on her? Had he gone through her drawers and closets? Had he studied her family photographs and gone into her desk and read her journal?

What if David was a killer?

What if he was Mr. X?

Andie struggled to quiet her agitated breathing, to slow her runaway heart. His age was right. His build and coloring. But why would he want to stir up interest in an unsolved murder case, a case in which he would be the prime suspect? That didn't make sense.

Besides, there were probably hundreds of men in Thistledown who fit David's general description. And how many men were there in this town, she wondered, who had experimented with light bondage during sex, who had a need to control and dominate women? A couple dozen? Less? More? Edward Pierpont had even fit that description, only he had controlled and dominated through fear, intimidation and physical abuse.

She was letting Nick get to her. Nick would do anything in hopes of solving the Robertson case; he had all but told her so that night over dinner. Her ethical responsibility to her patients and her profession didn't mean dip to him, not compared to catching a killer.

It'd be no skin off his nose if she turned David over to him and he wasn't anything more than a guy with a problem that he had sought help for. So what if he was wrong and David Sadler was publicly shamed and her integrity lost?

What's that oath worth, Andie? Is it worth dying for?

"Dr. Bennett?"

She jumped, startled. David was standing not three feet from her, his bright, light eyes unblinkingly upon her.

"I'm sorry, David. What did you say?"

"You look about ready to make a run for it."

"Excuse me?"

"You're perched on the edge of your chair." He motioned with his head.

She looked down at herself. *She was.* "So I am." She scooted back in her seat, struggling to compose herself. She smiled, though it felt as if her cheeks might crack with the effort. "Sorry. I'm distracted today. Go on with what you were saying."

"I was saying, things aren't always what they seem."

"What do you mean?"

"People, their motivations. Everybody has an agenda. It's just a matter of discovering what it is."

"You don't think you might be projecting onto others your own inability to be fully honest in your relationships?"

He thought for a moment, then shook his head. "Not at all. But I see by your expression that you disagree."

"I do disagree. I think it all comes down to trust, David. Being honest and expecting honesty in return. That's the essential core of all interpersonal relationships. Without honesty, how could anybody ever really know anybody else?''

"Exactly."

"So, you're saying that nobody really knows you? That they never have?" He simply smiled. The cat with his mouse. "What's your secret agenda, David? If everyone else has one, you must, too."

He leaned toward her. "Do you trust me, Dr. Bennett?"

About as far as she could toss him. "I'd like to, David. I really would."

He laughed. "You're so good at that evasive bullshit. *'I'd really like to,'''* he mocked. "Which means, of course, that you don't."

"Should I?"

"That's for me to know and you to find out."

Suddenly she was tired of his evasions, his games of cat and mouse; she was tired of Nick's warnings and her own fear, of wondering if David was the one harassing her.

Suddenly, she was pissed off.

She met his eyes evenly. "If you have a secret agenda, David, I want to know what it is. You owe me that."

"I owe you that?" He arched his eyebrows. "You're very naive, aren't you, Doctor? A real Goody Two-shoes."

She stood, all but shaking with fury. She felt played with and vulnerable and like a sitting duck. And she didn't like it. "If we're going to continue working together, I have to have complete honesty from you. Are you what you seem to be, David? Or do you have a hidden agenda? Another reason for these sessions with me?"

One second became several; the silence crackled between them. Then he lifted his gaze to hers. In that moment he looked more like a lost little boy than a man she feared capable of murder. "No secret agenda, Dr. Bennett. I want your help. That's all."

58

Julie was up to her old tricks again.

Raven hung up the phone, quaking with fury, with betrayal. All the signs were there, they had been for weeks. Her friend was acting guilty and distracted, giggling inappropriately or refusing to look Raven in the eyes. She had been evasive about how she was spending her time, and though she was never available, she wouldn't say where she had been or who she had been with.

Raven narrowed her eyes. One thing was for certain, however, Julie hadn't been with her. She hadn't been with Andie.

Did she think Raven was stupid?

Raven fumbled in her desk drawer for her cigarettes, lit one and dragged deeply on it. Why did she even bother with Julie? The girl was as loyal as a bitch dog in heat. Didn't she remember how her biological family had washed their hands of her? Didn't she remember how Raven and Andie had been her friends when no one else would give her the time of day? Or how, over the past ten years, she had turned to Raven again and again, for support and love, for money, a place to live, everything.

Whatever she had asked for, whatever she had needed, Raven had always given it to her. And each time Julie had promised that she had changed, that she had come home to stay, and Raven had believed her.

All Raven asked of her was loyalty. Such a simple thing. One that should come naturally. Raven brought the cigarette to her mouth again. Why did she love the girl so much?

Because she was family. Because you didn't give up on family until you were absolutely forced to.

Raven rolled her shoulders, trying to relieve the knots of tension there. What if Julie wasn't lying? Andie had spoken with her and had been convinced that Julie hadn't fallen off the wagon. Raven took another drag on the cigarette and crushed it in the crystal ashtray on her desk. She needed proof. To set her own mind at ease or to confront Julie with. And if necessary, to use to elicit Andie's help.

Maybe, if they both confronted her, if they both laid it, their friendships, on the line, she would get her act together and realize what was important.

After all, they had never actually delivered Julie an ultimatum before. Perhaps it was time they did, Raven thought.

Raven glanced at her watch. Julie had used having to work as an excuse for their not being able to get together tonight. That would be easy enough to check.

Raven picked up the phone, dialed the country club, then had the operator connect her with the bar. The bartender on duty answered; Raven asked for Julie. When he said she wasn't there, Raven asked if she would be in later. She wouldn't be, he replied. She had the night off.

Lying little whore. Disloyal bitch.

Raven slammed down the phone and got to her feet, shoving away from the desk so forcefully that her chair, a Louis XIV reproduction, crashed to the floor. She was going to find out exactly what Julie was up to and with whom. Then she would deal with her.

Laura rushed out of the back room, expression alarmed. When she saw the chair, she made a sound of dismay. ''Raven, are you all—''

''I'm leaving,'' Raven snapped, snatching up her briefcase. ''There's something I have to take care of. Lock up.''

* * *

Raven waited until dusk to drive over to Julie's, so her friend would be less likely to spot her BMW. If Julie did happen to see her, she would say she had stopped by on her way to dinner, just to make sure she hadn't changed her mind about going out.

Raven saw she was in luck as she pulled into the building's parking area—Julie's car was there. She chose a spot at the back of the lot, one where she wouldn't be noticed but one that afforded her a clear view of both Julie's car and the building's entrance.

Then she waited. As she did, her mind wandered. To the times she, Andie and Julie had spent together, of the way they had laughed together and supported one another. They had been like one person instead of three. More than friends, better than sisters.

Remembering hurt. When had her family gotten so far away from her? When had everything changed between them? Once upon a time they had been so close. Once upon a time they had shared everything.

The summer of '83. Mr. X's summer. She closed her eyes, thinking of that time, the similarities between then and now. Andie had been uncommunicative and distracted then, too. Julie had been lost in a world of her own making, and she, Raven, had been unhappy and worried, scrambling for a way to bring them all back together.

She was always the one, it seemed, who was scrambling to keep their family together.

She reopened her eyes. And there he was, driving by in his bright red Jaguar. David Sadler. Their Mr. X.

She blinked, thinking at first that her memories had materialized him. They hadn't. He pulled his car up at the building's entrance, swung out and headed inside.

What was he doing here? she wondered, glancing around. This wasn't what one would call classy digs. Not his typical stomping ground. Not the kind of place he would have friends.

Julie. He had come to get Julie.

The pulse began to thrum in her head. The inside of her mouth turned to dust. She called her thoughts ridiculous. How would David know Julie? How would he have met her? This was some sort of weird coincidence.

But it wasn't.

After only a couple of minutes, David emerged from the building. With Julie. She was laughing and gazing up at him, obviously smitten. Raven curved her fingers tightly around the steering wheel, fighting to catch her breath.

David Sadler was Julie's mystery man.

Feeling light-headed and sick to her stomach, she leaned her head against the rest. She closed her eyes and breathed deeply through her nose.

David Sadler was screwing Julie.

He was doing business with her, Raven.

She opened her eyes. What was he doing with Andie? Because he *was* involved with her, Raven was certain of it. Most likely as a patient.

The truth of that had her sitting bolt upright. David Sadler was involved with all three of them.

How could she not have seen it before? How could she not have at least *suspected* that he had tried to contact her friends, the other two girls who had been involved with him and Mrs. X?

She brought her fists to her forehead. *Dummy. Stupid. Stupid.* Of course he had contacted them. He had to be the one behind the clipping they had all received; he was probably the one behind Andie's obscene calls and was no doubt the one who had left the music playing in her house.

But why? she wondered. What did he hope to accomplish with his little campaign of terror?

She dropped her hands, beginning to sweat. Dear God, what did he know about the three of them? What did he know about her and the part she had played in the events of fifteen years ago? Did he suspect that she had been in that house with him and Leah Robertson? That she had seen *everything* that had happened? Many times she had thought he was aware of her presence. He had looked her way, looked toward the closet door and smiled.

Raven worked to get hold of her runaway thoughts. He didn't know, she told herself. He couldn't. He was playing with them. The way he had played with Leah Robertson. He was getting pleasure from their fear, from thinking he was in control, from his anonymity.

The son of a bitch. The sick bastard.

Julie. Mrs. X. Raven brought a hand to her mouth. *Jesus.* If Julie was having an affair with David Sadler, Raven would bet they were into the same kinky game that Mr. and Mrs. X had been into.

Hands shaking, this time with fury, Raven started her car. Mr. X had come back into all of their lives and like before, he had begun tearing them apart. He was to blame for Andie's distance and Julie's evasions. Just like the summer of '83. And just like then, Raven was being forced to scramble around, to find a way to make everything right again.

Andie and Julie were hers. Her friends, her family.

Nobody messed with what was hers.

59

"Raven," Andie said, surprised, swinging her front door open. "What are you doing here?"

"I didn't think I had to call first."

Andie's smile faded at her friend's words and tone. "I didn't mean that. Of course you don't. It's a work night, that's all." She swung the door wider and stepped aside so the other woman could enter. "What's up?"

"I thought we could go to dinner."

"Dinner?" Andie repeated, looking down at herself. When she'd gotten home from the office thirty minutes ago, she had thrown on some baggy shorts and an old T-shirt. "Now? Tonight?"

"Why not? You haven't eaten, have you?"

"No, but…" But she'd had a hectic day, one filled with numerous crises. Tomorrow promised more of the same. The last thing she felt like was going out. "I just sat down with a sandwich."

"Screw that. Let's go to MacGuire's. I'm dying for one of their burgers."

Andie frowned. Raven was behaving strangely. Almost manic. Usually quite self-contained, she was gesturing and fidgeting, her gaze darting from one point to the next as she spoke. She even looked strange—her cheeks were flushed, her eyes unnaturally bright.

"Is something wrong?" Andie asked.

"What could be wrong?"

"You tell me."

Raven laughed, crossed to the living room and plopped

down on the couch. She folded her arms behind her head and stared up at the ceiling. "You're doing that shrink thing again. Go change, I'm hungry."

Andie let out an exasperated breath. "The things I do for my friends. But I warn you, it has to be a quick dinner, I'm meeting with Martha and her lawyer first thing in the morning."

Twenty minutes later they were sitting in a booth at MacGuire's, food ordered, drinks on the table in front of them. An Irish pub–style restaurant that served a variety of hearty fare, including the best burgers in town, it was crowded even now, after eight-thirty on a weeknight.

"So, what's this all about, Rave? Not food, I'll bet."

Her friend looked her in the eyes. "I've missed you, Andie."

"Missed me?" She smiled. "But I haven't gone anywhere."

"Haven't you?" Raven fumbled in her purse for her pack of cigarettes, found them and glanced at Andie in question. "You mind?"

She said that she didn't, and Raven lit one and dragged deeply on it. Raven tipped her head back and blew a stream of smoke toward the ceiling, then met Andie's gaze once more. "Think about it. When's the last time we had dinner together?"

Andie thought back, and was surprised to realize it had been over two weeks. She smiled ruefully. "I've been busier than I thought."

"Just like Julie."

At the mention of their mutual friend, Andie slid her gaze guiltily away. She had hated lying to Raven about Julie; she felt like a heel. She and Raven had always been, with only a few exceptions, completely honest with one another.

"She's seeing someone."

Andie snapped her gaze back to her friend's. "How do you know?"

"I followed her. Tonight."

Andie couldn't believe what Raven was telling her. "You didn't."

"I did." She took another long drag on the cigarette, then stamped it out and immediately reached for another. "I knew she was lying to me, so I got proof." She blew out a puff of smoke. "The little bitch."

"Raven!"

"Here you go." The waitress arrived with their food. She set it in front of them, asked them if they needed anything else, then walked off.

Raven laid her napkin in her lap. "What do you expect me to call her? She lied to me, looked me in the eyes and lied her ass off."

"She didn't want to disappoint you."

"Please." Raven picked at a French fry. "I mean, she lied to you, too. Doesn't that make you feel like shit? Doesn't it make you mad?"

Andie took a deep breath. She had to tell her friend the truth. It would eventually come out, and when it did, it would be that much uglier. "Julie didn't lie to me, Raven. She confessed she was involved with someone." At her friend's stunned expression, Andie leaned toward her. "I know, I'm sorry. I hate that I kept the truth from you. Please try to understand. She begged me not to tell you. *Begged*, Raven. She was terrified of your finding out."

Raven didn't speak. She pushed her plate away and turned her gaze to the window.

A lump formed in Andie's throat. "She has a sickness, Raven. An addiction. It has control of her, not the other way around." Andie let out a long breath. "She loves you so much. She really does."

Raven looked at her then, her cheeks bright with color. "What about you, Andie? Do you love me, too? Or do you only love Nick Raphael now?"

Andie's mouth dropped, and she sat back in the booth,

stunned. Where in the world had that come from? Her friend sounded like a jealous lover.

"Is that what's going on, Andie? Are you dumping me? Is that why I never see you anymore?"

"No!" Andie struggled to hold on to her dismay. "First of all, I haven't even *seen* Nick Raphael since the night we had dinner, and I'm most certainly *not* in love with him. Second, you're my best friend. Even if I were in love with Nick Raphael, I wouldn't 'dump' you. With everything we've been through and been to each other? My God, don't you know me any better than that?"

Raven's eyes filled with tears. "What do you expect me to think? I've been feeling so left out of your life. We hardly speak on the phone, we almost never see each other." She smoothed and resmoothed her napkin. "How many messages have I left you? How many messages that you haven't returned?"

Andie swallowed hard, upset at the way she had hurt Raven's feelings but disconcerted nonetheless by her friend's anger and combativeness. Her possessiveness. "I'm sorry," she said again. "I've been so involved with the Pierpont trial and this whole...thing, the clippings and calls, the music. I just didn't think."

"No, you didn't." Raven signaled the waitress that she would like another glass of wine. "This is beginning to remind me of the summer of '83."

When Mr. and Mrs. X had come into their lives. When they had been torn apart, their lives changed forever.

"Excuse me. You're Andie Bennett, aren't you? Dr. Andie Bennett?"

Andie turned toward the woman who had come up to their table, stiffening slightly. The last time she had been asked that question, the person had threatened to put a noose around her neck. "I am. Can I help you?"

"You don't know me. I'm Gwen White, one of Patti Pierpont's teachers. Her English teacher."

Andie smiled, feeling somewhat better. She hardly

thought this staid-looking high-school English teacher the type to threaten her, especially not in the middle of a busy and popular restaurant. "Nice to meet you."

"I just wanted to ask, how's Patti doing? She's such a sweet girl, and so smart, I hate that this terrible thing has happened to her. And I wondered, if you see her, will you tell her I'm thinking of her? That we all are."

"Thank you," Andie said. "That's very nice. I'll tell her."

The woman's gaze darted to Raven, then she looked back at Andie. She lowered her voice. "I knew something bad was going on in the Pierpont home, but I didn't know what. Patti always seemed so unhappy. Not like the other girls at all."

Andie opened her mouth to comment, but closed it as the teacher continued. "And she was so angry. Some of her essays... It's really tragic."

"Angry?" Andie said. "How do you mean?"

The woman flushed. "I shouldn't have said that. I didn't mean anything bad by it. Like I said, she's a lovely girl." The woman took a step backward, looking uncomfortable, obviously feeling she had said too much or spoken inappropriately. "Please, if there's anything I can do to help her, call me. And tell her I said hello."

Andie promised she would and watched the woman walk away, thinking about what she had said. Patti had been unhappy. Angry. She had, apparently, revealed both through her writing.

Just as Andie had always told Martha—her daughter had known everything that went on in that house.

"Andie?" Raven leaned toward her. "What is it? You look strange."

Andie glanced back at her friend. "Something that woman said, I don't know, it just struck me funny." She shook her head. "What's new with you?" she said, abruptly changing the subject.

Whatever demon had held Raven in its grip before the

teacher had stopped by their table was gone. Raven seemed almost her old self, confident and sarcastic and funny.

She launched into a description of what she had been doing on the Gatehouse development. "In one way David Sadler's a dream to work for. He has style and class. He understands the importance of quality, he lets me do my job without questioning my every choice. I'm the professional in this area, and he lets me do my job. In another way," Raven finished, looking Andie in the eyes, "he's a real jerk."

"What do you mean?" Andie asked, despite herself. She was treading on dangerous ground here, discussing a patient this way. She should try to change the subject, try to steer Raven back to her actual work on Gatehouse. Her curiosity got the better of her instead.

"He's got this thing about women. It's kind of creepy. You know what I mean?"

"I don't think I do."

"It's a sexual thing. He's always trying to get me in bed, but that's not it. I can handle that overt crap. It's something…sly. Like he's watching me or…playing some sort of game."

Andie reached for her water; her hand trembled slightly. "It sounds…unsettling."

"Do you know him?"

Andie met her friend's gaze, startled by the direct question. "Excuse me?"

"Do you know him? David Sadler?"

Andie's heart stopped, then began to thud heavily. She lowered her gaze to her plate, pretending great interest in her Caesar salad. "I'm sure I've seen him around town."

"Have you met him face-to-face?"

"Perhaps," she murmured evasively. "His family's prominent, we might have served on a few of the same committees."

"But you don't remember?"

"If we served on some committees?" Andie speared some of the crunchy romaine. "No, I don't recall."

"And you don't recall if you met, out and about in Thistledown?"

Andie brought the forkful of salad to her mouth. Raven was definitely pumping her for information about David Sadler. Could she know he was a patient of hers? Could she suspect? Why would she care?

Andie chewed slowly, pretending to search her memory. She swallowed, then patted her mouth with her napkin. "Met him out and about? I'm not sure."

Raven narrowed her eyes, as if she suspected Andie of lying. "If you'd met him, you'd remember. There's something startling-looking about him. He's quite handsome, actually."

"Well, there you have it," Andie murmured. "So, tell me, when will the first model be complete?"

60

Andie slept poorly. She tossed and turned, kept awake by thoughts of Raven and their conversation that evening. Raven's behavior had been so bizarre, so off. She had chain-smoked. She had only picked at the hamburger she had professed to be starving for. She'd ordered a second glass of wine. She'd rambled.

All were highly unusual for Raven. Raven was nothing if not completely in control, all the time.

Raven had never, in all the time they had known one another, behaved quite like that. It had been strange, like being with a person she had known all her life but suddenly not recognizing her.

Andie thumped her pillow, trying to plump it, her thoughts turning to Nick and the discussion they'd had about people who had lived through intense traumas.

So, what happens if the person's anchors are suddenly taken away? Do they go bonkers?

Did Raven feel as if her anchors were being pulled away? Andie wondered. Was that why she had acted jealous and angry? Was she striking out in fear of being abandoned? It made some sense.

Or was something else going on? Something she hadn't shared with Andie?

Finally, around dawn, Andie gave in and got up. She made coffee and sat on her patio, sipping the strong brew and enjoying the early-morning light and the sweet scent of the new day.

She tilted her head back and breathed deeply, her

thoughts turning to Nick. She hadn't been quite truthful with Raven the night before. She had seen Nick that one time since their dinner together, when she had gone to the station.

Why hadn't she told Raven? she wondered, bringing the mug of coffee to her lips. Why had she kept it from her? Her visit had been business only. There had been nothing personal between them.

She shook her head, acknowledging another lie, this one to herself. Nothing personal? Nothing but the way her body had hummed when she'd looked at him. Nothing but the things she had been thinking—dizzying things, thoughts that had taken her breath away and made her pulse pound.

He, obviously, hadn't been affected the same way. He had been all-business, brusque, to the point. The macho cop doing his job.

So why had she kept the visit a secret from Raven?

Because she'd been afraid of her friend's response. The last time she had confided her feelings for Nick, Raven had ridiculed her. She had pointed out to Andie every reason why Nick was wrong for her. Why he would break her heart. Her reasons had been valid; they had been the same things Andie had pointed out to herself.

They had also *not* been what she'd wanted to hear.

Andie sighed. She was a little old for an adolescent crush, although that was what she had. And she was a good enough shrink to see what was going on here, see how her present feelings for Nick were tangled up with the part he had played in her past. Fifteen years ago, he'd been her knight in shining armor, even if only for a couple of weeks. He had comforted and protected her. He had come along when, still reeling from her father's abandonment, she had been desperate for a strong, steady male influence in her life.

She brought the coffee to her lips, a smile tugging at

them. Good thing Detective Raphael wasn't playing along with her fantasies.

If he did, she feared she wouldn't be able to say no.

That he wasn't playing along had been painfully obvious the other day. He had used her visit as an opportunity to grill her about Martha Pierpont, hoping to trick her into revealing God only knew what. She had to admit, after the intimate evening they'd shared, his cold-blooded professionalism had rankled.

And it had thrown her for a loop. She had been left standing there, remembering their evening and wanting to trust him, and feeling cornered and resentful.

The truth was, Nick Raphael made her feel.

The sun had risen, the birds had broken into a full morning chorus. Andie checked her watch and saw, unbelievably, that it was already time to go inside and dress. She had an early meeting at Martha's mother's with Martha, who was living there while out on bail, and Robert Fulton. He had asked her to join them. He intended to talk about Martha's defense and attempt to convince the woman to allow Patti to testify. So far, Martha had been adamant that she not.

Just as she had been adamant in her denial of Andie's suspicions concerning Edward and his daughter. Every time Andie tried to bring it up, Martha either shut down or became childishly defiant. Maybe they would have more luck today.

With a last glance at the beautiful morning, she stood and went inside to dress.

An hour later, Andie was greeting Martha Pierpont and her mother. Robert had not yet arrived, they told her as they invited her inside. Andie handed the older woman a box of pastries from the Little Switzerland Bake Shop, home of the best pastries in Thistledown. "I couldn't resist," she said. "Their apple strudel is to die for."

Rose Turpin smiled. "Thank you so much. I'll go put these on a plate."

Left alone with Martha, Andie turned to her. She caught the woman's hands. "How are you?"

Martha squeezed her fingers then drew her hands away, her small smile distant but unerringly polite. "Fine, thank you. And you?"

The last few times she had seen Martha, it had been the same thing—the woman had been distant but polite, refusing to face emotionally anything that was happening to her, even if only by admitting to fear, pain or regret.

Andie had tried to convince her to return to therapy, they could meet at her mother's, she had offered. Martha had refused, claiming she couldn't afford it. When Andie had assured her there would be no charge, she had found another excuse, then another.

Denial had gotten Martha through most of her adult life, and she had turned to it now, to get her through this.

"Martha," Andie said, "please, talk to me. I know you're going through a difficult time. A horrible time. Not acknowledging your feelings will only—"

"I told you, I'm doing very well."

"Can't I say anything to convince you to return to therapy?"

"There's no need now. Ed's gone."

"There's every need." She lowered her voice. "I'm not the enemy, Martha. I'm here for you. I want to help."

Martha stared at her for a moment, her expression blank, then smiled brightly. "Thank you, Dr. Bennett. I do appreciate it." She glanced at her watch. "Robert should be here any moment. Why don't we get you a cup of coffee?"

Martha started for the kitchen without pausing to ask if Andie wanted a cup. Andie followed her. Rose met her eyes as they entered the kitchen. She looked worried.

The doorbell rang. "That'll be Robert," Martha murmured. "I'll get it."

As soon as she left the room, Rose turned to her. "Something strange is going on, Dr. Bennett. Between Martha and Patti."

"Strange? What do you mean?"

"I heard them arguing. Patti was begging her mother to let her do something. Martha was very short with her and Patti left the room in tears. Before she did, she shouted that she hated him."

Her father, obviously. "Has Patti confided anything to you about the night her father was killed? Anything contrary to what she and Martha have told the police?"

"No, of course not." Rose frowned. "What are you getting at?"

Patti entered the kitchen, her cheeks bright pink, her expression guilty. Andie suspected the girl had been standing just beyond the doorway listening. "Hi, Gram." She slid her gaze toward Andie, then looked quickly away. "What are these?" she asked, going to the platter of pastries. "Can I have one?"

"Of course." Rose put an arm around her granddaughter and kissed the top of her head. "Dr. Bennett brought them."

"Sorry I'm late," Robert said as he and Martha entered the room.

Martha saw her daughter and paled slightly. "Patti, honey, why don't you get a pastry and go back to your room. We have some things to discuss in private."

"I want to stay."

"Not today, sweetheart. Get yourself a strudel and—"

"No." Patti cocked up her chin. "I'm not a baby anymore. You can't just send me to my room."

"Oh, yes, I can. I'm your mother. And this conversation is for adult ears only."

"Actually," Robert murmured, "I have no problem with Patti sitting in. After all, it has to do with her, as well."

"See!" Patti exclaimed.

Martha began to tremble. "I said, go to your room."

The girl dug in, facing her mother defiantly. "Why? I

know what you're going to talk about. Me. About me testifying." She turned to the lawyer. "I want to do it."

Martha sucked in a sharp breath. "No. Absolutely not."

"Why?" Patti cried, her expression anguished. "I should. You know I should."

"This has nothing to do with you."

"Nothing to do with me? Dad's dead, and you're charged with his murder, and you say it has nothing—"

"That's enough, Patti."

"No, it's not." She lowered her voice, sounding suddenly more adult than Martha. "It happened, Mom. All of it, no matter how much you want to deny it. It happened and it's not going away."

The woman struggled to compose herself. "I'm your mother, I know what's best for you." She held her daughter's gaze. "I don't want to hear another word about this."

Robert stepped in. "If you're worried about her time on the stand, Martha, let me reassure you, the prosecution will go easy on her. It's an unspoken rule, minors get the kid-glove treatment. And believe me, that's not because prosecutors are such nice guys. They know that even a hint of badgering could turn the jury against them."

"I said no." Martha's voice shook.

"But, Mom, you and I both know I should do this." Her voice thickened with tears. "I want to help you. Why won't you let me?"

Martha crossed to her daughter and gathered the girl's hands in hers. "You have your whole life ahead of you, honey. A long, happy life. I've made so many mistakes, baby. Let me do this for you."

"I don't want you to go to jail," she whispered, voice quivering. "I don't think I could stand it if you did. I love you, Mom."

"I love you, too." She hugged her daughter. "It'll be okay. It really will. Go on now. I want to speak to Dr. Bennett and Mr. Fulton alone."

"Come on, Patti-pie," her grandma said, holding out a

hand. "I'll go with you. We'll work on that quilt we started."

After one last, pleading look at her mother, Patti left the room. Andie and Robert exchanged glances, then Robert cleared his throat. "Martha, your daughter wants to testify and we need her. Why not at least consider—"

"No." She crossed to the coffee service and poured herself a cup. "Anyone else?" she asked.

Robert followed her. "Patti, more than anyone else, knows what Ed was like. She was here that night and—"

"We'll do without her. We have Andie. She'll testify about Edward. And so will I." She held a cup out to Andie. "Cream? Sugar?"

Andie shook her head and took the cup from the woman.

Robert tried again. "You're standing trial for murder. Your word, in the jury's eyes, is suspect. After all, you're trying to save your own skin. And, as far as Andie's concerned, she's a good witness except for the fact that many people have a general mistrust of therapists. There's also the matter of your outburst in Andie's office. If she's on the stand, that's fair game for the prosecution."

At mention of the outburst, Martha looked accusingly at Andie. The woman still denied it ever happened. She swore she never said, let alone shouted, that she wanted to kill her husband.

"Children," he continued, "are perceived as completely trustworthy and incapable of lying. Good, emotional testimony from her would take us a long way toward a not guilty verdict."

"We'll do it without her." Martha walked past him to the tray of pastries. She perused it, then selected one. Robert looked at Andie as if to say, "What now?" Andie lifted her shoulders, letting him know she didn't have an answer.

"The prosecution could call her," he said. "You do understand that?"

Martha looked at him, pastry halfway to her mouth. "I won't allow it."

"You can't stop it."

The blood drained from her face. "Of course I can. I'm her mother. She's a minor."

"She's fifteen, not five. The judge may very well allow it. If they ask."

Martha fumbled behind her for one of the chairs, pulled it out and sat down heavily. "Hasn't she suffered enough?" she asked, almost to herself. "Hasn't she endured all she should have to?"

Andie crossed to her. She squatted in front of her so the woman would be compelled to look her in the eyes. "What aren't you telling us, Martha? What really happened that night?"

"I told you. I told you exactly what happened."

"Did Ed hit Patti? Is that why you—"

"No." She shook her head. "No."

"Did he…touch her? Did he force himself on—"

"No! She was in her room. She only came out when she heard the shots. I told you!"

"Martha," she said gently, trying another tack, "I ran into Patti's English teacher, Gwen White. She told me Patti wrote about her father, about her anger and despair. Testifying could be a good thing for Patti. You see it as a negative, as frightening and traumatic. It might be freeing instead."

Martha began to shake her head, and Andie caught her hands. "Hear me out. This is a chance for Patti to *do* something to help you. Up until now she's been forced to sit back and watch. Her whole life, Martha. Helpless and hurting."

Martha's hands were ice-cold; Andie warmed them. "Do you see? Now she's a victim. And by forcing her to sit back and just watch what happens to you, without being given the opportunity to try to help, she stays a victim."

The woman tried to look away, but Andie didn't allow it. "She's been forced to sit back and watch all her life, Martha. Let her try to help."

Martha's face crumpled. She seemed to age ten years before Andie's eyes. "I know how much you love her," Andie said. "Give her this. Let her testify."

For one moment Andie thought Martha would relent. She saw it in her eyes, in the way she sagged in her chair, as if she didn't have the strength of will even to sit straight anymore. Then she pulled herself together and freed her hands from Andie's.

"No," she said, then louder, almost shouting, "No, I won't allow it."

"But why?" Andie got to her feet. "I'm not the enemy," she said, repeating her words from earlier. "Neither is Robert. If you would just tell us what you're afraid of, we could help you."

"I have to know everything, Martha," Robert said. "To defend you, there can't be any secrets between us. You have to be one hundred percent honest with me. If you're not, we could lose."

Martha paled. "That's right," he said, "we could lose. Believe me, the prosecution will unearth something, be it a witness or testimony and I'll be left floundering. The jury will know. They'll see it. They'll lose confidence in me. And then, we're dead."

He crossed to her. "I have to be prepared. And my job is to defend you, to the best of my abilities, no matter what. If you were to tell me you killed him in cold blood, I would still defend you to the best of my abilities."

"But I didn't!" she cried. "I told you what happened! I told you the truth. Edward was trying to kill me! He was going to do it. I shot him. I had to." She dissolved into tears. "He was going to kill me."

Robert and Andie exchanged glances. He took another step toward Martha. "If you've told me everything, then what are you so afraid of? If you've been completely honest, what are you trying to protect Patti from?"

Martha raised her eyes to Robert's. The despair in them took Andie's breath.

"Ask yourself this, Martha," he said softly. "Do you want to spend the rest of your life in jail?"

61

Two days later, Martha showed up unexpectedly at Andie's office just before lunch. "Martha," Andie said warmly, relieved to see her. Since the meeting the other morning, she had been unable to stop thinking about the woman. She had worried about how alone she must feel, how desperate. She worried that she might act on those feelings, do something crazy.

"Hello, Dr. Bennett," Martha murmured, twisting her purse strap around her index finger, obviously nervous. "I was hoping... I thought we..." Her voice trailed off.

"Of course we can. This is the perfect time." Andie caught the woman's hands. "I'm glad you're here. Come into my office." Andie turned to her receptionist. "Missy, no calls, no interruptions."

The receptionist nodded, her gaze following Martha. "You got it."

Once in the office, they took their seats. Martha clasped her hands in her lap and averted her eyes. Moments ticked past.

"What is it, Martha?" Andie asked softly. "What's bothering you?"

She looked up, then away. "I was afraid you wouldn't agree to see me, with the way I've been acting."

"I would always see you, Martha. And you're entitled to the way you've been acting. You're going through a great deal."

Silence fell between them again. Andie decided to take a chance. "This is about Patti, isn't it?"

Martha looked up, her expression anguished. "Yes, it—"

Her intercom buzzed; Martha Pierpont bit back whatever she had been about to say. Andie frowned. Her receptionist knew "no calls, no interruptions" meant just that. And she understood why—moments just like this one.

"I'm sorry, Martha, this must be an emergency. Excuse me." She picked up the phone and buzzed her receptionist back. "Missy? What is it?"

"I'm so sorry, Dr. Bennett." The woman sounded rattled. "But Raven's here. She *insisted* I interrupt you."

"I'll be right out." Andie excused herself again and hurried out to the receptionist area, closing the door behind her. Raven sat on the edge of Missy's desk, chatting, though the receptionist looked anything but happy. "Raven, what's wrong?"

"Hey, Andie. We have a lunch date. Remember? You, me, rabbit food."

"A lunch date," Andie repeated. "Didn't Missy tell you I was with a patient?"

"Yeah, but we had plans."

Andie didn't hide her annoyance. "I'll have to take a rain check."

Raven stood. "But I need to talk to you about Julie. It's important."

"So's this. I'm sorry, but you and Julie are going to have to wait."

Hot color flooded her friend's cheeks. "So what you're saying is, this patient's more important than me? Than us?"

Andie stiffened, angry. She glanced at Missy and saw that her eyes were huge with disbelief. "Yes," Andie said. "This is more important than a lunch date with you and yet another discussion about our mutual friend's problems. Now, excuse me."

She turned to go; Raven caught her arm, her grip almost painful. "You're blowing me off. Again. I don't like it."

"Sorry about that. I'm doing my job, it comes first."
She extricated herself from Raven's grasp. "I'll call you
later."

Without a backward glance, she returned to her office
and Martha Pierpont. "I'm so sorry," she said, taking her
seat, trying to pretend that her lifelong best friend hadn't
just shocked her with her insensitivity and selfishness.
"Please go on."

Martha looked at Andie's closed office door, then back
at Andie. "I've gotten you in trouble with your friend."
She collected her purse and started to stand. "Maybe I
should go."

"Please," Andie said, holding out a hand, "don't worry
about that. You came here today for a reason, don't leave
until we've discussed things."

Martha hesitated; Andie cursed Raven's interruption.
"Tell me about Patti," she urged. "That's why you came.
Tell me, Martha."

For the briefest of moments, the woman looked as if she
was going to refuse, as if she was going to draw into herself once more. Then she began to speak, softly, haltingly.
"It started a few months back, maybe six, though I didn't
know about it at first. Edward…he—"

Martha's throat closed over the words and she tried to
clear it. "Patti didn't tell me. She…wanted to try to hide
it from me." Martha lifted her eyes to Andie's, the expression in them that of a woman who had lost everything,
even hope. "The way I always tried to hide everything
from her. The way I always tried to…to pretend everything
was fine."

Andie nodded encouragingly, a fist of tension settling in
the pit of her gut. She had a pretty darned good idea where
this was heading. "Go on."

Martha reached for a tissue and immediately began
shredding it. "Edward, he…apparently, he came home…
unexpectedly one afternoon. After Patti was home from
school. I was gone somewhere…I don't even know

where. He was angry. Spoiling for a fight. So, he started in on Patti.''

Martha sucked in a broken breath. "She tried to ignore him. She put on her headphones. She went to her room. But he...he followed her.''

Andie let Martha find the words, even as she fought to keep her own anguish from showing. "She begged him to leave her alone. She begged him to...to go away. But he...he...''

Her voice dwindled to nothing. Andie prodded her gently. "What did he do, Martha?''

She shook her head, throat working, eyes bright with tears.

"Did he call her names?''

"Yes.''

"Did he strike her?''

"Yes.''

She drew in a deep breath. "Martha, did he rape her?''

For long moments, Martha gazed blankly at her, as if she hadn't heard the question or couldn't face the answer. So, Andie asked her again. "Did he rape her?''

"Yes,'' she whispered, bringing her hands to her face, dissolving into tears. "Yes. He...raped my baby. My precious, precious girl.''

Emotion choked Andie, and she struggled to find some semblance of objectivity. She hadn't created this situation, it wasn't her fault. She felt somehow responsible, though. She felt as if she should have been able to do *something,* anything to help Martha and her daughter.

But she hadn't been able to. She and Martha had been working together for a year, and in all that time, she hadn't done a thing.

"He started coming home in the afternoons, when he knew I'd be gone. I don't even know how...how many times—'' Her words ended on a wail of despair. Andie went to her and held her while she cried, wishing she could do more. Wishing she could have changed the course of events. After a while, when her tears had abated slightly, Andie asked her how she had found out.

"I came home," she whispered. "I caught him."

"When was that, Martha?"

"I don't know, a month or so ago. Maybe two."

"What did you do?"

Martha grew still. She drew herself up, meeting Andie's eyes clearly. "I told him I'd kill him if he ever touched her again. I meant it, Dr. Bennett. I'd never let him touch her again."

"Oh, Martha." Andie caught the woman's hands and squeezed them. "Is that why you don't want Patti to testify? Are you afraid the jury will—"

"No!" She shook her head. "I don't care about that. About the jury or what they might think. I have to protect her, don't you see? I haven't up until now. I—" Her voice cracked, and she cleared it. "You were right, Dr. Bennett, all along. Patti knew about me and Edward. She always knew. She's suffered enough, I won't make her go through that."

"Listen to me, testifying will be good for Patti. I believe that. She needs to do something. Let her help instead of making her stand back and watch, helpless to do a thing. The way she has her whole life."

"But if she testifies, everyone will know what he did. They'll know, they'll point and whisper. She'll never be able to go anywhere without people knowing. She'll never be the same, she'll—"

"Martha," Andie interrupted as gently but firmly as she could, "it doesn't matter if other people know, *she* knows. She can't go back. To deny this happened to her will only damage her more."

"But…her life, it'll change forever."

"Edward's already done that. It's what happens now, how we help her cope with his abuse that will change her life."

After that, there had been nothing left to say. With Martha's permission, Andie had called Robert and repeated what Martha had told her. Then he had spoken with Martha and set up a time for them to meet the following day. This would change their defense, he had been certain. He wouldn't know just how much until he had heard the entire narrative from Martha and Patti, then taken some time to analyze the situation.

Martha's story, her pain, had haunted Andie for the rest of the day. She had thought of it during other patients' sessions and found herself feeling responsible and defeated.

She had dragged herself through the afternoon and evening, packed with back-to-back patients, exhausted and spirit-weary. Her patients seemed to pick up on her despair and had reacted accordingly, becoming more frightened or angry or confused than they usually were.

By the time she had seen the last one at eight and arrived home, all Andie wanted was the cleansing oblivion of sleep. She tossed the stack of mail on the entryway table, even though she saw a letter from her mother. Past hunger hours ago, she made her way through the dark house, not even bothering with lights.

When she reached her bedroom, she flipped the switch. Light flooded the room. Her gaze went to the bed; a scream flew to her lips. Someone had left a gift for her, a kind of obscene calling card.

Not just someone, she realized with horror. Mr. X.

Across her white bedspread lay a noose and a black silk scarf.

62

Andie called Nick from her cell phone. He came right away. She met him in the driveway, never in her life being so grateful to see someone. "Thanks for coming, Nick. When I saw... I didn't know what to do."

"You did the right thing." He caught her cold hands and rubbed them between his warm ones. "Are you all right?"

"Fine." A hysterical laugh bubbled to her lips. "No, scratch that. I'm not all right. Why is he doing this, Nick? Why is he terrorizing me this way?"

"I don't know. But I'm here now, and everything's going to be okay." He squeezed her hands, then released them. "You wait out here, and I'll go—"

"No! I'm coming with you." She sucked in a deep breath, not wanting him out of her sight.

He hesitated a moment, then nodded. "But stay right with me."

She laughed nervously. "Don't worry. We're talking glue here."

They made their way slowly through the house. Nick checked every closet and cubbyhole, he checked behind and under furniture and to see if each window was locked. He found that the one in the laundry room was not. It was open a crack and the screen was loose, as if it had been pried open from the outside.

Andie looked at it, then Nick, frowning. "That's not right. I'm sure it was locked, just like all the others."

Nick only nodded, then went to work. He moved his

gaze slowly over the window, sill and screen. Andie had the sense that he saw everything and missed nothing. From there, he shifted his gaze to the floor below the window, and beyond to the overflowing basket of dirty laundry, a bra and a pair of her lacy panties right on top.

Her cheeks burned, and she bent and snatched up the garments and stuffed them into her trouser pockets. "I'm a little behind on my laundry," she muttered.

A smile touched his mouth. "No problem at all. Nice undies, by the way."

He squatted and carefully studied the wall and floor, eyebrows drawn together as if pondering a question he wasn't yet ready to voice. "Does this door lead outside?" he asked, indicating the one at the opposite end of the room.

"Yes. That's the walkway to the garage."

"I want to check for footprints."

There were none. The bushes under the windows looked undisturbed, the siding unmarred. "It doesn't mean this wasn't his point of entry, it hasn't rained in a while so the ground's hard and dry. But still, I thought there'd be something."

"Like what?"

He only shook his head. "Where's your bedroom?"

She led him down the hall to her room. They stopped in the doorway. The overhead light blazed.

He touched her arm. "Wait here."

This time she did as he asked without a murmur. He checked her closet and bathroom, checked the windows and under the bed. "Just vacuum in here?" he asked, returning to the doorway.

"My cleaning service came this morning."

He nodded. "Whoever he is, he's not a big man."

"How do you know that?"

He pointed to the plush carpeting at their feet. "See the indentations? Footprints." He squatted; she followed. "There are yours." He touched a print. "See, same size, same shoe style. There's mine.'' He indicated the marks. ''Size twelves. I've got big feet.''

''Then those are…'' Her words trailed off.

''That's right, those belong to your mysterious friend.''

She gazed at the prints, her throat constricting. She swallowed hard, past fear. In a way, looking at the prints was like looking at the person who was terrorizing her. And Nick was right, the person's foot was considerably larger than hers, but smaller than his. They'd worn a heelless shoe, like an athletic shoe.

''You're amazing,'' she said.

He met her eyes, one corner of his mouth lifting into a lopsided smile. ''Thanks, but any first-year rookie would have noted that.''

Andie doubted that, though she knew nothing about police work.

''Let's go take a peek at your little surprise package.''

''I'll stay right here, if you don't mind,'' she said, averting her gaze. She couldn't look at the bed, at the noose and scarf. Not without imagining the noose around her neck, not without feeling the burn of the rope, not without picturing herself blindfolded and dangling from it.

''Are you all right?'' he asked again. ''You look pale.''

She gritted her teeth. ''I'm okay. Just do what you have to do and get rid of it.''

''A couple minutes. Hold on.''

True to his word, a handful of minutes later, he told her the coast was clear. He had examined the area and bagged the evidence.

''I'll take this downtown, give it to the lab guys and see what they can come up with. But don't hold your breath for any big revelations.''

They walked down the hall, toward the front door. The closer they got, the more she realized she didn't want him to go.

''Would you like a cup of coffee…a drink, or something? I have beer,'' she offered, remembering his niece, Sam, asking if he would like one.

"Yeah?" He looked at her. "Why not? I'm off duty."

"Good." She smiled. "Have a seat on the couch. I'll get it."

He did, and moments later she returned with a beer for him and a glass of wine for herself. She handed him the beer, then took a seat on the other end of the couch.

She peeked at him, then glanced away, her cheeks warming. She liked the looks of him on her couch, in her house. He filled the place with a different kind of energy, male and electric. Looking around now, the teal walls seemed too sweet, the chintz couch fussy, the flowered window treatments downright saccharine.

She peeked at him again; this time he caught her. And she felt like a high-schooler who'd been caught admiring the P.E. teacher's buns.

"What?" he asked.

"Nothing. It's just..." She looked away, then back. "I'm not used to having men on my couch." His eyebrows shot up, and she brought a hand to her mouth. "I didn't mean that the way it sounded."

"So, I shouldn't ask where you're used to having your men?"

Her face burned. "No, definitely not."

"I like the way you look when you're embarrassed."

"About two shades brighter than a boiled lobster?"

"At least." He took a swallow of his beer, then rolled the can between his palms. "You want to hear what I think about this whole thing?" When she nodded, he went on. "What you've got is a small man, lithe and fastidious."

At her incredulous look, he smiled. "Hear me out. He made it through your laundry-room window, not a large window, I might add, without disturbing the basket of laundry or knocking over the plant on the ledge beside it. He left no tracks, no clumps or specks of dirt. No dirty handprints on the white woodwork, no shoe scuffs on the wall, inside or out.

"I didn't dust for prints for two reasons. One, it would have been futile. Whoever he was, he took the time to wipe everything in sight. I could see myself in the brass fittings, they were so shiny."

"The other reason?" she asked.

Again, one corner of his mouth lifted. "Even if we managed to get a clean print, it wouldn't have helped. We wouldn't have found a match. This isn't a career guy, I'd bet my life on it."

Andie struggled to breathe. "So, am I in...danger?"

He met her gaze evenly, his devoid of all traces of humor. "I don't know. But, if I had to guess, I'd say no. I'd say somebody's getting perverted pleasure out of terrorizing you. Somebody's feeding on your fear and enjoying watching you sweat. But I don't like to guess."

Perverted pleasure. She swallowed hard. *Mr. X. Leah Robertson.*

David Sadler.

She squeezed her eyes shut a moment as fear rampaged through her. She fought to get a grip on it. She couldn't speculate that way, not about a patient. She had no proof that David was anything but a confused man who needed her help. And even if she did, what could she do? Refuse to treat him and that was about it.

"By any chance, tonight did you call Raven or Julie?"

Andie brought a hand to her mouth. "No. I didn't even...do you think he might—"

"Have left them a little surprise package, too? He might have, though I doubt it."

"He's singled me out."

"Yes." Nick cleared his throat. "Would you like me to get a uniform to give them a call or stop by—"

"No. I'll do it."

"Why don't you try them now."

Andie nodded, stood and went to the phone. She tried

Raven first, then Julie. Neither friend was home so she left both a detailed message outlining what had happened, that Nick was with her and that she was okay. She asked both to call her if they'd had any problems.

She returned to the couch; she looked at Nick. "I'm scared."

"I know."

"You don't have to…you don't have to leave just yet, do you? I mean, Mara's not—"

"She's with her mother."

She looked down, realizing she clutched her wineglass in her hands, that she hadn't even taken a sip. She set it carefully on the coffee table. "What should I do?"

"Play it safe," he said quietly. "Make certain every window and door is locked. You could think about having a security system installed. Or getting a watchdog."

He took another swallow of beer, draining it, giving her time, she suspected, to adjust to what he was telling her. He moved his gaze over the room. "I like your house."

"Thanks."

"It's a little too girlie for my taste, though."

She smiled, grateful for his attempt to divert her. "That's what happens when you're a girl."

"I'd heard that." He set his beer can on the table. "I should go."

"Don't. Please." He looked at her in question, and she clasped her hands together, not believing what she was saying. "I'd like you to stay. With me."

He reached across and cupped her cheek in his palm. "Beautiful, smart, sweet Andie."

She flushed, pleased. "Do you really think that?"

His lips curved up. "I always thought that."

She covered his hand and leaned toward him, aching for the feel of his mouth against hers, despite all she knew to be safe and smart. She lifted her face to his. "If I asked you to kiss me, would you still think I was smart?"

"No," he murmured. "I'd think I was lucky."

He brought his mouth down on hers.

She didn't know what she had expected from his kiss, but not this...explosion of arousal, this heat. She curled her fingers into his cotton pullover, but whether to hold him to her or anchor herself to this world she wasn't sure. She only knew that kissing had never been like this before, the simple connection of one mouth to another, had never left her gasping.

This was heaven. It was shattering. Cataclysmic. It stole her breath and her good sense.

He groaned and shifted his weight, easing her against the couch's deep pillows, tangling his fingers in her hair. "It's been so...long," he muttered, dragging his mouth from hers, finding her ear, the curve of her neck, the sensitive skin where the front of her blouse parted.

"Too long," she whispered.

He kissed her again, and again, until she was light-headed and weak with arousal. He drew away from her, breathing heavily. "Is it the fear?" he asked. "Or is it me?"

She gazed into his dark eyes, realizing she didn't know. Not really, not completely. The fear, the desire, both were firsts for her.

He must have read the truth of that in her expression, because he let out a long breath and sat up. "Shit." One corner of his mouth lifted in the lopsided smile she realized she was beginning to love. He dragged a hand through his hair. "Me and my big mouth."

"It doesn't matter." She held out a hand. "It doesn't."

"Yes, it does. To me."

She didn't know what to say, so she said nothing. He rested his forehead against hers. "You don't have to sleep with me to get me to stay."

"I know."

"Do you?"

He brushed his thumb across her lower lip; she felt the caress all the way to her toes, almost like a jolt to her system. She shuddered and reached for him. He caught her hands, brought them to his mouth, then set her away from him.

"I'll stay, Andie, but I won't sleep with you. When we make love, I want to know it's *me* you want. Not a cop. Not a bodyguard or a diversion from fear."

He was right; she knew it with her head. She should be grateful for his cool head and gentlemanly ways. She wasn't. She was disappointed. She ached with unspent passion.

She made a sound of frustration. "I suppose you think I should thank you?"

"But you won't?"

"Hell, no. I'm too pissed off."

Laughing, he kissed her again, hard. "I'm glad to hear that. If it's all the same to you, I'll take the couch."

63
***

Julie lay on the front seat of David's car, her head in his lap as he drove. He had promised her a special surprise tonight. Something new and delicious. Something exciting.

She gazed up at him, heart thundering. She loved him. More than she had ever loved anyone. He made her feel cherished, protected, adored. He understood her and loved her for what she was; he didn't judge her or want her to change. The way everyone else always had, even Raven and Andie.

In recent days, he had begun taking care of her most basic needs, ones for food, shelter and clothing; he chased away her fears and satisfied her physical desires. He had chosen her clothes in the morning and washed her hair at night. He decided what she would eat and how much.

Because he loved her. Because he wanted to be her everything.

And he was never stingy with her, didn't deny her the things she longed for. Instead, he indulged her every whim. All those Easters ago, as she had stood in front of her bedroom mirror, admiring herself, she had promised herself a closetful of princess dresses one day. That day had never come. Until yesterday. She had shared her long-ago dream with David and he had taken her shopping. Now she had a closetful of dresses that made her look like a princess.

All she had to do in return was trust him.

"Where are we going?" she asked, moving her head in

his lap, rubbing against his erection. Whatever he had planned for her, it excited him. Very much.

"The Gatehouse development."

"My surprise is there?"

He smiled. "It is?"

"Will I like it? Will it—"

"Shh." He brought one of his hands to her face, lightly caressing her cheek. "I don't want to talk now. I want to prepare."

So, obediently, Julie quieted. They had left the lights of Thistledown behind minutes ago; the car was dark save for the glow of the instrument panel. It tinted his skin red, and from her vantage point below, his dark eyebrows, sharp nose and cheekbones became more prominent, making him look half man, half bird of prey.

Or like the devil.

Julie caught her breath and squeezed her eyes tight shut. David was an angel not a devil. He was a savior not a destroyer. She breathed deeply, chasing her fears, the demons, away. She tuned into the feel of the road beneath them, the sound of David's breathing, the smell of their growing excitement.

Before long, David slowed and turned, as if onto a lane or into a driveway. Within moments of that, he stopped and turned off the car.

"We're here, sweetheart. Sit up."

She did as he asked. They were parked in front of a spectacular-looking house. It, and two others within easy distance, rose up before them, showplaces in the middle of nowhere. The three models, Julie realized. The ones Raven was working on.

"It's beautiful, David."

"Wait until you see the inside."

They climbed out of the car and went up the front walk. David unlocked the door, disabled the security system, then flipped a switch on the wall to his right.

Light flooded the house's interior. Julie caught her

breath. It was the most beautiful place she had ever been in. Like a castle.

He chuckled and pressed a kiss to the top of her head. "I see by your face that you like it."

"I love it."

"Your friend Raven has done a wonderful job. Nothing short of miraculous, really. I've never known a designer who moved so quickly or inspired others to work so hard for her. Several laborers, the floor installers, for one, put other jobs on hold to accommodate her."

"Raven's like that. She's always been able to get people to do whatever she wants." Julie swept her gaze over the interior. "And she's so talented. I wish I—"

"No," he murmured, turning, cupping her face in his palms. "You're the special one, Julie. She's not. Remember that." He kissed her, then brought his hands to hers. "Now, close your eyes so I can take you to your surprise."

She did, giggling, and he led her forward. They stepped off wood floors onto thick carpeting. He stopped, and flipped another switch.

"Okay," he said softly. "Surprise."

She opened her eyes.

And almost fainted.

A rope hung from one of the living room's exposed beams, its end tied into a noose. Beneath the rope sat a tall stool, beside it a smaller one, so she could step up.

A cry spilled from Julie's lips, and she took a step backward. She met the wall of David's chest. His arms circled her, anchoring her to him. Against her shoulder blade, she felt the wild beat of his heart. His breath came in short, agitated puffs.

He pressed his mouth to her ear. "I want you to give yourself completely to me. Will you do this, my darling? Will you put yourself wholly in my hands, trusting me with the very breath you need for life?" He turned her to face him, kissing her again and again, sucking all resistance from her. "Give yourself to me, Julie."

He removed her shirt and bra, caressing each place he revealed, murmuring words of adoration, of encouragement and thanks.

Tears streamed down her cheeks. She was afraid, so afraid. Yet, she was powerless against his hold on her. Even as a part of her screamed to break away and run for her life, she allowed him to manipulate her this way and that, a puppeteer with his living doll.

When she was naked, he bound her wrists, then last, lovingly, he blindfolded her. "You're so beautiful," he murmured, his voice quivering with excitement. "This will be good, very good."

David helped her up onto the stool. Sobbing, she stood on tiptoe, feet apart, and he fitted the noose over her head and around her neck, then eased back to the flat of her feet.

The rope tightened. It squeezed at her throat; she struggled to breathe even as she told herself to let go. Her entire life had led her to David and this moment. Fate had brought her to his window all those years ago, it had brought her here.

He was going to kill her.

Panic exploded inside her, with it a kind of acceptance. She wanted to die, she realized. She had always wanted to die.

He stood before her; she felt his breath against her knees, her thighs, her sex. He began to make love to her. With his hands and mouth, his heart and soul. She writhed under his ministrations, sensations rippling over her, pleasure mixing with pain, shame with arousal.

With each movement, the rope worked its terror, soon she was gasping and light-headed.

"Now you know who I am," he whispered. "Now you know."

She did know, she thought, panting, light-headed. She had always known.

He was Mr. X.

And she was Mrs. X.

She didn't want to die, she thought suddenly, arching against his mouth, stars flashing in front of her eyes. She wanted to live.

She orgasmed violently; her knees buckled. The rope jerked tight. Light exploded in her head. Then darkness.

She was in his arms, crying like a baby, grateful to him for her life. He rocked and petted her, brushing the tears from her cheeks, cooing. "You see, my darling, I didn't kill Leah. How could I have? I loved her. Like I love you. I could never hurt you."

She lifted her face to his, her vision blurred with tears, her neck so sore she winced at the movement. He smiled tenderly.

"Someone else killed my Leah. And the way I figure it, you and your friends are the only ones who might know who."

64

Nick couldn't sleep. Andie's couch had been designed for midgets. It had lumps. The mantel clock ticked with the force of a sledgehammer striking stone. The pillow was hard, the blanket scratchy.

And Andie slept not twenty feet away, in a big soft bed made for two.

He groaned, punched the pillow, then dragged it over his face. When he lay perfectly still and held his breath, he swore he could hear her's—soft, rhythmic, sensual. And if he breathed deeply through his nose, he could smell her—her perfume, her shampoo, her soap. The whole damn place smelled like her, he thought, tossing the pillow aside.

Screw his sense of honor and responsibility, he thought. Screw his concern for her opinion of herself in the morning, and most of all his own, ridiculous, overblown ego.

So what if it had been fear that had inspired her to invite him into her bed? So what if she hated them both in the morning? He could be wrapped up with that glorious body of hers right now. He could be asleep, sated and satisfied instead of lying here, hard, horny and totally pissed off at himself.

Fool. He grabbed the pillow, punched it again and stuffed it under his head. *Asshole.* When was he going to learn that in love, nice guys always finished last?

He smiled suddenly, amused by his own thoughts. Oh, man, what a woman Andie Bennett was. What a kiss they had shared. He hadn't been kissed like that, with such passion, in a long time. He'd felt like a kid, untried, a mass of raging hormones and a supercharged libido.

He turned his head toward the hallway and Andie's closed bedroom door. What would she do if he went to her now? If he told her he wanted her, that he couldn't sleep from wanting her? Would she open the door or slam it in his face?

Damn the consequences.

Nick stood and started for the hall.

His beeper went off.

Swearing, he doubled back, snatched it off the coffee table and checked the display. *Shit. Headquarters.* This time of night—morning, he corrected, seeing that it was nearly five—the call was most certainly bad news. The kind of news that would, without a doubt, take him away from carnal possibilities with Andie Bennett.

He found a phone and made the call. A drug bust had gone bad, there was one dead and two wounded. The chief wanted him there, a.s.a.p.

Nick went back to the living room and collected his gun, badge and shirt. He glanced at Andie's bedroom door again, thought about leaving a note and slipping out, but decided he couldn't do that to her. Especially considering what had brought him here in the first place.

He went to her door, uncertain whether he should knock or go in. He did both. After tapping softly, he eased the door open and stepped inside.

Her bed was a jumble, the sheet and blanket tangled around her legs—as if she, too, had been tossing and turning.

"Andie," he said, taking another step into the room. "I've got to go."

She stirred, then when he called her name again, sat up. The sheet fell away from her as she did, revealing a pale pink gown made of some delicate, shiny fabric. Through it he could make out the soft swells of her breasts and the dark outline of her nipples.

Arousal was swift and stunning. He sucked in a sharp breath and cursed the fact he hadn't simply left a note and gone.

"I've got to go," he said again. "There's been a homicide."

"Nick?" Her voice was thick, slurry with sleep. She reached up and pushed the hair out of her eyes. The movement brought her breasts into relief against the sheer gown. As if realizing what was happening—what she was doing—she dropped her hands and grabbed the sheet, yanking it up to her chin.

He returned his gaze to her face. Her cheeks were bright red. He supposed it would have been nicer if he hadn't stared, but some things were simply beyond a man's control. Besides, he was done being Mr. Nice Guy.

"I got a call. I've got to go in." He slipped into his shoulder holster. "Are you going to be all right?"

She watched him, eyes wide. "Yes, of course."

She said it so evenly, with such unruffled adultness. But she looked anything but confident and unruffled. She looked young and vulnerable and completely lost.

"Are you?" she asked.

"What?"

"Going to be all right?"

He smiled. "Oh yeah, bullets bounce off of me."

"Funny." She didn't smile. "I'm going to get up, could you turn around, please?"

He did as she asked. A moment later, she gave him the all clear. She had put on a robe. One that, in his opinion, only enhanced what she hoped to conceal.

"I'll make coffee."

"I don't have time." He went in search of his jacket; she trailed after him. He found it and put it on, then turned back to her. "How'd you sleep."

"Like a baby. You?"

"Same," he lied, irritated that he'd asked the question, but more irritated that sleeping within a handful of feet of him hadn't disturbed her slumber. "If you'd like, I'll check on you later."

"That's not necessary. I'll be fine. Really."

"Good." He found himself staring at her mouth and wanting to kiss her. He dragged his gaze away and headed toward the foyer. "Lock the door after me."

"I will."

He started through. She stopped him. "I... Thank you. For...everything."

He opened his mouth to tell her she was welcome. Instead, he muttered something unintelligible even to his own ears, dragged her against his chest and kissed her hard and long. For one moment she stood stiffly in his arms, then she melted against him, curving her arms around his neck, matching the fervor of his kiss with her own.

Finally, regretfully, he pulled himself away. "I've got to go," he whispered. "Be careful today."

Nick didn't look back as he made his way down the walk and into his Jeep; he fought the urge while he started the engine and backed down the drive. He gave in then. And his heart turned over. She stood just where he had left her, breeze stirring her filmy gown and robe, the morning sun spilling over her, making her look like an angel.

Shit, he thought, catching his thoughts. He was deep into it now. So deep he wasn't sure just how he was going to make it back out.

65

Julie pulled up in front of Andie's house and gazed at her friend's bright windows. She shifted David's Jaguar into neutral, but let the car idle, uncertain if she was going to stay.

Andie would help her. Andie would know what to do.

Julie leaned her head back against the rest and closed her eyes. As she did, she recalled the pressure of the rope around her neck, recalled her twin feelings of shame and arousal, resistance and acquiescence.

She brought a hand to her neck and trailed her fingers across the rope's path. Though the bruise was several days old, her skin still bore the mark of the rope; if she tipped her head just right, her neck muscles screamed in protest, though not loudly, as they had at first.

She was losing her mind.

In the days since her and David's encounter at the Gatehouse model, the lines between fantasy and reality, self-preservation and pleasure had blurred. The past and present flowed one into the other in her head, creating a distorted, frightening mix.

At night she dreamed of David and Leah Robertson; by day memories of that summer consumed her thoughts. Memories of her, Raven and Andie's friendship and the things they had watched David and Leah do.

David was Mr. X. But he hadn't killed Leah Robertson. He wasn't capable of such an act. She believed that with all her heart.

He'd loved Leah.

He loved her.

But she couldn't tell Andie that. She couldn't tell Andie—or anyone else—who David really was. Julie curved her fingers tightly around the steering wheel, her heart thudding heavily against the wall of her chest, so heavily she had to fight to breathe. Andie would pat her silly friend on the head, then promptly phone the police. She would try to convince Julie that her life was in danger, that David meant her harm.

Julie turned her gaze to Andie's bright windows once more. She simply wouldn't understand. She would insist David had been the one terrorizing her, the one who had left the noose and scarf, the one who had done it all.

But he wasn't the one. David could never harm anyone. He had proved that to her the other night.

But if David hadn't killed Leah, who had?

The way I figure it, you and your friends are the only ones who might know who did do it.

Had one of them seen something they hadn't shared with the others? Julie wondered. She caught her lower lip between her teeth. Had one of them kept a secret from the others? If so, why?

Julie shifted the car into first and eased into Andie's driveway. She shut off the engine, flipped open David's cell phone and punched in Andie's number, quickly, before she lost her nerve. Her friend picked up on the first ring.

"Andie, it's me, Julie. I have to talk to you. It's important."

Julie heard the desperation in her own voice and wondered at it. Was that the way she felt? Desperate? Lost and out of control?

"Where are you?" Andie asked sharply, obviously concerned.

"In your driveway. I...don't want to see anyone else, Andie. Are you alone?"

"Yes." The phone line crackled. Julie saw Andie's

front blinds move. She heard her friend's quick intake of breath. "Where did you get that car?"

"It's a friend's. Andie, I can't...you're not expecting anyone, are you?"

She meant Raven.

Andie would know that. She would wonder why.

"I'm not expecting anybody. Julie—" her friend hesitated "—are you...is everything all right?"

To Julie's surprise, her eyes flooded with tears. "I don't know. I—" Her voice broke on a sob. "I'm coming up. Okay?"

Andie said it was, and in a matter of moments, she was in her friend's house and arms, being cooed and fussed over. Andie got her settled on the couch, cushioned by big, soft throw pillows.

"Can I get you something?" she asked. "A drink? Some coffee or—"

"No, nothing." Julie blinked against the tears that filled her eyes. "Thanks though."

Andie sat on the other end of the couch, legs curled under her. "Talk to me."

Julie shifted her gaze, unable to look Andie directly in the eyes. "I don't know where to start."

"So start anywhere."

"Like the part where I tell you I'm falling apart?" A hysterical laugh tumbled past her lips. "Where I tell you I think I might be losing my mind?"

"You're not losing your mind," Andie said softly, "even if it feels that way."

"You know what it really feels like?" She lifted her gaze to Andie's. "It feels like I'm dying. And you know what? I'm not all that upset about it. What does that mean?"

The color drained from Andie's face.

Julie brought her shaking hands to her lips. "I can't stop thinking about Mr. and Mrs. X. About what they did together. I feel so weird all the time, like somehow I'm re-living the past. Reliving their affair.''

"Let him go,'' Andie said. "Don't see him anymore, Julie.''

"I can't.'' Julie shook her head, tears spilling down her cheeks. "I want to but…he has this hold on me, Andie. This power. It's scary, I…I don't think I can live without him.''

"You can, baby. You can. I'll help you. Raven will help you.''

This wasn't going the way she had meant it to, Julie realized. She had meant to talk about the past, about Mr. and Mrs. X. She had meant to help David.

"Julie, sweetheart, talk to me. It's him, isn't it? He's done this to you.''

Julie dropped her hands, her gaze with them. "No.'' She shook her head. "No.''

"Listen to yourself,'' Andie said, her voice quivering. "Look in the mirror. You are falling apart. You're killing yourself. He's killing you.''

"He wouldn't hurt me!'' Julie cried. "He loves me. And I love him.''

"Then what's happening?'' Andie scrambled across to her, catching her hands. "You can come live with me. Quit your job, get into a program. I'll help you, he won't know where you are.''

"You don't get it, do you? I've been dying for a long time, maybe forever. He didn't do this to me.''

"Julie, please, listen to me. Before this man, you were trying to change. Trying to get a hold of your life. You were in control—''

"Jesus, Andie! Don't you get it, I was never in control! My whole life, I—'' She swallowed the words, their taste bitter against her tongue. "That's not why I'm here.'' She curled her fingers around Andie's. "I have to know some-thing, about the past. About that summer. It's important.''

Andie nodded. "All right.''

"Remember that time Raven was in the house alone with Mr. and Mrs. X, that time we got out but she didn't?" Andie nodded again and Julie continued. "Do you think...could she have seen something...something more than what she told us?"

Andie searched her friend's expression. "What are you suggesting?"

"Do you think Raven—" Julie drew in a deep breath, using the seconds it took to choose her words carefully. "Remember how obsessed she was with Mr. and Mrs. X? Do you think she ever...that she could have gone back to watch them without us? Could she have gone back and not told us about it? Do you think that maybe she saw...something she shouldn't have?"

"Something she shouldn't have?" Andie repeated. "We all saw something we..." Andie's thought trailed off, then she widened her eyes. "Like what, Julie?"

"I don't know." Julie looked away. "Like who killed Mrs. X."

"Are you saying...you think Raven lied to us? To the police? To everyone? Are you saying, you think she actually *saw* Mrs. X's murder?"

Julie wet her lips, her heart thundering. "I don't know, I...yes, I guess I am."

For a long moment Andie said nothing, then she drew her eyebrows together. "Why would she lie, Julie? Why?" She shook her head. "Raven's your friend. You've known her almost all your life. Now, suddenly, you question her honesty? After everything she's done for you? Where's this coming from?"

The disappointment in her friend's expression cut her to the core. Julie ripped her hands from Andie's. "You always liked her better than me, didn't you? You always sided with her."

"That's not true."

"It is!" Julie jumped to her feet. "It was always 'poor,

silly Julie, the airhead.' You always felt sorry for me, you always humored me.''

"I've always loved you, Julie! I've always thought you—'' Realization crossed Andie's features. "This is coming from *him,* too, isn't it? This man you're involved with?''

"Of course not.'' The words sounded like a lie even to Julie's ears; she could imagine how pathetically false they sounded to Andie. So she said them again, defiantly.

"It is this man.'' Andie followed Julie to her feet, pleading. "He's dangerous. He's alienating you from us, your friends. He wants you to be alone and vulnerable. He wants you to feel like you have nowhere to turn but him.''

Tears choked her. That was the way she felt. But it was the way she had always felt—like she had nowhere to turn.

"Listen to me.'' Andie reached out a hand to her. "I can get you into a program. It'll take time, but you'll feel better, Julie. Don't you want that? Don't you want to be happy?''

Julie shook her head, her tears welling again, threatening to spill over. "How do we know the truth, Andie? How do we know what's real? Aren't people…aren't things sometimes not what they seem?''

"What you see is real, Julie. What Raven and I have been to you, that we've been there for you. That's real. That's love. Not what this man is contorting you into. Not this man's perverted version of love.''

"You don't know.'' Julie took a step backward, away from her friend. "You don't understand.''

Andie reached for her. "He's dangerous,'' she said again. "He's hurting you.''

"David loves me.'' She took another step. "I shouldn't have come here. I should have known you would try to turn me against him.''

"David?'' Andie repeated, a look of horror crossing her features. "Did you say his name's…David?''

Andie had figured out that her David was Mr. X. Julie snatched up her car keys. ''I've got to go.''

Andie grabbed her arm. ''Julie, I have to know. What's his name? David who?''

Andie would go to the police. She would turn him in.

''No!'' Julie yanked her arm free, turned and ran. She reached the door, fumbled with the lock, then tore it open. She stumbled out into the night, Andie only steps behind her.

She made it to the car and scrambled inside, slamming the door just as Andie reached it. She punched down the lock.

Andie grabbed the door handle and tugged at it, then pounded on the window. ''Wait!'' she cried. ''Julie, please!''

Hands shaking so badly it took her three tries, Julie shoved the key into the ignition, twisted, and the powerful engine roared to life. She slammed the stick into reverse, hit the gas and screamed out of the driveway, Andie's calls to wait ringing in her ears.

66

Andie watched Julie go, the blood rushing to her head, panic with it. Dear God. Could David Sadler be Julie's lover? Could Julie be the special woman he had talked about during their sessions?

I don't want to hurt her, Dr. Bennett. Help me, please. I don't want to hurt her.

Andie began to shake. She thought of David, of what she knew of him from their work together. She remembered the things he had said about his sexual preferences, how he had described women and his need to control them, his need to subjugate them.

She squeezed her eyes shut, picturing the rope burns she had seen on Julie's wrists the day she'd visited her friend at her apartment. And tonight, she had seen Julie wince and bring a hand to her throat, as if she was hurting, the gesture instinctive. Did she have bruises there, too? Bruises from a rope?

Mrs. X, dangling from the end of a rope. Her once-beautiful face distorted in death.

Fear took Andie's breath. She took a step backward, toward her house. If David Sadler was Julie's lover, that meant he was involved with all three of them. Her, Julie and Raven. Best friends.

Her heart began to thrum, adrenaline to pump through her. It could be a coincidence, she told herself, struggling to get hold of herself. Sure it could be. He could simply have—

What? Thistledown was a small town, but was it that

small? One man, involved with the three women who had been involved in Thistledown's most notorious crime?

Two, a coincidence. Maybe. But all three? No way.

Andie thought of the calls and clippings, thought of Mr. and Mrs. X's music and the noose and black silk scarf. She recalled the way Raven had questioned her about David Sadler, as if pumping her for information about him. As if she had already known about him and Julie and wondered if he might be involved somehow with Andie.

Why was he doing this? Why had he sought out the three of them? What would be the...

Her blood went cold.

David Sadler really was Mr. X.

With a cry of pure terror, Andie turned and ran back to her house, slamming and locking the door behind her. She raced to her purse and rummaged through it, looking for Nick's card. She found it and reached for the phone.

Nick would know what to do. He would find David Sadler and lock him up. She and her friends would be safe.

She punched in the number, then hesitated as it began to ring. What if she was wrong? She was upset. Frightened for Julie. For all of them.

Emotion clouded good sense, rational thought. Could be David Sadler was just what he said he was. His being involved with the three of them could be, if not purely coincidental, relatively innocent.

What he and Julie were involved in was dangerous, but as far as she knew, not illegal. Wasn't that what those cops had told her all those years ago? And all those years ago, she had followed her instincts and her world had been blown apart; her friends, and their families, had been hurt.

She had much more to lose now. Her career was at stake. Her reputation. Her safety, that of her friends.

She dropped the receiver back onto the cradle. If she went to the police, to Nick, she would break her oath of confidentiality. She could be exposing an innocent man to embarrassing, even damaging, scrutiny; a man she had made a promise to. If she didn't, she might be allowing a killer to roam free. Or worse, she might be allowing him the opportunity to kill again.

I don't want to hurt her, Dr. Bennett. Help me.

Andie brought the heels of her hands to her eyes, recalling the day David had told her about the special woman he'd met. He'd been taunting her, she realized. Asking if she wanted to know the woman's name, all the while knowing his lover was one of her best friends.

David Sadler had been playing with her all along.

No, Andie thought. That wasn't quite true. Half the time he had been playing a twisted game with her, the other half he had been begging for her help. He wanted her help; in that, he was being sincere. She believed that with every fiber of her being.

What did she do? Suddenly, her house seemed too big, too quiet. Her questions, the decision she had to make, pressed in on her. She didn't want to be alone. But she didn't want to be with just anybody.

She wanted to be with Nick. If she confided in him, he would know what to do. If she didn't, he would still make her feel safe.

Without giving herself the time to change her mind, she went to the phone book, hoping against hope that he was listed. She found an N. Raphael on Marigold. In The Meadows subdivision, she realized. She had looked at a house on Marigold, way back.

Saying a silent prayer of thanks, she grabbed her purse and headed out the door.

67

Fifteen minutes later, Andie stood on Nick's doorstep, torn between praying he was home and hoping with all her heart that he wasn't. She lifted her hand to knock again, then thought better of it and turned to leave.

Before she could, the door opened behind her. "Andie?"

She spun back around, tears flooding her eyes. She opened her mouth to speak, but unable to find her voice, just gazed helplessly up at Nick.

He searched her expression a moment then without speaking, swung the door wider. She stepped through it and into his arms. For long moments, she clung to him, finding more comfort than she could have imagined in his strong arms that surrounded her, in the steady beat of his heart under her cheek. If only she could find the answers she sought as easily and as well.

He cupped her face in his hands and tipped it up to his. "What's happened?"

She shook her head, overcome with emotion. "I...can't. I—"

"Andie, if—"

"Daddy! Who's—" Mara barreled around the corner, skidding to a stop when she saw Andie, her face falling.

Andie's heart broke at the look. She remembered what it was like to have to share her father with a stranger. "Hello, Mara." Andie smiled at the child, then looked at Nick. "I'm sorry," she whispered, making a fluttering motion with her right hand. "I didn't know... I should have thought that it might be your weekend with Mara."

"It's all right." He winked at his daughter. "Isn't it, sweetie?"

The girl said nothing for a moment, as if thinking it over. Then she nodded. "I guess. But you have to do what we want to do."

Nick opened his mouth as if to reprimand his daughter, and Andie stopped him by touching his arm and jumping in. "Of course I will."

"We made popcorn an' we're playing Battle." She narrowed her eyes. "Ever play it before? It's real fun."

"Battle?" Andie repeated. "What is it?"

"A card game," Nick offered. "We called it War when I was a kid."

When Andie still didn't recall, the girl took her hand and led her toward the living room. "That's okay," she said. "It's pretty easy. I'll teach you."

The child sat on the floor and she pointed to the place across from her. "Daddy can sit next to me."

"How about a glass of wine?"

"Thanks." Andie smiled up at Nick.

"Bernard *never* plays what me and Mommy want to." The little girl wrinkled her nose. "We always have to do what he wants."

"That doesn't seem fair," Andie said lightly.

"It isn't." Mara sighed and propped her chin on her fists. "I liked it better when my mommy and daddy were together."

"I know what you mean," Andie said, mimicking Mara's body language, propping her chin on her fist. "My mommy and daddy moved to different houses, too."

"They did?"

"Uh-huh. And I was really sad."

Mara reached out and patted her hand. "Me, too."

"But you know what?" She smiled at the girl. "One day I woke up and I wasn't sad anymore."

"Did your mommy and daddy get back together?"

"No." Andie shook her head. "But I realized that even though we were living apart, they both still loved me as much as they always had. And that made everything...okay."

Mara thought about that a moment, then cocked her head. "You looked sad tonight," she said. "When I first saw you."

"I was," Andie answered.

"How come?"

Andie thought a moment, wanting to be as honest as she could be with the six-year-old. "A friend of mine is in...trouble."

"My daddy helps people who are in trouble." Mara's face lit up with love and pride. "Is that why you're here?"

Andie lifted her gaze. Nick stood in the doorway, watching them. She met his eyes, and her heart did a funny little something. Was that why she was here? That's what she had told herself when she left her house and headed over here. She had told herself that he would have answers, that she would know what to do when she saw him.

She had been lying to herself. The truth was, she hadn't thought about those things since she walked through his front door. The truth was, she was here because she hadn't been able to stop thinking about him, because she liked him and liked being part of his little family, a lot more than she should. The truth was, she had been wanting to be with him again, ever since the night he had spent on her couch.

"Yes," she murmured, "that's why."

He crossed the room, never breaking eye contact. He bent and handed her the glass of wine, a smile tugging at the corners of his mouth as he whispered, "Just can't stop working, can you, Dr. Bennett?"

She took the wine; their fingers brushed.

Nick announced that there had been enough talk, it was time to get back to the game. With Mara's consent, he reshuffled and dealt new hands, so Andie could be included.

The game went from zero to fast and furious with the first throw, which turned into a triple battle. Mara was quick; she knew her numbers and the value of face cards, and quickly cleaned up. After several hands of that, they moved to a rousing three-game round of Candy Land.

Finally, Nick called it quits. It was late, and though Mara protested loudly and vigorously, she was out on her feet.

"Sorry, shortcake—" he stood and held out a hand "—time for bed."

"Daddy!" She drew the word out, sounding adult and exasperated, one last attempt to wheedle a few more minutes out of him. "I'm not tired."

"Sorry, kiddo, tired or not, it's ten o'clock. If you don't go to bed, you're going to be a grump tomorrow, and your mother will have my head."

"Okay." She dragged herself to her feet. "But I want four stories."

"Two," he countered, smiling.

She looked at him long and hard, then held out three fingers. "And no less."

Nick laughed and met Andie's eyes. "I'll be back."

He and Mara started off, then Mara stopped and ran back to her. She gave her a hug and a kiss on the cheek. "'Night."

A lump the size of Texas formed in Andie's throat. "Good night," she managed to say, her voice choked.

Mara skipped back to her dad, and Andie watched them go. Dear God, what was she doing? Falling in love with Nick? With his daughter? She squeezed her eyes shut, acknowledging the truth.

She was falling in love with a man who wasn't really free. A man who wasn't ready for a relationship, a man who had a daughter who still dreamed of her mom and dad getting back together. A man who was nothing like anyone she had ever imagined herself being with.

Then why did being with him feel like a dream come true?

Stupid. Stupid. She knew better. She was setting herself up to be hurt. The Big Hurt. A broken heart.

Andie opened her eyes and glanced toward the front door. She could jot a quick note of apology and goodbye to Nick, and be long gone before he emerged from Mara's room.

So why didn't she? Her cheeks heated at the truth. Because she didn't want to. She was afraid, but not that afraid. For the first time in her life, she realized with a sense of shock, desire overpowered her instinct for self-preservation. Nick Raphael was worth the risk.

Desire. Andie brought a hand to her mouth, feeling giddy, light-headed and short of breath. She burned with it. With the need to be with a man, this man, with the need to mate with him.

Another first.

Andie stood and crossed to the bookcase, her legs shaky. She scanned the titles without really seeing them. Was this how Julie felt about men? she wondered. Hot and achingly alive, distracted and flushed and more than a little bit out of control?

If so, she could understand now how her friend allowed herself to be ensnared by one unsuitable man after another, how she managed to embroil herself in one disastrous love affair after another.

Here she was, sensible Andie Bennett, on that very precipice herself.

"Mission accomplished. She's asleep already."

Startled, Andie spun around, cheeks on fire. "Nick."

He slipped his hands into his pockets and cocked his head, studying her. His lips lifted. "You were expecting someone else?"

"Of course not. I…you move quietly."

"I'm a cop. It's one of the tools of the trade." He took a step into the room. "I wondered if you would still be here when I came back out. I half thought not."

"Intuitive, too." She smiled nervously. "Another asset?"

"Uh-huh." He crossed to stand before her. He reached out and trailed his index finger down her cheek. She felt his touch to the tips of her toes, and tipped her head into the caress. "What happened, Andie? When you got here, you looked like the devil himself was chasing you."

She feared he was. "I'm better now."

"That's not what I asked."

Her lips lifted. "I know."

"Andie—"

She laid her fingers against his mouth. She saw the concern in his eyes, the speculation. She didn't want either, not right now. And she didn't want him to be a cop—only a man.

"I can't," she said again. "Not yet." She searched his gaze. "Give me some time. Okay?"

He caught her hand and held it against his mouth a moment more, then brought it to his heart. "You said I was right, that you almost sneaked off while I was putting Mara to bed. Why?"

Underneath her hand, his heart beat strong and steady. She curled her fingers into his cotton pullover, longing to be closer, to feel that beat against her own breast. "Because," she murmured, her voice thick, "if I stayed, I knew what would happen."

The tempo of his heart increased. "And what was that?"

She lifted her gaze boldly to his. "I knew we'd make love."

For one moment he stood frozen, surprised, she knew, by her sudden daring. Then he kissed her, deeply, passionately, drawing her into him as surely as the sun drew a flower to its bright heat.

She kissed him back, long, drugging exchanges that went on forever, yet not nearly long enough. Never breaking contact, he swept her into his arms and carried her to the bedroom, closing and locking the door behind them.

He dispelled her second thoughts with the brush of his fingertips, a murmured endearment, a throaty sound of passion. He dispensed with her clothes the same way, and she with his. They sank to the bed.

Being naked with him was a sensual delight, his hard body made for her softer one. She explored at her leisure, and he at his. His body fit hers as if they had been made for one another.

She had never known, never believed, sex could be like this, magical and renewing and perfect. She had never imagined a man could be so gentle, so willing to give and receive in return. He made himself vulnerable to her, he told her what he liked, he asked for what he needed.

He expected her to do the same in return.

At first she was afraid. Asking for what she needed came with risks. So did sharing what she really wanted. Once he knew what really mattered to her, she would be completely vulnerable to him.

"Tell me what you need," he whispered against her mouth, as if sensing her hesitation. "I'll give it to you, Andie. I promise."

So she did. She opened herself to him in all ways but the last. She asked for what she needed, what she wanted, she told him what was in her heart, what really mattered to her.

And when she opened herself in that final way, he took what she offered and sank into her. Their hands met as their pelvises did; he laced his fingers with hers. He caught her mouth, taking the very breath she needed to survive, drawing it from her lungs and into his own. Then in the moment she was sure she would die, he gave it and her life back to her.

Nick Raphael breathed life into her.

She arched against him, crying out her pleasure. Her release. He muffled the sound with his mouth, with his own sound of pleasure. His own release.

Afterward, they lay on their sides, facing one another. He brushed his fingers over the curve of her hip to the dip of her waist and back, seemingly content just to gaze at her.

"I should go," she said, dreading the moment, dreading how she would feel an hour or a day or even a minute from now. Already hating her worries, her hopes, the anxious hours she would spend waiting or wondering.

It had started already. Nick wasn't a free man. He had uttered not one word of love, no promises, no mentions even of the day after tonight or the minute after this one.

He tangled his fingers in her hair. "I don't want you to go. Not yet."

"Mara—"

"Won't be up for hours. She's a sound sleeper."

"You're sure?"

"Positive."

She smiled. "I don't want me to go, either."

He moved his gaze over her face, then lower, taking a leisurely path. When he found her gaze again, she knew that her cheeks were pink. "You're perfect, you know that?"

A smile of pure, feminine pleasure stole across her mouth. If she were a cat, she would purr and rub herself against him.

"I mean it, you know. It's not just because we made love." His lips lifted. "Or because I want to make love again."

She arched her eyebrow. "You promise?"

"Which?"

"Either. Both."

"It's not." He rolled her on top of him. "But I do."

She lowered her mouth to his. "I do, too."

68

Raven sat in her car, staring at the modest house in the middle of the block, watching and waiting, her thoughts chaotic. Moonlight filtered through the windshield, bathing the car's stifling hot interior in cool blue.

Sweat trickled between her breasts and shoulder blades. She gripped the steering wheel, her palms slippery. Her heart thundered, and she struggled to breathe in the closed, airless car.

Raven feared she might suffocate.

But still, she didn't open a window. She didn't want anyone to hear her breathing. Anyone, but most of all Andie.

Andie would recognize her breathing, just as Raven would recognize hers, even from fifty or a hundred feet away. When she emerged from that house, she would sense her friend's presence, the way a mouse did a cat's. The way a child did her mother's.

Or maybe she wouldn't.

Her world was coming apart.

Panting, desperate for breath, Raven brought a hand to her forehead and wiped away the sweat. Andie had turned away from her. She had taken to keeping things from her. Turning to others for comfort and support. The way Julie always had.

But Julie was weak, her character deeply flawed. She had always been broken goods, right from the beginning. Raven had learned to expect less from Julie, to deal with her as she would a naughty child.

But Andie…she had always been Raven's rock. Strong and centered. Completely loyal. Always faithful. Except for the summer of '83.

And except for now.

Nick Raphael.

Now, Andie turned to him—just as she had once before. Now, she shared her dreams and secrets with him. She longed to be family with him. She didn't need Raven anymore. She didn't want her.

A moan eased from Raven's parted lips. The sad sound surprised her, because what she felt was hatred. It burned in her chest and in the pit of her gut, huge and hot, with a life force all its own.

Tonight, she had followed Andie here. She had been watching her friend for days now. She knew Julie had paid a visit to Andie tonight and that they'd had some sort of a fight. And she knew the noose and scarf had sent her running.

But not to Raven. Not to the one who had always loved and cared for her. Not to the one to whom she had promised her undying loyalty.

She had run to Nick Raphael.

Raven narrowed her eyes on the house, willing Andie to emerge. Willing it with all her love and loyalty, with every fiber and molecule of her being.

And Andie did. She stepped out of the house and onto the small front porch.

Only to be drawn back into *his* arms for a long kiss. Raven watched, consumed with hatred and jealousy, her mouth dry and bitter-tasting.

Andie broke away. She was laughing. She looked happy, happier than Raven had ever seen her. Andie was in love with him, Raven realized, catching her breath. She knew her friend well enough to know that. What was happening between Andie and Nick Raphael wasn't just sex.

Love. Andie was in love.

She could lose her forever.

Raven clutched the steering wheel tighter, fighting off despair, fighting off the possibility. She wouldn't allow it to happen. She couldn't. Somehow, some way, she would take care of it. She would make certain Andie didn't leave her.

David Sadler. His image popped into her head, realization with it. This was his fault, she decided. They had been happy until he'd come into their lives—now and fifteen years before. He was the problem. The one stirring up trouble, causing Andie to be confused and afraid, causing Julie's slide into the abyss.

Raven started her car. The air conditioner shot a blast of tepid air at her face. Tepid and foul, but air nonetheless. She sucked it in greedily, gasping, revived. She was going to fix this. The time had come, she was going to make Mr. X pay.

69

Raven decided she would give Julie one more chance to prove her loyalty. One more chance to prove herself worthy of Raven's continuing devotion. To earn it, Raven had decided, Julie would have to choose their friendship over her affair with David Sadler.

Raven didn't hold out much hope, not intellectually anyway. But in her heart it burned bright and hot. She had to try. She loved Julie. She was family.

David Sadler was going down. That was a given now. She, Raven, was bringing him down. And Julie was either with her or against her. Completely loyal to her or dead to her. It was as simple as that.

Raven had stopped by Julie's apartment several times over the past two days; she'd never found her home. When she ran into a couple of Julie's neighbors and asked about her, they said they hadn't seen her around much lately. Curious, Raven called the club to find out when Julie would be working next. That day, the man said. She opened at ten-thirty. It would be her last day, he added. She had up and quit.

Raven hung up the phone, saddened but not surprised. If her friend hadn't moved in with David Sadler yet, she would soon. Julie was doing the same thing she had always done, tossing aside her own life, a life with her friends, to be with a man.

One last chance. She had to give her one last chance to choose her family.

Raven checked the time. Perfect, she thought. She

should be able to arrive at the club just behind Julie. She grabbed her purse and car keys and headed for her car.

Raven walked into the bar at ten thirty-five. Julie stood with her back to the door, counting the money in the register, getting ready for the day.

"We don't open until eleven," she called, not turning.

"I'm not here to drink."

Julie spun around, her cheeks hot with color. Her friend looked as guilty as a six-year-old who had gotten caught playing doctor with the boy next door. "Rave!"

"Hello, Julie." Raven slid onto one of the stools. "I've been looking for you. We need to talk."

"Now?" Julie cleared her throat. "I mean, I'm at work."

"It won't take long. I thought we could chat about the affair you're having."

Julie widened her eyes in exaggerated innocence. "I'm not having an affair, Rave."

"Don't lie to me, Julie. I know everything. Even that you asked Andie to lie for you."

Julie nervously clasped and unclasped her hands. "She told you that?"

"What did you expect?" Raven made a sound of disgust. "She's a better friend than you, Julie. More loyal. She always has been."

Julie's eyes filled. "I'm sorry."

Raven waved off the apology. The tears. "What does that mean to you? If I had a nickel for every time you said that to me, I'd be bloody, fucking rich."

Julie hung her head. Silence fell between them. After several moments, Raven cleared her throat. "Do you have anything to say to me? To ask me? Or is this it?"

Julie lifted her gaze. "To ask you?"

"That's right. Don't you even wonder why I'm here?"

"I know why." Julie sighed and looked away. "I can't believe Andie told you... I'd hoped that this time, that she might choose..."

Julie let the thought trail off, and Raven narrowed her eyes slightly. What was Julie getting at? Obviously, Andie had *not* told her everything.

"Of course she told me," Raven said. "We're best friends. The way you and I are *supposed* to be."

"I'm sorry." Julie took a deep breath, her face pale, her expression distraught. "I didn't mean anything by it. I just...I was wondering about that summer. I had some questions, that's all."

The summer of '83.

And Mr. and Mrs. X.

"Here I am. Ask me."

Julie twisted her fingers together, something Raven had seen her do a thousand times when she was uncertain or nervous. "I just wondered if that summer...if maybe you saw something you didn't tell me and Andie about. Something you were afraid to tell the police."

"We were always there together, Julie. How could I have seen something different?"

"I know, but...if you ever went over without us. Maybe you stopped by and forgot to tell us. Or...or something."

Disloyal little bitch. After everything she had done for Julie, she repaid her with this? With suspicion? With doubt about her honesty and her loyalty?

Raven shook with fury at the betrayal. It was yet another slap in the face from someone she had called family. She leaned toward Julie, heart thundering, breath short. "Why are you asking me this?"

Julie shrank back. "I just wondered."

"You just *happened* to be thinking about Mr. and Mrs. X? You just *happened* to be wondering about events that are fifteen years old?"

"Yes," she murmured, shifting her gaze, "that's all."

"You're a rotten liar, Julie Cooper."

"I'm not lying! You have to believe me, I wouldn't lie to you."

Raven reached across the bar and grabbed her friend's

hands, squeezing them so tightly Julie gasped. Raven lowered her voice to a deadly whisper. "You don't think I see through your questions? You don't think I know who's behind them? Your *boyfriend,* of course. David Sadler. You're pathetic, Julie. Really pathetic."

"Let go of me!" Julie cried, tugging against Raven's grasp. "You're hurting me!"

Raven tightened her grip. "Don't you get it? Don't you see? He's using you, Julie. He's involved with all three of us. He's planning to bed us all. You certainly didn't think you were his one and only, did you?"

"That's not true. It's not!"

"But it is." Raven laughed. "He's already tried. But Andie and I aren't easy like you. We don't fall into bed with every dick that happens by."

Julie was crying now, tears streaming down her cheeks, tugging futilely against Raven's strong grasp. "No...no. That's not true. David loves me. I know he does."

Raven glanced at the bar doorway, then turned back to Julie, lowering her voice. "Of course he's using you. Why is he asking about the events of fifteen years ago? Is he getting off on it? Or maybe you and he are into that same kinky stuff that Mr. and Mrs. X were into. Maybe David Sadler is Mr. X?"

"No!" With an almighty tug, Julie ripped her hands from Raven's. "Leave David alone. He hasn't done anything to you."

"Maybe I should call the police," Raven said evenly, getting to her feet. "I'm sure they'd find your boyfriend's sexual proclivities very interesting. Especially considering that he's found a way to entangle himself with the three girls involved in the Leah Robertson murder case."

Julie crumbled. "Please, Rave," she begged. "Don't go to the police. My David didn't kill Leah Robertson. He couldn't. He loved her. He loves me."

"And I don't love you?"

"It's not the same," Julie whispered. "You're not a..."

"A man?" Raven supplied, making a sound of disgust. "You're willing to believe this sick bastard, a man who's only just come into your life, over me, after everything I've done for you? After everything I've been to you? You're willing to think *I* did it? Please."

"I didn't say that." Julie shook her head and took a step backward. "I never suggested that you—"

"You're such a fool, Julie." Raven placed her hands flat on the bar and leaned toward her. "When it comes to men, you always have been. You never saw what was important in life. Friendship and family. The things Andie and I gave you. We're the ones you should be pledging your loyalty to."

"You're crazy," Julie whispered. "You're obsessed with loyalty because of your nutty old man. You're as nutty as he was."

Raven froze, feeling her friend's words like a sharp slap to the face.

She had her answer. Julie had betrayed her for the last time.

Raven walked toward the door. When she reached it, she turned and looked back at her former friend. Julie stood with her head and shoulders bowed, her arms wrapped around her middle. The picture of vulnerability and defeat. Tears pricked Raven's eyes, but she hardened herself to them. And to the place inside her that yearned to forgive her friend and welcome her back home, anytime, no matter what.

She couldn't do that. She wouldn't.

Julie Cooper was family no more.

"I suggest you watch yourself," she said softly. "If you don't, you might end up just as dead as Mrs. X."

70

Raven planned carefully. If she was going to bring David Sadler down, she was going to have to do it carefully, so as not to incriminate herself in any way. To simply walk into the police station and announce that she had been in that house all those years ago, that she had witnessed things she hadn't admitted to before, would open herself to questions. To speculation and suspicion.

She wanted no part of that.

David needed to be caught in the act.

So Raven followed Julie and David, waiting for the perfect opportunity to strike, knowing him well enough to know that it would come. The man was as predictable as a set clock.

Raven discovered immediately that David and Julie were, indeed, playing the same sick and dangerous game that he and Leah Robertson had been. In fact, David was orchestrating the scenes to be exact duplicates of the ones of fifteen years before. Which put him exactly where she wanted him to be.

She followed them to the Gatehouse community, to the model home whose interior she had put so much of herself into. His taking Julie, the woman she had once loved and cherished, to that house—*her house*—was an obscenity. The ultimate insult.

She wondered if he thought of it that way; wondered if he got a kind of vicarious sexual thrill from it.

She wondered, too, if he had any inkling that now, like all those years ago, he was being watched.

He took her former friend to the formal living room, with its exposed-beam ceiling and the waiting rope. Raven crouched beneath a window and peered over the sill, the night oppressively hot and still. The heat and humidity settled atop her like a smothering blanket, sweat rolled down her back and pooled under her arms.

As she had known he would, David blindfolded Julie and bound her hands. Then he led her to the stools and the noose. As Raven watched, the past and present mingled in her mind, twisting and turning together until she was uncertain where one began and the other ended.

Her mind galloped back and forth between her twelfth year, her fifteenth, this one. Her head filled with the sound of her mother and father's last fight, the image of the shovel coming down on her mom's head, blood flying; then with Leah Robertson's throaty laughter and the way her body had twitched and jerked in her last moments of life.

And it filled with thoughts and images of Julie, her sweet, sweet friend. That first day they met, in the church yard, the sun sparkling in her blond hair; on the morning of her first wedding, radiant and hopeful; the way she had been a year later, marriage over, as she had turned to Raven for comfort and support.

And the way she was now, demeaned and unfaithful, as low to the ground as a snake's belly.

Poor Julie, she thought, tears stinging her eyes. Poor weak, confused Julie. If only she were stronger. If only she had more brains or a bigger heart. Even though she had hurt Raven time and again, even though Raven had washed her hands of her, she still loved her. The way, she understood now, her father had never stopped loving her mother.

And like her father, she would mourn Julie's loss forever.

Raven knew everything David was saying to Julie, though she couldn't hear him. She knew he uttered the same words he'd uttered to Leah Robertson all those years ago; they were burned on Raven's brain. Julie was at his mercy; he could do anything he wanted to her, even kill her. If she didn't obey him. If she didn't please him.

All it would take was one little kick to the stool.

David made love to Julie. With his hands and mouth, bringing her friend, Raven saw, to the point of orgasm, again and again. Suddenly he stopped. Raven wasn't surprised, this was part of the game, too, one she recognized from years before. One only she knew about.

Raven understood. He was asserting his total dominance over his lamb. Reminding her that she was his, that her fate was totally in his hands. He owned her.

To prove his point, he left her. Alone in the dark. To wait. And worry.

Her time had come.

Raven waited until David had driven off, then went around to the front of the house. She didn't know how much time she had, so she would have to act quickly. Raven unlocked the front door and stepped inside. She heard Julie crying softly, whimpering in fear. With a disgusted shake of her head, Raven crossed to the security system's keypad, entered the code, then breathed deeply, taking a moment to enjoy the new-house scents of the fresh paint and newly milled wood.

She snapped the door shut behind her.

Julie's whimpering stopped. "David?" she called. "Is that you?"

Raven smiled. It wasn't David who mattered now, wasn't David who was in control. It was her.

Raven dipped her hand into her pocket and pulled out a pair of rubber gloves, the kind surgeons wore. She slipped them on, working her fingers all the way in. That done, she headed for the living room, heart thundering, adrenaline pumping.

Her first look at her friend turned her stomach. The taste

of bile was bitter on her tongue. She forced it back. "Hello, Julie," she said.

For one moment of crackling silence, Julie was still with shock. Then she turned her head in Raven's direction. "Rave," she whispered, "is that you?"

"None other."

Julie opened her mouth, but no sound came out. Raven could only imagine the chaos of the other woman's thoughts—her shock and shame, her questions.

Raven laughed softly, deciding to cut her some slack, considering the circumstances. "I followed you and David here. I knew he was up to the same sick tricks as fifteen years ago."

She circled the other woman, pleased to see that she trembled. "You should see yourself now, Julie, trussed up like a Christmas goose. It's disgusting. Where's your pride?"

"Let me down," Julie whispered, the tiny sound broken by tears. "Please, Raven."

Raven ignored her plea. "All those years ago, I hand-picked you to be a part of mine and Andie's family. Because you needed us so much. I thought that would make you loyal. How could I have been so wrong?" Raven clucked her tongue and shook her head. "You never got that, did you? You were our friend because *I* said it was okay. *Me.*"

Julie started to cry, quietly at first, then with increasing force. Her sobs shook her, nearly unbalancing her. She begged Raven, over and over, to let her down.

"So, now you need me, is that it? Now that you want something from me?" Raven narrowed her eyes. "I hate him, you know. Though I didn't always. I admired him. Maybe I even fancied myself in love with him." Raven shrugged. "He taught me about power. About wielding it over others. He taught me about control.

"He opened a whole new world for me." Raven smiled, remembering, her heart thundering. "Things I'd had only glimmers of before. Suddenly I understood...everything. Who I was. What was important. What my father meant by loyalty and the extremes one must go to protect the ones you love.''

Inside the rubber gloves her hands began to sweat. ''That's why I sneaked into the house all those years ago, to watch. And to learn.''

At Julie's involuntary sound, Raven giggled; the girlish sound echoed through the big room. ''You were right. I did go back and watch them. I hid in the closet. I saw and heard everything. That's how I knew what David was doing with you, where it would lead.''

''You...killed...her,'' Julie choked out, her words partially obscured by her sobs. ''Didn't you?''

Raven clicked her tongue. ''No loyalty. He has you strung up like a sacrificial lamb, and you're thinking *I* killed Leah Robertson. That's why I'm here, Julie. That's why—''

She bit the words back, angry suddenly. Furious. At David Sadler for bringing them to this. At Julie, for allowing it to happen. ''He should have stayed out of our lives. He should have stayed as far away from us as possible. But he didn't. He thought it would be fun to mess with *my* family. Just like fifteen years ago.''

She took a step closer to Julie. She smelled her fear, she smelled sex and sweat. ''I've decided to be rid of him, once and for all. Unfortunately, you have to be a part of the plan. I can't do it without you.''

She lifted her face to her former friend's, wishing she could remove the blindfold, wanting to look at her beautiful face one last time. ''Mrs. X was easy,'' Raven murmured, reaching out to Julie but stopping short of touching her. ''I wanted her to die. But you... I'm sorry, Julie. I am. I wish this could be different. I wish you had been more loyal.''

"Let me go, Rave," Julie begged. "Please, don't do this. I love you. You're my best friend. Rave, plea—"

"Too late, Julie. Way too late."

Raven kicked the stool out from under her.

71

The snapping of Julie's neck ringing in her ears, Raven looked frantically around her. She had planned carefully for this moment, so she would make no mistakes. Why couldn't she think? Why couldn't she remember?

She was sweating. It dripped into her eyes, burning them. She rubbed them, horrified to realize how badly she trembled. This had been so much more difficult than Leah Robertson. She hadn't cared about her. Watching her die had been a curiosity. A rush.

But Julie...

A sound of denial and grief raced to her lips, and she choked it back. Raven couldn't look at her. She averted her eyes and focused on the reasons she'd had to do it; she forced herself to focus on her plan.

Think. Think. Her eyes fell on the stool. Of course, she remembered, the stool. She took a clean handkerchief from her pants pocket, stooped and carefully rubbed away the smudge her shoe sole had left on the white wood.

She looked at the floor. She had been careful to stay on the plastic runners and off the carpeting. There would be none of her footprints in the plush pile around the body. She held out her hands, knowing she had worn gloves the entire time, but wanting to reassure herself.

She thought back, carefully, to each step she had made. Before she had put on the gloves, she had touched the doorknob and the security keypad. Her prints on both would be expected: she was in and out of this model every day. Same with any other trace evidence they might find that would indicate her presence.

No, all the real evidence would point to one person, the one who owned the house, the one whose fingerprints and other biological evidence was all over the stool, the scarves, the rope. Julie's body. The one whose footprints were embedded in the plush carpeting all around the corpse.

Just to be safe, Raven followed the plastic walkway to the kitchen, then back around to the foyer, down the hall and back to Julie, making a continuous line of impressions beneath the plastic. Now, she thought, checking her watch, finding it difficult to think over her pounding heart, for the last piece of evidence, the one that would link David Sadler to Leah Robertson's murder fifteen years before.

Leah Robertson's wedding ring. Her trophy. The little insurance policy she'd snatched from the scene all those years ago. She took it from her pocket and holding it carefully, along the rim, she manipulated it against Julie's lifeless fingers, then let it slip from her own. It pinged against the stool, then bounced, landing on the carpet a few feet away.

Raven dared a glance at her friend then, tears pricking her eyes. She whispered goodbye, then let herself out, careful to rearm the security system and lock the front door.

72

The call had come in at 3:01 a.m. An anonymous tip. Something weird was going on over at the Gatehouse development site, the caller had said. They had seen lights.

Something weird, all right. A homicide.

Nick stood beside Bobby, listening to the coroner, his chest tight, stomach churning. Horror and revulsion warred with excitement. Excitement because they were going to get the sick son of a bitch this time. Nick felt it. In his gut. This was no copycat. This was the guy, the one who'd slipped through their fingers fifteen years ago. He wasn't going to do it again. Not this time.

"Can you ID her, Nick?" the coroner asked, removing the blindfold with tweezers, tapping the body so it swung slightly in his direction.

"Holy shit," Nick muttered, taking a step backward, her identity hitting him with the force of a blow. He struggled to speak, aware of the others looking at him, waiting for a response. "Yeah," he managed to say, his voice thick. "I know who she is. Name's Julie Cooper."

"Julie Cooper," Bobby repeated, drawing his bushy eyebrows together in thought. "Why do I recognize that name?"

Nick averted his gaze from the once-beautiful face, bloated and red in death. "She was one of the teenagers involved in the Robertson homicide fifteen years ago."

And she was one of Andie's best friends.

How was he going to tell her?

Bobby whistled under his breath. "Son of a bitch."

"No shit."

"Fellas, you want to take a look over here?"

They both turned. One of the uniforms was bent over, examining something on the carpet.

"What do you have, Mallory?"

She looked up. "It appears to be a wedding ring."

They crossed to and squatted beside her. It was a lady's ring, a plain gold band of medium width. Using tweezers, Nick lifted it from the carpeting. He held it up to the light, studying it.

"Was Julie Cooper married?"

"Several times, as I understand it. But not currently." Nick squinted. "It's inscribed. With love, 2–14–80."

"1980?" Bobby scratched his head. "This isn't her ring, then. Not unless she was a child bride."

"Maybe her mother's?" the uniform offered. "Or another family member's?"

"No," Nick murmured, the excitement growing, pulling at him. He forced himself to ignore the emotion, to go slow, to be careful. "It's not Julie Cooper's wedding ring, it's not her mother's." He looked at the coroner. "Remember, Doc?"

The man met his eyes, understanding. *Leah Robertson.* "Are you asking me if Robertson was wearing her wedding ring? It'd be in my records."

"Ours, too." Nick looked at his partner. "But I'd bet we have a match here."

Bobby nodded, following. "I'll check it out, first thing."

"Bag it, Mallory." She took the tweezers from him, and he stood, thinking of Andie again. He glanced toward the door. *How was he going to tell her?*

"What about next of kin?" Bobby asked.

"I'll take care of it." Nick glanced toward the door once more, then back at his partner. "I need to go see Andie. I need to tell her before…the media gets wind of it. I need to—" He passed a hand over his forehead, cursing the job he had to do. Knowing no one else could do it; that he wouldn't allow anyone else to. "And I need to question her. She might have some information. She might know who Julie's been seeing."

"Just watch your ass," Bobby said. "Considering her history and what's been going on, she could be in danger, too."

If Andie knew who the killer was, she could be in danger, too. Of course. So could Raven.

Without even taking the time to respond, Nick flew out the door.

73

The phone awakened Andie from a deep sleep. It was Nick calling.

"This is important, Andie," he said, cutting off her sleepy, pleased greeting. "Is everything all right there?"

Andie sat up, instantly awake. Alarmed. "Yes," she said, reaching to turn on her bedside light. "I think so."

"Good. I'm in my car, on my way over. I'll be there in two minutes. Don't answer the door for anyone but me. Got that?"

"Nick, wha—"

"Got that?" he repeated, barking the words at her.

She said she did, and he hung up. She held the receiver to her ear for a moment, heart thundering. She moved her gaze over her bedroom, grateful for the light.

Something had happened. Something terrible.

With a squeak of fear, she jumped out of bed and ran to the bathroom. She grabbed her robe and brushed her teeth, then scurried to the front door to wait for him.

He arrived moments later, swinging into her driveway and screeching to a halt. He leaped out of his car and ran for her door. She swung it open, and taking one look at his face, made a sound of alarm. "What is it?" she asked. "What's wrong?"

Instead of telling her, he took her into his arms and kissed her. Long and deeply, holding her in a way that frightened her, holding her as if he had thought for a moment that he might never be able to hold her again.

"Thank God," he muttered. "Thank God you're here and safe. I was so afraid…I—"

She broke away from him, shaking, terrified. "Tell me," she managed to say, her voice a croak. "What's happened?"

"Inside," he said. "Not here."

"Nick—"

"Please, Andie. Just do as I ask." She nodded and led him inside, into the foyer. He shut the door behind them. "It's Julie," he said. "She's… Andie, Julie's dead. Murdered."

Andie stared at him, certain she had heard wrong but knowing she had not. She felt the color drain from her face, the warmth from her body. She shook her head, her mouth working, though no sound came out.

"We got a call a couple hours ago," he went on. "An anonymous tip. The caller said there was something weird going on at the Gatehouse development. We found Julie there. Andie, she…"

"No!" Andie cried. "No, it's not true!" She looked wildly around her, knowing she should be doing something, but not having a clue what. She began to tremble violently.

"I'm sorry," he said, going to her, drawing her into his arms. He held her tightly. "I'm so sorry."

She shook her head again, swamped with tears, unable to catch her breath. She curled her fingers into his shirt, clinging to him.

"Listen to me, Andie. There's more."

He told her then, how Julie had died. Quickly and with little emotion, as if to lessen the blow of his words.

Mrs. X. Hanging by her neck. Her face bloated and red, grotesque in death.

Andie squeezed her eyes shut, seeing Julie the same way. Her stomach rushed to her throat. She held the sickness back, gasping, light-headed.

Julie… Dear God, not Julie.

"Andie, honey—" Nick caught her hands and rubbed them between his. "You need to listen to me. It's important. I need your help. Julie needs your help. Was she seeing anyone? Do you know anyone who could have done this?"

"David," she said, lifting her gaze to Nick's. "David did it."

74

When Raven heard about Julie, she seconded Andie's shock and despair. She, too, gave the police a statement about Julie's involvement with David Sadler. About her suspicions that Julie had been involved in something kinky.

But the police didn't have to act only on Andie and Raven's suspicions; the circumstantial evidence implicating David Sadler was overwhelming. He owned, and therefore had complete access to, the property where the murder had been committed. The ring found at the scene was, indeed, Leah Robertson's. David Sadler's prints were on the stool, the scarf that bound Julie's wrists, on the one that covered her eyes. The footprints embedded in the carpeting around the victim matched his. Hair, fiber and other trace materials had been sent to the lab in St. Louis for analysis.

Once again, quiet little Thistledown made big news. Once again, Andie, Julie and Raven were in the spotlight. Only this time, Julie was dead.

Only this time, a murderer wouldn't escape justice.

Within forty-eight hours, David Sadler was arrested for the murders of Julie Cooper and Leah Robertson.

Of course, as all criminals did, he proclaimed his innocence loudly and vehemently.

But nobody listened. Nobody at all.

75

Two weeks after the murder, the medical examiner released Julie's body for burial. Raven insisted on making all the arrangements herself, and Andie let her. She didn't have the energy or heart to tackle more than getting up in the morning and dragging herself through something that resembled her routine.

She was numb with grief, racked with guilt. "If onlys" tormented her. If only she had given David's name to Nick. If only she had been a better, braver friend and tried harder to help Julie. If only she had been more astute at her job. If only she hadn't been so naive, so trusting.

She should have seen through David Sadler. She should have known that he was Mr. X. That he was a killer.

If she had, Julie would still be alive.

But no, like the too-trusting, Goody Two–shoes Raven had always called her, she had wanted to believe in David, in his motives. She had wanted him to be what he said he was, a man who wanted help. Who wanted to change. And she had longed to help him. To be Super Shrink, or something.

So, she wondered bitterly, had it been her naiveté that had gotten Julie killed—or her ego?

She stood at the graveside, the pastor's words floating on the morning air, and though Andie listened, she couldn't recall a word he said. She missed her friend. It hurt. She felt responsible.

She had gone through the motions when forced to: with her patients, with her family, who had called the minute they'd heard; with the reporters, who for the first week, had hounded her every step.

Mostly, she had chosen to hole up alone in her house, refusing even to see Raven. Raven had been hurt by her refusal, but Andie had needed to grieve alone. Nick, on the other hand, had given her time, space. He had let her know that if she needed him, he was there. Then he had let her be. She missed him, ached for him, but she couldn't bring herself to reach out to him. Or anyone else.

Beside her, Raven wept. Across the way, two young women Julie had worked with sobbed openly. Julie's family hadn't come. When Raven had called them, Reverend Cooper had told her that Julie had been dead to them for a long time. Her mother had sent flowers, though. A wreath of daisies and baby's breath. Julie had adored daisies, choosing them over roses or orchids or any other more exotic bloom. Her mother had remembered that. In that small gesture of love and remembrance Andie had found comfort. Julie had been loved, even if secretly and without courage; she would be missed.

The service ended. Andie turned to go. And saw Nick. He stood at the edge of the gravesite, beyond the small circle of mourners.

She crossed to him. Their gazes met and she felt as if a ray of sunshine was spilling over her. The first in two weeks. "Thank you for coming."

"Are you all right?"

She looked away, then back, eyes swimming with tears. "No."

He reached out and cupped her cheek in his palm. She tilted her face into the caress, comforted.

"It's not your fault," he murmured. "Don't blame yourself."

How did he know her so well? She swiped at her runny nose, brokenhearted. "He was my patient, Nick. I should have known. I should have turned him in so many times. When I learned he was the one that she was having an affair with. When I realized he was involved with all three of us. When I learned what—'' Her throat closed over the words, and she cleared it. ''When I learned the things they were doing together. I had so many opportunities to save her.''

''You had an oath to uphold. Without proof of his guilt, you had no reason to break that oath.''

''We have proof now,'' she said bitterly. ''Plenty of it. Only problem is, Julie's dead.''

''He wants to see you.''

Andie froze, knowing who he must mean but unable to believe it. ''What did you say?''

''David Sadler's asking for you.''

She recoiled, sickened by the thought of facing him. ''No.'' She shook her head. ''I can't. I won't.''

''He wants to talk, Andie. But he won't speak to anyone but you.''

''Why me?'' She searched Nick's expression. ''He must know how I feel about him.''

''He wants to be heard, to be understood. You were his shrink, you're the most likely candidate.''

''I'm not his shrink anymore. Tell him to find another one.''

''Andie, he claims he's innocent. Of both murders.''

She met Nick's eyes, stunned, angry. ''How can he say that? How, when all the evidence points right to him?''

''There's more. He swears he didn't leave the noose and scarf on your bed.''

She felt his words like a blow. Heat flew to her cheeks. ''And you believe him?''

''I didn't say that. But he admits to the clippings and calls, to breaking into your house and leaving the music playing.'' Nick looked away, then back. ''It's odd, that's all. I wanted you to know.''

For a moment she said nothing, just digested what he'd said. She met his eyes again. ''If he didn't leave them, Nick, who did?''

"I don't know. Maybe you can find out. Maybe you can get us some answers."

She hesitated. The thought of sitting across a table from David Sadler repulsed her. She rubbed her arms, rubbed at the gooseflesh that crawled up them. "I just don't... know."

Nick touched her face again, tracing his thumb across her cheekbone. "Stop being a victim, Andie. Stop feeling sorry for yourself. Do something to help the situation."

His words hurt; but he was right. "All right," she murmured, chest tight. "But not as his doctor. He has to understand that. Nothing is confidential. If he agrees to that, I'll talk to him."

76

David sat across the table from Andie. He wore a bright orange prison jumpsuit; his hands, folded on the table in front of him, were cuffed. A dark, purpling bruise marred the side of his neck. She didn't ask where he had gotten it. She didn't care.

Everything had been prearranged. David hadn't wanted anyone present, not even his lawyer. Just outside the room's locked steel door Nick and a guard waited. The door had a small barred window; all she need do was glance over her shoulder and she would see them. She found that knowledge infinitely reassuring.

Screwing up her resolve, Andie looked David dead in the eyes. Something there, an eagerness, a hopefulness, reminded her more of a lost little boy than a man accused of two murders.

An illusion perfected over the years by a man who was a master manipulator. A cold-blooded killer.

"Thank you for coming, Dr. Bennett."

"Don't thank me," she said stiffly. "I'm not your psychologist anymore. Nothing you say is confidential. I'm not bound by any doctor-patient oath. Do you understand?"

He said he did and laid his hands flat against the table; the metal cuffs clicked against the wood. "Interesting twist of fate," she said. "Now you're the one whose wrists are bound."

The blood seemed to drain from his face. "I'm sorry," he whispered. "I know you're angry with me, but—"

She cut him off, so furious suddenly she could taste the emotion. "You know nothing about me or the way I feel. You're the slime of the earth, David, and the only reason I'm sitting here is in the hopes of learning something that will incriminate you. If I can help them fry you, I will. Do you get that?"

"Yes." His voice shook. "I get that."

"Then why do you want to talk to me?"

"Because I'm innocent, Dr. Bennett. Because I want to tell you my side of the story, I want you to believe me."

"But why?" She clenched her hands into fists. "What difference would it make if I believed you?"

"You'd stand up for me. I know you would."

Her stomach rose to her throat. No wonder he thought that, he had manipulated her to his will for weeks now. *She had made so many mistakes.* "I won't believe you," she said. "You killed one of my best friends. You lied to me, terrorized me—"

"I didn't mean to hurt you. You have to believe that. I only wanted—"

"Don't say 'only' to me! Don't you dare!"

Andie jumped to her feet. She swung away from him, fighting to catch her breath. What was she doing here? she wondered. Why was she subjecting herself to this?

She wasn't, not anymore.

"I'm leaving. I've heard enough."

"No! Dr. Bennett!" She heard him launch to his feet and she swung around, afraid. She saw that his ankles, like his wrists, were shackled. She needn't fear his sneaking up on her and overpowering her. She could escape easily, anytime she chose.

If only her thoughts, her self-recriminations, were so easy to escape.

"Please," he said again. "Let me start at the beginning. Then, if you don't believe me, use anything I say, I won't care."

She hesitated, then nodded. They returned to their seats.

And he began. "Yes, I was having an affair with Leah Robertson. Yes, we were into unusual, kinky sex." He cleared his throat. "We met at a charity event, one for the library." A hint of a smile touched his mouth. "Our eyes met and we both knew immediately. We were kindred spirits. She needed what I had to offer, I needed what she was willing to give me."

Leah had been one of the special ones. The ones he had described during their sessions.

So had Julie.

Andie looked away, repulsed.

"We began to meet," he continued. "It was dangerous. She was the wife of a public figure, I was prominent in the community. We could go few places without being recognized. Her place was out of the question. So was mine.

"So, we came up with a plan. She rented one of Sadler Construction's empty houses. There were so many then. We chose carefully, one on a nearly deserted street, one surrounded by other vacant houses and an undeveloped lot. One far away from our everyday lives. Leah made all the arrangements, directly through Sadler Construction. I was never involved."

He paused, as if choosing his words carefully. "We felt so free then. We became more daring. Bolder. More unconventional. We lived out things we had only been able to fantasize before, and our involvement with bondage, submission and dominance grew."

He drew a deep breath. "She was always a willing partner, Dr. Bennett. She got off on everything I did to her. I know you watched, so you know, I never forced her to participate."

Like Julie. Andie's eyes filled with tears. *Oh, Julie, why didn't you let me help you?*

"That…last day, we took the game further than ever before. I strung Leah up, then brought her to the brink of orgasm, but kept release just beyond her grasp. The waiting, the denial, she liked that. Then I left her there. Alone. And alive.''

He leaned toward Andie, pleading, his expression as earnest as an altar boy's. ''Don't you see? That was exciting for us. To leave her that way, alone and completely vulnerable. I could do anything to her, and she knew it. She found the knowledge, the fear, exciting. The ultimate aphrodisiac.''

A sound escaped Andie. One of terror and disgust. She slid her chair farther back from the table.

''I know I make you sick,'' he said. ''I know you can't understand the way I am. That I disgust you. You aren't the first.'' He cleared his throat again, this time sounding almost choked with emotion. ''But the point is, she was alive when I left her. I swear, Dr. Bennett, she was alive.''

When Andie didn't respond, he went on. ''When I returned two hours later, the house was surrounded by police. I didn't know what had happened. And considering who her husband was, I wasn't about to stroll up and ask. It wasn't until hours later, when I heard it on the news...that I learned Leah was dead.''

''Great story,'' Andie said softly, sarcastically. ''Wonderful work of fiction. But if you were so innocent, why did you run away? If you didn't have anything to hide, why didn't you go to the police?''

''Get real.'' David made a sound that was a cross between a laugh and a curse. ''I was innocent of murder, but not of fucking the police commissioner's wife. Even if all the evidence hadn't pointed toward me, I was as good as convicted.''

''So you just disappeared.'' She snapped her fingers. ''Just like that. Like a coward dog.''

''My father knew about me and Leah. He sent me to St. Louis to run that arm of the company.''

The rift between him and his father, the one he had spoken of during their sessions.

His family had covered for him anyway.

She wasn't about to.

He looked her in the eyes. "I didn't kill Leah," he said softly. "I didn't kill Julie. I loved them both."

"You didn't kill Leah," she all but spit at him, "but as soon as you returned to Thistledown, you not only looked me and my friends up, but you insinuated yourself into all our lives."

She swallowed past the emotion that welled up in her. "Then you began to terrorize us. The clippings and calls, the music, the...noose and—" She nearly choked on the words.

"I didn't do that! I told the police."

"But why should I believe that? Why should they? You're a liar, David."

"I'm not, not about that. Whoever left that is the real killer."

She made a sound of disdain. Of course. *The real killer.* "Fine. Tell me, David, what did you hope to gain with your little campaign of terror?"

"After Leah died and all your pictures were splashed across the papers, I was certain one or all of you knew more than you had told the police. Something you were afraid to say. I thought maybe it was the cops who did it. Or someone whose face you'd recognized from TV or the newspaper."

"Like the police commissioner?"

"Yes. Like the police commissioner. At first, it seemed simple. I thought, if I frightened you, made you think that someone, the person who really killed Leah, was after you, that you would come clean and tell what you really saw that summer." Urgency colored his words. "I thought one of you would crack and tell the truth. I focused on you because I figured out pretty quickly that you were the one most likely to do something. Just like that summer."

"The truth," Andie repeated, furious. "We told the police the truth. You're the one who lied, the only one with a reason to lie!"

"No! Please." He reached out with his bound hands, imploring. "One of you did lie! You all said you'd only been in the house twice. But one of you was there at least one more time. A couple of days before...before Leah...I found a hair ornament, the kind a teenager might wear. It was in the bedroom, peeking out from underneath the closet door. It was mother of pearl, shaped into a bo—"

"Shut up."

"It's true. I saved it all these years, in the hopes that it would help me find Leah's killer. I can show it to you."

Raven used to wear barrettes. Her father had liked her to wear them.

"No!" she shouted, standing. "You're Leah's killer. You killed Julie, too. You're a murderer and this time you're going to pay for your crimes."

"Don't you see! Whoever killed Leah and Julie left you the noose and scarf. I did the others things, but not that." He broke down, blubbering like a baby. "The game got control of me again, Dr. Bennett. I promised it wouldn't, I thought I could control it. With Julie, with all of you, it... I didn't mean for any of it to go this far. Please help me, Dr. Bennett. I didn't kill Julie. I loved her."

She shook her head. "You don't know what love is, David. You can't."

He got to his feet, hands out, pleading. "Ask yourself why Julie was killed. To get me. The same person must have done it, and he's still free. He could do it again."

"No." She backed toward the door. "You did it, you're going to pay." She reached the door; she turned and rapped on it. She saw Nick, his concern; the guard inserted the key.

"People lie," he called from behind her. "You have to listen to me! They hide their true selves to protect themselves or others they love. They have agendas. Secrets that have nothing to do with the appearance of things. Dr. Bennett, please, you have to listen.''

"No." The guard swung the door open, but instead of stepping through she looked over her shoulder at David. "No," she said again. "I don't have to listen. And I won't.''

77

Despite her avowals to David Sadler, Andie couldn't stop thinking about the things he had said to her. In the days that passed, his words, the conviction behind them, gnawed at her. She believed he was guilty. She knew he was a master manipulator and a sociopath who cared for no one but himself.

But even knowing those things, she couldn't put her meeting with him out of her mind.

If one of them had been in the house days before Leah Robertson's murder, that meant one of them had lied—to her friends and family, to the police.

It hadn't been her. Nor Julie, obviously.

That left Raven.

I found a hair ornament, the kind a teenager might wear. Mother of pearl, shaped into a bow.

Andie brought the heels of her hands to her eyes. Raven's father had loved his daughter's hair pulled back; he had bought her many fine, expensive clips for her hair. Too many times to count, Raven had laughed about it to her friends; he wanted her to stay a baby, she had said. A little girl, totally dependent on him.

But, why would Raven have lied about being in the house? And what about the noose and scarf? If David hadn't left it, who had?

Andie made a sound of frustration, pushed away from the desk, stood and crossed to her office window. She gazed out at the waning day. Fall was coming, she thought.

Its colors had begun to creep across the landscape, brushing it with hints of gold and rust.

She had seen her last patient over an hour ago and had let Missy go home early, preferring to be completely alone with her thoughts. She touched the warm glass, thinking of the past, of her friend, and of what she knew of both. Raven wouldn't lie to her. Period. She trusted and believed in her.

David Sadler, on the other hand, was a proven liar. She didn't trust him and never had. But she had allowed him to get to her. She had allowed him to manipulate her.

She was still doing it. She stopped now.

Andie turned away from the window and returned to her desk. Spread across it were patient files, correspondence from several civic organizations and a lengthy memo from Robert Fulton, detailing the status of Martha's case.

Robert had decided that Patti would testify, that the positives of her doing so far outweighed the negatives. He also felt that, in terms of their defense, Martha's fear for her daughter's safety added to state of mind and helped them. Martha had lived under terrible psychological duress for years; the events of the last months had provided the final straw.

Andie lowered her gaze to the memo and frowned. *Things, people, were sometimes not what they seemed.*

That statement had been niggling at her for weeks now. Ever since David had first uttered it, then Julie had repeated it. Andie caught her bottom lip between her teeth. What had he said yesterday? That people would go to great lengths to protect themselves or the ones they loved. That they had unexpected agendas, secrets that had nothing to do with the appearance of things.

Andie caught her breath, her mind suddenly whirling with snippets of conversations, with recollections of small, seemingly insignificant things. Martha at the benefit, looking effervescent in her sexy red dress. Stopping and chatting with the president of the chamber of commerce, the district attorney, the chief of police. All men. Touching this one on the arm or hand, smiling up at that one, laughing, flirty.

In her sexy red dress.

Andie frowned. Hadn't Martha told Andie many times how Edward insisted she wear dark colors or neutrals? Hadn't she told Andie that wearing the wrong thing would, and had, thrown him into a rage? Hadn't Martha, during their sessions, shared Edward's irrational, insane jealousy? That so much as her meeting another man's eyes had provoked him to violence.

So, why would Martha have worn that dress? Why would she have behaved so flirtatiously? Why, when she knew how jealous Edward was, how easily angered?

I know the things that incite him, Dr. Bennett.

Andie's heart began to pound, her palms to sweat. Edward's gaze had followed his wife. Andie had noted that. He had watched her move from one party patron to the next, smiling and laughing. Perfectly innocent behavior. Nothing to get riled up about.

Unless you were an abusive husband, a husband twisted by jealousy and possessiveness.

Andie caught her breath. What she was thinking, speculating, was ridiculous. Preposterous. Why would Martha have deliberately incited her husband to violence?

So she could kill him. In self-defense.

Andie shook her head. That was crazy. She was letting David, her grief over Julie's death, Raven's strangeness of late, all of it, she was letting all of it get to her.

Don't you think it's odd that Martha Pierpont encouraged her husband to buy a gun, despite the fact that he was a violent man?

That snippet of conversation with Nick had gone into her head, then immediately out. She remembered being surprised by it, remembering mentally denying it and tucking it away to mention to Martha or Robert. But she hadn't thought about it since. Until now.

*Don't you think it's odd that Edward Pierpont died by
his own gun, only a week or so after having bought it?*

Andie brought the heels of her hands to her eyes. Yes,
she did. She thought it very odd. Martha had told her that
she had begged—*begged*—Edward not to buy the gun. She
had suggested a bodyguard instead.

Who was telling the truth? She wanted to believe that
her patient was. Just as she had wanted to believe David.
But, why would the sales clerk lie? He had nothing to gain
or lose in this situation.

Martha did.

Andie thought of the threatening letters Edward had
been receiving. The first one had come around the time
Martha had learned her husband had been abusing their
daughter. A coincidence. Maybe.

Martha could have sent them. She might have. Even if
she hadn't, she had used her husband's fear to encourage
him to buy a gun.

Andie remembered then. Martha had been packing her
grandmother's china for storage in the attic. Edward hadn't
liked it. Too old-fashioned, he'd said. Too flowery. Martha
had come to one of her sessions with black stains on her
fingers. From newsprint, she'd said.

If Andie went to Martha's attic, if she found that boxed
china and unwrapped it, would she find newspaper pages
with holes cut out? Headlines with letters missing? Letters
used to piece together threatening words, words aimed at
frightening a man into buying a gun?

Andie stood. What she was thinking was preposterous.
But she had to ask. She would go see Martha, she would
ask her—about what the clerk had said, about the dress,
about everything. She had to know.

Andie grabbed her handbag and headed out.

When Andie arrived at Rose Turpin's house, she found
Patti sitting on the front-porch swing. Andie lifted a hand
in greeting and started up the flower-lined walk.

The girl smiled. "Hi, Dr. Bennett. What's up?"

"Not much." Andie took a seat beside her on the swing. "I just thought I'd stop by."

"It's pretty, isn't it. The night, I mean." She breathed deeply. "The quiet."

"It is nice." The swing swayed; every so often one or the other of them would push off with their toe to keep it in motion.

"I never knew quiet could be like this. So...empty." Patti looked at her. "Do you know what I mean?"

"Not really." Andie smiled, deciding she liked this girl very much. "Why don't you tell me?"

"At home the quiet was loud. Full." She searched for the right words, Andie could tell, to describe what she had felt. "Full of stuff. Anger. Fear." She looked down at her hands. "Unhappiness."

Her unhappiness. Her mother's. "I'm sorry."

She looked back up, her eyes swimming with tears. "I didn't always hate my father, Dr. Bennett. Once upon a time I loved him a lot. That was before I realized what...before I saw what he was."

She cleared her throat. "He was an awful person, Dr. Bennett. He was mean, you know? The kind of person who actually...*likes* hurting people.

"He especially liked to hurt Mom." Patti flexed her fingers, struggling, Andie saw, to go on. "I couldn't understand why she let him treat her that way, and I used to pray that she would fight back. Or that she would take me and we would run away together."

She smiled to herself, remembering. "I used to fantasize about places we'd go, how we'd escape. We would have had such fun. I bet you think that's silly."

"Quite the contrary," Andie said softly. "I think it's nice. Very nice."

"In a way, for a long time, I was angry at my mom, you know, for taking it. For not fighting back. And then he...I—" Patti drew in a shuddering breath, her tears brimming, spilling over. "Then I did the same thing. He

came after me, he called me...called me those awful
names, the ones he always called Mom, and I just tried to
ignore him. I thought, maybe, if I just...pretended it wasn't
happening, he'd stop.''

''But he didn't.''

''No,'' she whispered, bowing her head. Andie saw the
girl's tears dripping off the end of her nose and falling
onto her hands, clenched into fists in her lap. ''It hurts so
bad, Dr. Bennett. Can you...make it go away? Can you
help me forget?''

Andie covered one of the girl's hands with one of her
own. ''I can't help you forget, but I, or someone like me,
can help you learn to go on. We could help you put what
your father did to you, and your mom, in a place where it
won't hurt so much.''

The girl nodded and lifted her gaze. ''I don't want to
be like my mom. I don't want to...pretend. I don't want
to live my life hiding the truth from everyone, even myself.
Having things look like they're okay isn't the same as
them being okay.''

She sounded older than her fifteen years, Andie thought.
Tragedy had a way of maturing one. Andie knew that to
be true from experience.

''It's funny, but that night I was so proud of her, of
Mom. She had been defying him, in small ways, for days.
Then she wore that red dress. She looked so beautiful.''

The pulse began to thrum in Andie's head. ''I was there,
she did look beautiful.''

A smile touched Patti's mouth. ''I thought it was finally
going to happen.''

''What was going to happen?''

''That we were going to go away, just me and Mom.
That she was going to leave him.''

''Why do you say that?''

''She told me we were, not that she hadn't before. But
that night she told *him.* She meant it, too. She shouted it
again and again.''

He'd kill me if I ever tried to leave him. I tried once and he nearly did it.

Andie fought for an even breath. It didn't mean anything. It didn't.

Patti shuddered and rubbed her arms, as if chilled by the memory. "He went crazy. I had never heard him that way. He said he was going to kill her. I was so...afraid. I didn't know what to do. I decided I'd call 911, then I heard the shots."

Patti's eyes grew wide at the memory, and Andie knew by her expression that she was seeing, reliving, the events of that night. "The sound reverberated through the house." She brought a fist to her chest. "Through me. I felt it all the way to...to my bones or soul. I knew that he had done it. That he'd killed her.

"I ran into the hall. Blindly. Screaming her name. I went to their bedroom. The door was open. I saw...him. On the floor. There was lots of blood and... And Mom was...she was holding the gun. Alive. She was alive."

Patti brought her hands to her mouth, as if holding back some sound or thought, then dropped them and looked at Andie. "I was glad, Dr. Bennett. I was glad that he was dead."

Silence fell between them. The swing stilled. From a tree somewhere above them, a bird broke into a sweet, evening song.

"Dr. Bennett, what are you doing here?"

Andie looked up. Martha stood in the doorway, her pretty face wreathed in a welcoming smile. Andie returned the smile, though the curving of her lips felt stiff. "I stopped by to say hi. Saw Patti here and she and I have been chatting."

"How nice." Martha crossed to the swing, bent and pressed a kiss to the top of her daughter's head, then lightly stroked her hair. The gesture spoke of a deep, abiding and protective love. The kind of love that weathered any storm, that prompted one to go to unimaginable lengths or acts to keep the loved one safe from harm.

"Can I get you a glass of tea?" she asked. "Something else?"

"No, but thank you for offering." Andie took a deep breath. "Patti mentioned the red dress you wore to the benefit. I never told you how gorgeous you looked in it."

Patti beamed at her mother; the woman flushed with pleasure. "Thank you. I bought it special, for that night."

Because she knew how her husband would react to it? Leave it alone, Andie. "Did you?"

"Mmm. That seems a million years ago." Martha leaned against the gallery railing. "You know, since Edward's death, all progress on the women's shelter has ceased."

Patti stood. "I'm going to get one of Grandma's chocolate chip cookies. Anyone else want one?"

Neither woman did, though Martha told her to ask the older woman if she wanted to come out and join them.

"I heard that, about the women's shelter," Andie said when Patti had left.

"Considering what's happened and what's come out about Edward, who knows if it'll be revived." She sighed. "I'm sorry about that."

Sorry. As if she were directly responsible.

Andie opened her mouth to ask her about the sporting-goods-store clerk. About what Nick had said, about her suspicions. About the china, the red dress, the flirting. She opened her mouth to ask if she was right.

What did it matter if she was? Edward Pierpont was a cruel, evil man. He deserved to be dead.

Andie couldn't believe she had even thought that. If what she suspected was true, Martha had planned her husband's death. It didn't matter what kind of man he was, it was wrong to take the law into your own ha—

Even when you had nowhere else to turn? Even when

you were saving your own life? Even when you were protecting your child?

Right and wrong. Good and bad. Black and white.

Andie thought of everything Martha had told her over the year they had been working together; she thought of Patti, her despair, her fear and now, her relief. And she thought of the man Edward had been and the things he had done to these two women. Horrible, vile things.

He deserved to be dead. It was better that he was.

Shaken by her own thoughts, Andie stood. She didn't want to know what had really been going through Martha's head, Andie realized. Not now, not at this moment, anyway. Maybe tomorrow. Now, she needed to clear her head. To think. She needed to know the right thing to do.

"I have to go," she said. Martha looked at her in surprise, and Andie forced a casual smile. "There's something...I remembered. I...there's someone I need to see. Tell Patti I said goodbye."

Without a backward glance, she hurried to her car.

78

Without a conscious plan, Andie drove to Nick's place. She parked at the curb in front of his house and walked to the front door. He wasn't home, so she sat on the step to wait. Her thoughts whirled with bits and snatches from various conversations with Martha and Nick, Patti and Robert; with her own suspicions. With her confusion over what to do.

Could it be true? Could Martha have deliberately pushed Edward to the edge, to the point he would commit murder, so she would be forced to protect herself? So she would be forced to kill him, truly in self-defense?

Not only could it be true, it was. Andie knew it in her gut, without absolute proof.

What did she do now?

Andie lifted her face to the rapidly darkening sky, then glanced over her shoulder, at Nick's front door. This was becoming a habit, showing up here whenever she was frightened or confused. Whenever she needed answers.

Nick made her feel good. When she was with him, all felt right with the world. When she was with him, she felt brave. Fearless.

Only she was neither of those things.

When had she become a watcher?

Andie caught her breath at the thought, the truth of it. When had she begun to let fear control her? she wondered. Fear of being hurt. Of ruining her reputation. Of upsetting the status quo.

She shifted slightly on the step, uncomfortable. What

had happened to the courageous girl who had risked everything to help a woman she didn't even know?

When had she begun hiding from life?

She closed her eyes. She thought of the girl she had been at fifteen. Young and strong and brave. She thought of Raven, too. And of Julie.

That terrible summer had altered them, altered the course of their lives forever. She had lost her father that summer, had lost the perfect picture-book family she had thought she had. She had been introduced to a dark side of life that no young girl should know of; she had, for the first time, seen that actions had consequences, for better or worse. And once committed, an act could not be undone.

The changes in her had begun then. The uncertainty. The fear. The unwillingness to risk.

So she had eschewed risk. She had kept to the safe, the predictable, the easy.

Raven had been doing the same thing, Andie realized. Hiding from life. They had been using each other, depending on each other for everything—because it was safe. Easy. It came without risks.

She had to stop. They had to stop.

From across the street came a burst of childish laughter. Two children raced across the front yard, followed by their parents. The woman glanced over, lifted her hand in greeting, then dropped it, as if realizing Andie wasn't Nick's wife, that she didn't know her.

Sudden tears stung Andie's eyes. She wanted that woman to recognize her. She wanted to belong here, on this front step, inside this house. She wanted to belong to Nick.

She loved him. Sometime over the past weeks, she had fallen in love with him. The feeling swelled inside her until she thought she might burst with it. Even as she admitted her feelings to herself, she admitted she was afraid. He might not love her back. He might love her for a while, then leave her. The way her dad had left her mom.

She drew in a deep, shaky breath. But living without him sounded scarier still. It sounded lonely. How could she not have seen that before?

She was done running. The time had come to take a few risks. To put herself, her heart, what she believed, on the line.

And do what? Tell him she loved him? Blurt it out like an awkward teenager?

Yes, exactly that.

Andie stiffened. Words, resolutions, were easy. Saying them to herself, thinking them. But acting on them, following through, that was the tough part.

Take a risk, Andie. Tell him the truth; tell him how you feel. Andie glanced at Nick's door again, feeling buoyed, invincible. *Take a stand, not just about him, but about everything: Martha, Raven, life itself.*

The time had come to act on what was in her heart, on what she believed in—in her gut. No matter the consequences.

Even as the resolution formed in her mind, Nick arrived home. He pulled into the driveway. She watched him climb out of his Jeep and walk toward her. Her heart began to thud against the wall of her chest and a sensation filled her—one that was light and fluttery and breathless. She loved everything about him, she acknowledged. The way he walked. The way his eyes crinkled at the corners when he smiled, the sound of his voice, the way she felt when she was with him.

He stopped before her, his expression serious. "Hi."

She held his gaze. "Hi."

"What's up?"

"I was missing you."

He smiled and caught her hands, drawing her to her feet. "Funny. I was missing you, too."

His words went straight to her head. "Were you?"

"I left a message with your service."

She smiled. "I can't wait to get it."

"You can use my phone."

"Mara's at her mother's?"

"Uh-huh."

"So, we have the house all to ourselves? Just you and me?"

"All to ourselves." He cupped her face in his palms. "Just you and me."

He was so beautiful, she thought. So strong and good. He made her feel brave again, he made her *feel* again.

She traced her fingers across his lips. She loved him. God, that felt good. Wonderful. The most wonderful feeling in the world.

He lowered his mouth to hers. Andie sighed and looped her arms around him, drawn into his kiss, into the dizzy way it made her feel, kissing him back.

If she let herself, she could drown herself, her thoughts, in this. Nick's kiss, his lovemaking. If she let herself, she would take the easy way once again. The way without risks.

Take a risk, Andie. Go for it.

"Wait," she murmured against his mouth. She brought her hands to his chest. "Wait."

He broke away, meeting her eyes, his filled with questions. She smiled, nervous, her every instinct telling her to run for cover as fast as she could.

Instead, she met his eyes, his questions, evenly. "Could we talk for a minute? There's something I...I need to tell you. Before I lose my nerve."

"Sounds important."

"It is." She laughed suddenly and sat down. She lifted her face to his. "You didn't know I was just a big ol' chicken, did you?"

He sat beside her on the step, his expression amused. "Oh, sure, after capable, brilliant, independent and gorgeous, that's just what I'd call you. A chicken."

She smiled. "It's true, though. I didn't even realize how big of one until today."

He seemed to sense she needed time to compose her thoughts, and he gave it to her. He sat quietly, patiently, but with the kind of stillness that resonated with awareness. Nick Raphael missed nothing.

She loved that about him, too.

Andie drew a deep breath, marshaling her courage. "I have to say this for me, Nick. Just...because. But I want you to know beforehand that I don't...I won't expect anything from you after."

He turned to her, his gaze intent. "All right, Andie. I'm listening."

So, she said it. Blurted out the words even as part of her wanted to call them back, hide them away and retreat to the safe place she had depended on for so long.

"I love you, Nick."

He said nothing. One awkward moment became a dozen of them, and tears stung her eyes. She felt like an idiot. Like a fool, socially challenged, emotionally deficient.

She cleared her throat, determined to go on anyway. "I needed to be honest with you. I realized a lot of things today, and one of them was that I've been hiding from life. Afraid of being hurt. Afraid of losing...something. Even when it was something I was too afraid to go after."

She sucked in another quick breath. "It's okay that you don't feel the same. You don't need to say anything. In fact, don't say anything. It'll be better that way, and—"

"Shh." He laid a finger against her lips. "Don't apologize for giving me a gift, Andie." He smiled. "I'm glad you love me. And I'm glad you're here. Okay?"

Relief moved over her, as did disappointment. Relief because she had done it, taken her first step out of emotional hiding and the world hadn't come crashing to a halt. Disappointment because he hadn't said he loved her in return. But the feeling wasn't unbearable. It wasn't nearly as horrible as she had thought it would be.

She returned his smile. "You're so strong. You seem invincible. Like you always know which way you're going, like you never make a mistake. Have you ever, Nick Raphael? Made a mistake? Or are you as perfect as you seem?''

He gazed at her a moment, his smile fading. ''Mistakes? Oh, yeah. Take a look at my marriage. I couldn't have screwed that one up more if I'd been trying.''

Nick sighed, stood and crossed to the far edge of the small front porch. He gazed out at the street and the lights popping on up and down the block. ''Jenny was right,'' he murmured, almost to himself. ''The end of our marriage wasn't all her fault, though I told myself it was.''

He tipped his face to the sky for a moment, then looked back out at the street. ''I always knew what was important. Family. My marriage. At least I gave lip service to that.'' He laughed, the sound tight and almost bitter. ''Somehow, I let it all slip away from me.''

He met Andie's eyes; the regret in them took her breath. ''I screwed up. I put my job before my marriage. Before my family. It started before Mrs. X's murder, but her murder sent it spiraling out of control. I was so busy proving myself, proving I was Supercop. The best. The smartest. I worked on cases that weren't mine, I stayed late, did the overtime. When I wasn't doing that, I was rehashing the Robertson case, sure I would find something we had missed.

''I forgot what was important. Then it was too late. Jenny was gone. She'd turned to another man. She'd taken Mara with her. My family was gone.'' He snapped his fingers. ''Just like that. You can't get that back once you've lost it, Andie. And it really hurts.''

For long moments, she said nothing, thinking of Nick and his marriage, but also of her father. Had he felt that way, once he had lost them? Though it had been his choice to leave, looking back, had he had regrets? From things he had said over the years, she thought so.

She stood and went to Nick. She wrapped her arms

around him from behind and pressed her cheek to his back. "I'm sorry, Nick."

"It's over."

"Is it?" He stiffened slightly and she tightened her arms around him, hating what she was about to say, but having to say it anyway. "You could go to her. Try again."

He shook his head. "It's over. When she left, Jenny and I hadn't loved each other in a long time." He turned and circled his arms around her waist. "Besides, you're in the picture now."

She wanted to melt in his arms. She wanted to believe that her being "in the picture" made a difference. She didn't do either and met his gaze evenly. "Neither of those has a thing to do with what you just told me. You were talking about family. About your family. About missing them."

"That's not going to change."

"I know, Nick." She slipped out of his arms. "I also know what it's like to be the kid who wants her parents to be together again, more than anything. I know what it's like to resent the woman who took my daddy away. That doesn't disappear, even though my father and Leeza have been together for fifteen years and my mother's gone on with her life. Still, a part of me hates her for stealing my father and for busting up my family."

"You didn't steal me, Andie. The situation is totally different."

"I know that, too. I guess I'm wanting you to be honest with me, and yourself, about the possibilities. What if Jenny came back, Nick? What if she wanted you back? If she wanted to be a family again?"

He hesitated before answering, the seconds agonizing. "Jenny and I don't love each other anymore, and I don't think there's a snowball's chance in hell she'd want back with me, but I've got to be honest with you, I don't know what I'd do. Because of Mara."

His answer hurt more than anything had in a long time,

maybe forever. She swallowed hard, past the emotion, past the tears, determined to be a grown-up. She wasn't going to hide from things that scared her, not anymore.

"I'm sorry, Andie. I know that's not what you hoped to hear."

"It's what I expected, though. And I appreciate your being honest with me."

"Still a Boy Scout, aren't I?" A rueful smile tugged at the corners of his mouth. "Jenny always accused me of never seeing shades of gray in the world. She called me narrow, anal retentive, blind. That was me, Mr. Right or Wrong. Black or white. The perennial Boy Scout. Now, suddenly, I look around and see all sorts of gray."

"What do you mean?"

He paused before answering, though she was unsure whether searching for the perfect example or for impact. "Like the situation with your patient, Martha Pierpont."

Andie worked to keep her thoughts, her dismay, from showing. Did he know her so well now, he could read her mind?

"I've reviewed all the case notes, I've talked with the prosecutor, heard about Patti. And I think about how Martha lived, all those years with that sick bastard. I think about what he did to his daughter, and I think it's better that he's dead. It's sure as hell better that Martha killed him than the other way around. And he might have. He was doing his best to kill her slowly, day after day, year after year.

"But I can't think that, not officially. As a cop, if I have proof Martha Pierpont acted with premeditation, I'm bound by my job to act on that proof. To uphold the law. Black and white."

"But as a man?" Andie asked, loving him more now than she had even a moment ago. For his honesty. His humanity.

"As a man?" He looked up at the dark sky and the new moon. "The answer's not so black-and-white, is it? The

Erica Spindler

world's a better place without Edward Pierpont. Sometimes shitty people deserve to die. And sometimes innocent people, good people, get stuck in situations beyond their control. Situations they don't deserve.''

He looked her dead in the eye. In his, she saw herself, her thoughts, her suspicions about Martha. Nick Raphael was smart. He, like she, had put two and two together.

If he hadn't come to the same conclusion as she, with the certainty she had, he had toyed with it. He wondered. But he wasn't going to take it any further than that.

Andie crossed the porch, stopping in front of him. She lifted her face to his. ''Just you and me, Nick.''

He reached into his jacket pocket for his keys. ''The house, all to ourselves.''

She took the keys from his hands and unlocked the door. She drew him into the house, to his bedroom. She removed his clothes, and he hers. Then they made love, there on his bed, bathed in the early evening and the quiet. In the wonder of their being together.

And when, at climax, she cried out his name and that she loved him, she wasn't scared at all.

In fact, saying the words, what was in her heart, at that moment, felt right. Like the most right thing in the whole world.

79

Morning light spilled through the cracks between the blinds and across the bed. Andie moaned, deep in her throat, and rolled onto her side, snuggling against Nick's back, completely content.

She opened her eyes, taking in the sun, becoming aware of the sound of a bird singing outside the window. She smiled, thinking the sweet song appropriate. Saturday had come and gone. They'd left the house exactly twice—once to go to Nick's brother's restaurant for food, and once to rent movies they both could enjoy, an action flick with heart for him, a romance with a who-done-it to solve for her. The rest of the time, they had stayed here, in bed, making love.

Now, it was Sunday. Andie's smile faded slightly. She couldn't put off Raven any longer. Her friend would be home this morning; the Sunday paper, coffee and croissants were a ritual for her. Though Andie hated leaving this warm cocoon, she knew she would find no better time for what she had to say to her friend.

Take a risk, Andie. Go with your heart.

She pressed a trail of kisses and nibbles along Nick's shoulders. He stirred; she sensed his smile. "Good morning, sleepyhead," she whispered.

He rolled onto his back, though he didn't open his eyes. She had been right—he was smiling. "Morning to you."

She lay across his chest, liking the feel of her breasts pressed against his skin. "Sleep well?"

"Mmm. Dreaming of you."

"That's what I like to hear." She kissed him then drew away. "There's somewhere I have to go this morning."

He opened his eyes then, all traces of sleep instantly gone. She searched his gaze, wondering how he could awaken so quickly, wondering if it came from years of being a cop, of being expected to be alert no matter what time a call came in.

"What's up?" he asked.

She moved her hand and grinned. "You are."

"Vixen."

"Insatiable vixen," she corrected.

"Stay with me." He shifted to his right, half pinning her beneath him. "I promise to play nice."

She kissed him again, feeling her resolution waver. "I have to do this now, today, before I lose my nerve. Wait for me?"

"Only if you bring back doughnuts." He grinned. "From the Krispy Kreme, on Fourth."

Andie returned his smile. "Doughnuts? You're such a cop."

"So sue me. It comes with the job." He tightened his arms. "Mind telling me where you're going?"

"To see Raven," she said and sat up. "I need to see her. I feel like I have to tell her about us and all the things I realized the other day." Andie drew her knees to her chest and wrapped her arms around them. "Raven and I have been each other's everything for so long, and I...that's going to change. It already has. I don't want to hurt her, but we've depended on each other far too much, Nick. We've been using each other to hide from life, from other relationships."

She looked at him, troubled despite her resolve. "This has been coming for a while, I think she'll see it, too. I know she's felt it."

For a long moment, Nick was quiet. When he finally spoke, his softly voiced words caused a ripple of unease to move over her.

"Be careful," he murmured. "Raven's very...protective of your relationship. She may not take it well."

Andie looked him in the eye, shaking the unease off. She laughed. "For heaven's sake, Nick, you make it sound so ominous. What's she going to do, kill me?"

80

"Andie," Raven said with pleasure, swinging her front door wider. "How nice."

Andie smiled nervously, uncertain what she would say to her friend, more uncertain of Raven's reaction. It was one thing to experience an epiphany, it was quite another to have someone else's forced on you.

"Have I caught you at a bad time?" she asked.

"Don't be a jerk." Raven caught her hands and drew her inside. "What are Sunday mornings for besides best friends and good coffee?"

"The Sunday funnies?"

Raven laughed. "I have French roast brewing and some fresh croissants."

"Sounds great." Andie followed Raven to her kitchen. It was strictly gourmet, all the bells and whistles. The kind of kitchen a chef would envy and a decorating magazine would feature on the cover.

True to her friend's words, she had croissants and strawberries arranged artfully on a tray, the coffeepot burbled its last just as Raven reached for the cups.

It was all so picture-perfect.

"What do you say we sit out on the porch? It's pretty today."

Andie agreed and within a handful of minutes, Raven had the table on the screened porch set with pretty linen napkins and china dessert plates. As a final touch, she placed a crystal bud vase at the table's center, then added a bloom she snipped from her garden.

Picture-perfect, Andie thought again.

They took their seats. Raven smiled. "We used to do this all the time. Remember?" Without waiting for Andie to reply, she went on happily. "Sunday mornings. Fresh coffee and pastries. The newspaper. A walk in the park later."

She poured Andie a cup of coffee, then added cream for her, knowing just how she took it. Raven passed it across, meeting Andie's eyes. "What happened to us, Andie? How could we forget what was important?"

Andie shifted, finding something about the brightness of Raven's gaze unsettling. It was as if they were lit by an inner fire. "We got busy with our careers. We grew up." Her lips lifted. "Sort of."

Raven laughed, the sound high and girlish. "Silly, Andie." She held out the tray of croissants. "You can never be too busy for family. You know that."

Andie took a pastry and laid it on her plate, her appetite gone. Raven, too, selected a croissant. Andie watched as she ripped into it, noticing for the first time the size of Raven's hands, the strength in them.

Raven spread a bit of raspberry jam on the bread, then bit into it. Andie dropped a hand to her lap and curled her fingers around her napkin, repelled, though she couldn't say why.

"I've been waiting for you to come back around. I knew you would, Andie. When I opened the door this morning and you were standing there…my heart took flight. All my planning and waiting was paying off. Finally, I knew that everything was going to be all right again." Raven met her eyes, tears of happiness sparkling in them. "You've always been my special one."

Special one. David. A sensation, like ice water, trickled down her spine. Raven's words, the way she said them, seemed off. Not quite…right. It was as if someone had plugged her into the wrong-voltage socket, or wound her key too tight.

Erica Spindler

"I loved Julie," Raven went on, "you know I did. But she never meant to me what you do. I don't know—" Raven sighed and brought her coffee cup to her lips "—maybe because she wouldn't let me. She kept us both away on some level. No matter how hard I tried to be faithful to her, she kept...straying."

Talking about Julie this way was making Andie uncomfortable. As was the touchy-feely best-friends tone of this conversation. She understood the grieving process, she understood that talking helped lessen the pain. But she wasn't ready. It felt wrong. She told Raven so.

"You're right. I'm sorry." Raven reached across the table and covered her hand. "Of course you're not ready. How could I have been so insensitive?"

She had to say what she had come to. The longer it went on, the harder it was going to be. And the harder for Raven to take.

"Raven," she murmured, "I need to talk to you."

"So talk," Raven said, smiling, reaching for another croissant. "I'm right here. I'm always right here."

Andie stood and walked to the screen enclosure and gazed out at the golden fall day. This was going to be tougher than she thought. Raven was going to take it worse than she had imagined.

Andie thought of Nick, his words of caution, then looked back at Raven. "I realized some things. Important things. About me. About us. What we've been doing."

Raven's smile froze. The blood drained from her cheeks. "About us?" she repeated.

"Before I begin, I beg you to try to hear what I have to say. To try to understand. I really want us to talk about this."

"What are you doing, Andie?" Raven asked, a muscle working in her jaw. "Dumping me?"

"Of course not. You've been the most important person in my life almost forever, how could I—"

"But not anymore. Is that it?"

"I didn't say that." Andie fought back a feeling of alarm. This was spinning out of her grasp already, and she had hardly begun. "Raven, please. Try to listen. I realized that somewhere along the line, I stopped trying. I started taking the easy way, the way where I knew I wouldn't get hurt."

She went on, talking about how Patti Pierpont's desperation and Julie's death forced her to see, spoke of Nick and how he made her feel alive. How he had brought to the surface longings she had buried years ago.

Raven brought a hand to her throat. Andie saw that it trembled. "What are you saying?"

"That we've depended on each other too much. That we've used our relationship as a way to hide from other relationships. We made it easy not to need anyone else. That's hiding from life, Raven. I don't want to do that anymore."

Raven balled her hands into fists. "This is about *him,* isn't it. Maybe you're more like Julie than I thought."

At the comment, furious heat rushed to Andie's cheeks. Raven was hurting, Andie told herself, counting to ten. She felt betrayed and was lashing out. Otherwise, she would never have spoken of Julie that way.

"This isn't about Nick, though he has helped me see. This is about me. And you."

"That's bullshit!" Raven pushed back from the tiny table with such force, she upset the vase. It hit the tabletop, shattering. "You're in love with him, I know you are!"

"I am in love with him," Andie answered, her voice steady. "I want to be with him, no matter the consequences."

A sound of pain passed Raven's lips, high-pitched and terrible. Frightened, Andie hurried to her friend. She knelt before her and gathered Raven's cold hands in hers. "Don't, Raven. I still love you. You're my best friend. You always will be. But you can't be my everything. No one can be someone's everything."

Raven drew her hands away. She met Andie's gaze, hers swimming with tears. "Get out."

Tears flooded her own eyes. "Raven, please."

"Get out," she said again, voice shaking. "You're a traitor. Dead to me now. I'll never forgive you. Never."

81

Nick sat quietly, the squad room in chaos around him, his attention focused on Julie Cooper's autopsy report that lay on the desk in front of him. It told him the time and cause of death, what her last meal had been and when she had eaten it. It told him that except for the trauma to her neck, she had been the picture of health, told him that she had not had intercourse prior to being killed.

There was lots more it didn't tell him.

Nick frowned. Something didn't add up.

He shuffled the autopsy report to the side, shifting his attention to the lab report, just in from St. Louis. The trace evidence—hair and saliva left on Julie Cooper's body—had been analyzed. The lab hadn't found any conflicting DNA evidence; all the genetic markers pointed to only two people—Julie Cooper and David Sadler.

Fiber samples, footprints, fingerprints and now genetic markers. Ones from both crimes. All pointed to David Sadler. He was the guy. Cut-and-dried. Easy.

"Why the frown, partner?" Bobby ambled over and dropped the bag of takeout on the desk in front of Nick. "Ham and cheese on rye, brown mustard, no pickle. Salt-free chips."

Nick glanced up. "Thanks, man."

"No problem." Bobby folded his large frame into the chair across from Nick. "What gives?"

"The Cooper homicide." Nick reached into the bag, took out the sandwich and unwrapped it. "Why would a smooth operator like David Sadler kill Julie Cooper in one of his own model homes, then just leave the body for us to find?''

''Dunno.'' Bobby leaned back in his chair. ''My guess is he panicked. He didn't mean to kill her. They got carried away, the stool goes over.'' Bobby snapped his fingers. ''Pop. She's history.''

''So he runs? Leaving evidence that links him not only to Julie Cooper's homicide, but Leah Robertson's, as well?'' Nick took a big bite of his sandwich.

''He knows he's in deep shit. He can't think. He needs a plan. Or maybe he has one, but needs to get some pieces of it lined up. He takes off, before he can get back, we've been tipped and he's screwed, big-time.''

Nick washed the bite of sandwich down with cold coffee. ''That's another thing. This anonymous tip. There's something odd about it. Somebody just *happened* to be passing by the Gatehouse development. At that time of night? There's nothing out there, Bobby. Nada. How did this person happen to see lights? And what about the two-hour discrepancy between the coroner's estimated time of death and when the call came in?''

Bobby arched his bushy eyebrows. ''You tell me.''

''I don't know.'' He made a sound of frustration. ''What about the barrette?''

''The one Sadler *supposedly* found in the house? The one neither girl can positively identify? Give me a break. That proves dick. The guy's grasping at straws.''

Nick met his friend's eyes. ''It's all too pat, Bobby. Too easy.''

''That's the way I like 'em, partner. Get the perps off the street and in the pen without even breaking a sweat.'' Bobby stood. ''This one's personal for you, could be that's clouding things. Could be it has you making things hard.''

Nick frowned. He didn't like to think that was the case, but it very well could be. Every cop knew the best place to look for a suspect was close to the victim. ''Maybe so.''

''Excuse me. Nick?''

At the sound of his ex-wife's voice, Nick looked up. Jenny stood a couple of feet behind Bobby, her expression hesitant. Nick caught his breath, thinking immediately of Mara. "Is something...is Mara all right?"

"Fine, I—" Jenny moved her gaze between Bobby and Nick. "Sarge said I could come back. I hope that's okay."

"No problem," Nick said, standing. He flipped the Cooper file closed. "What can I do for you?"

She clasped her hands in front of her, her gaze flickering to Bobby once more. "Could we go somewhere...private? To talk?"

"Sure," Nick said with forced casualness, the blood beginning to thrum in his head. This had better not be about reducing his visitation time with Mara. Or about her trying to renege on his having Mara the entire week of her birthday. They had already agreed; he had put in for time off. "Bobby, anybody in interrogation one?"

"Not that I know of, partner."

"If you need me, that's where I'll be."

Nick led Jenny to the interrogation room, closing the door behind them. He faced her. "If this is about me changing my plans with Mara for her birthday, you can forget it, Jenny."

"That's not it. It's..." Her words trailed off helplessly. To his surprise, her eyes filled with tears. "It's about... us."

"Us," he repeated, thunderstruck. "What do you mean, us?"

"I...I think I've made a mistake, Nick. A big mistake." She crossed to him and laid her cheek against his chest. "I want to come back. For us to be a family again."

To come back. For them to be a family again.

Nick struggled to breathe evenly, past his surprise, his thundering heart. Hadn't he hoped for this, a chance for his family to be back together? Hadn't he prayed for it?

But now, all he could think of was Andie.

But this wasn't just about him and his life. It was Mara. Her life. What she wanted and needed.

"I'm so sorry," she whispered. "So sorry I did what I did. That I hurt you. I wasn't thinking clearly."

"But you are now?" he asked, openly skeptical. "Thinking clearly."

She tilted her head back to meet his eyes. Tears sparkled in hers. "Yes. I want to come home. Please take me back, Nick." She curved her arms around his waist, clinging to him. "Forgive me."

He breathed through his nose, thinking of Andie, the way she loved him—without demands or provisions, without hesitation. And he thought of the way it had been between him and Jenny, her dissatisfaction, her betrayal. "Why do you want to come back, Jen?" He freed himself from her grasp. "I thought you didn't love me anymore. That you weren't happy."

"I know I said that, but—"

"But nothing's changed. I'm the same man I was then, you're the same woman. We'd have the same life."

"It wouldn't have to be that way. You could change. So could I."

For long moments he simply gazed at her, the woman he had once loved, the mother of his child, a woman with whom he shared so much history. And yet, as he gazed at her he realized he felt little more than sympathy and indifference for her. As he gazed at her, he could only think of another woman. The one who had sneaked into his heart and stolen it.

A sense of wonder filled him. *Andie. Sweet, perfect, wonderful Andie.*

"I'm sorry, Jen, but it's too late. There's someone else. I'm in love with her."

"No." The word rushed past her lips, and she searched behind her for a chair. She found one, pulled it out and sank onto it. She lifted her watery gaze to his. "No."

Nick crossed to where she sat and squatted in front of

her. "What you said when you left, you were right. We didn't love each other anymore. We hadn't in a long time. Hell, we hardly liked each other." He reached up and touched her cheek lightly, then dropped his hand. "It wouldn't last. You wouldn't be happy."

"I would. I—"

"No, Jen," he corrected gently, "you wouldn't. And we both deserve better than a loveless marriage. So does Mara."

She sucked in a trembling breath. "Well, I guess I've made a monumental fool of myself. But I never thought you'd…that you'd—"

"Turn you down?" He laughed softly, but without amusement. "I might not have a week or two ago. A part of me can't believe I'm doing it now." He straightened and held out a hand to help her up.

She took it and got to her feet. "I guess I should…go."

"Jenny?" She met his eyes. "What about Bernard? Is that over?"

She lifted her shoulders. "We've been…fighting. He doesn't like being…tied down with a child. He likes to go out, to travel."

"So? Travel with him, Jenny. I'll keep Mara, anytime. You know how much I love her. Maybe we could do an equal-time custody arrangement? That would take some of the pressure off of you."

"But with your job—"

"I'll put in less hours. Think about it."

"I will."

From there, there was nothing left to say to one another. He walked her to the station's front entrance, then returned to his desk.

"So," Bobby murmured, grinning up at him, "what was that all about?"

"She wants us to get back together."

Bobby didn't often look totally dumbfounded, but he

did now. He whistled long and low under his breath. "What did you—"

"I said no, Bobby. Much as I want to be with Mara full-time, it's over." He slid into the chair behind his desk. "Besides, she doesn't really want me back. It's just that things aren't going perfectly with Bernard, so she came running back to where she felt safe. No big deal."

Bobby's eyebrows shot up. "No big deal?"

"Yeah, that's what I said."

"And you're okay with this?"

"Very okay."

"Did this decision have anything to do with a certain lovely headshrinker?"

"Yeah, it did," Nick said, surprising his partner for the second time in as many minutes. "It had just about everything to do with her."

Bobby narrowed his eyes. "You've been holding out on me."

Nick flashed him a grin. "Yup."

"That sucks, partner. Big-time."

"No," Nick said, lowering his gaze to the reports on the desk in front of him, "What sucks is David Sadler's story. What do you say we take another crack at him? See if he wants to add anything to his story?"

"His lawyer won't like it."

"His lawyer can bite me." Nick smiled. "Get the guy on the phone, I feel like going fishing this afternoon."

82

Hours later, Nick drove through Thistledown, heading for home. He opened his window to enjoy the cool evening air, thinking of David Sadler and his interrogation earlier that afternoon. The man had remained adamant about his innocence. Not only that, as he had all along, he kept talking about Leah Robertson's murder and about Andie, Raven and Julie's involvement in that crime. He'd insisted, again, that at least one of the girls had been in that house watching him and Leah, and that he believed that girl knew who the real killer was.

Nick drew his eyebrows together. Sadler claimed he hadn't left the noose and scarf for Andie. Nick found that weird. Illogical. Why admit to breaking into her house and leaving music playing, but not the noose and scarf? And why keep focusing on the past and the role of the three girls in Leah Robertson's death?

Sadler's story was getting to him. Something wasn't right about this whole thing. He smelled fish.

Everything kept coming back to Andie, Julie and Raven. Only now, Julie was dead. That left only two.

Nick smiled grimly. Maybe the time had come to pay a little visit to the third member of that little triumvirate. He had passed Rave Reviews, Raven Johnson's design firm, a couple of miles back. Though late, light had spilled out the windows and he'd noted a car parked in the lot beside the building.

He pulled a U-turn and went back. He reached the building and swung into the drive. Somebody was there, all right. And whoever it was, they drove a forty-thousand-dollar BMW. He parked beside it. Definitely not a secretary, he thought, climbing out of his Jeep and heading up the walk.

A sign in the window pronounced the business closed; Nick rang the bell, then rapped on the glass. Once, then again when no one appeared at the door.

A couple moments later, Raven emerged from the back of the store and came to the door. She looked agitated. Her eyes were red, as if she had been crying.

He flashed his shield, though he hadn't a doubt she knew who he was.

She cracked open the door. ''Yes?''

''Hello, Raven.'' He smiled. ''I wondered if I could have a couple minutes of your time?''

''What's this about?''

''David Sadler.''

She hesitated, then opened the door and let him in. He stepped inside, moving his gaze over the interior of the shop. Lots of high-priced froufrou. The kind of place a cop only went in to make a call.

''How can I help you, Detective?'' Though she smiled, he sensed real animosity directed toward him. Real anger. *Because of Andie.*

He pictured the house, the front door, the security system's keypad and its blinking green light. ''I was wondering how often you and David Sadler spoke during the week preceding the murder. How deeply you were involved with the development, and if you knew how many other people besides yourself and Mr. Sadler had continuous access to the properties.''

She folded her arms across her chest. ''I've answered all those questions before, Detective.''

He smiled again. ''Yes, I know. But there are a few points I'm not clear on.''

''Such as?''

Nick pictured the house's entryway once more. ''Well,''

he murmured, thinking on his feet, "it seems there's both a primary and secondary code for the model's security system. The primary code was David's, everyone else with access—" he paused for effect "—people like you, used the secondary code."

For a moment, a mere heartbeat of time, she was quiet, her expression blank. That tiny space of time spoke volumes. "I wouldn't know anything about that," she said. "I'm sorry you've come out of your way tonight." Raven checked her watch. "If you have any further questions, call my attorney and we'll come down to the station."

"Your attorney?" Nick cocked his head. "Is there some reason you feel you need a lawyer present to answer a few questions?"

"Of course not. But one can't be too cautious." She forced a stiff smile and reached for the door. "If there's nothing else, it's been a long day. And in case you've forgotten, I'm still grieving the loss of a dear friend."

"Of course," he murmured. "I'm sorry to have disturbed you tonight." He started through the door, then stopped, meeting her eyes once more. "There is one more thing," he said. "According to the alarm company's monitoring service, the night of the murder, the alarm was disarmed and rearmed twice. Once with David's code. Once with the secondary code."

Nick studied Raven while he spoke. Except for the tiniest flicker behind her eyes and a slight elevation in her breathing, she seemed totally unaffected by what he was saying. Raven Johnson, he decided, was one cool customer.

"You wouldn't know anything about that, would you, Ms. Johnson?"

"How could I, Detective? I wasn't there."

"Of course." He smiled again. "Sorry to have troubled you. Good night."

83

Raven Johnson did exactly what Nick had hoped she would: she waited about five minutes, which was enough time for him to drive a few blocks, U-turn and come back, before she headed straight out to the Gatehouse development. He guessed that the alarm system's instruction manual was kept there—that she had to see if he had been lying.

Nick whistled under his breath as he followed her at an inconspicuous distance. He didn't know if he had been lying or not; inspiration had struck and he'd run with it. What he did know now, however, was that Raven Johnson had played a bigger part in Julie Cooper's murder than just that of the grieving friend.

Nick turned into the Gatehouse development. Raven should have arrived several minutes ago, enough time to go inside to wherever the model's important paperwork was stored and begin tearing through it.

The house lay dead right. He turned. His headlights sliced across the road; the yellow police tape stood out shockingly bright against the black night. Nobody had taken it down yet. He flipped off his headlights and slowed to a crawl, finally easing his vehicle to a stop beside Raven's.

He climbed out, drew his weapon and started for the house. He peered into Raven's car as he passed. The driver's-side door wasn't quite closed, she had left her purse on the front passenger seat. She had obviously been in a hurry.

Nick, on the other hand, was in no hurry. He made his way stealthily toward the front door, pausing every couple of moments to listen.

He reached the door and let himself in. He glanced at the alarm's keypad and saw that the system was on but unarmed.

The house was dark save for the kitchen. He heard the sounds of someone moving about, opening drawers, shuffling papers. His lips lifted. *Bingo, baby. Gotcha.*

Weapon out, he made his way down the hall. When he reached the kitchen, he saw that he had congratulated himself too soon. The kitchen was empty. The contents of a drawer had been spilled across the floor. The back door stood wide open.

"Dammit." He lowered his gun and hurried for the door, forgetting stealth, wanting to catch and question her before she got away and he lost his advantage.

From behind him came the sound of a door flying open. Nick realized his mistake and spun around. He saw Raven, her face twisted into a mask of hate and rage, saw too late the length of plumber's pipe in her hand. Pain shot through his head, followed by a blinding white light.

His world went black.

84

Nick came to. He moaned, feeling as if his head was on fire. He tried to move and found he couldn't. He opened his eyes slowly, blinking to focus them. When they did, he discovered why his arms and legs refused to cooperate: his wrists and ankles were bound with silver electrical tape.

Then he remembered. Raven. The louvered pantry doors. The pipe.

He moaned again. How could he have been so careless? So stupid? He hadn't called for backup. Nobody even knew he was here. Those were the kinds of mistakes only a rookie would make. A dead rookie.

Dizziness overcame him, nausea with it. He closed his eyes and breathed deeply through his nose, using both to steady himself. He was in deep shit here, he couldn't be dizzy and sick. Not if he was going to get out alive.

Raven entered the kitchen. She carried a shovel and a roll of heavy-duty plastic. Light-headed again, he drew in another deep breath, struggling to hang on to consciousness. Not to puke. He couldn't go back under now.

"Hello, sleepyhead," she said, her lips twisting into an imitation of a smile. "I see you decided to come around."

"Barely," he croaked, his mouth and throat dry and bitter tasting.

She laughed. "An honest cop. Imagine that?" She leaned the shovel against the counter, then tossed the roll of plastic to the floor. She followed his gaze, smiling again.

"Curious, I see. That's good, for you, anyway. It means you still have your faculties."

"Lucky me." He coughed and tasted blood. He must have bitten his tongue when he hit the floor. It hurt like hell. "So, are you going to fill me in or make me wait until the party starts?"

"Why not?" She lifted a shoulder. "Earlier, did you happen to notice the big hole in the backyard?"

"Sorry, I was a little busy."

She stared at him a moment, her lips twisting into that freakish smile. "You're funny. No wonder Andie thought she liked you."

She turned. Nick saw her purse on the counter. *She had been out to her car. How much time had passed?*

She took out her cell phone and laid it beside her handbag, then dug around inside, coming out with a pack of cigarettes and a lighter. She lit one and drew deeply on it. "Anyway," she said after blowing out a stream of smoke, "the hole's a pool. Or rather, it's going to be. They're scheduled to pour tomorrow."

"And?"

"And you're going to become a permanent part of that pool."

He realized what she meant and silently swore. "The way your mother became a permanent part of your patio?"

"Exactly." Raven took another drag on the cigarette. "My dad wasn't so dumb."

"No? He got caught."

"Only because he underestimated me."

"The way Julie trusted you."

Her cheeks flamed red. She narrowed her eyes. "Julie was a traitor. She was disloyal to me, to our family. She got what she deserved."

"The way I'm going to get what I deserve?"

She took another long drag on the cigarette and smiled. "Yes."

"What're you going to do with the plastic?" he asked,

hoping that if he kept her talking long enough he'd be able to come up with a way out of this. "Wrap me in it so I don't start to stink?"

"You'll be under the cement, you won't stink." She dropped her cigarette in a disposable coffee cup that someone had left. He heard the tip sizzle as it hit the liquid. "Carpet runners," she explained. "They'll make it a lot easier to drag you outside."

He breathed deeply through his nose, fighting another wave of dizziness. "Do you really think you're going to be able to dig a hole big enough to dump me in, get it covered and smoothed over, all before the workmen arrive in the morning? I don't think so. If I were you, I'd take off now. You could be in St. Louis and on a plane for Rio before anyone found me."

"Nice try, Detective. But I have no intention of leaving Thistledown. This is my home. By the way, I'm not digging a hole for just one." She glanced at her watch. "Time to get your little girlfriend out here."

Andie. Dear God, no. Not Andie.

He couldn't hide his alarm, and she smiled. "That's right, Miss Andie Bennett. Traitor. Disloyal whore. I'm sure she'll come running when I call and tell her you're in trouble."

"Don't do that," he said, desperate, willing to beg if it would save Andie. "Please. She didn't do anything."

"Wrong again." Raven met his eyes, hers narrowed to angry slits. Bright spots of color stained her cheeks. "Did you really think I'd let you steal her from me? Did you really think I would let her go?"

She was completely insane. Obsessed with Andie and the notion of loyalty.

"I didn't come out here alone, you know," he said, struggling against the tape, trying to mask his total panic. "My partner will be here any moment. I called in my whereabouts, in a few minutes this place is going to be crawling with cops."

She laughed. "That's bullshit, Detective, and not nearly as clever as the bit about the two codes. That was good." She picked up the piece of pipe. "If anyone was going to show up, they would be here by now. No, you're all on your own."

She crossed to stand over him. "Say good night, Detective Raphael. I have a call to make."

And then she swung.

85

Andie pulled up in front of the Gatehouse model, parking her car beside Nick's Jeep. She climbed out and looked up at the dark house, heart thundering. Raven had sounded so strange when she'd called. Her voice had been high and frightened-sounding, the cell-phone connection weak and crackling. *"Something terrible's happened,"* she had said. *"To Nick. You have to come right away. He needs yo—"*

Raven's cell phone had gone dead. Panicked, without pausing for second thought, Andie had raced out here, driving as if the devil himself had been after her. Now Andie wondered if that had been wise. Maybe she should have called someone to come with her. Maybe whatever had happened would be more than she could handle alone.

Maybe David Sadler was telling the truth. If he hadn't killed Julie, a murderer roamed free.

At the direction of her thoughts, Andie scolded herself and hurried up the walk. David Sadler was the one who'd killed Julie. And Leah Robertson. He was where he should be, safely behind bars.

Andie opened the front door and stepped inside. The house was eerily quiet, dark save for a light from the opposite end of the hallway. She thought of Julie, of what had happened to her here and a wave of nausea rolled over her.

She forced it back, keeping her gaze averted from the living room and trained on the long hallway before her. "Raven?" she called. "Nick?" She took a step deeper into the house. "Rave," she called again. "It's me. Where are you?"

"The kitchen." Raven appeared in the lit doorway and motioned for her to come. "Quick. Nick's hurt!"

Alarmed, Andie ran. She reached the kitchen, crying out when she saw him. He was on the floor, wrists and ankles bound by tape, hair matted with blood.

"Nick... My God!" She ran to him, kneeling down at his side. He opened his eyes. In them she saw horror. But he wasn't looking at her. He was looking past her.

Andie twisted around. She saw Raven. And the pipe. A scream flew to her lips.

A moment later she saw nothing at all.

Andie awakened to the sound of digging. Her entire body ached. Her mouth was dry and gritty, as if she had eaten dirt. She breathed deeply; the effort hurt. A smell filled her head. Heavy. Fecund. The smell of damp earth, she realized.

She opened her eyes. She lay on her side on the ground, in some sort of dark pit, her cheek against something...slick. Unnatural. Plastic, she realized. At the same moment she realized her wrists and ankles were bound.

Like Nick's had been. A sound of fear slipped past her lips. *Where was Nick?*

The digging noise stopped. "Hello, Andie."

She lifted her gaze. Raven stood a few feet away, a shovel in her hand. "Raven?" Andie whispered, disbelieving. "What...what are you doing?"

Her friend smiled. Andie found something about the way her lips stretched over her teeth grotesque. "Taking care of my family."

"Taking care of... I don't understand."

"Don't you? You betrayed me, Andie. You were disloyal. Just like Julie. Just like my mother."

As if stirred by the memory, Raven went back to digging. Andie stared at her, horrified, not quite able to grasp what was happening. *Who was this woman? Not Raven Johnson, her best friend. Not the woman she had known and loved since she was eight years old. It couldn't be.*

Raven spoke again, suddenly, startling Andie. "I didn't want to kill Julie. But I had to. She was a disloyal little cunt." Raven paused in her work to look at Andie. "I'm sorry to use that language, but it's appropriate. She chose that piece of slime, David Sadler, over us. Over me."

Terror took Andie's breath. *Raven had killed Julie?*

"She had even begun to ask questions. Can you believe that?" Raven shook her head, as if she could hardly even grasp the concept of what she was saying. "Questions about Mr. and Mrs. X. About my being in the house with them, day after day. Hiding in the closet. Watching them."

She stopped and met Andie's eyes once more. Because of the dark, Andie couldn't see her clearly, but she felt the other woman's gaze like the icy hand of the grave. "You see, Andie, she'd figured out that I'd killed Mrs. X."

Andie bit down hard on her bottom lip to keep from crying out. To keep from giving in to terror and falling apart. How could she have been friends with Raven all these years and not really known her? How could she not have seen the monster lurking just beneath the mask?

She hadn't wanted to see, Andie realized, thinking back. Signs of her obsessiveness had been there. Of her extreme dysfunction. Her twisted values. Signs Andie had chosen to ignore. Because she'd loved Raven, loved the person, the girl, she had thought Raven to be.

Nick moaned and stirred, obviously in pain, but alive. She squeezed her eyes shut, saying a silent prayer of thanks. When she hadn't been able to see him, she'd been afraid, so afraid that Raven...

Andie couldn't even finish the thought. She had to convince Raven to release her. There had to be a way.

Raven paused in her work again, panting with exertion. She wiped the sweat from her brow. "To get rid of David, I needed Julie. She had to die. But still—" Raven's voice

thickened with emotion ''—I wouldn't have done it if she
had been loyal. I gave her a choice, Andie. She chose him.
She broke my heart.''

A choice, Andie realized. She had one chance; that was
it. If she couldn't pull this off, she was dead. So was Nick.

''You have this all wrong, Raven,'' Andie said, voice
quivering. ''I choose you over *him*. He's nothing to me.''

Raven laughed bitterly. The sound crawled along Andie's nerve endings, ugly and dark. ''That's not what you
said the other day. 'We depend on each other too much,'
you said. 'I love him and want to be with him, no matter
the consequences.' Well, here they are, Andie Bennett. *The
consequences*.''

''That's not true!'' Andie cried. ''I didn't choose him!
Check your answering machine. I called at least a dozen
times tonight. To apologize. To beg your forgiveness. I
was crazy the other day, Raven. Blinded by grief. Confused. He tried to trick me into loving him, to steal me
away from you. He almost succeeded.''

She ended the last on a sob and looked up at Raven,
pleading. ''I love you. We're family, Rave. Family always
sticks together, no matter what.''

Raven shook her head, though Andie could see that she
fought tears. ''Why should I believe you? How do I know
you're telling the truth? All you've done is lie to me, let
me down.''

Raven sucked in a shuddering breath. ''I left the noose
and scarf on your bed, Andie. To punish you, because I
was angry at the way you were shutting me out. And it
was a test. You failed. You ran to *him*. That nothing. Not
to me, your family, the one you had always turned to. I
knew then, but I prayed I was wrong. The way I prayed
with Julie. That you would see the light.'' Her voice broke.
''You really hurt me, Andie.''

Andie started to cry. *This was it. Her and Nick's last
chance.* ''I have seen the light. Check your machine.
You'll see all my calls. You'll hear how I begged you to

forgive me and take me back. You'll see. I made a mistake, Rave. I'm sorry.''

Raven glanced at her wrist, at her watch. She shook her head, looking upset. ''I could retrieve...but my cell phone's...the time, there's no time.''

Andie seized on Raven's hesitation. ''We can do this together, Raven. Take care of him together. Like we've always done everything. A team. A family.''

When Raven only stared at her blankly, a sob of defeat rose to her lips. She hadn't done it. She and Nick were lost.

Then Raven was kneeling in front of her, working at the tape that held Andie's wrists, peeling it away. Andie began to tremble; her heart beat so wildly she could hardly breathe. She tried to control both, to keep her head, afraid Raven might notice and realize she had been tricked.

''We'll have to hurry,'' Raven said. ''There's not that much time left.'' She tipped her face up to the still-black sky. ''We need to finish up here, clean up the kitchen, then dispose of Raphael's car.''

She caught Andie's hands. ''You're trembling.''

Andie swallowed hard. ''I'm just so happy we're back together.''

''Me, too.'' Raven brought Andie's hands to her mouth, then dropped them. ''Undo your ankles, then come help me. The hole's almost deep enough.''

Andie nodded and began working frantically at the tape that bound her ankles. She hadn't heard anything from Nick in a while, and afraid for the worst, she glanced his way. His eyes were open. He was looking at her.

Afraid to signal him in any way, she tried to communicate with her gaze. To let him know how she really felt, to tell him she hadn't meant any of those things she had just said.

''Andie? What are you doing?''

''Finished,'' she said, tearing the last of the tape away

and jumping to her feet. Her head screamed protest and she swayed.

"Are you all right?"

"Fine," she managed to say. "Just a little dizzy."

"Feel well enough to dig?" Andie nodded. "Good. You finish the hole, I'll drag Raphael over. I think he's still out."

Andie crossed to her, scrambling for what to do next. Raven was bigger than she was. She was stronger. She, unlike Andie, wasn't reeling from a blow to the head.

Andie took the shovel and glanced around with what she hoped was nonchalance. "Where's Nick's gun?"

Raven looked sharply at her, and Andie wet her lips. "After all, we can't bury him...alive. That would be too cruel."

"Why do you care?"

Andie pretended to bristle at her friend's suspicion. "Right's right, Raven. You know that."

A smile touched Raven's mouth. "You always were the kind one, worrying about everybody. Taking care of us all. If it'll make you feel better, fine."

"Thank you."

Her smile disappeared. "But don't think I'm handing the gun to you. Sorry, Andie, but until I've heard those messages, I can't completely trust you."

"Of course. I don't blame you." She shifted her grip on the shovel. The handle was warm against her palm. She looked at it, then back up at Raven, her stomach rising to her throat. "We better get busy. Time's running out."

Raven took one last measured glance at her, then nodded, turned and started for Nick.

Last chance. She had to do it.

Andie hoisted the shovel; she swung.

The blade connected with the back of Raven's head with a sickening crack. As if in slow motion, Raven turned, her expression one of surprise. Blood spilled down the side of her head and face, turning her angel hair dark. She took a lurching step toward Andie, reaching her hand out.

"Andie," Nick shouted from behind her, "watch out! She's got the gun!"

Only then did Andie see it. The steel barrel gleamed cold and bright in the moonlight. With a sound of fear, Andie took a step backward, the shovel slipping from her grasp.

"Liar," Raven managed to get out, pointing the weapon. "Cheating whore. How could you...I always...I loved—" She crumpled.

Andie brought her hands to her mouth. For a moment, she stared at the woman she had called friend, then with a cry, ran to Nick. She knelt beside him. "Thank God...thank God..." She clawed at the tape at his ankles, freeing them. "I thought—"

"I'd lost you," he said, struggling to sit up. "I thought I'd never get to tell you—"

"Oh, Nick..." She moved her hands frantically over him, his face, the back of his head, his chest and arms just to make sure he really was all right. "I was so afraid...I thought you were, that she'd—"

"Shh... I love you, Andie. I love you so—"

A howl of pain and rage filled the night air. Andie spun around. Raven was on her feet, the gun in her hands. "I won't let you go!" she shrieked. "I won't!"

Andie launched to her feet and dived at Raven, taking her by surprise. The gun flew from her hand. She and Raven hit the ground. Andie saw stars, the wind knocked out of her.

Andie fought past both, struggling to her knees. She scrambled to her right, looking for the gun, though she had no idea where it had landed. Raven grabbed her feet and pulled her back, panting with the effort. Andie twisted and kicked. Her foot connected with something; she heard Raven's grunt of pain.

A moment later, she was free. Andie got to her feet, sobbing. She had to find the gun. She had to—

"Andie! Out of the way!"

Raven had the shovel. Andie fell backward, bringing her arms up to cover her face. An explosion split the night air. Then another. Raven reeled backward, the shovel over her head, her expression one of shocked disbelief. She teetered on the edge of the hole, the graves, she had dug for Nick and Andie, then toppled in.

Andie turned. Nick was on his knees, gun clutched awkwardly in his still-bound hands. Their eyes met, and relief, like the light of day, spilled over her. Getting to her feet, she stumbled to Nick. She freed his hands, then fell into his arms, trembling, clinging to him.

"It's okay, baby. It's over." He tightened his arms around her. "It's over."

She nodded, pressing closer to him, realizing how near they had both come to death; realizing, too, how grateful she was to be alive. And loved.

Nick started to speak. She stopped him. She wasn't ready to talk—not about what had happened or what would come next. "Not yet, Nick," she whispered. "Just hold me for a little bit longer." She lifted her face to his. "Okay?"

He held her gaze. "Forever, Andie. If you want, I'll hold you forever."

Epilogue

The courtroom was so quiet you could hear a pin drop. Andie sat in the witness stand, all gazes pinned on her. She had been on the stand more than two hours already, carefully answering Robert Fulton's questions, hopefully painting a clear picture of Martha, her marriage and the duress she had suffered under. She had described in detail the characteristics of a victim of long-term spousal abuse. In general, then in relation to Martha Pierpont. She had described, also in detail, what she knew of Martha and Edward's marriage, sharing one violent event after another.

As she spoke, she had heard a stir from the jury box, from the gallery. The information she had given, the tragedy of it, was discomfiting. Much of it was downright horrifying.

She kept her gaze trained on Robert Fulton. "The human psyche can take only so much trauma," she continued. "Before it snaps."

"Before it snaps," he repeated, circling around the witness stand so he faced the jury. "Like a muscle or a rubber band," he asked, "stretched beyond its limit?"

What happens then? Does the person go bonkers?

Andie thought of Raven, as she often did, with a mixture of horror and pity, and suppressed a shudder. "Yes," she answered clearly, "you could describe it that way."

"All right." He nodded. "Now that we have a picture in our heads, perhaps you could describe for the jury just what that means."

"A momentary or permanent alteration in thinking patterns. The person loses their sense of reality, their ability to coolly reason." *We're family, Andie. Family sticks together. No matter what.* "Emotion, such as blind fear, takes over. The person is no longer capable of thinking or acting rationally."

"So, you believe—" As if anticipating an objection, he corrected himself. "Is it your professional opinion, based on your research and experience, that Martha Pierpont...snapped?"

"Yes," she said, looking at the jury. "It's my professional opinion that Martha Pierpont's psyche was stressed to the breaking point. It is also my opinion that the night of the murder, she snapped."

"Is it also your professional opinion, Dr. Bennett, from your many sessions with her, spanning a year in time, that when Martha Pierpont shot her husband she acted in self-defense?"

"Absolutely. It's my professional opinion that Martha Pierpont feared for her life. From my work with her, I know she was convinced that her husband could, and someday would, kill her. I believe, without a doubt, that when she pulled that trigger, she was certain she was going to die if she didn't."

"In your professional opinion?"

"Yes."

A ripple moved through the courtroom. Robert smiled. "No further questions, Dr. Bennett."

The judge called a recess for the day. He gave the jury their instructions, reminding them that they were not to discuss the case with anyone or even among themselves, then released them.

Within minutes, the courtroom was empty save for Andie and Robert Fulton. "You did great," Robert said. "It's going well, I think."

Andie collected her purse and coat. "I'm glad. I want this to work out for Martha. She deserves some happiness."

Robert slid his notes into his briefcase, then snapped it shut. "What do you have on tap for tonight?"

She smiled. "Home. A sandwich and a bowl of soup. Maybe a back massage."

He laughed. "Just get some rest. Cross is first thing in the morning and the prosecution will be gunning for you."

"Thanks for the tip, I will."

He told her good-night, then went out to face the reporters. Andie, on the other hand, slipped out the side door to avoid the throng.

As she knew he would be, Nick waited for her on the courthouse steps. Mara was with him, and he was looking down at her, laughing at something she was saying. Andie stopped a moment just to gaze at him, letting the sight of him fill her head and heart like a sweet spring breeze. Letting it chase away the shadows.

Mara and Nick caught sight of her simultaneously and Mara squealed and barreled for her, arms out.

Andie squatted and hugged the child. "I missed you today. Did you have fun?"

Mara proceeded to tell her all the things she and her daddy had done, down to his forcing her to eat her entire lunch in order to get an ice cream for dessert. Andie lifted her gaze to Nick's, amused. "You cad," she murmured. "Her entire lunch?"

"But I let her have a double dip." He smiled and drew Andie to her feet and into his arms. "How'd it go?"

"It went well. Robert's feeling confident."

"Good." He bent and brushed his mouth against hers, then searched her expression, his concerned. "But I'm more interested in how you're feeling."

For a fraction of a moment, she thought of Raven, then

she smiled and touched her fingers to his mouth. ''I'm happy, Nick. Really, really happy.''

He kissed her again. ''Me, too.''

Taking Mara's hands, they headed home.

Turn the page for
an exciting preview of

Cause for Alarm

*Erica Spindler's chilling new
psychological thriller available from
MIRA Books in April 1999*

Prologue

Washington, D.C.
1998

The fashionable Washington neighborhood slept. Not a single light shone up or down the block of high-priced town homes, the only illumination the glow from the gas street lamps and the three-quarter moon. The November night was damp, the air heavy with the scent of decay. Winter had come.

John Power climbed the steps to his ex-lover's front door. He proceeded purposefully but without fanfare, his movements those of a man whose life depended on not being noticed. Dressed completely in black, he knew he appeared more shadow than man, a kind of ghost in the darkness.

Reaching the top landing, he squatted to retrieve the house key from its hiding place under the stone planter-box to the right of the door. During the spring and summer months the planter had been filled with vibrant, sweet-smelling blossoms. But now those same flowers were dead, their stems and leaves curling and black from the cold.

John turned the key in the lock. The dead bolt slid back; he eased open the door and stepped inside. Easy. Too easy. Considering the parade of men who had come and gone through this door over the years, retrieving this same key from its hiding place, he would have thought Sylvia would be a bit more careful.

But then, forethought had never been Sylvia Starr's strong suit.

John closed the door quietly behind him, pausing a moment to listen, taking those valuable seconds to ascertain the number and whereabouts of people in the house, whether they were sleeping or awake. From the living room to his right came the steady ticking of the antique mantel clock. From the bedrooms beyond, the thick snore of a man deeply asleep, a man who had probably drunk too much during his evening with the ever-enthusiastic and sometimes gymnastic Sylvia.

Too bad for Sylvia's friend. He should have gone home to his fat, dependable wife and their ungrateful, cow-faced children. He was about to learn the hard lesson of being in the wrong place at the wrong time.

John started for the bedroom. He took his weapon from its snug resting place—the waistband of his black jeans, at the small of his back. The pistol, a .22 caliber automatic, was neither powerful nor sexy, but it was small, light-weight and at close range utterly effective. John had purchased it, as he did all his weapons, secondhand. Tonight he would give it a watery grave in the Potomac.

He entered Sylvia's bedroom. The couple slept side by side; the bed was rumpled, the sheet and blankets twisted around their hips and legs, only half covering them. In the sliver of moonlight that fell across the bed, Sylvia's left breast stood out in relief, full, round and milky white.

John crossed to where the man slept. He pressed the barrel of the gun to the man's chest, over his heart. The direct contact served two purposes; it muffled the sound of the shot and assured John a swift, clean kill. A professional took no chances.

John squeezed the trigger. The man's eyes popped open, his body convulsed at the bullet's impact. He gasped for air, the gasps turning to a gurgling sound as fluid and oxygen met.

Sylvia immediately awoke. She scrambled into a sitting position, the sheet falling away from her.

The man already forgotten, John greeted her. "Hello, Sylvia."

Making small, squeaky sounds of terror, she inched backward until her spine pressed flat against the bed's headboard. She moved her gaze wildly back and forth, from John to her twitching, bloody companion.

"You know why I've come," John murmured. "Where is she, Syl?"

Sylvia moved her mouth, but no sound escaped. She looked only a breath away from complete, incoherent hysteria. John sighed and circled the bed, stopping beside her. "Come now, Syl, pull yourself together. Look at me, not him." He caught her chin, forcing her gaze to meet his. "Come on, sweetheart, you know I couldn't hurt you. Where's Julianna?"

At the mention of her eighteen-year-old daughter, Sylvia's chest heaved. She glanced at her bed partner, still and silent now, then back at John, working, he saw, to pull herself together. "I...I know...everything."

"That's good." He sat beside her on the bed. "So you understand how important it is that I find her."

She began to shudder, so violently the bed shook. She brought a hand to her mouth. "H-how...young, John? How young was she when you began leaving my bed to go to hers?"

He arched his eyebrows, amazed at her outrage, amused by it. "Are we feeling maternal suddenly? Have you forgotten how only too happy you were to let me care for her whenever you needed to be free?"

"You bastard!" She clutched at the sheets. "I didn't mean for you to defile her. To...to take my trust and—"

"You're a whore," he said simply, cutting her off. "All you've ever cared about was your parties and men and the pretty baubles they could give you. Julianna was nothing but a pet to you. Another of your baubles, a means for the tired old whore to buy a bit of respectability."

Sylvia lunged at him, claws out. He knocked her backward, easily, the heel of his hand connecting with the bridge of her nose. Her head snapped against the headboard, stunning her. He brought the barrel of his gun to the underside of her chin, pressing it against the pulse that beat wildly there, angling it up toward her brain.

"What Julianna and I share isn't about *fucking,* Sylvia. It's not so base as that, though I doubt you could understand. I taught her about life." He leaned closer. He smelled her fear—it mixed with the scent of blood and other body fluids, earthy but very much alive. He heard it in the small feral pants that slipped past her lips.

He tightened his grip on the gun. "I want to know where she is, Sylvia. What have you done with her?"

"Nothing," she whispered. "She...went on her...her own. Sh-she..." Her gaze drifted to the dead man beside her, to the ever-growing pool of red creeping across the white satin coverlet. Her voice shuddered to a halt.

With his free hand John grabbed a handful of her hair and jerked her face back to his. "Look at me, Sylvia. Only at me. Where did she go?"

"I...I don't know. I..."

He tightened his grip on her hair and shook her. "Where, Syl?"

She began to giggle, the sound unnaturally high, otherworldly. She brought a hand to her mouth as if to hold it back. "She came to me...you wanted her to have an abortion. I told her...you're a...monster. A cold-blooded killer. She didn't believe me, so I called Clark." Her giggles became triumphant, bizarrely so, given her situation. "He showed her pictures. Proof, John. *Proof.*"

John froze, his fury awesome, glacial. Clark Russell, CIA grunt man, former comrade-in-arms, one of Sylvia's lovers. One who knew much about John Power.

Clark Russell was a dead man.

John leaned toward Sylvia, the gun forcing her head back, her chin up. "Clark sharing classified information? I guess you're a better lay than I thought." He narrowed his eyes, disliking the way his heart had begun to hammer, his palms to sweat. "You shouldn't have done that, Syl. It was a mistake."

"Fuck you!" she cried, her voice rising. "You won't find her! I told her to run, as fast and as far as she could…to save herself and the baby! You'll never find her. Never!"

For a split second he considered the horror of that possibility, then he laughed. "Of course I will, Sylvia. It's what I do. And when I find her, the problem will be eliminated. Then Julianna and I will be together again, the way we're supposed to be."

"You won't! Never! You—"

He pulled the trigger. Brains and blood splattered across the antique white headboard and onto the pretty rose-patterned wallpaper beyond. John gazed at the mess a moment, then stood. "Goodbye, Sylvia," he murmured, then turned and went in search of Julianna.